A z u R   L I k e   I T

Quotes TK

Quotes TK

# AzuR LIke IT

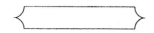

by

## WeNDY HOLDeN

A PLUME BOOK

PLUME

Published by the Penguin Group

Penguin Group (USA) Inc., 375 Hudson Street, New York, New York 10014, U.S.A.

Penguin Books Ltd, 80 Strand, London WC2R 0RL, England

Penguin Books Australia Ltd, 250 Camberwell Road, Camberwell, Victoria 3124, Australia

Penguin Books Canada Ltd, 10 Alcorn Avenue, Toronto, Ontario, Canada M4V 3B2

Penguin Books India (P) Ltd, 11 Community Centre, Panchsheel Park,
New Delhi –110 017, India

Penguin Books (N.Z.) Ltd, Cnr Rosedale and Airborne Roads, Albany, Auckland 1310,
New Zealand

Penguin Books (South Africa) (Pty) Ltd, 24 Sturdee Avenue, Rosebank, Johannesburg
2196, South Africa

Penguin Books Ltd, Registered Offices: 80 Strand, London WC2R 0RL, England

Published by Plume, a member of Penguin Group (USA) Inc. Previously published in
Great Britain by Headline Books Publishing, in somewhat different form.

First Plume Printing, January 2004

10  9  8  7  6  5  4  3  2  1

® REGISTERED TRADEMARK—MARCA REGISTRADA

LIBRARY OF CONGRESS CATALOGING-IN-PUBLICATION DATA

Printed in the United States of America

PUBLISHER'S NOTE

This is a work of fiction. Names, characters, places, and incidents either are the product of
the author's imagination or are used fictitiously, and any resemblance to actual persons,
living or dead, business establishments, events, or locals is entirely coincidental.

Dedication TK

Acknowledgments TK

"So how exactly would you define star quality?" Kate, pen poised over her reporter's notebook, looked up at the new landlady of the Punch Bowl. "When you're booking bands for your new Live Music Nites, I mean?"

It being morning, the pub was closed, but the door was open to encourage fresh air inside. None, so far, had taken up the invitation. A mixture of beer, stale cigarette smoke, and aging gravy filled Kate's nostrils. However scintillating the Punch Bowl's future—and Kate had just spent the best part of an hour hearing it spelled out in unsparing detail—its present looked and smelled the same as always. Even down to the usual fat black fly, throwing itself halfheartedly against the grimy lace-curtained windows.

Despite the new proprietress's plans for complete refurbishment, it seemed unlikely, for the moment at least, that the Punch Bowl would cease to be known as the Punch Out. This affectionate local nickname arose from the pub's location as the last of many that stood along the main drag of Southgate, thus forming the final stop on the notorious drinking route known as the "Southgate Stagger." By the time they reached it, the clientele were generally in a combative mood.

Even the unusually bright day outside did not improve matters inside. A brilliant beam of sun highlit the hideous patterned carpet that had been there since time immemorial. It shone pitilessly on sticky marks on tables and dust rising from red plush banquettes whose gashes bled dirty yellow foam. All soon to be replaced, apparently, by brass rails, colonial fans, and something called "a fusion menu." Jolene Shaw's ambitions—as Kate was now hearing—also included the launch of the Punch Out as a showcase for local live music acts. The ones who had rehearsed, that was, rather than the ones who staggered out after closing time roaring "Four and Twenty Virgins."

"Star quality?" Jolene drew confidently on her cigarette. She was a thick-nosed blonde of a certain age whose short skirt exposed an acreage of bare thigh that looked as if you could strike a match on it. She belonged, Kate recognized, to the tribe of women Dad described, not entirely disapprovingly, as "ridden hard and put away wet." "World's best at talent-spotting, me," she asserted. "Know straight away, I do, whether they're going to be any good or not."

Kate was intrigued despite herself. "Really? So what's the magic ingredient?" Talent-spotters, in her experience, were few and far between in Slackmucklethwaite; no one, at least, had spotted her genius as a journalist yet. It would be interesting to know what the town's answer to Simon Cowell thought constituted star quality.

"Good looks?" Kate pressed. "Great songs? Stage presence? Um . . . Keeping in tune?"

Jolene raised her eyebrows. "Round 'ere? You're joking, aren't you, love?"

"Originality?" Kate thought of Darren the junior reporter's rock band. Original was one way of describing them. Perhaps the only way.

Jolene shook her choppily cut yellow head which, stylistically speaking, occupied the midpoint between Anthea Turner and Joan of Arc at the stake. "No. What it all boils down to is whether they stand up or not."

Kate's pencil dropped out of her fingers. *"Stand up?"*

"That's right. Bands what sit down look borin' and aren't as easy to see in a pub. So the first thing I ask 'em when I'm booking 'em— even before I've asked 'em what sort of music they play—is 'can you stand up?'"

You had to laugh, Kate reflected as she left the Punch Out. Even if you sometimes felt like doing the exact opposite. After all, it wasn't as if what had just happened was unusual. Barely a day went by in the *Slackmucklethwaite Mercury*—locally known as the *Mockery*—without some scarcely credible incident. In last week's edition, for instance, the ARE YOU AN ANIMAL LOVER? headline had provoked complaints from readers about the media's obsession with sex, despite its being intended to drum up volunteers for the neighborhood dog shelter.

Jolene Shaw's intention of staging the local equivalent of *American Idol* rang warning bells in itself. *Art Beat*, the *Mercury's* culture section, was, after all, no stranger to controversy. Only recently had the furor caused by Kate's coverage of the Slackmucklethwaite Players' production of *Romeo and Juliet* begun to subside. That the role of fourteen-year-old Juliet had been taken by the Players' customary leading lady, fiftysomething chairwoman Gladys Arkwright, had caused a mild sensation among the audience. "That Gladys Arkwright may be no Gwyneth Paltrow, but she sure as 'eck nows 'ow to lean over a balcony," Alderman Bracegirdle was heard to remark appreciatively afterward. The sentence had ended up as the final line of Kate's review, with disastrous consequences. However exemplary Gladys Arkwright's balcony skills, she was not noted for her sense of humor. And the *Mercury's* editor had temporarily lost his too, after Gladys sought exemplary libel damages in the county court.

Oh well, Kate thought, dropping into the front seat of her battered Peugeot, Mrs. Shaw's stand-up rule was definitely good news for her colleague Darren. His band, which had been having trouble getting bookings, must at least have mastered the art of balancing on two legs. Or so one would have thought.

Jolene's last words grated in her ear. "I'm expecting a good write-up in t'*Mockery*, you know. Don't forget that quarter-page ad for t'Punch Bowl I've taken out."

If only, Kate thought, she *could* forget. Since the recent takeover of the paper by tycoon Peter Hardstone, extremely rich, extremely unpleasant, and clearly intending to squeeze the 249-year-old *Mercury* until its pips squeaked, advertisements had become far more important than editorial. Editorial had, in fact, become advertorial: flattering pieces supporting ad space bought by local businesses such as Jolene

Shaw's. Or the newly opened Use Your Noodle, self-styled Biggest Chinese Restaurant in the World, which had recently fired up its woks in one of Slackmucklethwaite's many former Methodist chapels.

While the restaurant's popularity among the post-pub crowd had been instant and immense, the transformation of the vast, pew-lined, Palladian-fronted temple into a pink-tableclothed Peking Duck palace had not been to the taste of older readers. Nor had their remarks been to the taste of Peter Hardstone. Weeks of unfavorable comment on the *Mercury*'s letters pages had ended, not in victory for the complainants, but in the axing of the page altogether. A shame, Kate thought, that a forum whose first letters had condemned the Black Hole of Calcutta should be brought down over a row about black bean sauce.

She rummaged amid the flotsam and jetsam of the passenger seat for the scribbled-in notebook that served as her reporting diary. Next up was the Women's Institute Lunch followed by—joy of joys—a date with Alderman Ernest Fartown, president of the local Chamber of Commerce.

She groaned. Admittedly, the *Mockery* hadn't been her first choice of employer. Long ago, having scored the county's second-top marks in French A-level, she had dreamed of a job simultaneously translating at the United Nations. Yet the cost of the necessary four-year-degree course was out of the question—the thought of plunging Mum and Dad thousands of pounds into debt was simply untenable, although, self-sacrificing to the last, they had not tried to influence her decision. Which had been, in the end, to do a "media module" at a nearby community college and try for a job on the *Mercury*. She had kept up her French as best she could, although admittedly there wasn't much call for it in Slackmucklethwaite. Or on the *Mercury* come to that.

But she had been thrilled to get the *Mercury* job at the time. Almost as much as the UN, newspapers had seemed full of potential. The gateway to a wider, more exciting world. It seemed incredible that, four years later, this was as far as her journalistic career had got. She could be interviewing the president of the United States by now, rather than that of the Chamber of Commerce. Or be working on a national paper in *some* capacity. That was the point of provincial papers, wasn't it? You learned your trade, then went to ply it in the capital. Countless ambitious young provincial journalists had gone on to glory this way.

But she had been unable to follow them. Few of the London papers she had applied to had bothered to reply, and those that did said no. This despite the fact that her—literally—groundbreaking story on what had been unearthed during the digging up of the school drains had catapulted her on the long list for the *What the (Local) Papers Say Investigative Local Journalist of the Year Awards*. Her report on how the children had gone into the classroom waving femurs from a forgotten, ancient part of the nearby churchyard had been her finest professional hour so far. Which, possibly, summed it all up.

The offices of the *Mercury* occupied the ground floor of a former butcher's shop. Although the cleavers, mincers, and chopping blocks were long gone, an odd smell was detectable on occasion, particularly in hot weather. Other reminders of the shop's former usage were the legends etched indelibly into the glass of the large front window—*Black Fat*, *Weasand*, and *Pig Bag*, all referring to varieties of tripe. These delicacies were now replaced in the window by curl-edged, sunfaded shots of local people and events taken by the paper's veteran photographer Colin and published in various issues of the *Mercury*. Each carried a small identification number in case—this being the main purpose of the display—anyone wanted to buy them. No one ever did.

Darren's skinny frame was hunched over his desk as Kate entered. He jumped slightly, sending jewelry rattling all over his body. Earlobes, neck, wrists, and a variety of nose rings tinkled like wind chimes.

"Only me." Kate grinned, throwing her leather jacket in the direction of the coat stand and feeling disproportionately delighted when it landed on a hook.

"Hello, gorgeous," the junior reporter said, smiling. That he really found her gorgeous Kate doubted: Darren's sexuality was a closely guarded secret even from her. But it was nice of him to say it. Especially as she had been wondering lately whether her decision to grow out her highlights was the right one. Years of being an assisted blonde dyed hard.

"No, honestly, keep it as it is—the natural look suits you," Darren advised. "You've got lovely skin and those big blue eyes—pale brown hair goes really well with it. It *is* sort of mousy, yes. But glamorous mouse."

"Glamorous mouse?"

"Yeah. And you hardly need any makeup—just a touch of mascara on those long lashes of yours. Bit of lippy and you're done."

Darren, it had to be said, was an unlikely advocate of the natural look. He had lashings of mascara and a lot of lippy on today; lipstick that was, moreover, black. His hair stood erect in shining purple-black spikes that contrasted with his dead-white face. Gusts of patchouli wafted from his tight black jeans and shirt whenever he moved. His boots were large, black and, like his belt, covered in silver studs and chains.

Walking through the town in full Goth rig was something only one with the junior reporter's love of drama and unstoppable belief that stardom was just around the corner could possibly have contemplated. Especially as, in Darren's case, what was usually just around the corner was a group of youths shouting, "Weirdo!"

Good old Darren. Hardworking, clever, humorous and, unlike certain of his predecessors, completely without issues about donating to the office tea-bag fund.

Kate smiled at him. "So what did I miss? What happened while I was out?"

"Believe it or not, something actually did happen for once."

"Let me guess. Hold the front page, there's a new bus timetable just come out?"

"Better than that, even. Slackmucklethwaite's own Beverly Hills has disappeared down a huge hole."

"What? Slack Palisades, you mean?" Kate's eyes widened. This really was a surprise. The luxury development of Slack Palisades, ten miles west of Slackmucklethwaite, with its brick drives, plastic porticos, "heritage" carriage lamps, and optional helicopter landing pads had appeared almost overnight as it was. That it had disappeared in the course of a morning seemed appropriate, if incredible.

"But Peter Hardstone lives in Slack Palisades, "Kate remembered. A thrilling possibility gripped her. "He's not fallen down this hole as well, has he?"

Darren shook his head. "'Fraid not. There haven't been any casualties at all, amazingly. Apart from people's egos and properties. Here's my report. I've just finished." He pushed it towards her. Kate took it and read.

HEAD: That Sinking Feeling

STORY BEGINS: As angry residents of the exclusive development of Slack Palisades prepared to spend the night in the local Ramada Inn, some of them relived the terrifying moment when their back gardens plunged into a 56-foot hole. Actor Greville Thomas, 50, lost his entire lawn and outdoor Jacuzzi in the landslip. "Fortunately I was inside having an, er, massage at the time," commented the actor once familiar to viewers as *Emmerdale*'s libidinous Squire Thirkettle. "My girlfriend said she felt the earth move. But I thought she must mean me."

SUBHEAD: Nightmare

Meanwhile, pop star Julian Bridgeman arrived back from a 1980s revival tour of the Baltic States to find that his front door had shifted on its hinges and wouldn't open. "My cleaner was stuck in the downstairs bog and in a right state," recalled the one-time singer with Computeroid, who reached number 5 in the charts in 1983 with the single "Budapest." "Then I heard this almighty bloody crash and turned round to see my outdoor recording studio disappearing into this, like, mega-hole. Along with all the original tapes of Computeroid's old hits which I was just about to remix with Fatboy Slim. Bloody nightmare, basically."

SUBHEAD: Rats

The entire luxury estate appears deserted by its residents. Those now in the Ramada Inn claimed they had no intention of returning to what remained of their exclusive, hi-tech homes and would pursue legal action against developers Fantasia Ltd. A Fantasia spokesman rebutted rumors that well-to-do rats were deserting a literally sinking ship. "Many of the residents are on holiday at the moment, that's where they've all gone," claimed the spokesman, who was reluctant to give his name. "It's a blip, that's all. People have overreacted. There was no suggestion this was going to happen right up until we arrived at this point."

"A blip!" Kate exclaimed, looking up. "Well, I'd like to see them telling Peter Hardstone that."

"He must be incandescent," Darren agreed. Kate returned to the report.

SUBHEAD: Mickey Mouse Hits Out

Freya Ogden, 41, President of the Slackmucklethwaite Conservation Society, hit out at the claim that there had been no intimation of the landslide to come. "Everyone knows there are centuries'-old mine workings beneath the heritage land Slack Palisades is built on," stormed Ms. Ogden, a part-time fire-eater. "Those early mine shafts are the entire reason it is a protected site. Or was. I have been warning Fantasia and the

Council ever since building began there that something of
this sort would happen."

"Wow." Kate handed the report back with raised eyebrows. "So that
mad hippie had a point after all by the looks of it."

In a more general social context, she knew, Freya Ogden wouldn't
be seen as particularly eccentric. Yet in Slackmucklethwaite, a formidable six-foot environmentalist vegetarian fire-eater was viewed with a
certain amount of trepidation. While it was hard not to admire the
passion of her convictions, it was impossible, too, not to view her as
mildly insane.

"Freya certainly did have a point," Darren said grimly. "And I'm
interested in hearing a few more of her points to help me get to the
bottom of this story. There's more where this came from, I'm sure."

"We should just about have time to get it in this week's edition,"
Kate said excitedly.

"I'm sending it off now." Darren was marching over to the fax.
"This'll be a story right up Hardstone's street. As it were, ha ha."

Kate hoped so. It would be a relief to be at last doing something the new proprietor approved of. So far, bullying and criti-
cism had been the order of the day. Every day since the tycoon had
taken over.

The ink—or, as Darren had remarked with ghoulish relish,
*blood*—had hardly dried on the takeover contract before Hardstone's
gold Ferrari, complete with tinted windows, slid to a halt alongside the
*Mercury* offices and his management style began to make itself felt. His
chubby, beringed hands, it emerged, were to be very much *on*. "I'm a
straight talker," Hardstone boomed at the staff collected to greet him.
"I say what I bloody well like and I like what I bloody well say."

Orange-tanned, buck-toothed, aggressively plump, and sporting a
toupee of staggering obviousness, Hardstone spent the rest of the afternoon clomping stoutly around on his built-up heels emitting sulphurous bursts of flatulence and communicating his vision for the
paper to Denys Wemyss, the *Mercury*'s gentlemanly but elderly editor.

"I'm not bloody asking you, I'm telling you," Hardstone roared at any attempts on Wemyss's part to suggest alternatives to the wholesale shedding of staff being proposed. "Shut up, Grandad, and bloody well get on with it."

By some miracle, Denys Wemyss, Kate, Darren, and Joan the motherly sales manager were left on the full-time payroll. Albeit with salaries slashed by a third and instructions that the *Mercury*'s editorial direction must now be composed of 60 percent ads. Otherwise, both people and pages were ruthlessly axed.

Mystic Mavis, the astrologer, took her dismissal particularly badly. "Must have been crap then, or she'd have bloody well seen it coming," was Hardstone's retort to Wemyss's plea for clemency. The *Mercury*'s sports pages had also gone; no point, Hardstone told the editor, in giving Slagheap United all that free publicity when the pages could be used for advertising. After all, "the Slags," as they were popularly known, could always take a weekly half-page if they wanted. Wemyss's pointing out that almost all the clubs were battling for financial survival and couldn't possibly afford such an outlay left the proprietor unmoved. "I'm not in the business of subsidizing bad management," he snapped at Wemyss. "At football clubs or anywhere else," he had chillingly added.

"Anyway," Darren remarked now, returning from the fax. "Wanna hear my band's new song?"

"What do you mean—new?"

Darren's was a cover band, although not in the normal way. Their name, the Denholme Velvets, came from the sign on a local fabric factory which had, as he passed it twice daily in the bus, gradually exercised a powerful hold over the junior reporter's imagination. During trips to and from work, he had slowly dreamed up the concept of a group specializing in the Velvet Underground's greatest hits "recrafted" as he put it, with a special twist. Hence "Gladys in Furs," "Sunday Morning (Chapel)," "Halifax (Will Be the Death of Me)," and "Uncle Ray," the Denholme Velvets' version of "Sister Ray." And now, it seemed, he had written another.

"It's called 'Waiting for the Bus.'"

He walked to the center of the worn carpet, narrowed his eyes, cocked his hip, beat rapid time against his thigh with the palm of one hand and crooned into the upheld fist of the other.

> Ah'm
> Waiting for me bus
> Twenny-six pence
> In me hand . . .

Kate clapped. "Fantastic."

> It's never early, it's always late
> First thing you learn is that you've always gotta wa-ait
> Oh, Ah'm
> Waiting for me bus . . .

He stopped suddenly as the door behind them swung open. It was the editor.

"Now then," said Denys Wemyss genially. "What's going on here? I know you're excited about your Slack Palisades story, Darren, but that doesn't mean there's not work to be getting on with."

"I'm editing *What's in a Name*, Mr. Wemyss." Darren leaped back to his desk with a rattle of bracelets. "Copy's just come in and I was showing Kate what this week's surname was. You know how much she looks forward to it." The editor nodded approvingly and passed into his telephone-box–sized office.

*What's in a Name* investigated the history of a different local surname every week. One reason it had survived the Hardstone ax was because it was what Wemyss rather pompously called a "curtain-raiser" to *Hatches 'n' Matches*, the *Mercury's* personal announcements section, in which it was intended to stimulate interest. The other, and main reason it remained, was that it was written for free by a retired teacher with an interest in etymology. The column was a standing joke between Kate and Darren because of the invariable extreme obviousness of the surnames "explained." "Is your name 'Butcher'?" Darren declaimed now. "'If so, there is a distinct possibility that one of your ancestors may have been a butcher, or otherwise involved in the meat trade.'"

Kate sat down and reluctantly began her own least favorite editorial task—compiling the collection of forthcoming pensioners' outings, Mothers' Union lunches, and other excitements that the regular *Mercury* reader found listed snappily under *Coming Events*. This list, always extensive, had expanded under Hardstone's regime as the proprietor considered that the clubs and pubs serving as meeting places might be persuaded to advertise.

"Go on," Darren urged. "Give me the highlights."

"Um . . . well, next Friday the Slack Bottom Methodists are organizing a whist-drive in the Village Hall."

Darren sniggered appreciatively. "Try and keep me away, that's all I can say."

"And the Sixty-Ninth Grimsdyke South Boy Scout Troop are looking for Beavers."

"I bet they are," snorted Darren.

"And the next meeting of the Hard of Hearing Club will be held on the fourteenth . . ."

"Eh? You what?" shouted Darren, cupping his ear.

"And from Friday there'll be regular Live Music Nites at . . . Christ, I forgot to tell you!"

Kate filled him in about her encounter with Jolene Shaw. Darren blazed with excitement beneath his white foundation. "You reckon she'll book us?"

"Definitely."

"Where is she?"

"The Punch Out."

*"The Punch Out?"* Darren's excitement lost some of its force. "Are you *joking*? I thought their idea of live entertainment was kicking Manchester United supporters to a pulp."

"Not any more, apparently. Jolene Shaw's taking the place upmarket and wants to feature local bands."

Darren's thin, beringed hands plunged agitatedly into his gelled and backcombed black-purple hair. Through the kohl rims, his eyes shone. "Wow. Sounds right up our boulevard. I'll give her a ring. Today Slackmucklethwaite," he added with a grin, "tomorrow the world."

2

"What's happened?" Kate arrived in the office the next day to find Darren in a fury.

"Just this." He thrust the *Mercury* at her. NEW BUS TIMETABLE CAUSES CHAOS AMONG PENSIONER read the front-page headline. "That's a typo, by the way. *Pensioners* should have been plural."

Kate stared. "But what's happened to the Slack Palisades story? Was it too late for the printers?"

"No," Darren snarled. She had rarely seen him so angry. "I filed it in plenty of time."

"So why hasn't it run? It was an amazing story."

"That's just what Hardstone said to Denys. You know he vets all the front-page stories now."

Kate nodded. The news that the proprietor intended to do this had arrived on a fax the day before. "But if he thought it was amazing . . . ?"

"The official line was that it was a bit too amazing," Darren spat.

"What do you mean, official line?" Puzzled, Kate screwed up her eyes.

"The official line is that bad publicity for the area, particularly about developments, will result in a loss of business."

"Does Hardstone not want us to run it at all, then?"

"No."

"But it was in his interests. It's about why his house disappeared down a huge hole."

"Actually, his house wasn't too badly affected, as it turns out. He's still living there, apparently."

"Whatever," Kate sighed, exasperated. "But surely the point is, it was the start of a campaign to expose Fantasia and whatever went wrong in the building of Slack Palisades, which would be a good thing for the area—high standards of probity and all that. Environmental conscience too. Freya was going to tell you everything she knew."

"Quite. That's the problem."

"What are you talking about? Why is it a problem? Is it just Freya's mad conspiracy theories or something?" Admittedly, that had always been a danger.

"Not exactly. The main problem is that Freya's turned up quite a lot of amazing stuff. The Council are implicated for a start. Alderman Bracegirdle's in it up to his eyebrows, not to mention his girdle."

"Really?" Kate's eyes were out on stalks. "The Council?"

"Well, they have to be, if you think about it. There's got to be something dodgy. Slack Palisades was built on greenbelt that hasn't changed much since the Three Field System. And built next to Slack Top, an eighteenth-century weaving village with protected heritage status. Backhanders to the Council are probably only the start of it. It's all extremely whiffy."

"But," Kate burst in, "that's all the more reason why Hardstone should let us run the story. It's dynamite." Her heart started to pound in excitement. "It might even go national."

"Except that it won't," Darren said flatly.

"But it's what the *Mercury's* supposed to be all about. Like it says on the front-page banner under the title. FIGHTING LOCAL BATTLES FOR LOCAL PEOPLE. Kate snatched up the copy of the *Mercury*. She frowned. "Oh. There's been a mistake. It says BRINGING LOCAL NEWS TO LOCAL PEOPLE on this one."

"Not a mistake. That's what it's going to say from now on. Our battling days are over."

"So is that the reason," Kate asked slowly, "we can't run the Slack Palisades story?"

"No. The real reason is," Darren took a deep breath, "that when Freya and I checked with Companies House to see who the directors

of Fantasia Ltd. were, it turned out that one of them was a certain Mr.
P. Hardstone."

"What? He built Slack Palisades?"

"'Fraid so. He's even more sleazy than we thought."

"It can't be true. Are you sure?"

"I'm certain."

"But he's never said anything about it. Although, come to think of
it, we have run quite a bit of advertorial. I've written a couple of blurbs
myself, which was tricky as I'd not been there."

"Precisely. He's been using the paper to promote it. The whole
thing's about as dodgy as it gets, basically. A sordid tale of heritage land,
historic mine shafts and more backhanders than a Wimbledon final."

Kate looked doubtfully at her colleague. It all struck her as a bit
dramatic. Deception and fraud on that sort of scale were hardly typical of the area. The town's only previous big corruption story was
when some unauthorized person made off with the proceeds of the
OAPs' Annual Blackpool Outing Fighting Fund—whether the fight
was for or against had never been satisfactorily established. As for the
Hardstone saga, she wouldn't put it past Darren to be exaggerating
ever so slightly.

"What does Denys say?" she asked tactfully.

"That it's all very complicated and not worth taking the risk."

"I can see his point," Kate said gently. "I hate to say this," she
added practically, "but even if it is true, Hardstone owns us anyway.
Unless you've got a job on another paper, you're probably best forget-
ting about it."

Darren relieved his feelings by shoving the *Mercury* in his
wastepaper bin. "And that's not all. He's not only gagging us, he's
damned near obliterating us."

"Uh?"

"Hardstone's ordered the ink bill at the printer's to be cut by half.
The type'll be so faint nobody'll be able to read it anyway. Basically,
what any hip young gunslinger of a journalist should realize by now is
that it's time to bail out, Kate."

Time to bail out. Kate knew that all right. The question was—

where to? It was all right for Darren—he was going to be a rock star. Or so he fervently believed, which was half the battle anyway. And for her? Even in its reduced state, working at the *Mercury* was one of the better options Slackmucklethwaite offered. Bailing out, until she had something to bail to, was therefore out of the question.

"Ahem."

Kate and Darren whirled round. The editor had come out of his goldfish bowl and was standing in the middle of the floor behind them. "A word if you please," he said in his courteous fashion. "In my office."

It was clear that what Wemyss was about to impart demanded a certain amount of ceremony. He was big on ceremony. Formality was his thing. He might, Kate thought, be old, increasingly batty, and hopelessly marooned on the *Mercury*, but there was something romantic about him nonetheless.

Wemyss's appearance was singular. His pointy little white beard, Homburg hat, and silk cravat were all redolent of a more formal, more romantic age of journalism. Kate, at her job interview, had listened spellbound as the editor reminisced, misty-eyed, about the days when senior staff on the *Times* had their own oak-paneled offices with coal fires and were served tea and cakes every afternoon by nice ladies with trolleys.

Adding to the editor's singularity was the fact that his surname was correctly pronounced *Weems*. Peter Hardstone considered this impossibly pretentious and went out of his way to address the editor as *Wemiss* on the grounds that, "If it's spelled that way, why the hell don't you say it that way? Bloody amazing you ever got anywhere in journalism."

With three people, the editor's office was crammed to the maximum. Besides Wemyss's desk, there was room for just one other piece of furniture, a small and wobbly chair on to which Kate lowered herself with even more trepidation than usual. She looked anxiously at Darren and saw from the bobbing of his Adam's apple that the same thought had occurred to him. The moment really had come at last. They were here to have the last rites read over their careers.

Wemyss pulled at his mustard silk cravat. He raked a liver-spotted hand through his thin white hair. Panic rose in Kate's throat. As the editor prepared to speak, the knicker factory reared up in her imagination, huge, dark and dominant, blocking out the light.

Then came the unexpected bit. "Great news," Wemyss announced, beaming. "Glad tidings of great joy."

Kate and Darren slid amazed looks at each other. "Glad?" ventured Kate.

"The *Mercury* is to have the most colossal honor bestowed upon it," Wemyss quavered, eyes shining with emotion. "We are about to receive royalty into our midst."

"What, the queen's coming?" gasped Darren.

Wemyss shook his white head. "Not that sort of royalty. One rather closer to home. Nathaniel Hardstone is coming to spend some time on the *Mercury*!"

"Nathaniel Hardstone?" Kate mused. "Peter Hardstone's son, you mean?"

"The very same! Son of the proprietor. Son and heir, more importantly. Marvellous news, isn't it?"

"Why?" asked Darren.

"Why?" repeated Wemyss.

"Yes, why?" Darren's finger tweezled a leather-strung silver cross lying against the bones of his skinny chest. "Why would he want to come *here*?"

Wemyss beamed. "To learn the business from the bottom up, of course! Nathaniel will be taking over one day, after all." His voice trembled; he was, Kate realized, viewing the whole affair as a ringing endorsement. "Of all the newspapers in the entire Hardstone Holdings empire," the editor added tremendously, "the one Nathaniel's chosen to come to is . . . the *Mercury*!"

"Kate?" Mum's fist banged on the thin wood of the bedroom door. "What the blitherin' 'eck are you doing in there? It's nearly eight. *Get a move on!*"

Kate rushed into the bathroom and under a tepid shower. As

usual, all the hot water had long been used up, but she knew better than to complain—"what else do you expect, woman, when you get up when you do?" was Dad's unbending view of the matter. She dressed hurriedly and went into the kitchen, which—again as usual at this time of day—was the temperature of a forge. Heat billowed from both the roaring grill and the constantly-boiling kettle.

Kate sighed as she reached for a piece of toast. At this point in her career, in her life, she should be perched stylishly at the breakfast counter, Matthew Williamson spoon over Jade Jagger china bowl, gazing across the shining blond wood floor of her fashionable riverside apartment to where the sweet Thames ran softly beyond floor-to-ceiling windows.

But she wasn't. Thanks entirely to the fact that she invariably had a lot of month left over at the end of her money—all the more since the advent of Peter Hardstone—here she was with Mum, Dad, and Gran in a semi called Wits End.

To be fair to her parents, the house was called that when they bought it. Neither of them, Kate knew, either noticed the name or cared. It didn't embarrass them the way it did her. Once, years ago, she had suggested to Dad that he change it to numbers, but he had merely observed—with, she recognized, some truth—that if she had nothing more than *that* to worry about, she was bloomin' lucky.

The only person with a more embarrassing address was Darren, whose family seat, Erzanmyne, paid tribute to his parents' joint ownership. It also paid tribute to their smoking; the walls and ceilings being dyed a light tobacco brown and the whole place suffused in the vinegary smell of stale cigarette fumes. Darren always said he'd never even seen his parents until he had grown past their knees, so obscured were they in dense clouds of Superkings.

Toast in hand, Kate mooched into the sitting room where her grandmother, as usual, was knitting and half-watching the TV that Dad had left on. Dad never, at any time of the day, sat down to watch television, preferring always to stand and thus give the impression he was on the point of some pressing household task.

"Hi, Gran."

"Hello, love."

Her grandmother was sitting in her chair by the window. A special old-person's high-seater to facilitate ease of getting up, it was swathed in an elastic nylon cover on which brown autumn leaves swirled against a brown background. Gran had had it in the sheltered accommodation she had shared with Grandad before his death and it had afterwards moved with her to Kate's parents'. It had been accompanied by a flotilla of ornaments including an ashtray from Southsea, a candle-powered mobile of revolving brass angels, a triumvirate of plastic wise monkeys, and a framed picture of Gran's wedding to Grandad. All were arranged along the windowsill at her side, apart from a plastic clock with pictures of birds instead of numbers that emitted a different "ornithological" sound for each hour of the day and night. This was mounted on the wall.

"What's that you're watching?" Kate squinted at the screen. A tousled blonde with huge teeth appeared to be planting a bonsai garden on top of a large stone tomb and surrounding it with decking. "Give the resting place of your loved one a happening edge," she said, beaming.

"Oh, I don't know, love. Some rubbish. I'm not really watching." Gran was concentrating on her knitting; her needles a blur of activity. Kate had never known her grandmother not be knitting, apart from when she was eating, and even then she often managed to fit in a couple of stitches between bites. "The devil makes work for idle hands," she would say as she busily clacked away—in bed, in the pension queue, even waiting at the bus stop. "She could knit for England," Mum would say indulgently, and Kate wished she would. David Beckham was about the only person she could imagine carrying Gran's creations off.

Although even he might find this one a challenge. Kate eyed with apprehension the length of bright yellow and zinging tangerine nylon dangling from beneath Gran's needles. All week she'd been hoping it was either a tea cozy or a coat-hanger cover, but that egg-yolk-colored edging was looking suspiciously like a neck hole. Please God it wasn't another tank top. Worse still, a poncho. Her bottom drawer was stuffed with both. Surely the day wasn't far off when even Gran, who had one glass eye and another failing rapidly, would notice she never wore any of them.

"Suit you, this will." Gran waved her needles and rolled her good eye at Kate. "You'll look a picture."

What sort of picture was the question. Orange and yellow wouldn't do a great deal for arms and legs so white they were almost blue.

"Nice summer colors," added Gran with satisfaction.

"I'll see you later." Kate bent to kiss her grandmother, inhaling as she did so the Camay soap scent of her skin.

Passing through the hall, she glanced at herself in the mirror. Did she look dowdy? Was Darren right about her highlights?

"Be back for tea, will you?" Mum's tone was tinged with hope. Kate knew that, in her mother's opinion, she should be out with her boyfriend. Or even better, in with her husband and children like most of her contemporaries from school. But Kate, having seen one too many former classmates heaving huge double pushchairs up and down the shopping precinct, had long ago decided against such a route. There had to be something better out there.

"Yes," she said, looking Mum in the eye. "I *will* be back for tea."

Mum shook her head sorrowfully. "Such a shame it didn't work out with that lovely Nigel Herring."

Kate felt a sharp dig of irritation. Several weeks before, to her mother's chagrin, she had finally dumped Nigel Herring. They had been in the same year at school and had met again after Kate was sent by the *Mercury* to profile Nigel's father's firm of solicitors. A relationship of sorts had ensued, based on what Kate had initially assumed was a shared desire to get out of town.

"Such a nice boy," sighed Mum.

Mum had been thrilled with Nigel. He was what she called "a proper man." A professional with prospects, in other words. The heir to a business, A-levels, a degree, and a company Punto. Prince William couldn't have ticked more of Mum's boxes.

"So nice to his mother too. Lovely lady, Mrs. Herring."

"Bit Hyacinth Bucket," objected Dad.

Dad had enjoyed Kate's reports of how Nigel's mother had different sets of china for dinner and breakfast and laid out the latter in the dining room nightly before retiring. He had been even more gratified by her obsession with an ancient pair of dachshunds whose frequent loud farts were put down to the fact "they have very tight skins, poor darlings."

But none of these was the reason the relationship had ended. Nor was it because Nigel Herring wasn't sexy or because, whenever he kissed her, his teeth clashed with hers and his glasses got caught in her hair. No, the deathblow had been Kate's discovery that Nigel's ambitions did not, after all, extend beyond inheriting Herring & Co., Commissioners For Oaths. A future with a man commissioning whatever oaths Slackmucklethwaite chose to swear was not one Kate wished to contemplate.

"Oh, *do* stop going on about Nigel Herring, Margaret." Gran shuffled into the kitchen. "You sound like a record that's got stuck."

Kate flashed Gran a grateful glance. At times like this she could almost forgive her for the fact that she had insisted she be christened Kathleen after Kathleen Ferrier, her grandmother's favorite singer. Dad, always keen to crack down on anything he considered pretentious, had teased his daughter endlessly when the change to Kate had been mooted. But Kate had stuck to her guns and now, like the rest of the family, he referred to her original title only in rare moments of anger.

"I'm not saying he wasn't a nice boy, but *really*," Gran added. "Our Kate can do better than that."

"Do better?" Mum raised her eyebrows. "Not round here she can't."

"I'm not talking about round here," Gran replied vehemently. "Kate needs to leave *round here* if you ask me. A bit of adventure, that's what she wants. Believe me, I should know."

"Didn't realize *you'd* had such an exciting life," Dad remarked.

"Oh, I've had me moments."

Kate wondered what moments. Her grandmother's life, so far as she knew, had been fairly uneventful. Perhaps the "moments" were to do with Grandad. The marriage had, like that of her parents, been an extremely happy one. Grandad may have been dead for five years, but not a day went by without Gran wistfully polishing their black-and-white wedding photograph with a hand where the plain gold time-worn wedding ring had long since sunk immovably into its fleshy red finger. Whatever relationship she eventually ended up with, Kate hoped it would be half so happy.

"Such a shame you don't make more of an effort, "Mum lamented, looking her daughter critically up and down. "You've got such lovely eyes and nice clear skin. Scrub up well when you try, you do."

Kate, who thought of her looks as ordinary at best, was conscious of looking some considerable distance from that best this morning. That best and herself were, in fact, several continents apart. Her nails were bitten. Besides being unhighlighted, her hair was unwashed.

"Would have thought you'd make an effort today of all days," she said, sighing. "Boss's son's coming, isn't he? Or so you were saying last night."

"Nathaniel Hardstone?" Kate made a face. She'd almost forgotten. The prospect of his arrival may have rung all Wemyss's bells at once, but it did precisely nothing for her.

"Nay," said Gran, emerging from the kitchen. "Leave the lass alone, Margaret. She'll find the right bloke in her own good time."

"Just as long as it doesn't run out on her," Mum said darkly.

"What—time or the bloke?" joshed Dad.

"Ha ha," grumped Kate.

"Boss's son might be nice though," Gran suggested. "You never know."

Kate ground her teeth. Actually, she *did* know. Nathaniel was, for a start, a ridiculous name. Podgy and petulant, redolent of red velvet pageboy suits, basin haircuts, and Little Lord Fauntleroy. Definitely not a good-looking sort of name, although there was no chance of that anyway. Hardstone's son, like Hardstone himself, would be short, florid, and thoroughly nasty.

Kate dashed through the rain to the car, glowing with a delicious secret. Unbeknownst to Mum and even to Gran, she *did* have a man in her life. And not just any man. Mark was faint-inducingly handsome, sexy beyond belief, smoothly personable, and as convinced as herself that real life lay elsewhere.

It was Mark who had, for some time, kept Kate from appearing punctually at breakfast. Mark who enticed her into her bedroom early and kept her up half the night with his charm, good looks, and endless erotic inventiveness. The only problem with Mark was that he wasn't real. He was fictional, the hero of the novel Kate was writing in her bedroom under cover of night and the duvet.

She'd got the synopsis more or less worked out now. Admittedly, the imaginative leap required had not been enormous.

*Local newspaper reporter Mark lives with his parents and grandmother out of financial necessity. He is bored out of his mind. He wants excitement, glamor, women, money, and fast cars. . . .*

The story had come upon her in a flash at a bottom-numbing Women's Institute meeting chaired even more uninspiringly than usual by Doreen Bracegirdle. It would trace Mark's escape from suburban strangulation by pleasuring the local bored housewives before—in a link she had not yet quite worked out—he graduated to pleasuring the bored mansion wives of Knightsbridge. After this, he would take various glamorous foreign locations by storm—the South of France most urgently.

For research purposes as well as her own sybaritic curiosity, Kate longed to visit the glittering Côte d'Azur, rite of passage of every celebrity known to man and general byword for luxurious excess. Admittedly with little hope, she had nagged Denys Wemyss on an annual basis to let her cover the Cannes Film Festival for the *Mercury*. Miraculously, earlier this year—on the assurance that she would cover her own expenses—she had almost succeeded in persuading him. An especially bitter aspect of the Hardstone takeover was that permission for all such trips had now been withdrawn.

Kate's hopes for the ultimate trip—a home of her own and inde-

pendence—were being increasingly pinned on this novel. That *Northern Gigolo* would become a bestseller was her most cherished and
fiercely secret daydream; even Darren knew nothing of it. He had the
Denholme Velvets. She had Mark.

As the engine finally started, Kate ran the paragraphs written this
morning over in her mind. It seemed likely that, when the dreamed-of
publishing deal was finally struck, she might have to change a few
names.

> Glancing in the dressing-table mirror, Mark passed a hand
> through his dark gold hair. It was thick and springy, unlike
> the thin gray strands plastered over the spongy head of the
> alderman-vice president of the Chamber of Commerce. No
> wonder Doreen Bracegirdle preferred him to her husband.
>
> "Aaah. That's it, lad, just there. Oooh." Beneath him, on
> the bed, Doreen Bracegirdle ground her fleshy pelvis upwards
> in ecstasy. Mark watched as one slack, blue-veined breast
> slipped down the side of her well-covered rib cage. Christ,
> how many more of these flabby old bags did he have to get
> through before he escaped? He closed his eyes and thought of
> all the firm-breasted third wives of billionaires reclining on the
> decks of their husbands' Cannes-moored yachts. The world—
> and, more importantly, his wife—were waiting for him. But
> how was he going to get to them?
>
> "You're beautiful," he murmured to Dor—-

It was at that point that Mum's knock had exploded on her bedroom
door. Still, Kate mused, driving away, such was the lot of literary types.
Coleridge had had the Person from Porlock to contend with: she had
Margaret Clegg of Wits End.

It was a surprise to turn into the street that was home to the newspaper offices, and see that she had been beaten to it. Standing beneath
the *Mercury* sign was someone—a man—holding a huge umbrella
against the now-torrential rain. Kate hurried along the shining pave-

ment. She could be wrong, of course. Certainly, this wasn't the short, podgy figure she had anticipated. He was tall—very tall. His long dark coat had a stylish sweep about it. On the other hand, he was peering with what almost looked like interest—although it could have been horror—at the photographs in the window. Given the rain, he had to be standing there for a reason. No one, even in good weather, hung about outside the *Mercury* offices for fun.

She quickened into a run, feeling the puddles splashing up into her trousers. "Mr. Hardstone?"

The tall figure turned. Beneath the gloom of his umbrella she glimpsed brownish hair and level brows.

"I'm Kate," she said, rummaging violently for the keys and blinking as the rain dripped off her hair into her eyes.

"And I'm fucking soaked."

He wasn't, she saw, exaggerating. Despite his umbrella, every last inch of him was wet. The rain soaked his hair and ran in rivers down his nose.

Kate ushered him into the office, surveying him discreetly as the fly-studded strip light shuddered into action. Nathaniel Hardstone was well over six feet, she estimated. His eyes were big, and very blue. Their thick lashes were clumpy with moisture.

Kate felt her palms pricking. A blush rushed hotly up her neck. *This* was Peter Hardstone's son? This vision—this *god*—was the offspring of the short, ugly, bullying proprietor?

She regretted intensely not bothering with makeup. She could feel water coursing over her lips. Her insides were racing.

His large red mouth was shiny with water. His nose was straight, with delicate nostrils. There were patches of rose in his tanned cheeks, a lean, perfect swoop to his jaw. It wasn't just that she had never seen anyone this handsome in Slackmucklethwaite before. She'd never seen anyone this handsome *anywhere*.

3

Aware that she was gawping, Kate was relieved when the telephone rang. The relief was short-lived.

"That t'*Mockery*?"

"The *Mercury*, yes."

"I think I were right t'first time," said the other end of the phone sourly. "It's Adrian Grimshaw here."

Trouble was clearly afoot. Kate glanced apprehensively at Nathaniel Hardstone. Having draped his soaked coat on the stand, he had perched his rangy, dark-suited form on the end of Darren's desk and was plastering back his rain-slicked hair with a long, brown hand.

"Hello, Mr. Grimshaw. How can I help you?"

"My wife's just given birth to a six-pound baby boy called Joseph."

"Very many congratulations," said Kate sincerely, wondering apprehensively why she was being told.

"What did you say?"

"I said congratulations. That's wonderful news."

"Well, it *would* be bloody wonderful," interrupted Grimshaw testily, "except that it says in your *Hatches 'n' Matches* column that he's called Jacob."

"Jacob's a very nice name," Kate hedged.

"But it's not *his* name. Why would I want to call my son after a *biscuit*?"

Kate noticed Nathaniel Hardstone's full lips curling in amusement. His hair, drying, had began to gleam a thick, dark gold. As a long hank of it detached and dropped fetchingly into an eye, he shook it back with the insouciance of a supermodel, revealing cheekbones that could probably be spotted from the moon.

"Er, right . . . I'll make a full investigation and ring you back." She slid her eyes over to Hardstone again. Her heart leaped in alarm. Not only was he watching her now with obvious interest, but was clearly listening too. Something in her voice had alerted him. Fear, probably.

"Right." Kate attempted to sound in control, as if some valued tip-off from a reliable source was being transmitted down the telephone wires. "That's great, thanks."

She lowered the receiver and forced an indulgent chuckle in the direction of Nathaniel Hardstone. "One of our local stringers. Bursting with stories, as ever, ha *ha*."

"Stringer from where?" asked Nathaniel Hardstone.

"Erm," Kate plucked a name out of the air. "Slack Palisades."

"Yeah?" Hardstone's eyes narrowed. "Is that right?" He lingered sinuously on the *s*. "I didn't realize anyone lived there now except Dad."

"Ah." Bugger, Kate thought to herself. How *stupid* of her to have forgotten the estate had gone down the pan, or, rather, the mine shafts. She wondered anew whether Hardstone's involvement in Fantasia wasn't just a figment of Darren's and Freya's fevered imaginations.

"Hang on, though." A faint smile irradiated the Hardstone features. "I'd forgotten, but there *is* someone else living there. Next door to us, yeah?"

Saved. Kate nodded confidently.

"Some footballer," Hardstone went on. "Called Igor Blavatsky, plays for United."

Kate beamed in a manner intending to suggest that this indeed was the stringer.

"Can't speak a word of English though," Hardstone added with a wicked smile.

The door opened and Darren strode in, streaming wet, the buckles on his boots rattling like the bells on Santa's reindeer.

The smile faded from Nathaniel Hardstone's face. He stared at the plastic bag Darren had perched on his head to protect his backcombed coiffure from the rain. Despite such precautions, Darren's foundation was weather-beaten, his mascara had run, and today's lipstick was heart-attack white.

"This is Darren," Kate muttered to Hardstone. "My colleague."

Darren gave Hardstone a cursory nod before shooting over to Kate and enfolding her in a gleeful bear hug. His ex-army greatcoat, soaked through, smelt strongly of creosote. Behind his smeared mascara, his eyes boggled with excitement. "The Velvets got a gig! *Yee-hah!*"

"You've rung Jolene then? Darren's in a band," Kate explained to Nathaniel Hardstone.

The proprietor's son shrugged. "Whatever."

Darren shot him a look of dislike. "Jolene Shaw," he said to Kate. "She asked me a really odd question."

"What?"

Darren carefully removed the plastic bag from his head and raked his hands through his hair. "Well, I was giving her all the sales talk—about the Velvets being a high-concept cover band etc. and she just interrupted me. Said she couldn't care less about all that and what she really wanted to know was whether the Velvets could, well . . ." He paused and looked puzzled.

"Stand up?" Kate suppressed a smile. She sensed Nathaniel Hardstone's expression switch from contempt to incredulity.

"Yeah." Darren blinked with surprise. "How did you know that? But yeah, just stand up. Like, on your feet. Weird."

"So what did you say?"

"I said that, sure, the Velvets can stand up. Boy, can we stand up. We stand up straighter and better than anyone else in the business. So we play on Friday." Darren punched the air. "Result or what."

"So what do you think?" Kate hissed at Darren.

Denys Wemyss had by now arrived and, in a fluster of excitement, swept Nathaniel Hardstone into his tiny office.

"I think," Darren said, "that there's still a bit of that cake Joan brought in last week.

"I'm not talking about cherry cake." Kate rolled her eyes towards Wemyss's office. "I'm talking about *him*. Nathaniel Hardstone."

"Ah." Darren twisted one of his nose rings and looked wise. "Mr. Sex-On-A-Stick, you mean."

"Now you mention it, he is rather good-looking. I *suppose*."

"Yeah. You look as if you supposed that." Darren slid her a mocking glance.

Kate bridled.

"Good-looking creep if you ask me though," Darren added. "There's something about him I definitely don't like."

"And would that something," Kate teased, "be the fact that he wasn't very impressed by the Denholme Velvets' booking?"

"I think you're confusing me with someone who gives a toss what he thinks." Darren's eyes flashed with anger. "Come on, Kate. Surely you can see what an arsehole he is."

"He's got a lovely bottom, if that's what you mean."

"It's *not* what I mean," Darren snapped.

There was, Kate decided, no point pursuing the subject. She watched him lever off the lid of the cake tin.

"Hooray. Plenty left. Fancy a slice?"

"No, thanks."

Using the knife that was a permanent resident of the tin, Darren hacked himself a hefty lump. He held it up in skinny white fingers tipped with chewed, black-lacquered nails. "Awesome," he sighed.

Deciding to make a proper tea break of it, he reached for the *Mirror* and Kate snuck another glance in the direction of the editor's office. Wemyss, she could see, was on fire with the urge to pass on his half-century of newspaper experience; Hardstone's beautiful face, on the other hand, looked leaden with boredom.

How handsome he was. But there was no point in getting excited. You didn't have to be Darwin to know the law of nature dictating that men who looked like Nathaniel didn't go for women who looked like her. The hard-bodied blondes in glittery dresses who peopled the glossy magazine party pages were more his scene. Beautiful, expensive women with huge white smiles and perfect highlights. Not scruffy types with a foot of mousy regrowth like her.

"Christ Jesus," Darren muttered.

"What?"

"Champagne D'Vyne." He waved the paper. The purple spikes shook in disgust.

"That It Girl?" Kate was mildly interested. "That model, or actress, or mattress or whatever she is who was on . . ." She paused, reluctant to admit, even to Darren, that she had watched *Hello Sailor, I'm A Celebrity.* The blame could in all fairness be laid at Gran's door. An adoring fan of all travel programs, she had been addicted to this recent *Celebrity Big Brother* spin-off in which a novice crew of "personalities" including Champagne had set off on a voyage around the world, eliminating each other as they went. Champagne's rudeness to her fellow sailors had quickly proved compulsive viewing, despite her role in the proceedings being short-lived. As the first one voted out, she had been made to walk the plank—into a launch full of cameramen—just outside Dieppe. Yet her few days on board, or rather her few clothes on board, had proved hugely popular with the public. As a result, Champagne's profile was higher than it had been for several years.

"The one who was on *Hello Sailor, I'm A Celebrity*?" Darren supplied. "Yes. The very same. She's coming to live up here."

"Here? *Slackmucklethwaite?* Why?"

"Because she's going out with Igor Blavatsky, of course."

"Really?" Kate widened her eyes. Blavatsky, whose reputation was that of the quiet man of football, "a safe pair of legs" as the United manager had put it, was not the sort one would have imagined falling into the clutches of a notorious star scalp-hunter like D'Vyne.

"Igor's been suffering from groin strain recently," Darren mused. "Missed some important marches because of it. You don't think it's anything to do with her, do you? Never knowingly overdressed. Or dressed at all." He held up the *Mirror* to Kate. A beautiful blonde was lying across the center spread, back to the reader, pouting lasciviously over her shoulder. Her buttocks, between which could be glimpsed a tiny gold thong, were as round, full, and brown as a couple of newly-risen brioches. EEH BAH BUM read the headline.

In the paragraphs accompanying her bottom, the "model and actress" gave what the paper termed her "colorful opinions" about moving to the north of England. *"Have I ever been up north?"* muses the Hello Sailor, I'm A Celebrity *star. "God no, you must be joking. What the hell would I go there for? You should see this place Slackmucklethwaite—that name, for a start! The shops are crap, the food's disgusting, the peasants are ugly and stupid and I can't understand a word they say. By the way, that tape recorder's not running, is it?"*

"Unbelievable." Kate shook her head, eyes glittering with fury. "Go down a storm with the locals, that will." Her fists were clenched with anger. How dare anyone, least of all birdbrained Champagne D'Vyne, speak about her hometown like that? She felt violently defensive of Slackmucklethwaite; its Doge's Palace Town Hall, its funny, kind, hardworking people, the beautiful countryside surrounding it. "Of all the stupid, stuck-up, snobbish—" Her voice shook with anger.

"Steady on. Who cares what that silly tart thinks, anyway?"

"Yes, I know, *but* . . ." Kate huffed furiously through her nostrils.

Darren stood up. "Better be off anyway. Got an exclusive with the owner of an electrical appliance shop who's taken a half-page ad in the *Mercury. Live Wire* is almost certainly going to appear in the headline. He'll be a real shocker. And he'll certainly be expecting plenty of plugs."

The telephone was ringing when Kate got back from the loo. She crossed her fingers as she answered it.

"Hello?" she asked cautiously.

"About fucking time," growled the other end of the line. "Why the *fucking fuck* isn't there anyone in the fucking office?"

"Good morning, Mr. Hardstone."

"Can't see what's so fucking good about it. Where've you fucking been? I've been ringing for fucking ages."

"I've been—"

*"I don't want to hear excuses,"* the proprietor thundered immediately. *"You want a fucking job or don't you?"*

"Yes, of course, Mr. Hardstone." Kate forced syrupy tones through gritted teeth. "Now what can I do for you?" *A few tranquilizers, maybe? An injection? A restraining jacket?*

"Is that useless bastard of a son of mine there yet?"

"Yes. I mean, Nathaniel is. Do you want him?"

"No, I bloody well don't. I want to talk to that stupid old twat Wemiss. He *is* there, I take it?"

"Yes."

"Only last time I rang, he'd taken the entire fucking afternoon off."

"That's right. Mr. Wemyss was at his mother's funeral."

"Yeah, and what sort of an excuse is that? It wasn't as if the old bag was going to know he was there."

There seemed no answer to this.

"Who are *you* anyway?" Hardstone demanded. "What's your name?"

"Kate Clegg."

"Oh yeah. You're that reporter with the big tits."

Kate blinked. "Er . . . I'm *a* reporter, yes."

"Yeah. Okay-looking girl, you are. Be quite attractive if you lost a few stone."

Kate's throat contracted with fury. "I'll try," she muttered.

On the other end, Hardstone roared, *"Don't be fucking clever with me! I'm the clever one round here."*

"Sorry."

"Put me through to that fucking useless editor. *Now.*"

"He's in a meet—"

"I said *NOW !!*" bawled Hardstone.

"Could you just hold on for a minute, Mr. Hardstone?"

A stream of abuse came floating out of the receiver as she laid it on the desk.

"It's Peter Hardstone," she hissed, putting her head round Wemyss's glass door. She avoided meeting Nathaniel's eyes, but could feel them sliding over her body like the cool—*very* cool—water in that morning's shower. It was an effort not to shudder.

The editor's face contracted with panic. "Er, right. You'd better put him through, dear. Tell you what, why don't you take Nathaniel out for a bite to eat? Show him round town a bit. Take him for lunch somewhere." He looked at his age-worn gold watch. "It's . . . er, well, *almost* lunchtime, after all."

Kate looked at her own watch. 11:45 precisely. "Well . . . okay. I'll take him to Billy's."

Wemyss looked alarmed. "Are you sure?"

Kate understood his concern. the local beau monde Billy's was not. Then again, what was? And Billy's at least combined the cardinal virtues of being cheap, hot, quick, and near the office.

Billy's Café occupied a corner of the town's covered market. Its eponymous owner, a tense, quiffed fiftysomething whose red face spoke of drink or stress or possibly both, presided from behind a counter on which chips, bacon butties and beans were regularly plonked with considerable force. A shelf serving as a table ran round the café's inside, underneath which were a number of low stools. On these stools squatted Billy's regulars. Old ladies resting their legs during shopping. Young mums with squirming, squealing children. Aimless teenagers smoking over everyone.

Nathaniel Hardstone was examining a pinned-up sign advertising *Billy's Small Breakfast*—*bacon, tomato, sausage, fried slice, beans, mushroom, egg, toast.* He whistled. "That doesn't sound like a small breakfast. That sounds like a massive heart attack."

"I'd have a bacon sandwich if I were you."

"Whatever."

Having placed the order with Billy, Kate returned to her seat, aware of Nathaniel watching her.

"It's unreal, this place," he remarked, staring round. Although, Kate considered, *he* was the most unreal aspect of it. His beauty and air of unfettered privilege, remarkable in any surroundings, seemed almost shocking in those of Billy's. Like seeing an angel in a bus queue.

"Billy's?" She smiled. "It's unique, I'll give you that."

"Not just here. The whole fucking shooting match? Slackmucklethwaite-by-bloody-Slagheap." He rubbed his eyes with his hands. "Can't believe I've got to *stay* in this dump."

Annoyance rippled through Kate. "I thought you wanted to come to the *Mercury*," she snapped. "We were told that you'd chosen to."

The head shot back up. Blue as gas flames, the eyes burned mockingly into hers. "Ooooh, *sorry*. Didn't realize you actually *liked* living here."

"It's my home," Kate said defensively. "I've never really lived anywhere else."

"Course it is. *Course it is.*" His face was serious now. He was nodding understandingly, the front of his shining hair lolling up and down. The glance trained on her was rueful. "I'm sorry, yeah? Take no notice of me. I hate my home so I think everyone else does as well."

"What, you mean you hate Slack Palisades? Living with your father?"

Kate tried not to look as utterly riveted as she felt. Experience had taught her that insouciance invites more confidences than an eager-for-information face.

"Yeah. I hate him most of all."

Nathaniel Hardstone hated his father! She should, she supposed, not be surprised. Working for the tyrannical tycoon was bad enough. Living with him must be a nightmare. Being related to him hardly bore thinking about. The surprise, Kate realized, was not so much what Nathaniel Hardstone was telling her, but that he was telling her at all.

"My father's a bullying bastard," Nathaniel said with feeling. He looked at her expectantly.

Kate smiled diplomatically. She was not yet certain she trusted him.

The eyes looking into hers narrowed. The voice dropped to an intimate murmur. "Is it true he's trying to get you to do *stripping features*?"

Kate's features flinched in fury. "What?"

"Well, maybe I've got it wrong, eh?" He flashed her a brilliant smile. His eyes as they lingered were hypnotic. "Call me Nat, yeah?" he purred. "All my friends do. And I'm hoping . . ." he leaned meaningfully forward, "that we can be friends."

Kate felt her heart bounce round her rib cage.

Two loud thuds from the counter. "Two bacon butties," yelled Billy.

"I'll go," Nat offered, rising to his six feet plus.

Returning, he picked up a bacon sandwich and, an expression of fastidious disgust on his face, was examining the thick white doorstops of bread separated by a greasy pink filling of meat.

"So what *are* you doing here?" Kate prompted when he returned. "If you don't want to work on the *Mercury*, that is."

"Got chucked out of Oxford, didn't I?" He bit into his sandwich.

"*Oxford?*" Kate put down hers, untouched. Her stomach might be rumbling, but the risk of what was known in the *Mockery* offices as a "Billy's beard"—a stream of bacon fat cascading down one's chin—stopped her answering its call. "You got sent down . . . from *Oxford?*"

"Thass right."

She stared in amazement, trying to imagine throwing away such a chance. "What happened?" she asked, forcing her attention back to Nat.

He raised his blond-flecked eyebrows and grinned. "Combination of things really. To be specific, a combination of cocaine and marijuana that the senior tutor found in my room."

"*Drugs?*"

Nat chuckled mockingly. "Can see why you're a reporter. Mind like a steel trap." He put his hands up as her face contorted with fury. "Sorry! I was joking, yeah? Anyway," he said, grinning, "the senior tutor was seriously pissed off. Would be even more pissed off if he knew I'd been shagging his wife." He gave a self-satisfied smile.

"Oh. Right." Kate tried to sound disapproving rather than fascinated.

"So that's why I'm here. It's my punishment. I've been put in solitary in Slack bloody Palisades and made to work on the *Mockery*. Basically, my bastard of a father's gated me."

"Deep fried eyeballs," shouted Billy, thumping more plates down on the counter.

"Joke . . . *yeah?*" Kate grinned at Nat's horrified expression. "That's what Billy calls his deep-fried boiled eggs."

"Very funny." As he smiled at her—a crinkle-eyed, intimate

smile—she felt herself melting again. He leaned forward and touched her hand. "Tell me, Kate," he said softly. "What is it that you'd really like to do if you had the chance?"

"Well . . ." Kate hesitated. "It's not that I don't *like* working on the *Mercury*."

Nat nodded vigorously. "Course not. *Course* not."

"But I wouldn't mind moving on to another paper at *some* stage."

Nat's face was all encouraging seriousness. "Course you wouldn't. And who could blame you?"

"Somewhere like . . . London?"

He nodded emphatically. "Sure. Well, it's the obvious place, yeah?"

"And another thing," Kate sighed, her reticence melting in the face of his sympathy. "I'd love to do some more—well—*interesting* stories. For example, before your father took over the paper I was supposed to be going to Cannes, to cover the film festival. . . ." In the shadowy depths of her mind she felt the buried dream stir.

She had not anticipated the effect this modest admission would have. Nat's mouth dropped open. "Cover the film festival? For the *Heckerslike Mockery*? I mean, the *Mercury*?" His voice was incredulous.

"The *Mercury* connection was for the press accreditation really," Kate could not stop herself confessing." To be honest, I just wanted to go and see what the festival was like. And to try to get my name about a bit. If I'd struck lucky with a celeb interview I might have been able to sell it to a London paper or something." She blushed.

"Good thinking." The blue eyes had kindled again. Kate shivered with pleasure in their warmth. "You know, that's an amazing coincidence," he added gently.

"What is?"

"The film festival. I'm supposed to be going to a party there next week. It's going to be at this amazing villa on Cap Ferrat and it'll be *crawling* with directors and casting agents."

"And actors?" Kate guessed, wondering what was so exciting about casting agents.

"Sure. All the A-list."

"Wow." Kate stared at him enviously. Then a thought struck her. "Your father going to let you go, is he?"

Nat jabbed a cigarette between lips as sulkily beautiful as any supermodel's, tore a flame into being, shook the match out with a long brown hand, and inhaled deeply. "That old tosspot's not going to stop me doing *anything*. Especially acting."

"Oh I see. You want to be an actor?" As always when matters thespian were mentioned, Kate's thoughts flew to Gladys Arkwright as Juliet.

"Everyone at college was convinced I was the next Hugh Grant. Until the fucking senior tutor stuck his nose in. And then my beloved father, of course."

"Oh dear." So it wasn't just *her* artistic career Hardstone had stunted. He'd done the same to his own flesh and blood. "What a shame."

"Your trip to the South of France." He had leaned urgently forward. "Who was going to pay for that? Not Dad, surely."

"You must be bloody joking . . . er . . . I mean no, actually."

"So who was stumping up?" He was looking at her intently.

"Me, of course," Kate said proudly. Thanks to his father, her independence was limited. But nonetheless, it existed. "Out of my savings."

Mum had been horrified at the cost Kate was expected to bear personally, believing she should put her savings towards the first rung of the property ladder. Gran, on the other hand, urged her to spend it on having some fun.

"After all, you can't take it with you," the old lady pointed out. "There's no pockets in a shroud."

"A shroud!" Mum had exclaimed. "Our Kate doesn't need one of them yet, surely?"

"You don't think so? She's sure as heck buried alive here. *Never* forget," the old lady told Kate, "that adventure is the flower of life."

Not that, Kate thought glumly now, it's one I'm ever going to see. Much less smell. Or pick.

She looked miserably at Nat Hardstone. He was smiling at her.

Smiling, moreover, the kind of smile that made her knees shake and her insides tumble. In the poky surroundings of Billy's Café, it was as if the sun had suddenly come out.

Kate smiled back. Perhaps she'd been wrong about that flower of Gran's, after all.

4

$G$ran leaned toward Kate over the breakfast table. "You look very nice, love." Her good eye shone behind her glasses. "Have you met someone?"

"Not really." Kate tried to sound as enigmatic as possible through a mouthful of toast.

"By gum, look at you," Dad snorted, entering the kitchen. "All dressed up like a pox doctor's clerk."

"Leave 'er alone," Gran admonished, needles whirring away. "You look grand, love. Smart as a carrot." She winked at her granddaughter.

Kate managed a faint smile. Neither carrot nor pox doctor's clerk was the look she was aiming at. Subtly sexy was more the idea. She felt exhausted. It had taken half an hour to track down the stretchy black short skirt worn half a stone less ago, then another thirty minutes to reacquaint herself with her makeup bag. All hope of a quick session with *Northern Gigolo* had been finally abandoned as Kate had rummaged frantically for the right shade of lipstick. Was red her color?

"Any tea?" she asked. Her mother sloshed a stream of powerfully brown liquid into a mug bearing the legend *Slackmucklethwaite in Bloom*. It was, Kate saw, the end of the pot; the sort of tea that tasted almost dry and made you feel even thirstier. And exactly—she ducked a glance under the kitchen table—the color of Gran's support tights.

"Am I to take it then," Dad asked pointedly, "that you've finally finished in the bathroom?"

Kate glared at her father. Had it been her fault the special hair conditioning treatment had to be left in for fifteen minutes? Which she'd put to good use anyway, shaving her legs, armpits, and bikini line.

"Never mind 'im," Gran hissed comfortingly. "He should think 'imself lucky. When I was a girl we never even *had* a bathroom. We'd have a pan of water and we'd wash down as far as possible, and we'd wash up as far as possible." She leaned over and cackled. "Then, once everyone had left the room, we'd wash possible."

Kate exploded into her tea. "Oh Gran. You've ruined my lipstick." From the Birds of Britain clock, the coaltit announced nine. "I'd better go," she gasped. "I'm late."

As she left, she shot a cautious glance at her grandmother's knitting. The tank top—for it could be nothing else—was looking worryingly close to completion. "Had to wait forty minutes for a bus yesterday," Gran said, beaming, waving her needles. "Got the whole of the back section done."

To Kate's intense disappointment, the proprietor's son was not waiting outside when she arrived at the office. Glumly, she let herself in. Half an hour passed before the office door finally opened. Kate whirled round, ablaze with anticipation, to see not sleekly groomed sexy Nat, but Darren looking even more Gothic than usual. Besides blue-streaked spikes he sported metallic blue lipstick, blood-colored nails, and heavy purple eyes.

"Amazing eye shadow," Kate remarked.

"It's not eye shadow. Let's just call it a sartorial disagreement with some footballers outside a nightclub."

"What—they were laughing at your clothes?"

"No. We were laughing at theirs." He rubbed a skull-ringed hand across a forehead of Elizabethan pallor. "We were pissed as farts. God, I feel rough."

"Hangover?"

"At least six on the Richter scale. And there's a new driver on the bus who takes every corner as if it's Monza. Your kidneys are in your throat by the end."

"Who were you with?"

"The Velvets. Celebrating the Punch Out gig."

"Bit previous, isn't it, celebrating now? The gig's on Friday."

Darren nodded and grimaced. "Ouch."

"So why not wait until afterwards?"

"You know the Punch Out. If we go down well they'll throw their beer glasses at us in appreciation. And if we don't . . ." His Adam's apple bobbed nervously up and down. "Well, anyway, we thought we'd get our beers in early."

"Oh get a grip, Darren." Kate grinned. "Fame is your destiny. Or so you keep telling me."

"Yeah, I know. Last-minute nerves, I s'pose."

"Don't worry. If anyone can control the Punch Out regulars, it's Jolene Shaw. She's a black belt in karate." This was one of the more unusual personal details the landlady had vouchsafed.

"But her regulars are all black belts in drinking and inciting wanton violence."

"Well, you're not doing too badly on that front yourself. Getting beaten up by footballers."

"For your information, we didn't get beaten up by footballers. They got beaten up by us. Speaking of clothes, though . . ." He peered at her closely. "*Wow.* Haven't seen you this dressed up since Richard Whiteley switched the Christmas lights on."

Kate blushed. "It's just a skirt, that's all."

"A pretty short one though. I'm surprised," Darren said. "Wouldn't have thought you'd have wanted to go along with the new directives from On High."

"What new directives?"

"The ones Hardstone rang up about yesterday. While you were out having your *lo-ong* lunch with Lover Boy."

"He's not my Lover Boy. . . ."

"Well, you obviously wish he was," Darren said sourly.

"No, I don't."

"Do."

"Don't . . ." Oh, what was the point? Darren and Nat obviously hated the sight of each other. And besides, everything he had just said was true. "What did Hardstone say, anyway?"

"Basically that the attempts to increase revenue through more ads haven't worked."

"Can't see what that's got to do with my skirt."

"He wants us to try a different tack. Wants more . . . er . . . *glamour* in the paper."

"Glamour?" Kate repeated suspiciously.

"Hardstone's told Wemyss that, to survive, we need to dramatically boost the circulation—or 'stimulate interest in our organ,' as he puts it without the *least* hint of innuendo." Darren's purple-ringed eyes rolled ironically. "The bottom line, if I may put it that way, is that we need more sex."

"*More* sex!" Kate tried and failed to imagine the *Mercury* with sex in it at all. Wemyss had, memorably, once removed the word *nipple* from a front-page story about a breast milk scandal. But that had been in the days when the paper had carried proper news.

"Our great patriotic leader sent something over for you. It's on your desk, I think."

Kate shot across to where a couple of folded-up pieces of paper torn out of a newspaper magazine supplement sat atop the pile of supermarket press releases and general rubbish. She smoothed them out. BAREFACED CHIC blared the headline. Her eyes flicked over the first few paragraphs before looking up in fury at Darren. "It's about why stripping is trendy, by some reporter who did a course at the London School of Striptease."

Was this what Nat had been talking about yesterday? Her cheeks burned as the penny dropped. "Hardstone wants me to take *stripping* lessons?"

"Yep."

"And write about it for the *Mercury*?" She looked down at the article again. There seemed to be more to stripping than one might imagine. Casting "lascivious glances" was mandatory for a start. Along with what the piece described as "bottom work."

"If it's any comfort," Darren offered, "I've been told to advertise myself as a superstud in *Hatches 'n' Matches* and write about my raunchy nights out with whoever answers. I'm just praying it won't be Gladys Arkwright."

"The *humiliation* of it." Kate ground her teeth. "The cheek of it."

"There is a way round it, of course."

"Which is?"

"Get your new best friend Nat Hardstone to have a word with his daddy."

Kate hurled him a burning glance, which ended up at the office clock. Ten already. Where was Nat?

"Oh, he'll be along in a minute, I'm sure," drawled Darren, effortlessly reading her mind. "I expect he's a bit tied up at the moment. Probably reclining on a chaise longue surrounded by grape-peeling slaves and flicking through the latest Porsche catalogue."

"Ha *ha*."

Darren groaned as he sifted through a pile of photographs for the news pages. "Hardstone's insisting we put this one in." He waved a glossy photograph recognizably not one of Colin's.

"What is it?"

"The Organizing Committee of Charity Quiz Night and Dinner at Soddington Hall."

"Why are we running that? I thought all charity coverage had been banned on the grounds it doesn't make any money."

"You may well ask," Darren said ironically. "Could it be that, for all her colorful past, our new proprietor's wife is something of a social astronaut? A certain Mrs. P. Hardstone appears among the names on the back of the picture."

"A picture of Mrs. H? Ooh, let's have a look!" Kate snatched the photograph. Third from the left in the lineup of large ladies in little black dresses was a brittle-looking blonde in a very little black dress. "*That's* her?"

The proprietor's third and current wife was an object of fascination to Darren and Kate following Darren's discovery she was not only a former Stringfellow's pole dancer but an erstwhile actress whose greatest hit had been an all-naked biopic of the wives of Henry VIII called *Sexecution*. This latter titbit had been unearthed when, strictly in the name of research—the new proprietor having instantly axed the

*Mercury's* own Internet connection—Darren had been surfing porn sites in Slackmucklethwaite Library. Further elucidation had been impossible as Darren was asked to leave by library staff.

"It's her all right. If you ask her nicely she might be able to give you some pointers about bottom work."

"Sod off."

"The whole quiz night only raised five hundred pounds." Darren waved the photograph as he waltzed away. "Bit pathetic considering how many four-wheel drive concessionaries and battery hen barons they had crammed under one roof. A pig-out with a conscience if you ask me."

Kate raised her eyebrows and turned back her computer. Every so often she looked longingly at the door, hoping that Nat would walk through it.

Across the room, Darren was muttering to himself.

"What's the matter?" Kate asked.

"Spellchecker on my computer's playing up. Weird. It was fine *yesterday morning.*" He looked at her meaningfully. Kate remembered, as she remembered everything about yesterday afternoon, that Nat had spent some time at Darren's desk when he was out. The junior reporter had been visibly annoyed to discover him sitting there on his return.

"Maybe it's a virus," she suggested.

Darren snorted.

"Oh come on," Kate urged. Really, it was getting ridiculous. Darren, clearly jealous of the handsome prince of the press, was obviously looking for things to accuse him of. Most likely his computer problems were due to wear, tear, and the impossibility, given budget restrictions, of doing anything about either.

"Oooh, sorry." Darren's kohled eyes were wide with mock shock. "Touched a raw nerve, have I?"

"I'm only saying it might not be his fault." Kate was aware she might have gone slightly over the top.

An uncomfortable silence descended.

"Doing anything special this weekend?" Darren asked eventually.

"Shouldn't think so."

As much as was possible beneath its white foundation, Darren's face darkened. "You've *forgotten*."

"Forgotten what?"

"Friday."

Kate stared blankly at him. "Friday?"

"You *have* forgotten," Darren accused. "Since Lord Snooty came on the scene you haven't had a thought for anything else."

"That's not true," Kate insisted, knowing it was. "Just tell me what you mean. *What's* happening on Friday?"

"The Denholme Velvets, of course! At the Punch Out."

"Oh. Yeah. Course."

"You *are* coming?" Darren's eyes searched hers. "You've got to. You set the gig up for us—"

"Hang on a minute," Kate interrupted. "I only told you that Jolene Shaw was looking for acts."

"—and you're my *friend*," finished Darren. His voice was pleading. "You've got to support me. Fight for me, if necessary. You know what that pub's like."

"But you've just fought off all those footballers," Kate pointed out

"That's *nothing* compared to the Punch Out. They're *seriously* hard in there." He looked at her imploringly. "Say you're coming. Please."

"Er . . ." Kate's heart sank. A normal Friday night in the Punch Out was bad enough. Friday night in the Punch Out watching Darren singing humorous songs before an audience of unamused regulars was enough to make her bladder shrivel like a well-salted slug. And Darren was right; it seemed more than likely that the Denholme Velvets were about to receive a full and frank appraisal of their talents from what was probably known in the business as a challenging audience. No wonder he looked worried. Kate gritted her teeth and accepted the inevitable. He was, after all, her friend. She had to stand by him. "Of course I'm coming, you nutter. Try and keep me away."

"No need to go over the top." Darren looked genuinely relieved. "Bring as many people as you can."

*Like who?* Kate wanted to ask, but didn't.

To Kate's delighted amazement she picked up the telephone later that afternoon to find Nat on the end of it.

"Oh, hi," she said, trying to sound as if she had forgotten his existence, as if handsome millionheirs rang her up every day of the week. "How's it going?"

"It bloody isn't," Nat grumbled. "Dad got another call from the bloody senior tutor. His bitch of a wife's told him everything. So now I can't even leave the bloody house? It's like being the Man in the sodding Iron Mask. In which, incidentally, I would have been a damn sight better than Leonardo DiCaprio."

Kate slid a look at Darren, ostensibly concentrating on the Quiz Night but obviously eavesdropping madly. It was a relief when the doorbell buzzed to announce the postman and Darren reluctantly got up to answer it.

"So," Nat purred, "what about coming over on Friday night? Slack Palisades may be hideous in daylight but at night parts of it are positively atmospheric. Can't see the socking great craters in it then."

Kate chewed her lip. "Er . . . I've got a date."

"You *have?*" She tried not to be offended by his obvious amazement. "Who with?"

Fifty drunk men in a pub. That's atmospheric as well."

On the other end of the phone, Nat snorted with annoyance. "You're *not* serious. That Goth's gig? Chuck it, can't you?"

"But I *promised.*"

"Promised? Oh grow up. Are you seriously telling me you'd rather watch Edward Scissorhands being bottled off than go out with me? Or stay in, rather," he added sourly.

"Of course not." Kate jiggled in her seat in agony. But she had no choice. Darren would never forgive a no-show. Bugger. If only she'd never gone near Jolene Shaw and her blasted pub in the first place.

"I'll see you around," Nat said coldly, before the line went dead at his end.

Friday afternoon rolled round without any further word from Nat. The seal was set on a miserable day when Kate returned home to find that not only had Gran completed the disgusting tank top but, thanks to the last-minute decision to attach a crocheted egg-yolk-yellow butterfly, it was even more hideous than anticipated.

Defiantly ignoring the vicelike-grip of her trouser waistline—in a frenzy of comfort eating, she'd demolished the entire pack of office biscuits—Kate helped herself to a vast portion of Mum's stew and dumplings. It was especially good tonight; a rich sea of gravy swirling round succulent islands of meat.

The apple tart that followed was equally delicious. Kate had seconds of that too, telling herself she needed something substantial to survive watching the mauling the Denholme Velvets would inevitably get later that evening.

Just as she finally put down her spoon, Mum turned the subject to that of Gran's knitted top. "Aren't you going to try it on?" she urged. "Your gran's been slaving over that for you."

Kate looked at the mass of screaming orange and assertive yellow suspended from a coat hanger on the back of the kitchen door. It looked like an accident in a citrus processing factory. Reluctantly, she got up and seized it.

In the privacy of the bathroom, Kate stared in despair in the mirror. The tank top was too tight and incredibly hot; had Gran knitted it with asbestos? The too-small chest panel strained over her own too-large one. She'd had to take her bra off to drag the thing on, with the result that her breasts had been forced downwards and her nipples appeared somewhere around her navel.

The drooping effect was reinforced by the yellow crocheted butterfly sagging four inches or so above where her breasts ideally should have been. Worst of all, thanks to Gran's dodgy measuring, her arms were revealed in all their fleshiness right up to the middle of the shoulder and the acid colors only emphasized their blue-white pallor. Glumly, Kate raised them and inspected her incipient bat wings.

"Kate?" Her mother's fist pounded against the door. "*Kate!*"

"I'm still trying to get it on." Tugging the too-short bottom of the garment downward, Kate played for time. What was the hurry to see her modeling Gran's worst creation yet?

"There's someone to see you. At the door," Mum hissed through two layers of MDF.

Kate saw her reflected eyes in the mirror widen with surprise. Someone to see *her*? Darren in the grip of serious stage fright, no doubt. He'd clearly been heading that way; as she had left the office, he had responded to her valedictory "good luck" with a croak of terror.

The bungalow's frosted glass door was ajar. An unidentifiable human shape was standing behind it. Bare breasts chafing against the nylon wool, Kate opened it fully—and gasped. Not Darren.

Instead, the cool, appraising gaze of Nat Hardstone raked up and down the monstrous tank top, and Kate's violently reddening face above it. His eyes lingered, incredulously, on the crocheted butterfly. "Wow. Crazy outfit."

*Oh no.* This couldn't be happening. Not *now.* Not wearing *this.*

Nat himself looked like a Gap advert. Out of his suit, he seemed handsomer than ever; faded jeans hanging loosely from his hipbones, knitted woolly hat that would look ridiculous on anyone one whit less beautiful, and a complex type of trainer no doubt currently huge in Hoxton.

Why the hell, she wanted to scream, hadn't he phoned? Given her some warning—a week, preferably? As Kate hovered on the threshold in an agony of indecision, the halftime *Coronation Street* theme music wailed out of the lounge behind her, followed by the blare of the adverts.

"Glad to see you too," Nat drawled. "Actually, I thought we had a date. Edward Scissorhands, remember?"

"But . . . I thought you were under house arrest."

He flashed a triumphant grin. "I am, strictly speaking. Dad's set all his CCTV cameras on me. But fortunately I'm pretty good with computers, so I hacked into the house's central system and deactivated the electronic gates. A few disconnected wires I can reconnect later, and I'm a free man."

"I didn't realize you *wanted* to see Darren," Kate gasped.

"I didn't. But it sounds a lot funnier than anything on telly."

"Kate!" bellowed Dad from the lounge. "It's bloomin' freezing. Put t'wood in th'ole!"

Nat's eyebrow raised. "What did he say?"

"He means shut the door," Kate mumbled, knowing Dad had chosen the most obscure possible means of conveying the request expressly to tease her. "Come in."

Once inside, Nat stared unapologetically around. Kate imagined it through his eyes; the swirling Axminster carpet, Mum's extensive collection of mail-order animal dishes on the hall walls accompanied by some choice examples of the school photographer's art. Nat's lip curled in amusement as he surveyed these; Kate's toes meanwhile curled in shame.

"We're in here, love," Mum called from the sitting room. "Bring your friend in."

Excited noises from Gran. "Eeh, Kate. Come in 'ere and let me see what that top looks like on."

"She knitted it," Kate explained to Nat.

"To be honest I didn't think it was Stella McCartney," he muttered back, hesitating in the sitting-room doorway.

"Come on in," Dad shouted at him. "You're standing there like a spare dinner that's fallen on a mucky rug."

At this, Dad's traditional epithet for someone not obviously engaged in useful occupation, Nat's level brows shot defensively into his luxurious hairline. "What the hell does that mean?" he hissed at Kate.

"Nothing." Kate's bitten nails drove into the soft flesh of the palms of her hands. It was clear Dad was not impressed with Nat. Nigel Herring had received the same treatment. She could just about bear it if only, *if only,* he resisted the temptation to call her Kathleen.

"This is Nat," she announced, fixing Dad with a warning stare.

"All right?" Nat inquired in his Mockney drawl.

"Nat eh?" Dad remarked in dangerously light tones. "What, like the insect?"

"*Nathaniel,*" Kate said testily. "He works with me at the *Mercury.*"

"Lovely hat," commented Gran, peering at Nat over her bifocals. "What sort of wool is that?"

Nat looked at her curiously before saying shortly, "Dunno."

"Come and sit down, Nat," Mum said, beaming.

Nat looked irritated. He glanced at Kate. "Er, actually we're just about to leave, yeah?"

"What?" chortled Dad. "With our Kath . . . I mean our *Kate* wearing *that?*"

"What d'you mean? She looks grand in that top," Gran said indignantly, staring at her granddaughter's torso. "Doesn't she?" she urged Nat.

Nat cleared his throat. "She looks . . . er . . . interesting."

Kate stared at the floor and longed for it to sink beneath her.

"I'll go to our 'ouse on a pig," sighed Gran blissfully. Kate groaned in despair. All that remained now was for Dad to observe, as he invariably did when wanting to embarrass her, that the temperature outside was cold enough for two hairnets and the night itself was as black as the inside of a cow. "I'll go to t'foot of our stairs," Gran added, bestowing on her creation her ultimate accolade of delighted disbelief.

Meanwhile Mum had folded her plump hands and begun to give Nat an amiable third degree. "And what does your father do, Nat?"

"Well, he, um, sells papers, I suppose."

"You mean he's a newsagent?" Mum was clearly disappointed.

"He's in the newspaper *business,*" Nat corrected. "He, er, owns the *Mercury,* actually."

"'E owns t'*Mockery?*" Mum's voice was a deep, joyful baritone.

"I'll just go and get changed," muttered Kate, unable to bear for another second either Mum's excited face, Dad's darkly suspicious one or imprisonment inside Gran's hideous tank top.

In the privacy of her room, she tore the loathed column of nylon violently over her head. It scratched at her arms and clawed at her face as it went, a thing almost alive. A few minutes later, mascara'd, lipstick'd, and wearing a new white shirt with a pair of jeans that, after violent persuasion, had miraculously agreed to zip, Kate rejoined her family. Nat was refusing a piece of cake Mum was trying to press on him.

"Very good cake, that is." Dad's tones were offended.

"I'm sure it is, Mr. . . . er . . ."

"Clegg."

"Clegg, but I don't really *do* cake, yeah? Anyway," he said, spotting Kate with too-obvious relief, "we'd better be going. Wow," he murmured as he hurried into the hall, Kate after him. "I always thought Alan Bennett made it up."

Kate bridled. "They're all right," she muttered defensively.

"Bit of a grumpy old sod, your father."

"Just protective," Kate said loyally, thinking that when it came to grumpiness Nat's father swept the board. Not that she said so. She didn't want to argue, not now and not with Nat of all people. Her insides were churning with tension—over her family, herself, Nat, the knitted top, and even Darren, who by this time had surely arrived at the Punch Out. She pictured him, skinny and vulnerable, facing an audience of catcalling regulars with all the size and charm of the proverbial brick shithouses.

"Have fun!" bellowed Mum after them. Dad accompanied them to the door and peered out into the inky oblong of night.

"Black as t'inside of a cow," he remarked as Kate's teeth ground over each other.

Then, as Nat looked at him as if his sanity was in question, he leaned over and enquired mock-solicitously of his daughter, "You sure you're warm enough? It's cold enough for two hairnets out there."

5

It was late on Monday morning when Darren eventually appeared in the office. He looked just as shell-shocked as when Kate had last seen him at the Denholme Velvets concert. An evening every bit as unforgettable as she had anticipated.

Kate watched as he flung his soaked army greatcoat in the direction of the coat stand and grimaced as it crashed heavily on to his keyboard.

There was a silence, interrupted only by water dripping through the hole in the ceiling into the now-empty cake tin on the floor.

"What did you think?" Darren shot her an anxious look. "All right, was it?"

"*All right?*" Kate raced across the office to her colleague. "All right? *You were fantastic,*" she helped, hugging Darren so hard she felt something crack in his back. "Ooh. Sorry."

"S'okay," said Darren, looking pleased. "Getting quite used to being mobbed by female fans now, as it happens. Got recognized at the bus stop by two different women this morning."

"That was lucky. It's pissing down."

"I'm not saying they gave me a *lift.*" Darren grinned. "Fame's a cumulative thing, I suppose. Probably not even the Beatles got lifts at bus stops straight away. Particularly not if they were all together . . . anyway, like we say in Waiting for the Bus . . ." He strummed an imaginary guitar:

> It's never early, it's always late
> First thing you learn is that you've always got to wa-ait
> Ah'm
> Waitin' for me bus . . .

Kate guffawed, remembering the mixed roars of laughter and appreci-ation when, at the end of the concert, to wild applause, the Denholme Velvets had performed the number as a second encore.

Like the rest of the audience, she had been amazed—there was no other word for it—at the band's perfect comic timing and im-peccably po-faced performance. And in particular at Darren. He had not only looked the pop-star part, but played it to perfection. Strut-ting about the Punch Out stage, clearly in his element, he had even looked sexy.

"No, it wasn't bad." Darren grinned hugely.

"It was brilliant!"

"'Gladys in Furs' went down well."

"A triumph."

"And 'Uncle Ray.'"

"Everyone was dancing."

"Especially," Darren added, eyes glowing, "after all those students from the Andy Warhol Society turned up, thanks to Alex, our bass player—he's doing engineering at the university, although I'm not sure whether it's a degree or just mending the pipeworks. Anyway, it was him who told them about it."

"God, yes. They *really* got things going. They looked amazing. All that makeup and blond hair. Certainly gave Jolene a run for her money. Mind you, she was giving it some as well." The landlady had in fact been so delighted by the success of her first Live Music Nite that she had—with help—heaved herself on to the bar and performed an impromptu cancan of such spirit that several pints had gone west and many packets of pork rinds were stomped to powder.

"I was a bit worried about them at first," Darren confessed. "Keepers of the Velvet Underground flame and all that. Thought they might not approve of what we'd done to the songs."

"But they loved them. They were dancing on the tables to 'Farm Fatale.'

> All that muck
> You'd better watch your step

It's gonna break your leg in two
It's troo-oo-oo ⌄

Kate sang. "I loved that one. Hilarious."

"The whole place was going wild," Darren recalled joyously. "People were even throwing their knickers at the end."

Kate blanched slightly.

"Lord Snooty enjoy himself?" Darren asked lightly, but with an amused twist of his mouth. "I saw you'd brought him."

"Er . . ."

Nat had been fine at the beginning of the evening, when every woman in the Punch Out was staring at him with unbridled lust and every man with unbridled envy. Once Darren and the rest of the Denholme Velvets had, in every sense, taken center stage, it was hard not to notice that his interest had notably waned. He had, in fact, spent the second half of the set answering a stream of text messages on his mobile.

"He must have done. It was brilliant," Kate assured her colleague. "I've never seen anything like it round here."

As Kate and Nat had left, the air outside the Punch Out had been full of excited shouts. Yet they had climbed back into his silver MX5 in silence. Nervously, she had tried to lighten the atmosphere. But Nat merely sighed at everything she said and held the black leather padded steering wheel with one hand, almost losing control as they rounded a precarious bend.

"Shit!" hissed Kate. Nat looked at her in irritation. She stared miserably at the floor. She had no one but herself to blame for the disaster of the evening. The suggestion Nat should come to the Punch Out had been one of the most unbelievable idiocy. He'd obviously hated every minute, and would certainly never ask her out again. She wanted to kick herself, yet was prevented from doing so by the flotsam and jetsam in the passenger footwell. Old papers, a pair of battered and frankly smelly trainers, cigarette packets, chocolate bars for some reason without their wrappers.

They drove on without speaking for what seemed like forever.

When Kate looked up it was to see the car drawing up outside Wits End. So this was good-bye. Oh, and see you in the office—maybe. She pulled back her lips into a breezy smile, determined to put a brave face on it.

Nat leaned over. Beneath a top note of cigarettes and beer, the scent of expensive aftershave wafted toward her. "Come for tea on Monday," he murmured.

Kate gripped the leather seat edge in excitement. Another date! "Great," she said, trying to sound casual. "Monday, you say?"

"Dad'll have left by then."

"Left?"

"Gone to London to see his accountants. To try and dig himself out of all the shit he's in."

"Oh, right." Kate tried not to look either as thrilled as she felt or as if she knew what he was talking about. Did Darren and Freya's investigations, then, have some truth after all? She tried to blank Nat's assessing look.

"Yeah, he's in a lot of shit. Up to his eyeballs. Didn't you know?"

Kate shrugged.

"But who gives a fuck about him, eh?" Nat said violently. "While the twat's away and all that. Seems a shame to let the old homestead go to waste. There's a private cinema, swimming pool . . . everything." His eyes shone wickedly. "Not to mention teabags. And I'm sure there's some cake somewhere."

Out of the corner of her eye she saw the Wits End sitting-room curtains twitch. Alarm shot through her at the prospect of Dad stomping down the path with a flashlight. "I'd better be going."

"Yeah, before that scary dad of yours comes out and beats me to death with a black pudding."

"Ha *ha*."

Nat grinned. His teeth gleamed in the dashboard light. "Come about four. Tell that old git of an editor you're judging a ferret-throwing competition or something."

*     *     *

Something was moving and rattling in front of her face. Darren's braceleted arm, Kate slowly realized. "Hello? *Hello-o?* Anybody in there?"

"Uh, sorry," Kate muttered, homing back in on the office, Monday morning. "I was miles away."

"You must have been. You didn't react at all when I told you the most amazing thing about Friday night."

"Which was?"

"So I'll just have to tell you again." Darren sighed elaborately. "Did you happen to notice a smallish bloke in a black T-shirt standing at the back of the room?"

"No. Should I have?"

"Turned out he was A and R for Chip Shop."

"Which translates as what in English?"

Darren rolled his eyes. "Spots talent for this really happening new record label. They've been looking for one more act to take on a European tour. The A and R man was only here because he broke down on his way to check out some eighties revival band in Blubberhouses. *And guess what?*" Darren thumped the table. There was a clatter as part of the computer detached itself. "Chip Shop want to sign *us*! The Denholme Velvets! They reckon we've got star quality!"

Excitement flashed through Kate, swiftly followed by envy. She grabbed her colleague by the shoulders. "Darren! That's *fantastic*! Oh God, you're going to be *so* rich and famous!"

"Well, probably not *immediately*," Darren admitted. "The money's not much and the record company's pretty new. We're hardly Oasis, but at least it's a start." His eyes burned with joy. "Tour sounds great though. Italy, Spain, and France, and we finish with a couple of dates on the Riviera."

The phone rang. As he answered it, Kate felt another wave of hot envy smash over her head. The South of France. Oh, it wasn't fair.

She reeled herself hastily back in. Her chance would come eventually. It had to. It always came to those who waited, after all. And at least she had four o'clock to look forward to. Never had she anticipated a cup of tea so much.

*      *      *

Kate parked on the outskirts of the Slack Top settlement and walked through the lovely old village. She breathed in the fresh, sharp air of the high country and admired the perfectly preserved eighteenth-century weavers' cottages with their rows of high windows to let in light to work by. She peered down the shadowy passages, up the sweeps of shiny cobbled lanes. Passing the handsome Georgian Weavers' Arms, Kate glanced with interest at the pub's gourmet restaurant, Spinning Jenny's. Thanks to the establishment flatly refusing all attempts to persuade it to advertise in the *Mercury*, it was beyond the reach and, sadly, the stomach of the *Eating Out* compiler. The average *Mercury* reader was possibly not the target audience anyway, to judge from the crowd of gleaming Jaguars and BMWs outside. The ostentatiously well-heeled of the area, "the ten-bob millionaires" as Dad liked to call them, had obviously taken the place to their hearts.

She looked at her watch and saw that it was ten to four. Tea was at four.

A few minutes later Kate was dashing through the huge gilt entrance proclaiming *Slack Palisades* in elaborate ironwork. The place was deserted and, up close, even uglier than expected. From behind huge and brutal automatic gates, drives of custard brick wiggled between rampant *leylandii* hedges. No house seemed complete without a bolt-on plastic conservatory and vast, awkward bay windows hung with colossal curtains. Each garden featured fake dovecotes, concrete heraldic beasts, and patios with alfresco ovens. Also standard were stableyard-effect multicar garages and Elizabethan-style weather vanes.

The landslip damage, Kate saw, was impressively widespread. In most drives, ragged bits of brick hung like loose yellow teeth over the edges of gaping holes. If what Darren said was true, Hardstone had shafted himself. She smiled at the thought.

"Don't know what you're looking so pleased about," grumbled a voice beside her. Kate came down to earth with a shock. A tall, broad, and formidable woman with a shiny red face, large red-framed glasses, spiky hennaed hair, and layers of flappy aubergine clothes had emerged from behind some *leylandii* and was regarding her balefully. Kate recognized Darren's coinvestigator.

"Hello, Freya."

The hands of Slackmucklethwaite's leading vegetarian fire-eater and conservationist, gloved in multicolored woollen stripes, gripped a wooden pole atop which a placard commanded PETER HARDSTONE GO HOME in lime-green neon letters. Seeing Kate looking, she twirled it testily to reveal, on the back, DODGY PETER PLANNING DEPT CHEATER.

"There's nothing to smile about up here, you know," Freya huffed. "This is prime historic greenbelt land that's been ruined by unscrupulous developers." She waved her banner emphatically.

"A shame," Kate commiserated, reluctant to be drawn into the debate, or at least the Hardstone part of it. She was still not entirely sure she believed Darren's allegations. She looked hastily around. And should Hardstone appear, being seen with Freya would do her career prospects—such as they were—little good. Then, with a rush of relief, she remembered Hardstone was away.

"You bet it's a shame," returned Freya. "*Greenbelt land!* Just *look* at it!" She flung out her free arm, which featured more bracelets even than Darren's. These, together with the vast dangling earrings dragging down her lobes, made her rattle like a win on a Las Vegas slot machine. "Ruined! All that biodiversity down the toilet! Peter Hardstone's more of an environmental fucking disaster than a chain-smoker in a black rhino-skin coat holding an ivory cigarette holder on the deck of a leaking bloody oil tanker." She brandished her placard. "But he's cruising for a bruising, let me tell you. I've dug up more dirt about him than *he* dug up to build this pile of crap in the first place."

"Darren told me," Kate said, wondering how best to make her excuses and leave. "You're working on it together, I understand."

"*Were* working on it together," Freya corrected. "He tells me he'll get sacked if he does any more on it. Man of straw. But it won't stop me, oh no. Sooner or later everyone's going to know what happened here. That arsehole Hardstone can't gag me. He's heading for a fall—down one of his own bloody holes." She thumped the placard.

"Freya, I'm sorry, but I have to go. I'm going to be late for something."

"We're all late for something," thundered the environmentalist. "Saving the planet, for instance. And we've got people like that bastard Hardstone to thank for it." As, again, she smashed the base of her pole against the pavement, Kate hurried off, feeling thoroughly guilty. Freya was right, of course. It *was* incredible that something as crass and brashly vulgar as Slack Palisades could be built within spitting distance of lovely Slack Top. Particularly on protected land riddled with historic mine shafts. Although, in a sense, it seemed the land had got its own back.

Besides, Kate had other issues on her mind just now. Such as having forgotten to ask Nat which of these houses he actually lived in. On the other hand, it should be easy. Hardly anyone lived here now, after all.

It didn't take long to spot it. Behind arrowhead-topped gates in a particularly lurid shade of gold was the biggest, peachiest building of all, the one featuring more glass excrescences than any other. The gateposts, each topped with a concrete unicorn, bristled with more security than a world leaders' conference. The concluding piece of evidence, however, came from the sports car in the driveway; the house was inhabited.

In the center of the huge gold gates was mounted a large coat of arms. For some odd reason it seemed to be charred, but Kate could make out an unrecognizable lump quartered with something that bore an improbable resemblance to a high-heeled shoe. Neither made much sense, and that they had been approved by the Royal College of Arms seemed doubtful.

The brass-finished closed-circuit TV cameras swiveled suspiciously in her direction. She pressed the buzzer on the gatepost.

"Sod off!" yelled a female voice through the roaring crackle of an intercom. Kate started in surprise. Hadn't Nat said he was home alone? Or was this some sort of servant? She should have realized Peter Hardstone would have a staff of thousands to supervise his personal comfort, if not to run his newspaper. Not much of a greeting though, whichever way you looked at it.

"Er, Nat's expecting me," Kate yelled back.

The cameras whirred and clicked and the gates opened with more of a shudder than their hi-tech appearance implied. Dodging the occasional chasm, Kate followed the yellow brick road.

Two hideous concrete busts—one male, one female—were set into shallow circular alcoves on either side of the front door. The man's head was an astonishingly idealized interpretation of the brutish features of Peter Hardstone. Astonishing, Kate thought, because she had not believed idealizing them would be possible. The woman's head featured cascades of hair and what seemed even in cast concrete to be remarkably plump lips.

The white-paneled entrance was heavily festooned with brass door furniture. Kate was trying to locate the bell amongst it when the door suddenly flew open. The first thing to emerge was a powerful gust of perfume, closely followed by a skinny, miniskirted and very tanned blonde some considerable distance from the first flush of youth. Her hair had a curious, fried appearance. She wore high heels and a pink sequined T-shirt bearing the legend *Uber-Babe* through which thrust a turbo-charged bosom. An enormous number of necklaces disguised a possibly less than youthful throat. Her heavy makeup seemed excessive for a quiet Monday afternoon.

Kate knew from the Soddington Hall photograph that this was the third Mrs. Hardstone, erstwhile Stringfellow's pole dancer and star of *Sexecution.* And while this dashed her hopes of being alone in the house with Nat, meeting this legendary figure was compensation of a sort.

Mrs. Hardstone III looked Kate up and down. "Hellair," she said in fluting, girlish, and determinedly upmarket tones. "I thought you was that ridiculous vegetarian woman trying to set fire to the gates again."

"Freya Ogden." Kate tried not to feel offended at being confused on the CCTV with the considerably larger environmental campaigner. Perhaps the third Mrs. Hardstone was unusually shortsighted. An inability to view the full extent of her husband's repellent appearance would certainly aid marital felicity.

"You *know* her?" The rhinoplastic nostrils flared.

"Er no, not really," Kate lied hurriedly.

The blonde regarded her with suspicious and thickly mascaraed eyes. "So who maight you be?"

"A friend of Nat's."

The thin brown arms folded. "He never mentioned he was expecting anyone."

What exactly did this woman think she was going to do? "He's asked me," Kate said wearily, "for *tea.*"

"Indeed." The shiny red lips twitched with amusement. "*Tea.* So that's what he's calling it now."

Kate gave her a level state.

Mrs. Hardstone III stared back. "May I ask how you know my stepson?"

"We met," Kate explained patiently, "when he came to work on the *Mercury*. I'm the senior reporter, Kate Clegg."

"So you work for my husband?" The woman flashed a tight, complacent smile. "I'm Brogan Perks-Hardstone," she added, extending a limp brown hand on which several large and expensive stones glittered. "*Mrs.* Peter Hardstone. Suppose you'd better come in."

Kate followed the sinewy calves into the hallway. "Wow."

"Glad you like it," trilled Brogan. "It's all brand new. A surprise for my husband. He's away for a few days so I thought I'd decorate the house to surprise him. Stamp my personality on it."

Some personalities, Kate decided, were best left unstamped.

"Amazing, don't you think?" prompted Brogan.

Amazing, Kate thought, was the word. Other possible words were *kitsch, camp,* and *completely tasteless.* She had never seen an interior as grotesque in her life.

A dark red velvet pelmet heavy with swags, tassels, and fringes ran around the top of the walls. From this streamed lengths of purple velvet looped back with red silk ropes to expose layers of gold brocade and leopard skin. Mounted on the leopard skin were pairs of ornate gold candle sconces flanking mirrors in gilt frames writhing with carving. Below these, parked against the wall and facing each other across a zebra-patterned carpet, were two huge gilt and purple satin thrones festooned with fringes and silk tassels and heaped with gaudy cushions. Dotted everywhere were small tables swathed in silk and satin, their surfaces crowded with fussy little china dishes.

"Wow," Kate said again, groping for the words. "It's . . ."

"Baroque-and-Roll," crowed Brogan.

"Sorry?"

"That's what my desayner calls it. Sort of seventeenth century meets rock-star glam."

"I see." Keeping her expression noncommittal was a challenge; with every second that went by Kate felt it struggling towards a snigger.

"He did the lounge—I mean drawing room—as well." Beckoning Kate to follow her, Brogan strode through into a room whose ceiling was padded with amethyst velvet pierced with huge buttons covered in the same material. The effect was like looking up at the seat of a huge, purple piano stool.

"Ceiling upholstery!" beamed the mistress of the house. "It's my desayner's speciality. His signature look. Some of those frames have twenty-four Karat gold in them." She pointed to where more ornate mirrors, mounted against the red-brocade-covered walls, hung out at perilous angles from oversize pearl chains.

"Incredible," Kate remarked, taking in the groups of satin-swathed ottomans and brocade sofas clumped about the leopard skin carpet.

"Furniture with attitude," Brogan corrected. "Every single piece done specially for me by my desayner."

You don't say, Kate thought. "Who *is* this designer?"

"Who? *Who?* Marc de Provence, of course. Would have thought that was obvious. Don't you ever read *Wallpaper?*"

*"Marc de Provence?"*

"*Only* today's most happening desayner," Brogan sneered. "A French aristocrat from a very old and very rich family who bases all his designs on the simply *fabulous* château he grew up in. Have you *really* never heard of him?"

"No."

Brogan tried and failed to pucker her obviously Botoxed brow. "But he's famous on seven continents!"

Kate blinked. *Were* there seven continents? "Oh, right."

"Well, I suppose he's not really *aimed* at people like you," Brogan said pityingly. She gave an affected little titter. "I mean, with a pair of candle sconces going for upwards of eighty thousand pounds, beds at around a hundred thousand pounds, and each bit of material you see on the wall here costing more than a thousand pounds a meter, he's not really in your league."

"No," Kate said, trying to strike an appropriate note of regret while resisting the urge to squeal with laughter. Brogan had paid more than five times her annual salary for those tawdry candle brackets? On the other hand, given the short financial leash Hardstone kept his staff on, that wasn't funny at all. It was bloody annoying.

The proprietor's wife seemed oblivious to her insensitivity. More likely, Kate realized, she didn't care. "The Hollywood stars *love* him," she gushed on. "Practically every single one of them's got his signature sateen throne. That's where I first saw his work."

"What, in Hollywood?" *Sexecution* must have been more successful than any of them had imagined.

"On an episode of my favorite program, *Celebrity Homes.* I knew then and there that I just had to have him. He did the whole look in two days!"

Kate agreed that two days was remarkable. That so much rubbish could have been imported in a mere forty-eight hours defied belief. Irritation swept through her, and not only because of the decor.

Where was Nat? Why hadn't he come down to welcome her?

Just then, a tall figure appeared in the doorway opposite the room's entrance. It wore blue-and-red striped pajamas. It leaned against the gilded doorframe, yawned, stretched and seemed to do a double take on seeing her.

"Nat!" A mixture of relief and indignation coursed through her. He *hadn't* forgotten. *Surely.*

"Just got out of bed, darling?" Brogan drawled archly. "*Rather* rude of you. Especially when you'd invaited um, sorry-I've-forgotten-your-name here for tea."

Before Nat, now recovered and smiling smoothly again, could re-ply, the front door slammed with violent suddenness. "Anyone home?" roared an unpleasantly familiar voice. Brogan started. Kate froze. Hadn't Nat said his father was in London? She glanced over at him in the doorway. But the blue-and-red pajamas were no longer there. Along with Nat himself, they had vanished.

Then, nasty, brutish and short, Peter Hardstone stomped into the sitting room.

6

Hardstone was not alone. In his wake came a gray-uniformed chauffeur wearing a cap with a PH monogram. *"You fucking clown!"* Hardstone was ranting to his unfortunate companion. "You stupid clumsy *bastard.*"

"Dahling!" trilled Brogan, trotting nervously over to her husband. "We weren't expecting you back until tomorrow! What a mahvellous surprise!"

Hardstone looked at her with contempt before rounding back on his unfortunate driver. *"You blind or something?"* he roared. *"Why the fucking fuck didn't you look where you were going?"*

Kate felt sorry for the driver. She shot him, as one beleaguered Hardstone employee to another, a sympathetic fraternal glance. He did not return it.

Brogan placed a hand on Hardstone's arm in apparent demonstration of how easily she could tame the beast. "Surely he's not crashed the Ferrari?" She glared at the chauffeur. "After all, it would hardly have been the first incident of this nature, would it? That time you reversed into me when I was walking behind the F? Almost ran me over, you did."

There was something about the chauffeur's mutinous expression that suggested the *almost* was a source of regret.

Her husband batted her hand away. "No. The F's fine."

"So what's happened then, precious?" Brogan lisped, batting her eyes. "What's nasty driver done to upset my sweet little Petey-Weety?"

Despite her horror at seeing her employer, Kate found it hard to suppress an involuntary snort of mirth at this.

Brogan's sweet little Petey-Weety paused, then drew back his lips in a snarl. *"Only that he completely failed to hit that bloody stupid hippie who marches around with that sodding placard all day long."*

Brogan clasped her hands together in horror while flashing a glance of sneering triumph at the chauffeur. He stared insolently back. They had clearly crossed swords before.

"There she was," fumed Hardstone, "right in front of the bloody *bonnet.* And what does he go and do? Only swerves to avoid her, that's all. We could have flattened her!" he roared in anguish. *"No one would have bloody seen! She could have been squashed flat!"* he howled like a harpooned elephant.

"Wouldn't have been 'xactly legal though, would it?" the driver muttered.

The cords stood out on Hardstone's fat neck. *"Not legal? Who the hell cares if it's legal?* Legal's for wimps! Legal's for *little people."*

The chauffeur shrugged. "Didn't mean to offend, I'm sure," he said in a voice that implied the exact opposite.

"I sincerely hope you didn't," Hardstone snarled, pressing his large red face close to his driver's. "Because, as you know, I'm not a violent man. It's just that people who cross me have a tendency to meet with," his voice dropped to a threatening hiss, *"unfortunate accidents."*

There was an uncomfortable silence.

*"You!"* Hardstone said, suddenly swivelling his molten little eyes on Kate. "I recognize you. That girl from the *Mercury,* aren't you?"

Kate nodded.

"So how's my useless bastard of a son shaping up as an office boy?"

"Nat's a great help," Kate said through gritted teeth. How could he, how *dare* he, leave her alone to face his father?

"First time in his life he ever has been then," Hardstone said, addressing Kate's breasts. "By the way, how's the stripping going?" He smiled at her—a lascivious smile that made her shudder.

Kate looked at him speculatively. For a delicious minute, she pictured herself telling the proprietor exactly what she thought of him. A grand gesture that would, of course, be career suicide. "I'm working on it," she muttered.

He grunted with apparent satisfaction before demanding with terrifying suddenness. *"So why the hell aren't you in the office?"* he boomed.

"I've come to tea with Nat."

"Tea?" Hardstone snarled. "Is *that* what he does all day? Sits around sipping Earl Grey like some fucking old *dowager*? Hope you don't *fancy* him or anything."

Kate looked indignantly at the empty doorway formerly containing Nat. Had he disappeared for good, or was he just around the corner, out of sight? She did not answer Hardstone.

"You'd better not," Hardstone snarled. "Because, lazy arse though he is, he's too good for the likes of you. I want a daughter-in-law with a bloody title, at the very bloody least."

Just as Kate felt her self-control tug violently from her grasp, Nat reappeared in the doorway. "Oh, for Christ's sake, Dad," he muttered, "don't be such a bloody snob."

"Snob!" Hardstone roared. "Me? A snob?" He strode over to his son and poked him in the pajama-striped chest, emphasizing each word with a stubby finger. "How. Can. I. Be. A. Snob. When. I. Don't. Care. What. Class. I. Am?" he bellowed. "I'm neither working-class nor middle-class nor upper-class. *And I don't give a fucking damn. Know why?*" He directed this last at Kate. She shook her head.

*"Because I'm the only class that matters,"* Hardstone boomed triumphantly. *"Rich class."*

Behind him, Brogan tittered. But Hardstone's self-satisfied grin had already snapped off at the mains. As his gaze rolled around the decor, taking in the swags, the tassels, the fringes, his small, hot eyes widened and his mouth dropped slowly open. He stared at the leopard skin, the sconces, the signature sateen thrones. The fussy little china dishes.

There was a brief, heavy pause in which the tycoon's rasping, sticky breathing echoed round the sitting room.

Brogan flicked back her hair and arranged her frontage. Her eyes shone with the expectation of triumph. She opened her mouth, but the words were never uttered. They were drowned by Hardstone's sudden, mighty roar.

"What the fuckin' *fuck* . . ." He turned savagely on his wife.

Brogan's smile was locked and rigid. "A lovely surprise for you, Petey-Weety. I thought the place could do with a teensy overhaul. Something a little more . . . staylish?"

*"It's like the inside of Elton John's bloody knicker drawer."*

Kate watched Brogan's mouth slam shut and her eyes well. She was no fan of the proprietor's wife, but it was impossible not to feel sympathy at such abject failure. Although the chauffeur, visibly smirking, seemed to find it possible enough.

"Who did this?" Hardstone demanded in a low, dangerous voice. *"Who did this?"*

"The celebrated interior desayner Marc de Provence," his wife bleated. "He's famous on seven continents for Baroque-and-Roll."

*"Baroque-and-Roll?"* Spittle sprayed from the proprietor's mouth.

"Yes, like rock and roll," Brogan stammered.

Striding over to the fur-draped wall, he slammed his fat fist against it, his toupee fairly shuddering with the force of the action. As the company looked on, £80,000 worth of sconce crashed to the floor. Immediately afterwards, one of the mirrors slipped, slumped drunkenly outwards and then, as the pearl chain holding it snapped, fell heavily downwards and smashed into a thousand pieces.

"Whoever this French poof is, he obviously saw you coming," Hardstone snarled at Brogan. "Not that, given your films, everyone else hasn't at one time or another," he added brutally.

As Brogan burst into sobs and hurled one of the fussy little china dishes at her husband, Kate saw Nat making frantic "over here" gestures from the door. Her opportunity came as, continuing the domino effect of destruction that Hardstone had started, a corner of wall covering flapped off and a £1,000 swathe of red brocade sagged from its moorings. Slowly, one by one, the drawing pins holding Baroque-and-

Roll in place pinged out, hitting those present painfully in the face. Then, with a swooshing noise, the material slithered off, bringing down with it an entire haberdashers' department of black satin, purple velvet, and hot pink tassels. All of which entirely swamped Peter Hardstone who stood directly underneath.

Nat and Kate left Brogan to face the consequences. Within minutes, they had fled down a corridor, up a flight of stairs, and were in the safety of Nat's room behind a closed and locked door. Somewhere in the distance, a roar as of a maddened bear echoed, accompanied by shrieks and the crashing of china.

"I almost feel sorry for Brogan," Kate remarked. She had sat down on a pile of small, hard cushions that threatened to slip from beneath her buttocks at any moment.

"Don't be." From the bed, where he sprawled on his back, long legs crossed at the ankle, Nat's face was set and his eyes glowed angrily. "Look what she's done to my bedroom. I feel like bloody Barbie."

He had a point. The walls were draped in hot pink crushed velvet and over the circular pink bed in the center hung a white canopy of ectoplasmic muslin. Above this swung a huge and hideous chandelier bulging with china flowers. Tall incense burners of vaguely classical appearance stood at regular intervals round the walls. Between them squatted half a dozen sateen pouffes in pale lilac.

"Is Brogan the bust by the door?" It had been difficult to tell.

"For the moment. But frankly the turnover's so fast I don't know why Dad bothers having them cemented in."

Crash! Bang! The distant battle raged on.

"Not sure Brog's going to make it much longer," Nat drawled. "Dad's sacked wives for less than this. He'll probably be filing in the morning."

"Really? For divorce?"

"Well, I don't mean his nails, do I? Irreconcilable decorating differences, it'll be this time. No doubt Brogs'll get custody of the Jacuzzi, though. There's a particular jet called the Italian Stallion she's extremely into." Nat rummaged in his pajama pocket for a cigarette and snapped a lick of flame at its tip.

"The way Dad's going, he won't be running the company for much longer, either." He snorted. "The fat old sod's not as rich class as he'd like everyone to think."

"How do you mean? Why not?"

He exhaled again, flat on his back, the smoke rising like whale spume. "Would have thought that was obvious. You've noticed the cutbacks, I take it."

"You couldn't not. They've been pretty swingeing."

"They've had to be. Whole company's going down the pan. He's trying everything to drum up the cash. All his editors—even the ones in London . . ."

Kate felt a bolt of excitement. Hardstone had editors in London?

". . . Dad's new idea is to sack them unless they put up their houses as collateral to keep their newspapers afloat. Problem is, he heavily overinvested in Slack Palisades and now he's in debt up to his eyebrows. Banks'll foreclose soon, unless he can come up with some kind of rescue package."

Kate swallowed. She was beginning to feel uncomfortable and out of her depth. She took a deep breath. "Er, Nat—look, why exactly are you telling me all this? I work for your father, don't forget."

He stared at her. His eyes under their lowered lids had a spell-binding, slave-making quality. "Yes, but you hate him, don't you?" he said softly.

Kate blanched. Fear flashed warningly through her. She stared at him helplessly.

He smiled. "But you do, don't you? I mean, anyone normal does. The man's a complete c—"

"Look," Kate said hastily, starting to get to her feet.

Nat sat up. "Hey, relax babe. I'm on your side, doll, believe me. I hate my father's guts. He's a bully, a bastard, and a crook. No one could be more chuffed than me that he's in all this shit. And, since you ask, the reason that I'm telling you is that you're my friend, yeah? And you want as much as me to get out of this dump of a town . . . well, you know what I mean," he mumbled, catching Kate's defensive glance.

Kate leaned back against the wall and slid slowly down it on to the cushions. She did know what he meant. Only too well.

Nat patted the bed beside him. "Come over here," he whispered.

Praying for her knees not to crack, Kate heaved herself upward. She slid on to the bed with difficulty, the fringed and tasseled coverlet of crushed magenta velvet dragging against her trouser legs.

"Let's have a drink, shall we, babe?" Stretching one hand down the side of the bed, he hauled up a bottle of champagne from amid the muslin. It was, Kate saw, open.

"Er, I'd better not. I'm supposed to be at work, strictly speaking."

"I'd love to hear you strictly speaking," Nat smoldered. He waved the bottle. Krug. She'd always wondered what it tasted like. "Go on. Have a bit. It'll help you relax."

Okay then." How often, in the course of a normal day's work, did she get offered Krug anyway? Had he been lying here all morning tippling away?

Nat grabbed the grubby glasses and poured Kate a glass, grinning at her naughtily.

"Mmm," said Kate, savoring the yeasty taste. Krug really was amazing stuff. A sense of warm recklessness had possessed her. Her problems seemed miles away, years away, almost as if they didn't exist. She felt like a different person. Sexier, wilder, and more fascinating altogether. The sort of person who drank Krug in the afternoon on the beds of handsome millionheirs. "Cheers!" She beamed and took another deep draught.

"Cheers." Over the rim of his glass Nat regarded her intensely. "Has anyone," he asked suddenly, "ever told you that you're beautiful?"

Kate grinned ironically. "Oh, all the time."

But Nat was not smiling. He had raised himself on all fours and was moving towards her, each limb lithe with intention. She felt almost sick with anticipation.

"Good. Because you are." He was kissing her now, his lips moving smoothly, insistently over hers.

She felt him slide a hand under her shirt and ping open her buttons. A clutch of panic and then . . . aah. What did it matter? What *did* it matter that they had barely met? That her pale body was revealed in all its fleshy curves and probably striped with elastic marks into the bargain. All that mattered was the here and now. Gran was right. Adventure was the flower of life. And here, Kate smiled, pushing her hand downward, was the stem.

She closed her eyes. His voice seemed to be coming from miles away, beyond the rushing in her ears, the swirling in her stomach. "God," he was saying. "I want you. I've always wanted you."

"But you've only known me five minutes."

"But I've wanted you for every second of *that*."

His hand was between her legs now. Excitement pulled in her gut. The pleasure began to thrill through her pelvis, radiating outward, making her knees shake and buzz. She panted and gasped, every fiber of her being concentrated on the one thing in the world that mattered—getting Nat inside her before she burst with want.

Then, suddenly, she remembered. Her body now spread with a blush that had nothing to do with desire.

"Er, Nat . . ."

"Steady, tiger," he murmured, draining the last of his champagne before turning back to her.

"Er, the thing is . . ." Feeling his readiness—more than readiness—Kate fought her own longing and squirmed reluctantly away.

"What?" His voice was sharp with annoyance. "Oh for Christ's sake, this is a great time to come over all virginal on me."

"It's not that," Kate whispered, weak with embarrassment. "It's just that . . . you know . . . safe sex . . ."

"A bloody condom, you mean?" He jerked away and rolled over on to his back and, in his favorite gesture, raked his hands through his hair. "Don't you trust me?" He was clearly offended.

"Er . . ." Kate was knotted with awkwardness, fairly sweating with shame. Weren't men supposed to be understanding about this? It wasn't an unreasonable request.

"Where do you think I've *been*, for God's sake?" Nat demanded.

"It's not *you* . . ." Kate whispered in anguish. Yet she was determined to hold firm. Who knew where the senior tutor's wife had been, especially if she allowed every Tom, dick, and student to storm her citadel? "I'm so sorry . . . but if you happened to have one . . ."

As he rolled off the bed, his erection jerked up like a swing band's brass section. After some bad-tempered rattling of drawers, he heaved himself back on top. A tearing of foil and a few expert touches later, he had keyed her up to a pitch of panting anticipation once again. They tensed, shuddered, and shouted together before slumping, exhausted, back on the bed.

"Wow." Kate, eyes closed, was savoring a series of delicious, subsiding throbs. "That was amazing."

"You know, Kate," Nat whispered after a minute. "We're two of a kind, you and I."

"Are we?"

A flicker of irritation swept Nat's face. Then the dazzling teeth appeared again. "Yeah. We're two of a kind in the sense that we're both stuck here. And we're both desperate to escape. Aren't we?"

Kate sighed and gave in. "You bet," she agreed ruefully. She remembered the earlier conversation. "Did you say your father had editors in London?"

"He has now." Nat yawned. "There was a takeover recently. The *Ealing Examiner*, the *King's Cross Chronicle*, and the *Islington Argus*."

Kate's heart hammered. Might there be intergroup opportunities for her? The long-awaited chance to escape to the capital? "I'd love to work in London." She looked at him hopefully. He owed her a favor now, after all.

"Sure." Nat smiled and traced her cheek with one long finger. "Look, babe, there's nothing I can't do for your career, you know. Matter of fact, I've been thinking about how I can help."

"You *have?*" She swallowed.

"Yep. And I've got a plan that'll get you out of here for good. Get both of us out, come to that."

All acrimony forgotten, Kate flung both arms round him in excitement. "We'll *both* go to London, you mean?"

"Er, not exactly."

"What, then?" Kate squealed, as Nat's fingers began to explore again.

"Tell you later," he murmured, his face lowering over hers.

7

"Seen the papers today?" Darren, bursting through the office door a few days later, waved the armful he had brought with him from the bus. Under the parsimonious new regime, having the national newspapers delivered daily to the office counted as a dispensable luxury rather than a professional necessity. Kate and Darren were therefore obliged to buy their own in order to have the faintest idea of what was going on in the world.

"Not yet. What's happened?"

"Lots of nasty articles about Champagne D'Vyne."

"*Good.* Hope they're tearing her limb from limb."

"Oh, I think they're serious. And United aren't seeing the funny side either. They're furious, apparently. That sort of thing could lose Blavatsky a lot of fans."

The telephone shrilled.

"Features desk!" demanded a smart-voiced woman who sounded as if her vocal cords had been rubbed with sandpaper.

Kate smiled. The assumption of some callers that the *Mercury* still had several employees, let alone several departments, was both touching and quaint. Time, she decided, for the "staff of thousands" routine.

"Features?" she replied in Moneypenny tones whilst waving frantically at Darren. "Just hold the line while I put you through to the features editor."

"Features," Darren barked in his best this-had-better-be-important manner. A few seconds later, his face had snapped into an expression of serious alertness. He even began to take notes. "I see," he murmured. "An interview. Right. Well, I'm sure it can be arranged. I'll get back to you." He replaced the receiver, his expression incredulous beneath his geisha-white foundation. "Unbelievable. That was someone called Xanthippe."

"*Xanthippe?* That *is* pretty unbelievable."

"What's more unbelievable is that she's from something called Harde and Phaste PR. They're Champagne D'Vyne's press people. She wants to do an interview with us. With the *Mockery!*"

Kate's eyes were out on stalks. "Champagne D'Vyne does? Why?"

"Fuck knows, frankly." Darren was shaking his spiky head in bemusement.

Kate thought for a minute. "Oh, I get it. She needs a nice article in a local paper in which she appeals for forgiveness and says she was hopelessly misquoted, taken out of context and all that."

Darren's gelled spikes waved as he nodded. "So we're part of her fightback campaign, are we? A bit of positive northern PR?"

"Exactly. Do we *want* to help get her off the hook, though?"

"That depends," Darren's eyebrows slanted speculatively upwards, "on what else we stand to gain out of it. An intelligent, nonhysterical interview with Champagne at the moment, given all the fuss she's caused, might well come to the attention of a few national editors. A really well-written piece could lead . . ."

". . . to all sorts of things," Kate breathed excitedly. "Freelance work, even a job!" She paused, remembering Nat, his promises and the escape plan. No sign of any of them yet. And here was an opportunity to take her fate into her own hands. "So when does she want to do the interview?"

"This afternoon if we can. In Blavatsky's house in Slack Palisades."

Slack Palisades! Even better. Kate's fists tightened in excitement. She had not heard from Nat since the unforgettable afternoon. He had warned her that, thanks to his father's surveillance, getting into town could be problematic. Phone calls were as tricky now his father had confiscated his mobile. Kate had been racking her brains for ruses to revisit the luxury estate. And now one had dropped into her lap.

"That's great!" she gasped.

"Isn't it just?" replied Darren levelly.

Their eyes met and maintained wavering contact. Technically speaking, there was no competition. Kate knew, and knew Darren knew, that the interview should go to her as the senior reporter. On the other hand, on their beat, encounters with celebrities—even minor ones like Champagne—were about as frequent as solar eclipses. Slackmucklethwaite's only habitués of the small screen were the men who came to repair them. Given the context, pulling rank would be bad form.

"Let's toss for it," she suggested.

After some difficulty, Darren managed to locate a pound coin in the pockets of his skintight black jeans. "Heads," said Kate watching, heart thumping, as the coin spun in the air, and remembering she had never won a toss in her life.

"Heads it is."

With a gasp of excitement, Kate grabbed the telephone and dialled the number for Harde and Phaste PR. That afternoon, once again, she walked through the triumphal entry to Slack Palisades.

To her surprise, Igor Blavatsky the footballer turned out to live in the peach palace next door to Peter Hardstone. As she passed it, Kate gazed through the gilded gates of the proprietor's mansion. If only there were a way of letting Nat know she was there. A mobile, for instance. But besides confiscating his son's, Hardstone had long since called in the one she'd used for work on the grounds that it was an expensive luxury. Which it was when you had to pay for it yourself on *Mercury* wages.

She reached the Blavatsky intercom to discover a strange, rhythmic noise issuing from it. It sounded like an animal grunting. Or else . . .

"Hello?" Kate asked tentatively.

A roaring crackle, followed by a series of orgasmic groans. No. No doubt now what was going on there.

"Champagne!" a man's voice could be faintly heard urging. "Someone's here."

More groans.

Rumors of the actress-model's rapaciousness had clearly not been exaggerated. Presumably that was Igor Blavatsky she was ravishing—up against the wall by the intercom, by the sound of it. Well, it certainly put the *entry* into entryphone. And his groin strain was evidently improving.

"It'll only be the bloody *Ecky Thump Mercury*," boomed a throatily upmarket female voice. "Let them bloody wait. We're busy. Oooh, do that again . . ."

*Ecky Thump Mercury* indeed. The calm, nonjudgmental interview line agreed with Xanthippe of Harde and Phaste was clearly going to be a challenge.

Suddenly a vision in violet came strutting round the corner of the house. It was tall, slender, deeply tanned, and wore a pair of excessively tight trousers. A matching purple jacket was worn over a lilac satin shirt slashed at the front to reveal a chest of marble smoothness. His face—the features were just about identifiable as male—was, if anything, smoother. His hair was short and gelled upwards into a coxcomb of bright brassy blond.

"Mr. Blavatsky?" Funny, but she had imagined him more muscular. Hadn't had him down as the purple suit type either.

"Not Mr. Blavatsky."

Kate reddened. "Oh, sorry." Blavatsky, of course, was probably still inside. Finishing off the business interrupted by her buzz.

The vision shrugged, pouted slightly, placed both hands on his hips and regarded her with narrowed eyes. "*Bonjour*," he said.

"*Bonjour, monsieur!*" It was a thrill to give her neglected language skills an airing. "*Comment ça va?*"

He sucked in his cheeks and looked rather taken aback. "You har ze journalist?"

She nodded. "Kate Clegg from the *Slackmucklethwaite Mercury*."

"*Bonjour*, Kate Clegg. I am," the vision announced with a *tarantara* pause for effect, "Marc de Provence."

"The interior designer?" This was the man who had wrought such style havoc chez Hardstone.

Irritation creased Marc de Provence's sharp little face. "Razzer more than zat, actually," he sniffed. "I ham not merely a designer. I am an interiors *visionaire*. Let me tell you hall about myself."

"Well, that's great," Kate began, looking over his shoulder into the house. "The thing is . . ."

"Ze hinterview? Champagne, she ees busy," the violet visionaire assured her rapidly. "She harsk me to harsk you to wait while she gets ready."

"*Ce n'est pas un problème*," Kate answered in French.

The chewing stopped. As before, he looked less than delighted at her attempts at his native tongue. But the French, Kate knew, could be very fussy about people speaking their language.

"Is my accent really that bad?" she sighed. "Can't you understand me at all?"

He shook his trim little head. "Ees bettair eef you spik Engleesh."

Kate felt disappointed. Lack of practice had clearly taken its toll on her accent. When, she wondered, would she ever speak French again?

"Come and seet down," instructed her companion, clacking briskly across the poolside patio in what Kate saw now was a pair of zebra-striped shoes. He pulled out two woven chairs, inspected the seats, sat down, crossed his legs, folded his hands, and looked at her expectantly. "You can hinterview *me* in ze meantime. I am verray keen zat any rich local ladeez should know I ham passeeng through for a few days. I might be able to take on certain commissions—eef ze price ees right."

"Well, I'm not sure." Following Peter Hardstone's assessment of the de Provence vision, an interview with the man himself was unlikely to impress the proprietor.

"Not sure!" De Provence drew himself up in his chair, pursed his lips and looked at her with eyes of an amazingly artificial-looking emerald. "Do you not realize what you are being offered? An exclusive interview with *moi*! Interiors magazines would kill for zees hopportunity."

There had, Kate recalled, been a murderous glint in the Hardstone eye too. Before it had been obscured by one of the £1,000 wallcoverings.

"I will explain *mon philosophie*," Marc de Provence announced with a flourish. "What I do ees haute couture for ze home. Baroque-and-Roll, you know?"

Kate nodded. She knew all right.

"I specialize in *fabrications*."

That was true too.

"Ees a very special look. Ze draperies, ze materials, ze hornate furniture. A look of hover-ze-top luxury. Beautiful to ze touch, beautiful to ze heye."

*Oh for Christ's sake.* "What would you say," Kate asked boldly, "to those who find your vision a little . . . tacky?"

The green eyes gave a warning flash. "Ees not tacky. Ees fancy."

"And *very* expensive," Kate challenged, remembering the sconces.

"Hexpensive?" Marc de Provence folded his lilac arms, exposing a huge watch of complex appearance. "Hey, lady, nice things, zey cost money. Zere is nothing I do for five thousant pound. Except put ze phone down, ha ha. I don't even get out of bed for an order for ten thousant pound."

"*Don't you?*"

He shook his brassy head. "Not worth ze heffort. *Mes clients*, they don't insult me weeth such peedling sums anyway. They can see I'm a genuine artiste."

"So what you do is art, is it?"

His nostrils flared. "*Mais oui!* Mes fabrications, zey are unique."

"So I saw." Kate recalled the effect of the fabrications on Peter Hardstone.

Marc de Provence brightened immediately. "You 'ave seen my work? On ze *Celebrity Channel*?"

"Er, no." Kate jerked a thumb behind her. "Next door."

The designer looked delighted. "Ah, yes. Brog*an*. What a dream palace I created for 'er. For 'er I create my specialitee, my paddet ceilings, my signature sateen thrones!" He threw a rapturous arm aloft. "She loved them. She was ze perfect *client*. Never once asked about ze price of anything."

He was obviously blissfully unaware of Brogan's husband's view of the dream palace. Kate glanced crossly towards Igor Blavatsky's house. Was she going to have to sit here all afternoon and talk about signature sateen thrones?

"You're very fond of purple," she observed.

"*Mais oui*. It is ze *lavande*, ze 'erb-flower of la belle Provence." He contorted his mahogany features in a grin. "And *moi*, I am ze *beau Provence!*"

There seemed no immediate answer to this. Eventually Kate thought of another question. "Did you train anywhere? Go to design college?"

De Provence looked outraged. "What could any college teach *moi*? Of course, I didn't go to," he twisted his lips contemptuously, "*design school.*"

"Um. So what attracted you to, er, interiors in the first place?"

He blinked back at her. "Ze money, of course."

"Oh." Kate paused, fascinated both by his amazing greed and even more amazing candor. "You don't mind admitting that? That you're motivated mostly by money?"

"Of course not. Why should I?"

Marc de Provence and his unique sensibilities could be accused of many things, but lack of direction, Kate decided, was not one of them. Although it now occurred to Kate to wonder why he was wandering about Igor Blavatsky's garden.

"Beezness," the visionaire explained. "Now I haf feeneeshed Brogan's 'ouse, I look aroun' for other opportunities. Zees estate looked *parfait* to me—full of pipple wiz money—but zen ze 'oles come." He looked with loathing at a small crater beside the swimming pool. "And now ze only other pipple here are Champagne and *zat footballer.*" He spoke the last two words with a grimace.

"You're working for *Champagne?*" It was all starting to make sense. Of a sort.

"*Oui.* We 'ave come up weeth ze most wonderful scheme togezzer. Fabrications all hover ze house. We are ready to go, everytheeng is set. But now we 'ave a problem."

"Which is?"

De Provence scowled and leaned confidingly forward over his folded arms. "Champagne's boyfriend," he hissed. "I tell you, he ees a nightmare. He criticizes my work, he offer hees opinion." He slapped his knees in fury. "But I ham not interested in being hoffered hees opinion! Ze only thing I'm interested in other people hoffering me hees *money*."

He threw himself angrily back in his chair. Producing a card case, he thrust a small metallic purple card into her hand.

Kate looked at it. *Marc de Provence. French Château Chic for Englishmen's Castles.*

Just then from somewhere about his person, a tinny, electronic version of "The Arrival of the Queen of Sheba" pealed out. Producing—amid flashes of magenta suit lining—a tiny purple metallic mobile, the designer held up the flat of a palm to Kate.

As he gushed fulsomely—presumably to a client—into the receiver, Kate looked speculatively at the house, and decided it was now or never. She made a dash for it.


"Hello?" Kate pushed open the front door of the house and peered into a pillared hallway leading to a huge central staircase. "Hello?"

A frenzy of yapping filled the air. "Aaagh!" Kate yelled, as something agonizingly sharp sank into both ankles. Looking down, she saw a small, squirming, fluffly bundle hanging off each of her legs. "Get off, you little bastards," she howled, pain pulsating through her calves.

"*Don't* talk to them like that," snapped a voice in the doorway. "They're very sensitive, you know."

"And so are my legs, thanks very much." Kate, hand-deep in bouffant dog coat as she tried to prise off her attackers, looked up, eyes watering with pain.

"Really? You surprise me."

Lounging in the doorway dressed in nothing but a man's shirt, cigarette dangling from bee-stung lips, and watching from heavily fringed green eyes, was a stunningly lovely woman.

Kate was swamped with an instant hatred that derived only partly from the gratuitous insult. The other woman's elegant, effortless beauty made her feel two stone overweight and about as fashionable as spats.

Champagne's legs stretched slim and brown down to long, elegant feet. White-blond hair streamed straight and shining as silk over her bony shoulders, one of which was almost entirely exposed. Almost entirely exposed too, were a pair of magnificent, tanned breasts, in which pertness combined perfectly with generosity of proportion.

"Owwwww!" Kate yelped, as the dogs sank their teeth even further into her ankles. "Get off. *Get off!*"

"I said *don't talk to them like that.*" The green eyes glittered. "You'll hurt their feelings. Poor little angels."

"But they're hurting my legs!" Kate gasped.

Champagne looked pointedly at Kate's trousers. "Frankly, I'm surprised you can feel anything through all that. Gucci! Prada!" she cooed, bending over to the animals. Her shirt fell further open to reveal a length of taut stomach and the fact that she wasn't wearing knickers.

With a final crunch of their jaws that made Kate's eyes stream, the dogs released her ankles and hurled themselves on their mistress. "Poor doggy woggies," Champagne honked, kissing the ribboned tops of their heads. "Poor Gucci-goo and Prada-wada."

Kate rubbed her legs, thinking frantically about tetanus and rabies.

"So," Champagne demanded in her sticky, upmarket voice. "You're from the *Ecky Thump Mockery*?"

"The *Slackmucklethwaite Mercury.*"

Champagne threw back her head and emitted a scream of derision. The actress-model's campaign to win over northern readers, Kate thought sourly, had hardly got off to the most tactful of starts.

She fixed a warning eye on the frantically yapping dogs. Champagne or no Champagne, if they bit her again, she would batter them to death with whatever came to hand. Her own shoes, if necessary. Evidently sensing this, they kept their distance.

"Are you *really* the celebrity interviewer?" Champagne looked at her doubtfully.

"I'm the *everything* interviewer."

Champagne gave a diva-ish toss of her head. "Look," she honked haughtily, "I'm not used to being interviewed by *anyone*."

"I can see that." Kate smiled sweetly. "I've been waiting quite a while, you know. But I'm sure you'll manage to be on time eventually. When you've had a bit more practice."

The green eyes bulged with fury. "That's not what I mean. I'm an A-list star, okay? The *Slagheap Standard*'s really got lucky."

A-list! Kate fumed silently. Champagne's profile may have enjoyed a boost thanks to *Hello Sailor, I'm A Celebrity*. But she was hardly Madonna.

"Where's the photographer?" Champagne barked.

"On his way."

The bus was obviously running late. Colin, who had been spared the Hardstone cull on grounds of cost-effectiveness—he never took more than a few frames and used the cheapest film possible—traveled everywhere by bus with his OAP card. He had come to photography comparatively late in life, via an evening class started some years after he had retired. His idea of technical wizardry was to urge subjects to "give us a nice smile, love." And his camera shake had got infinitely worse recently. Mario Testino he was not, although Darren had taken to calling the blurry effect generally produced the "slack edgy" school of photography.

"I thought we'd do the interview first," Kate suggested.

"Better get it over with then," Champagne said ungraciously. "Come into the sitting room." She stalked ahead through the hall into a large room full of white sofas piled with gold cushions.

As an invitation to sit seemed unforthcoming, Kate took the initiative. The white sofa she sank into drew her down like quicksand. She'd need a winch to get back up. "Let's start with the reasons why you're so happy to be living in the North," she began pointedly. "That way we can clear up any misunderstanding that might have arisen from the unfortunate piece that ran in a certain national newspaper recently."

Not an iota of embarrassment registered on Champagne's features.

"Unfortunate! Misunderstandings!" she snorted. "Probably the only time in my life I've been quoted accurately."

Something, Kate thought, had gone wrong with the script here. Wasn't the point of their encounter for Champagne to soothe ruffled feathers among Blavatsky's fans and Northerners generally?

"Er, well, anyway, back to Slack Palisades," she tried next. "You've obviously got a lot of plans for this place. I met your, um, house artist outside. All very exciting."

Champagne's expression became thunderous. "But what's bloody boring is that Igor's being so stingy about the money." She exhaled petulantly. "I mean, what's a few million, okay, when you're a footballer? But he says he can't see what's wrong with the house as it is."

Kate surveyed the sitting room's expanse of white sofas, cream carpet, and vast glass-topped coffee tables. While the prevailing style was mild international tacky, everything was brand new, clearly expensive and, compared to the excrescences of Bra View, generally inoffense. She felt a certain sympathy with Igor.

"Bloody Igor!" Champagne stormed. "He's completely bloody useless. God knows what I'm doing with him—well, actually I do. He earns fifty grand a week—not that I ever see any of it," she added bitterly. "He's meaner than mouseshit. Only stayed here because he could negotiate himself a lower rent after all the other houses fell down holes."

Kate had been wondering what lay behind Blavatsky's decision to remain in residence. It seemed a reasonable enough idea to her—always assuming no more craters appeared.

"He's *such* a pain in the arse," Champagne added bitterly. "Especially now he's *got* such a pain in the arse."

"How *is* his groin?"

Champagne's beautiful top lip curled in scorn. "No fucking use, basically."

"Poor him," Kate said sympathetically. "Groin strain can be a nightmare for footballers, can't it? They're off for months sometimes. He must get very down about it."

"Down's the bloody word. Trust me to end up with the only multimillionaire twentysomething who can't get it up."

Kate was puzzled. If this were true, how could Blavatsky have been
ramming Champagne up against the entryphone? "Is Igor around?"
she asked carefully. "Great to have him in the pictures if he is."

Champagne swung her hair from side to side in a swishing blond
negative. "Playing away, thank God."

In that case, Kate thought, poor Igor wasn't the only one. So who
was Champagne's other lover? Marc de Provence? It seemed unlikely;
the designer had definitely struck her as being, as Dad would have put
it, "on the other bus."

She consulted another of her hastily prepared questions. "I imagine that going out with a Russian player has given you an interesting
insight into other cultures?"

"It would if I could understand anything he fucking said."

Kate frowned. Champagne was not only making no effort to get
herself out of the hole caused by her offensive remarks, but seemed determined to dig herself in even deeper. What, exactly, did she think
was the point of this interview? Either she had no idea why her press
people had arranged it, or she simply didn't care. Kate decided to give
her one last chance. "I was going to ask you what you particularly liked
about being in Slackmucklethwaite."

Champagne looked incredulous. "*Like?*"

"You love Slackmucklethwaite people because they're so friendly
and straightforward?" Kate offered.

"How the hell would I know? Oh yah, I'm sure they are. Look,"
Champagne suggested, unfolding her long, graceful length from the
sofa, "you've obviously got a knack for this. Why don't you just make
the whole thing up? I'll slip off and get ready for the photographer.
Save us all time."

Kate watched the slim back disappear into the hall.

She considered. Tempting though it was, doing a hatchet job on
Champagne would be risky. Admittedly, it might make her, the writer,
briefly notorious, but it would also instantly cast her as a stitcher-up of

celebrities. No one famous would thereafter touch her with a shitty bargepole, and, as interviews with the famous were all editors cared about, the chances of this strategy leading to a better job were unlikely. What was completely likely, on the other hand, was the trouble such a piece would cause with Peter Hardstone.

She was interrupted in her ponderings by Champagne dashing, shrieking, back into the room. "A *disgusting* old man's wandering around the outside of the house. He's looking in all the windows. Look!" she added hysterically. "He's there!" Kate followed the end of the pointing, quivering, manicured finger to where a disheveled, stooped, and bearded figure was peering uncertainly into the sitting room. "A bloody tramp by the looks of it." Champagne lunged for a telephone on a side table. "I'll call the police."

"No, don't," said Kate, reddening. "It's Colin. My photographer."

8

After having loudly and contemptuously expressed her surprise at Colin's lack of arc lights, silver umbrellas, and the full team of wardrobe and makeup assistants she was used to, Champagne flounced off to get changed. Reappearing in a silver bikini, silver stilettoes, and a fur coat, she fiercely objected to having to pose in the *Mercury* photographer's signature way. "I've been shot by the biggest names in the business," she roared. "Bailey, Demarchelier, Testino, you name it. And not one of them's *ever* asked me to give them a *nice fucking smile!*"

Proceeding to stretch herself out in a manner revealing more cleavage than Peter Hardstone could have hoped for, Champagne fixed Kate with a challenging green stare. A small silver mobile was, Kate saw, peeping out from the flimsy front of her bikini bottoms.

"Well?" she honked.

"You look very, er, nice."

"Not the bloody photograph." She looked contemptuously at Colin, fussing around with his camera at the edge of the pool. "What the hell's he got there anyway? A Box Brownie?"

Quite possibly, was the honest answer to that one. If not a one-reel party disposable.

"Aren't you going to ask me?" Champagne demanded.

"What?"

"The whole reason for this interview, of course," Champagne snapped, exasperated. "The whole reason for this interview, of course," Champagne snapped, exasperated. "The whole reason I bothered to get out of bed for your crappy little rag."

"Oh, right. I thought we'd done that bit. Wasn't the reason so you could be nice about the North?"

"You must be *joking*. Xanthippe's *obsessed* with the idea I might have upset a few local yokels but I told her she was confusing me with someone who gave a toss. I said I didn't mind talking about my *acting career* though."

"*Your acting career?*" Kate had imagined this to be dormant, following events a couple of years ago when Champagne had famously been booted off a film set for unreasonable behavior. Or unreasonable acting—it had never been clear. Did the crimes of *Hello Sailor, I'm A Celebrity*, besides hitting a new TV low, include convincing Champagne to foist her thespian ambitions on the world once more?

"So. Go on. Ask me about acting."

"Er, well. Who's your favorite actor?"

Champagne stared at her indignantly. "How the hell do I know?"

"Well, most actors have someone they admire, who inspired them—that sort of thing."

"Well, *I* don't, okay? Why should I be interested in *other people* acting?"

Kate took a deep breath. "What sort of *acting* are you interested in, then? West End theater?" Champagne would no doubt have her sights on a triumph comparable to Nicole Kidman in *The Blue Room*. Or Kevin Spacey or Gwyneth Paltrow in whatever they'd been in.

The green eyes were full of scorn. "I don't want to be in *plays*. Grotty little theaters, bazillions of lines to learn—what sort of mug would want to do that?"

Only half the Hollywood A-list, thought Kate. But what would they know?

Champagne tossed her ice-blond hair. "Not me, okay? I'm going straight to film."

"You've got a part, then?" Had some reckless director allowed her back on set?

"Sure I have." Thrusting her breasts out triumphantly, Champagne arranged the fur coat along the line of her thigh and smoldered at the hovering photographer.

"Keep still," said Colin.

"I bloody am still. It's your hands that are shaking."

"Aye, you're right," Colin said with mild interest. "Anyway, that's grand. Just a bit further back perhaps." As he reversed to frame his shot, Kate saw he was close to the very edge of the pool. "Go on now," he urged his subject. "Give me a nice smile."

Champagne bared her teeth in a contemptuous snarl.

"Thaa-at's it," Colin said, beaming. "Lovely. Really nice and sincere."

"This film part," Kate said. "Tell me about it. What's the film?"

Champagne paused before delivering, smugly, "The new James Bond."

"*James Bond!*" It was enough to make Kate fall off her chair—had she been offered a chair.

"That's what I said." Stretching herself out yet more comfortably on the padded sun recliner, Champagne studied her nails.

Kate's head rushed with disbelief. On the other hand, that pneumatic figure was straight out of 007 central casting. And *Hello Sailor* had indisputably raised her profile. But *this* much? "So you're the new Bond Girl?"

Champagne raised her chin haughtily. "Rather more than that, actually. I play a brilliant nuclear physicist who saves the world. She's a very complex character."

"She sounds it."

"I mean, obviously the brilliant bit will be easy-peasy. But I'm going to have to mug up on the physics. She's going to be a great challenge. Really stretch me as an artist."

Literally, Kate hoped, note-taking. Perhaps it would be one of those Bonds with excruciating rack-torture scenes. That went tragically wrong during filming . . .

"Yah. She's kick-ass, independent, a woman who knows her own mind and doesn't take any shit. Okay? She's emancipated, intelligent . . . all that stuff." Champagne yawned.

"She sounds very different from the usual Bond Girl stereotype."

"Yah. She is."

"So all that embarrassing, sexist crap with Mary Goodnight,

Plenty O'Toole, and the rest of them is finished?" It was, Kate had to admit as she scribbled all this down, a good story. There could be something in this interview after all.

"Dead as a dodo."

"No more innuendo and suggestive names?"

"Completely past its sell-by, all that. My character's a new heroine for the new millennium."

This worthless woman really had the luck of the devil. Trust Champagne to be in on the launch of a whole new type of Bond Girl. "What's the name of your character?" Kate looked up from her notebook.

"Miss Castle."

An unimpeachably respectable surname, commensurate with a change of Bond tack. "And what's her first name?"

"Bouncy."

Kate smothered a snort. "*Bouncy Castle?*"

Champagne stared back with unblinking green eyes. "What's so bloody funny about that? I'm *very* excited about playing her. And Pierce is apparently beside himself at the thought of working with me."

Kate could well believe it. "Has that been, um, *widely* reported? You playing Bouncy Castle?" There was no point going big on the story if it had already been in every arts section in the land. And given the paper-buying situation at the *Mockery*, she was hardly in a position to check.

Champagne looked cagey. "Not exactly. It's not been formally announced yet. So there you go—a real, live exclusive for the little old *Bogglethwaite Bugle* or whatever you call yourself."

"Just one more thing," Kate said levelly, clicking her pen top. "What's the name of the film?"

"*Azur Like It.*"

"Like the Shakespeare?" Kate was puzzled.

"What's Shakespeare got to do with it? That's what it's called, right? *Azur Like It.* It's set on the Côte d'Azur. *Obviously.*"

"Oh, *that* sort of Azur."

But Champagne's attention had drifted. Her eyes were on Colin who, having backed further towards the swimming pool, was crouching down, hands still shaking, to take another shot. "Further back," she ordered. "My skin's not looking its best at the moment."

As Colin obligingly backed away Kate noticed that Champagne's skin was unimprovably radiant and perfect. Her full, pink lips—the sort, annoyingly, that looked perfectly made-up even when they were bare—were curling slightly upward to the accompaniment of a slight buzzing sound. Kate watched while Champagne slid a hand towards her silver gusset and fished out the vibrating mobile. It was impossible not to overhear the ensuing conversation.

"Oh, *hi* big boy. No, no luck. He won't give me a cent, the mean bastard. How's *your* get-rich-quick plan coming along? *Is* it? Good."

"Keep still," quavered Colin, from over by the pool.

"Champagne stared at him. "Back off," she roared. "No, not *you*," she yelped into the receiver. "Bugger," she shrieked, shaking the mobile. "Hello? *Hello?*"

Kate looked concernedly at Colin. At Champagne's last command he had scuttled backwards even further and was really *very* close to the edge of the swimming pool now.

"Look, let's get this interview bloody well over with, shall we?" Champagne said irritably. "This film, right. It's set on the Côte d'Azur, yah? I'm going over there next week on location. And to the film festival too."

Kate ground her teeth. Why was it that everyone—Darren, Champagne, even the Northern Gigolo, if she ever got back to writing about him—seemed to be heading for the Riviera? Everyone except herself and Nat, that was. Gran would be announcing that she was off there next.

"And the festival kicks off," Champagne added, stretching out a length of bronzed calf and admiring it, "with a huge party on Cap Ferrat. Shouldn't be too much of a bore."

Kate's head jerked up. Hadn't Nat mentioned a party on Cap Ferrat during lunch in Billy's? Of course he had. Every word he had ever said to her was wrapped in scented tissue paper and stored carefully in her memory.

*Shouldn't be too much of a bore.* Damn her glittering spoiled green eyes. Kate would, just then, have done anything to push the arrogant blonde in the pool. It seemed like wish-fulfillment to hear a sudden, panicked yell, followed by a splash.

Sadly, however, the yell was male. Male, old and distinctly Colin-like.

Kate rushed to the edge of the pool. Colin was bobbing forlornly about, the long threads of his scrapeover trailing behind him like gray seaweed, exposing a boiled-egg–like dome of head. The gales of triumphant laugher from Champagne suggested that this was exactly what she had intended to happen.

More days went by without word from Nat. He had not come near the office, nor had he called. Kate was now miserably convinced either that she had imagined his entire existence—in particular their last encounter—or that, having seen her merely as a recreational screw, he had left town without telling her. Perhaps he'd got to the South of France after all—everyone else seemed to be heading there. The possibility made her sick with shame and disappointment whenever, as was often, it slid across her mind. What about the escape plan he had promised? It was impossible to think he would not be in touch again.

Darren was no help. "Oh, for God's sake, Kate. Good riddance, if you ask me." His eyes narrowed into kohl-rimmed slits. "Not in *love* with him, are you?"

"NYFB. None of your fucking business."

"Whatever." Darren pushed his spikes—auburn-tipped today—backwards, drummed his long fingers on the desk and began to sing the Velvets' unique take on "Sister Ray." "Just like Uncle Ray sez . . ."

But Darren, she knew, had troubles of his own. Work on the Slack Palisades bribery and corruption story—to which he had been contributing secretly and fitfully—had finally hit the rocks. Largely because something hard and fast moving had hit Freya Ogden. The conservationist had been knocked over in a mysterious car accident and was now recovering in hospital. This was irritating to Darren on more counts than just work. Hospital food, in Freya's view falling short of the macrobiotic ideal, he was currently spending his lunchtimes in a relay between Slackmucklethwaite's health food shop and Freya's bedside.

Darren, of course, suspected Hardstone was behind the accident. Remembering the scene with the chauffeur, Kate was absolutely certain that he was. Behind the wheel too possibly. Messing with Hardstone was obviously a very dangerous business. She longed to tell Darren everything she knew, but that would involve explaining about Nat and what she was doing in Bra View in the first place. Darren would certainly disapprove. Still, as long as Freya stayed in traction, Darren would hopefully stay out of trouble.

Compounding the general grimness of life was the fact that Wits End echoed constantly to Gran's and Mum's enquiries about when they were going to see that "grand lad" again. Enquiries in which Dad noticeably took no part.

Kate looked remorsefully over at her colleague. Things were bad enough without falling out with Darren as well. "Darren?"

He held up a warning hand. "Look, I'm expecting Chip Shop to call about the tour arrangements any minute. I need to think about my riders."

"Riders? Aren't you going on a bus?"

"Honestly, you civilians." Darren sighed in mock exasperation. "Riders—you know. Backstage provisions, all that stuff. Should I have Cristal champagne in the dressing room or boring old Moët? Will any scented candle do, or does it have to be Jo Malone?"

Had fame—even its most distant prospect—gone to his head already? Kate looked at him uncertainly, then realized his shoulders were shaking.

"Sorry. Your face!" Darren grinned. "You didn't actually believe me, did you? Cristal—you must be joking. We'll be lucky to get Ribena on this tour by the sound of it. Not that I'm complaining."

"When are you going?" Kate asked, trying to sound cheerful instead of jealous.

He beamed deliriously. "This weekend. I managed to wangle the time off from Denys by pointing out I hadn't taken any holiday this year."

Darren, Kate thought glumly, probably *was* about to be a rock star. On a small scale, to begin with, but it was bound to get bigger. He had the courage of his convictions. Whereas she . . .

Whereas all she had was a one-fifth finished novel. Channelling her frustration into early morning stints on *Northern Gigolo* was a tortuous process in which the adventures of her fictional hero were interrupted by stints of gazing into midair and thinking of her real-life one. Now Nat had apparently deserted her—although she still couldn't finally accept this—the book had taken on a new and almost desperate importance. It seemed the only escape route left.

*Between Mark's taut thighs, the Jacuzzi waters surged . . .*
That evening, in her Wits End bedroom, Kate scribbled frantically.

Her large purple nipples, rigid with desire, scraped against his muscular chest as Doreen Bracegirdle pulled him further into her. "Mark! You're so big . . ."

She sighed. Despite the inspiration of Brogan's Italian Stallion, Wits End on a rainy evening was hardly ideal for the composition of erotica. Especially not with Dad flushing the loo on the other side of the thin wall. Yet, like the Northern Gigolo himself, she was determined to keep at it.

. . . With each thrust Doreen lashed her head from side to side, whipping him with her long hair . . .

But perhaps this was taking artistic licence too far. The real Doreen Bracegirdle had a mannish gray crop and chronic back problems. It seemed unlikely she had a Jacuzzi either, although given Hardstone's backhanders to her husband to secure planning permission, the Bracegirdles probably had a full massage suite by now. In any case, she probably ought to change the names. Doreen, for example, could become Dorian.

Mark slammed into Dorian harder and harder, possessing her with a thrillingly brutal force. Her buttocks slapped against the tiles. Slam! Slap!

Massage suite or no massage suite, there would still definitely be tiles in the Bracegirdle bathroom. Avocado ones, probably.

Slam! Slap! "Oh, God!" gasped Dorian.

*Bang! Bang!* "Oh Christ!" exclaimed Kate. Her pen leaped, panicked, into the air as the thin wood of her bedroom door reverberated under the force of Mum's blows. "Kate! Tea!"

Kate hastily shut the exercise book and shoved *Northern Gigolo* under the mattress. "I'm coming!" she shouted, stealing Dorian Brace-girdle's next lines. She swung her legs off the bed.

"Your young man visiting again soon, is he?" Mum asked eagerly over the sausage and mash.

"He's not my young man," Kate sighed, taking a piled plate. In re-cent weeks she'd asked for half portions; what, now, however, was the bloody point?

"No bad thing if you ask me," Dad remarked.

"I wasn't asking you," Kate muttered. She noticed with trepidation a stretch of snot-green nylon dangling between her grandmother's needles. To Kate's trained eye it was showing early, dangerous signs of a polo-neck jumper nature. Please God it wasn't for her. Her ears were still sore from dragging off the butterfly top.

"Never mind, eh?" Dad said, slopping onion gravy all over his Himalayan pile of potato. "Plenty more fish in the sea."

Kate almost choked on her sausage. Was he joking? From a man point of view, the local seas were overfished to an extent to get Friends of the Earth in a flap. Although there was certainly plenty of plankton about.

She had hardly started on a second helping of Mum's homemade trifle when there was a knock at the door.

Mum looked up. "Ooooh, it'll be the Avon lady."

"I'll get it," Kate offered, eager to escape Dad for a few minutes.

"Tell her I haven't had the chance to finish looking through the brochure yet, but I'm thinking about some of that aromatherapy stuff for me funny legs."

Kate crossed the swirling carpet to the door, vaguely registering that the figure blurrily visible through the door panel was both taller and thinner than Mrs. Townend, cosmetics purveyor by self-appointment to the inhabitants of Wits End.

"Nat!" Kate clutched the doorframe in panic. "Where have you been?"

His eyes met hers unflinchingly. He looked even more devastatingly handsome than she remembered. "Sorry. Like I said, it's been a bit tricky keeping in touch, yeah? But I'm here now."

Surely there should be more to his apology than this. She had, after all, heard nothing. *Nothing*. For what had seemed like *ages*. Nonetheless, she felt herself grinning like an idiot.

"Well, aren't you going to ask me in?"

"Er, we're just finishing tea—I mean dinner . . ."

There was a movement behind her, accompanied by the unmistakable clack of knitting needles. "Eeh bah gum!" Gran, spotting Nat, exclaimed with delight.

Nat looked amazed. "I didn't realize people really said that."

"You coming in 'ere?" Gran paused by the sitting-room door. "I was just nipping in for the second half of *Emmerdale*."

"I don't know why you're bloomin' bothering," Dad yelled from the kitchen. "There's not a single old farming character left. They're all drug dealers, prostitutes, and pyromaniacs these days."

"That's why I like it," Gran shouted back.

"Who's that at the door, anyway?" Dad boomed.

"Our Kate's young man," Gran called back before she could be stopped. But Nat merely laughed, causing emotions from embarrassment to ecstasy to surge through Kate.

There was a disapproving silence from the kitchen followed by angry muttering ". . . must be wrong in't head," Kate heard Dad hiss in reply to placatory noises from Mum. "Go and sit down," Mum called.

Kate snapped into action. No way was Nat going back into that sitting room to be grilled by Mum and Gran. "We'll be in my bedroom if anyone wants me," she called determinedly.

"Right you are, love," Gran said, beaming meaningfully. "Don't do anything I wouldn't."

"Quite a character, your granny," Nat remarked, as Kate whisked him up the narrow stairs. "And knitting another masterpiece, I see."

Giggling, the ice broken, Kate thumped him hard on the back.

In her tiny bedroom, they sat on the edge of the bed. Kate felt her knees, trembling, knocking against the radiator on the wall at the bed's foot. She had no doubt what was coming next.

Nat pressed her gently backward on to the bed. His cool hand slid under her shirt. Then, slowly, the hand descended.

"Nat . . . *no.* Not here. You can't . . ."

"Can't I?" Nat raised himself slightly. His fingers continued exploring. "That's not the message I'm getting down here."

"You can't! You really can't!" Even as she spoke she wondered why she was bothering. He was irresistible and he knew it. What was more, he was achieving the unachievable by making the fact that her parents and Gran were downstairs watching *Emmerdale* seem sexy and dangerous. He deserved something for that, at least.

Eyes narrow with suppressed laughter, he opened his fly deftly. Kate swallowed. There had been no rustle of foil, no snap of rubber. Must she really stop him in his tracks again? Then there was the headboard, slamming against the wall. Even over *Emmerdale* it might be heard from the sitting room. She closed her eyes, knowing she was about to be swept away.

"Hang on," Nat said suddenly. Kate opened her eyes. He was bending over her, patting the side of the mattress. "Like the Princess and the bloody Pea," he was muttering.

"What is?"

"There's something crackling under here and it's, like, putting me off." His hand poised to slide beneath the mattress.

Oh God. The book. Her most fiercely guarded secret. "Don't look under there," Kate commanded, louder than she had intended. Purple swept her face and neck at the thought of Nat reading the sex scenes featuring Doreen—Dorian—Bracegirdle.

Fortunately, just then, Nat's mobile shrilled. "Sorry, s'urgent," Nat muttered, texting hurriedly back.

"Don't worry," Kate assured him, taking full advantage of the opportunity to reach under the mattress, pull out the book and drop it under the bed.

"Look," Nat was standing up and packing himself back in his trousers. "I've got to go."

"But you've only just got here."

"I know. I'm sorry, yeah? What you doing tomorrow night?"

What was she ever doing? Either soldiering on with the Gigolo or sitting in front of *It Shouldn't Happen At Celebrity Driving School* with Mum and Gran. "Nothing much."

"Great. Let's go to that restaurant."

Fear sprang into Kate's eyes. Surely he didn't mean the Italian Job?

"That one in Slack Top," Nat continued. "Only one round here that looks halfway normal."

"Spinning Jenny's?"

"That's the one."

Kate felt a surge of excitement, swiftly followed by apprehension. "Bit expensive, though."

He waved a dismissive hand. "Don't worry about that. My shout, babe."

"Ooh, thanks. I've always wanted to go there." The glamour! Dinner with the ten-bob millionaires! Dad would disapprove. Not that he needed to know, of course.

"There's something I wanted to talk to you about."

"Is there?"

"That plan I mentioned? To get you out of this dump . . . I mean Slackmucklethwaite?"

She smiled at him in the mirror as, with practiced fingers, he artfully mussed up his bronze hair. Catching her eyes eventually, he grinned at her dazzlingly. "So. See you there at eight?"

"Okay."

"And could you book it? It's just that I can't phone from home . . . you know—yeah?"

Kate nodded. "Yeah."

9

Kate smiled at Nat Hardstone from across the candlelit table. They had by now got through an entire bottle of champagne, with the result that Kate, while wondering if the escape plan would ever be revealed, was at least no longer worrying about whether she was wearing the right clothes or using the correct fork. Between endless bitter complaints about how his father was ruining his acting career, Nat had managed to plough his way through a dozen oysters and was currently following this up with a vast steak. Kate, remembering her manners and determined not to take advantage of him taking care of the bill, had stuck to the one modest plate of pasta. Imagining Gran's reaction—"Five pounds! For a plate o' bloomin' weeds!"—she had also resisted all attempts on the part of the forceful waitress to sell her fashionable side salads of dock leaves and dandelion heads.

Being a fashionably spare sort of place, Spinning Jenny's featured small, bare wooden tables packed very close together. These, combined with the grim-faced waitresses marching up and down between them, reminded Kate of sitting exams.

She looked eagerly around for the ten-bob millionaires. They were, she supposed, the trim and prosperous-looking men in their late fifties with light tans and jauntily-cut gray hair sitting opposite bouffanted, red-lipsticked females swathed in the layers of floppy beige. From time to time the air-conditioning flung in Kate's direction a ribbon of powerful aftershave or assertive scent from theirs.

"So," Nat said, smiling into her eyes. "How's the *Mockery*?"

Kate, who had begun to give up hope of ever being asked a question, grabbed her opportunity. She gave a mock groan. "Thrilling. The big story today is the new vicarage gates. Colin went to photograph them and rang me up about four times. Did I want them open or shut? With vicar or without vicar?"

"Still wanting to get away, then?"

"Desperately!" Her eyes widened expectantly.

He pressed his palms together around his nose and looked at her from over the top of his fingers. "I just don't know what you'll think of this, but remember you mentioned the Cannes Film Festival, yeah, and how disappointed you were not to be able to cover it for the *Mockery* . . . the *Mercury*, I mean?"

Kate sat bolt upright, electrified. "*Yes?*"

"Well, I talked to Dad about it."

"You did?" She frowned. "But I thought you didn't, you know . . ."

"Speak? Well, we don't not much. But he had to ask me if I'd be a witness for the divorce, agree the decorating was crap and all that."

"Divorce? So he *is* getting rid of Brogan?"

"Yeah. And I was right. She *does* want custody of the Jacuzzi. . . ."

"Anyway. Go on. So you spoke to your father? About me?"

"Yeah. He's always interested in talking about anything concerning his businesses. Anything concerning himself," Nat said bitterly. "Other people are of no interest at all. Look what he's trying to do to me and my acting. . . ."

"So what did you say?" Kate cut in, trying to steer the conversation back to the more pressing issue of her future.

"That you were a bit, um, demotivated . . ."

"You said *what?*"

"Hang on, it's cool." Nat smiled at her reassuringly. "Trust me, doll. I know what I'm doing."

Playing fast and loose with her job, by the sound of it. Panic gripped Kate.

"I told him," Nat said with matter-of-fact lightness, "that you were a brilliant reporter the paper couldn't afford to lose."

"*You did?*" Kate clenched her paper napkin with delight.

"Sure I did. And that one way of keeping you happy was to let you cover the Cannes Film Festival."

"You *didn't*!" As exultation swept over her like fire, she leaned across and grabbed his arm. "What did he *say*?"

Nat smirked at her triumphantly. "Agreed, didn't he? Was completely cool about it. Actually said he thought it was a good idea."

Kate sank back against the hard wooden school chair. "Oh Nat," she said weakly. "*Thank you*." She closed her eyes and immediately saw blue seas, white stucco hotels gleaming in the sunshine, palm trees and, wafting up and down the Croisette, more film stars than you could shake an Oscar at.

She snapped open her eyes again. "The festival's next week, isn't it? I'd better tell Denys."

"Don't bother," Nat said swiftly. "Dad's sorting it all out with him. Wemyss wasn't all that sold on the idea, to be perfectly honest. Needs persuading."

"Oh God. I knew it." With Darren off touring the globe, her absence for a week or even a fortnight would leave him with precisely no staff. Her eyes darted in panic between Nat's pupils.

". . . so it's probably better not to mention it to him," Nat added. "In fact, don't say anything to him, at all. Just assume it's okay. Leave it to me and Pops to sort out, yeah?"

"Well, if you're sure." Relieved to have escaped an unpleasant encounter with the editor, Kate settled to blissful contemplation of her good fortune. "So you'll sort out the press accreditation as well, will you?" she added.

Nat looked utterly blank.

"For the film festival? You know, all those funny colored passes they have."

"Oh *yeah*." He nodded vigorously. "Sure, yeah. I'll sort that all out."

Kate leaned over the candlelit table and hugged him with excitement. "Oh Nat! You are brilliant. That's *fantastic*."

"Hey, look out. You're setting your hair on fire . . . Er, there's just one thing," Nat said when she had, slightly singed, reseated herself. "Dad's not prepared to stump up for the fare or hotel, I'm afraid. The deal's as it was before, yeah? You pay for yourself."

Kate nodded. "Fine." There was enough in her savings, she had calculated, for a return fare in economy, plus a few days in some modest hotel, some carefully budgeted meals. Then a thought struck her sharply. He, of course, had been grounded by his father. He had not said he was coming too. Was he really arranging for her to go without him? "But what about you, Nat?"

"What?" His smooth brow disappeared under irritated creases. "I'm bloody coming, of course. That's the whole point of the exercise—apart," he added hurriedly, "from *you* getting to cover the film festival, I mean."

"So your father doesn't mind you going? After the drugs thing?"

"He's chilled about that now."

"And he doesn't mind you going with me . . . oooh!" Something was inching up her skirt and touching the inside of her thigh. Something that felt like a bare foot.

Kate gasped and fixed her eyes on him. "After all he said about women with *taitles* . . . *aaahh*." She suppressed a yelp. The foot had edged higher. As waves of excitement built between her thighs, Kate looked hurriedly around her. Fortunately, all the ten-bob millionaires seemed deep in the wine lists.

So she was finally, really, going to the Riviera. It was as if all the walls around her these many years had suddenly fallen down. The light of infinite possibility flooded in, blinding in its color and excitement. The Cannes Film Festival. The glamorous villa party packed with film stars on Cap Ferrat. Because of course, he would take her with him. She looked at Nat with shining eyes.

The foot had found the spot it sought now. Kate's breath was coming short and fast. Her eyes were wide. Gently but firmly the big toe started to flex.

"So, look," Nat was grinning at her wickedly. "All you need to do now is sort out our travel arrangements. Let's leave as soon as possible."

"Right. I'll be down at Fair's Fare tomorrow, as soon as they open." Kate spoke in a squeak. She was clenching the cutlery.

"You're sure?"

"Certain." Kate tried to concentrate as powerful pulses of pleasure shook her body.

"So you're cool about lending me the plane fare?"

*Ulp.* Kate stared. The throbs subsided. He—son of a multimillionaire—was asking *her* to lend him money?

"I mean," Nat drawled, increasing the delicious pressure again, "I *have* talked to Dad and Wemyss round for you, right? I'd ask Pa for some dosh but he doesn't realize I've blown my allowance already and he'll be well pissed off if he finds out. He'd probably change his mind about the whole shooting match."

"Oh no, well you mustn't ask him," Kate gasped, eyes watering and hot flushes bursting in her face like fireworks. "Of course I can lend you some money—if I have enough."

Nat's face blazed with satisfaction. "Oh, I won't need much. Just enough for a first-class round-trip ticket to Nice. You can manage that, yeah?" The toe pressed harder.

"Yes . . . yes . . . yes . . . *yesss!*"

The ancient family suitcase, as used by Mum and Dad on their honeymoon and every outing since, was standing packed by Kate's bed. After Mum's insistence on several million pairs of knickers, lotions, and medication for every eventuality and Gran's newest creation "in case it gets parky," there had hardly, in the end, been room for anything else.

With the utmost difficulty Kate stuffed in her sartorial staples; denim jacket, black trousers and white T-shirts, a red summer dress, a couple of shirts and pairs of jeans. As a concession to the glamour zone, Kate splashed out on a pair of smart flip-flops with flowers on the front big enough to cover the fattest bits of her toes.

Nothing in her wardrobe was of the floatily chic variety one wore to interview Leonardo DiCaprio on the poolside terrace of the Eden Roc. Admittedly, DiCaptrio's media schedule was unlikely to include half an hour for the *Mockery.* Nat's glamorous film party was, however, another matter.

He had proved as irritatingly difficult to pin down on the subject of clothes as on any other detail concerning the event. But hopefully the greenish-yellow linen jacket and trousers bought last year in the Whistles sale for her cousin's wedding would pass muster. Or mustard, reminiscent as it was of a pot of Colman's English. It would have to; there was no time to find anything else. Nor was there the money.

Dinner at Spinning Jenny's had seen to that.

Having dropped his Cannes bombshell, Nat had celebrated by ordering a large piece of lemon tart, some Roquefort, and a café cognac. When the bill arrived, he shoved it straight in her direction. "You can get this on expenses, yeah?"

Kate boggled. "I don't have an expense account. I thought . . ."

"That I was paying, yeah? Actually, I meant that Dad was—through the paper." His perfect nostrils had flared briefly with annoyance. "Look, if you get it, I'll pay you back, okay?"

He hadn't, not yet. Nor had he reimbursed her for his first-class ticket. He had been unwaveringly specific about the departure date and also that they left from London.

The cheapest flight Kate had been able to find herself was £40 the day after. "Yeah, sure it's a shame, doll," Nat remarked of the discrepancy. "But the sooner I get over there, the sooner I can start networking for you, yeah?"

Kate had cheered up at this. Her own lack of contacts among the Hollywood glitterati had vaguely started to worry her. If she was hoping to get interviews, this would definitely be a disadvantage. But if Nat was prepared to do some groundwork, her delay in arriving might be an advantage.

"See you at Nice Airport, yeah? I'll wait for you. Ciao, doll."

And with that, he had snatched the tickets, breathed on her lips and was off.

Her parents had been both suspicious and alarmed by the suddenness of the trip, but had come round once she explained it had Denys Wemyss's full approval. She had also had the foresight not to mention

Nat's part in the proceedings. Being promised Mel Gibson's autograph had, meanwhile, helped allay Mum's fears—well, he *might*, Kate thought guiltily, be at the film festival. One never knew, as Mum herself liked to say. And here was Mum again, wanting to swell the bursting suitcase with a bath towel—"because you never know"—a loo roll and a box of PG Tips.

"I'm not camping, Mum!"

"I'm just covering all eventualities," was Mum's riposte. "The *Mockery*'s hardly likely to book you into a five-star hotel, let's face it."

No, but Nat might, Kate thought happily. The hotel end of things, along with the press accreditation passes, had been left in his hands. And she had no worries about his competence; either he, or his father, had handled Denys Wemyss and the question of her time off so perfectly that Wemyss hadn't so much as mentioned it. Darren, who would undoubtedly have wanted to discuss it at length, was no longer around to do so, the Chip Shop tour having finally started.

The next morning, as she left for the first of several buses that would take her to the airport, Gran clasped her hard. "Make the most of it, love," she urged. Kate winced as the strong fingers, honed by years of knitting, dug into the soft flesh of her shoulders.

"I will, Gran," Kate said, her buttocks flexing with excitement as she thought for the millionth time about Cannes. Anything, after all, could happen now. Sheer persistence, coupled with a bit of luck, might throw her in the path of one of Hollywood's finest, resulting in the no-holds-barred interview that would make her name. There would be no going back after that. Particularly not to Slackmucklethwaite. Not that she would dream of ever saying anything so hurtful to the family now standing waving fondly on the drive. Kate forced the lump in her throat down hard.

At the airport, she found herself in the queue directly behind a group of large and loud Hoorays who, Kate gathered from their earsplittingly loud conversation, were headed for some smart wedding. Probably thirty, they looked at least forty; the loudest and largest, in fact, looked fifty. Kate hoped for the bride's sake that he wasn't the groom. Supremely unattractive, he wore standard Hooray summer issue of creased linen suit, the beige trousers of which made his hips look wider even than they were. His porcine face was as red and round as the setting sun and there was a vivid boil above the bridge of his nose that gave the impression he had been shot through the forehead.

The check-in girl droned through the formalities. "Did you pack this bag yourself? Did anyone give you anything?"

"Oh, now you mention it," brayed the red-faced one, "a bearded Arab-type bloke gave me this alarm clock with a sort of fuse thing attached."

As the other Hoorays roared, the check-in girl surveyed him coolly. "Hilarious, sir," she said flatly.

Another of the group stepped forward. "Er . . . any chance of an upgrade, sort of thing?"

The girl did not even look up." No, sir. None whatsoever."

In the lime-upholstered departure lounge, Kate looked around at her other fellow travelers. Various ostentatiously bored types were yawning into mobiles or, in the case of one flop-haired man, flicking through the *Hollywood Reporter*. Festival-bound Kate thought, with a leap of the heart. Like me.

The other passengers seemed a motley crew. Families trying to control wild packs of children; backpackers reading *A Rough Guide to the Riviera*; tanned Victor Meldrews buried in the *Daily Telegraph* and white-trousered blondes weighted down with Vuitton and *Vogue*.

Kate was distracted from her copy of *Heat* by a sudden commotion in the doorway. Bustling into the departure lounge came a tall, glamorous blonde. One whom Kate recognized instantly. She had, after all, interviewed her only a few days ago.

Kate's only regret in leaving was that she would miss the edition of the *Mercury* with Champagne in it. It would certainly have been destined for the cuttings book. In the end, Colin's photographs had been a chlorine-soaked write-off but the called-in image from the picture agency—Champagne sprawled seductively in a tight, skimpy T-shirt, nipples protruding in classic chapel-hatpeg style—in every sense embodied the sexy, starry new *Mercury* Peter Hardstone had in mind. The only teat-flashing celebrity ever pictured in the <u>Mercury</u>'s previous 249 years had been a sow with an outsize crop of piglets dug out by Kate for *Fifty Years Ago Today.*

"Yah, bloody nightmare," Champagne was shouting into the small silver mobile Kate had last seen poking out from her bikini bottoms. "Igor refused to stump up for first so I've had to fly bloody goat class."

"Charming," remarked a cut-glass–voiced woman next to Kate. "That makes all the rest of us goats, I suppose."

"Well, of *course* I bloody well tried to get upgraded," Champagne roared as she flounced past in a baby-blue T-shirt bearing the red-sequined legend *Tanorexic.* "And yes, the cow on the check-in desk knew perfectly well who I was. Stuck me in deep vein thrombosis all the same, though. *Bitch.*"

Kate's admiration for the check-in girl, already considerable, doubled.

"I absolutely hate to say so," said Kate's plummy neighbor, watching the slender brown legs stride away under a faded denim miniskirt that barely covered her bottom, "but isn't she that ghastly tart from *Hello Sailor, I'm A Celebrity?*"

"I'm afraid so." Kate smiled at Cut-Glass Woman. She was pale, fair and rather short; certainly not more than five feet four. And older than me, Kate thought. Late thirties?

"Hope she's not sitting next to me. Although it would thrill my husband to bits."

"For about five minutes," Kate said. "That's as long as any normal human being can stand."

"You don't understand. My husband isn't a normal human being. Or even a human being."

Kate searched the woman's face for signs that she was joking. There were none.

"He's a gossip columnist," the woman said contemptuously. "For one of the papers." She gestured towards the *Hollywood Reporter* reader. "That's him over there. Vile, isn't he?"

But handsome, Kate saw. Dishy in a reptilian way—long face, sharp dark eyes, oily, floppy dark hair. She wondered why, if the woman disliked her husband so much, she was still with him. But of course things—especially those sorts of things—were rarely pure and never simple.

"By yourself?" The woman nodded. "Lucky you. What I'd give to go somewhere without bloody Lance. Be single again, for that matter."

"Actually, someone's meeting me at Nice," Kate admitted.

"Actor, is he?" asked the woman. The question had a weary air. "Most of this lot are." She cast an unimpressed glance at the other inhabitants of the departure lounge.

'I thought so," Kate said excitedly. "All off to the festival, are they?"

"For what it's worth, poor sods. That's one of the things about being married to a showbiz columnist. I can recognize at a hundred paces every sad TV personality who's hoping to upgrade to full celeb status through being in a film. See that musclebound bloke over there? That's Bruce Goose from *Fire! Fire!* And the one reading the *Hollywood Reporter* upside down? Mandy Moran from *Surgeon, Surgeon.* Desperate to break into movies, apparently, but the poor dear doesn't seem to realize you have to be able to read first."

"You don't sound very keen on Cannes," Kate remarked, smiling. The woman obviously had issues, but she was funny.

"Don't I? Can't think why. Look, we'd better get on this plane."

Kate's seat was practically at the back of the plane, and by the window. Getting to her seat involved the disgorging of some Hoorays, all of whom were grumbling about being in "steerage." They stared pointedly at her breasts as she squeezed, apologizing, past them.

The plane taxied and took off. Kate fought to stop herself snapping at the child behind her who had twanged the pocket at the back of her seat from the moment she sat down. Annoyance turned to amusement once the plane had pierced the clouds and the child had peered out of the window, surveyed the fluffy scene and demanded, "Where's God?"

Kate stared out of the window. The White Cliffs of Dover gave way to the hazy blue of the Channel, then to the patchwork khaki fields of northern France. Here and there came a flash of silver as the sun caught the bends in the rivers. Gradually the terrain changed again to vast rocky brown plateaus, valleys and mountains, some capped dazzlingly with blue-white snow. Eventually Kate fell asleep and woke from a doze to hear the captain announcing the descent. Excitedly, she pressed her nose against the window for her first glimpse of the Côte d'Azur.

First came red-roofed villas in the hills, swimming pools glowing like aquamarines in their gardens. Then a pale mass of buildings that stretched from the foothills to the sea. The ocean was bright blue dotted with dazzling white boats.

Without warning, the plane swung out over the water, dropping so close to the yachts that Kate could almost see the lemon in the owners' gin and tonics. Convinced the next thing she would see was passing fish, she shut her eyes.

"*Mesdames et messieurs. Bienvenue à l'aéroport Nice Côte d'Azur. L'heure locale est midi et demi,*" announced a calm-sounding stewardess, apparently unaware she was descending to a watery grave. "Ladies and gentlemen, welcome to Nice Côte d'Azur Airport. Local time is twelve-thirty."

Kate kept her eyes tightly shut.

"Excuse me," barked a fruity voice near her ear. "That's actually rather painful, you know."

"God, I'm sorry," Kate gasped, unpeeling the fingers plunged tightly into her neighbor's arm.

A wave of euphoria swept her from top to toenail. She was alive. She was here. And somewhere just the other side of the arrival doors, Nat would be waiting to greet her.

Nice, however, had a far from nice surprise in store. Kate emerged excitedly through the arrival doors to find no Nat among the waiting crowd. No message, either; none of the portly, sunglassed, card-bearing men bore one with her name on it.

Standing, annoyed and stranded, amid the glittering marble of the arrivals hall was bad enough. Being swept aside as Champagne strode imperiously past, honking loudly into her mobile, a swarm of Vuitton-bearing porters scurrying anxiously in her wake, was worse. Kate gazed after her with loathing.

The Hoorays ambled up and stood in a little group next to her. They seemed to be waiting for someone.

"Did you buy from the list, Caractacus?" one asked. "I was quite tempted by the tennis-ball firer, I must say. Bit steep though at thirteen hundred and ninety-nine pounds. The eight-hundred-pound leather elephant was what I really wanted to give them but it had gone by the time I rang up."

Kate tried not to gasp. Her family's idea of an extravagant wedding present was a set of cotton sheets. Just what *was* a tennis-ball firer for £1,399? Tim Henman, presumably. As for an £800 leather elephant—she'd want a real one for that.

"These are the cut-crystal champagne flutes," said a third man, gingerly poking the box on top of his suitcase. "Or were," he added dolefully, at an answering rattle from within.

"Well, *hello* there. Fancy seeing you here."

Kate jumped. It was the woman from the plane.

"He didn't turn up then?"

Kate shook her head crossly. "But he'll be here soon."

She noticed with irritation the other woman's look of pity. "You look as if you could do with a drink. There's a bar up there." The woman gestured up an escalator.

"But . . ."

"You can see the concourse from it, so don't worry about missing him. If he comes, that is."

"He'll come," Kate said grimly. "Don't worry." He had better. Apart from anything else, Nat owed her a considerable amount of money.

"*I'm* not worried, darling. Not if *you're* not. Now come for that drink," urged the woman. "I'll be glad of the company. Lance is supposed to be sorting out the hire car but I can see from here that he's nobbling some tarty D-lister by the exit doors—interviewing one of our nation's great white celluloid hopes, rather. So he's obviously going to be ages. I'm Celia St. Louis, by the way. Come on, I'll help you carry your stuff. Bloody hell, what have you got in this suitcase?"

"You're covering the film festival for the . . . what?" In the bar, Celia's pale eyes were wide as she cradled her red wine.

The *Slackmucklethwaite Mercury.*" Kate grinned, feeling temporarily buoyed by her own glass of white.

"Wow. Lance works on the showbiz section of one of the Sundays, which sounds positively boring by comparison. What's the *Slackmucklethwaite Mercury* like?"

Kate told her about Gladys Arkwright and her balcony. Even Darren hadn't been such an appreciative audience. Celia wiped her eyes and took a deep draught from her glass.

"Are you a journalist too?" Kate asked, by now well into her second.

Celia shook her blond head adamantly. "No, I'm here as a plus one. We're so cheap and Lance is so bloody mean that this has to count as our holiday. He gets most of it back on expenses that way; in fact, he's even making a profit this year. Not only did he trade in the club-class tickets for those discount jobs, he's cancelled the smart hotel the paper booked for him and checked us into some godforsaken village up in the hills. Still," she said, sighing, "however bad it is, it'll be a change from St. Reatham."

"St. Reatham? Where's that?" Kate immediately imagined a sleepy country village. A picturesque sort of place.

"Streatham. Sarf-East London, darling."

"Oh, right."

Celia beamed at her. "So. Where are you staying?"

Beneath the numbing alcohol, Kate felt a stab of panic. "Nat was *supposed* to be sorting something out," she said as casually as she could manage. "But as I haven't got a mobile, he can't get in touch with me. And I don't have a French phone card."

"Borrow mine." Celia rummaged in her handbag.

"Gratefully, Kate took the proffered mobile and tried Nat's number. No answer. Fueled by the wine, she lurched from fury to fear. Had there been an accident of some sort? She pictured a crumpled car, blood on the sunlit road, the wail of ambulance sirens . . .

"Maybe his is out of battery." She tried to sound calm as she handed the phone back. "He does seem to use it a lot."

"*Does* he now." Celia gave her a wise look.

"But he's bound to turn up soon." Even to her own ears, she sounded panicked now. "He's got my passes to the film festival—everything. *And* he's supposed to be taking me to this amazing film party on Cap Ferrat."

"We're going to that," Celia remarked without enthusiasm. "Everyone who's anyone will be there. As well as everyone who isn't."

A comforting thought struck Kate. Nat could and should appear at any moment, of course. But if not, and failing all else, she would definitely see him at the party. The entire raison d'être of his trip was to attend it. "I'll catch up with him there, then," she said, relieved.

"Of course—always supposing you've got your invitation with you."

"Er . . . well . . ."

"You *haven't* got it?"

"Nat's got it, I suppose. But do I need one? Can't I just go there and, I dunno—*meet* him?"

Celia snorted. "Hardly, darling. The place'll be crawling with celebrities. Security'll be tighter than Gwyneth Paltrow's arse."

*Sod it.* Kate's stomach cramped with misery. Without an invitation, or any means of getting one, how exactly was she going to link up with Nat? Was her Riviera dream over before it had even begun?

10

Kate gazed helplessly at her new friend. The situation seemed to be getting worse by the second.

"And," Celia was pointing out now, "even if you *had* got an invitation, you've got nowhere to change because, as of this moment, you don't even know where you're staying. Am I right?"

Celia had, Kate realized, the uncomfortable knack of cutting the bullshit and slicing straight to the heart of a problem. "Oh God. This is so embarrassing. You must think I'm pathetic. But I'm not usually this hopeless, believe me."

"I do believe you." Celia reached over and patted her arm. "It's not your fault, darling. You've been completely swept off your feet. . . ."

Kate nodded.

". . . by a bastard who's let you down."

Kate's chin jerked up indignantly. "Hang on a minute. . . ."

Celia waved a silencing hand. "Believe me, I know the signs. It happened to me. When I first met him, Lance was all champagne and compliments." Her eyes flashed. "But it was Pa's money he was trying to get up the aisle, not me. What kind of an idiot was *I*?"

Kate felt defensive. Was Celia suggesting she was being a fool over Nat? There had to be a good reason for his nonappearance. That he'd just left her in the lurch was unbelievable. Impossible, unthinkable.

Something in her expression brought an end to Celia's tirade. "Anyway," she said briskly, "we're straying off the point. Basically," she placed both hands on the table for emphasis, "you're in a mess."

Kate grimaced. It was difficult to deny her situation lacked a certain promise.

"But," Celia announced, "there's a way round this. Here's what we do."

"*There* you are," a voice cut in some minutes later." Hitting the bottle, might have guessed."

"Hello, Lance." Celia smiled sarcastically at her husband. "Been enjoying an intellectual workout with the cream of Britain's acting talent?"

Lance pursed his lips. "Actually, Champagne D'Vyne was very interesting on the subject of the new Bond film. She's promised me an exclusive behind-the-scenes."

"I bet she has." Celia yawned. "I hear she promises a lot of those. Now, Lance, this is Kate Clegg. She's coming with us to the Cap Ferrat party."

"*What!*" exclaimed Lance in horror.

"She's supposed to be going anyway," Celia said firmly. "She's a reporter, and her boyfriend is an actor—am I right?" she added, turning to Kate.

Kate nodded. Well, she had the might of the *Mockery* behind her, didn't she? And Nat certainly *intended* to become an actor.

"What paper do you work on?" Lance had fixed her with a beady eye.

"Um, a local one. You won't have heard of it."

"Try me."

Kate took a deep breath. "The *Slackmucklethwaite Mercury?*"

'The what? Damn right I haven't heard of it." Lance curled his lip.

"So that's settled then, is it?" Celia interrupted. "Kate comes with us. And we're finding her a room in our hotel."

"But I won't need one," Kate protested. "At least, only until the party. Nat's sorted out accommodation. All I need to do is find him."

"Ye-e-ss." Celia's smile was gentle. "But let's book you one, shall we? Just in case."

"Case is right," grumbled Lance, regarding Kate's big brown suitcase with scorn. "That needs a whole bloody suite to itself."

*     *     *

Ste. Jeanne, the village Celia had been anticipating with so little enthusiasm, looked fine to Kate. More than fine. As, grumpily, Lance piloted the rented three-door Saxo—"Really, darling, you spoil me," Celia had observed on seeing it—Kate looked out, enchanted, from her squashed position in the back. "It's so *pretty*," she breathed.

Ste. Jeanne was the type of hill village to delight the heart of the broadsheet travel editor; a picturesque huddle of pale gold stone topped with orange and apricot roofs and crowned by a couple of belfried towers. The cobbled main road tunneling shadily to its heart wound steeply up beneath ancient terraced houses with walls like peanut brittle. At its steepest point it passed under a battlemented archway whose gate had long since disappeared. Once-defensive towers now bristled with bright clumps of flowering plants dangling down in the sun like colorful beards. Despite its great age, each building looked cherished and cared for—neatly roofed and solidly pointed, with lace-curtained windows flanked by pastel shutters and underscored with window boxes exuberant with geranium and bougainvillaea. More spilled from vast clay jars leaning against higgledy-piggledy doorways.

"Not bad is it?" There was a note of surprise in Celia's voice. "Sure you haven't made a mistake, darling?"

"Shut up and look out for the Hôtel des Tours," snapped Lance.

They drove slowly down the main street. "The rue du Midi," Celia said, peering out at the signs. It was a colorful riot of restaurants, shops, and awnings. People were browsing, chatting or merely wandering. They passed a cheerful market square, in the middle of which a blond stone fountain trickled into a circular, blond-walled pool. Above all stretched a cloudless blue sky.

"This says Place de l'Eglise," Celia announced as the rue du Midi opened out into an arcaded square.

"And here's the Hôtel des Tours." Kate gestured to where, beneath two of the arcades, tables had been set out with cheerful blue cloths. People sat drinking leisurely coffees and watching the new arrivals with curiosity.

"Except," Lance drawled, "the sign says *Café de la Place.*"

"Oh. So it does."

"So where the fuck's the Hôtel des Tours?" Lance glanced at his watch. "We've only got a couple of hours before the bash starts."

"Is that it?" Kate pointed opposite the Café de la Place. Beneath a rioting vine on the ancient wall, a few battered wooden tables stood emptily about. In contrast to the café opposite no one sat at them. The vacant, rusting sign-holder that protruded from between the leaves above suggested that some time had passed since anyone had.

"Well, there are a couple of *tours* in the square." Celia indicated the two church towers. "But it looks shut. More than that, it looks dead."

"It can't be." Lance glared at Celia. "I talked to them just the other day."

"You *dreamed* it, darling." Celia sighed. "Must have done. Your French isn't up to asking the way, let alone booking a room."

Lance's thin nostrils inflated with rage.

"There's only one way to find out," Kate said reasonably. She was fed up with being cramped in the back, where the feeling of being a five-year-old out with arguing parents was growing. "Let's go and have a look."

There was no doubt that the Hôtel des Tours was an unusual establishment. The impression it had given of being shut was erroneous. Behind the fringe of vine lurked an enormous wooden door bristling with ancient ironwork. It was slightly ajar to reveal a small, gloomy bar.

*Extremely* gloomy, Kate saw, once Lance had risked a hernia prising the doors apart. And extremely empty, which was unsurprising if those present were the regulars. By comparison, the Punch Out's clientèle seemed positively sparkling.

At one table, two men of intimidating appearance grumbled at each other in undertones. Both were hugely broad across the chest, although one was much shorter than the other. The taller had a red face, round black eyes and a white apron; the hotel chef, Kate imagined, although it was anyone's guess where the restaurant was. None of the tables either inside or out boasted as much as a salt pot, much less a menu. Next to the chef sat someone dark, burly, squat, and exactly fitting Kate's mental image of the troll under the bridge in *The Three Billy Goats Gruff*. Beneath the table stretched a huge Alsatian with malevolent yellow eyes. Catching Kate's wary glance, it bared its teeth.

Both men seemed oblivious to their presence. More oblivious still was a thin man of indeterminate age and wild salt-and-pepper hair. Slumped against the bar on a high wooden stool, he was working his way steadily through the bottle at his elbow. His ancient white trousers were liberally splashed with claret, as was his equally aged blue shirt. The general effect, given the deltas of magenta veins spreading about his nose and cheeks, was of a human tricolor.

"Bloody drunk," said Lance, not bothering to lower his voice.

"Hypocrite!" snapped Celia. "I've seen you in far worse states."

"Not on that bloody paint stripper. Nothing less than the Veuve for me."

"Shame," retorted his wife. "We might be marginally less in debt if you'd stuck to Thunderbird. Who's in charge here, do you think?" she hissed to Kate.

"Er . . ." Kate looked around. The women in the bar were, if anything, more intimidating than the men. The piercing gaze she felt burning into her back belonged to a crone with a twisted expression whose wrinkled, beringed, and red-taloned finger meditatively circled the top of a glass of red wine. The Gitane that roared like a forest fire in the ashtray beside her hinted at the origin of the single blond streak at the front of her pure white chignon.

At another table, a woman whose bulging eyes, wide mouth, and wounded expression were reminiscent of a tragedy-struck trout gazed imploringly into the middle distance. Her gray hair, swept loosely back into a bun, framed a face that was the wrinkled yellow of corn-fed chicken skin. Hands the size of spades spread beseechingly out across what looked like a large exercise book.

Scarcely more encouraging, through a good deal more attractive, was the full-lipped, high-cheekboned young woman slumped behind the bar gazing in sultry fashion at the Troll. Kate watched with inter-

est as he broke off his muttered conversation to gaze hungrily, hopefully back. The barmaid tossed him a glance of contempt and threw
back the black hair that streamed over her shoulders like oil. Twisting
a strand between long fingers, she surveyed the three newcomers
through huge, beautiful, and unenthusiastic brown eyes.

"How's your French?" Celia whispered as they lined up along
the bar.

"Okay-ish," Kate said modestly.

"I'd better do the talking then," Celia said decisively. "Because
Lance's is crap as well."

"Thanks very much," snapped her husband.

Celia's French was both perfect and prettily accented, even
though, oddly, the barmaid seemed to have difficulty understanding
it. The dark eyes looked blank. The full lips tugged down in helpless
ignorance. The black head shook from side to side in apparent incom-
prehension.

"You have a go," Celia muttered to Kate. "It might be my accent.
I spent two years in Paris after university."

Kate began to speak when the girl dipped and fiddled with something under the counter. A blast of eardrum-explodingly loud French
pop music filled the bar and Kate was forced to ask about the rooms in
a wild yell. As, suddenly, the music disappeared, Kate found herself
bawling in the silence like a drill sergeant. Someone sniggered.

Long lashes blinking innocently, the barmaid explained the radio
was *en panne*. Kate and Celia looked at each other suspiciously.

"It can't be broken. She did it on purpose. What a complete cow,"
hissed Kate. Too late she realized that she had said it in French.

The barmaid's eyes flashed dangerously. "About the rooms, you'll
have to ask Madame," she snapped.

"Madame" turned out to be the Trout. And Madame, to Kate's relief, understood perfectly, if not particularly politely. She sighed deeply
and leafed slowly through the exercise book—revealed now as an accounts ledger—as if Kate's enquiry were the most inconvenient imag-
inable. Yes, she had a booking for a Mr. and Mrs. St. Louis. Yes, there

was another room free if she wanted to book in herself. Kate collected the keys with the strong impression that there was no one else staying at all.

As the barmaid turned the music up again, the red-faced man at the bar put his pastis glass down. "I shay," he muttered in a slow, inebriated, patrician English accent. "I shay," he reiterated, attempting to prop himself up on the bar but sliding abruptly down again. Kate winced as his chin hit the wood. "Would you mind *awfully* shtopping that *frightful* row. . . ."

Kate watched as he swayed from side to side atop his bar stool. It was clear what was about to happen. Lurching heavily to one side and then the other, he slipped off the seat and fell heavily to the ground like a sack of potatoes. The arm he flung out to break his fall shot along the bar counter, sending everything flying off the end in a waterfall of bottles and ashtrays. His arrival on the ground was accompanied by a shower of smashed glass. By way of finale, the bar stool crashed to the floor.

Celia looked sardonically at her husband. "The most romantic place I've ever stayed in," she remarked.

Kate's room—at the top of the hotel—was better than expected. While basic, it was big. There was a large brass bed and a roomy wardrobe, while the "facilities"—a loo, basin, and shower cubicle—stood ranged against one wall. But the great glory of the room lay outside.

Opening a pair of white French doors, Kate stepped out on to a tiny red-tiled balcony, edged with a white-painted rail and containing a marble-topped table and white plastic chair. The warmth of the tiles seeped upwards through her feet as she leaned over the metal rail, breathing in the herby air.

The balcony commanded a magnificent prospect of the Place de l'Eglise. Kate surveyed the two church towers—one clock, one bell, both painted an optimistic peach—at the end. Then she examined the houses. The windows of the dwellings were scattered so randomly over the ancient walls it was impossible to tell where one house ended and another began. Dark with vine or gay with bougainvillaea, they varied crazily in height. Some stood four stories high; others, with covered balconies added to the top, had five; a lack of uniformity giving the roofline the appearance of uneven teeth.

Only one house in the square, that occupying the entire far end opposite the church towers, was not of this type. Grander and of more regular appearance than the rest, it boasted a large carved door topped with a stone coat of arms, a flight of imposing steps, and big, mullioned windows that were firmly and mysteriously shuttered. Kate looked at it with interest. It obviously was, or had been, the house of someone important.

Along the bottom of the square's two longest sides—it being actually an oblong—ran the thick-walled arches of the arcades. Divided by stocky pillars, they opened on to the square like cloisters. Inside ran a raised pavement on to which opened the doorways of the houses; an ancient sequence of haphazard shapes and heights.

Kate looked down, enchanted, at the heads and shoulders of people passing beneath. She looked across at the bustle of the Café de la Place. She smiled at the sight of five old women, resplendent in flowered overalls, sitting on a bench by the church in the sun. From their expressions it was clear that the world they were watching pass by failed to measure up to their expectations.

Finally, Kate turned back into her room. It was, she thought, the original room with a view. Almost a shame she'd have to leave it when she finally hooked up with Nat. She jumped as, behind her, a telephone shrilled.

"Ready yet?" asked Celia. "Lance is doing his nut. You have to be downstairs in ten minutes."

They tore along the coast road in Lance's Saxo. Kate stared out, enchanted, at the glittering sea. The approach into Nice was announced by a row of stucco hotels encrusted with balconies, carvings, and cupolas, all glowing richly in the evening sunshine. She gazed in delight at one particularly palatial facade, topped with a salmon-colored dome.

Lance, halted by a traffic light, was clearly outraged by the interruption. He rummaged impatiently in his inside pocket, struck a large hand-rolled cigarette in his mouth and applied a match to it. As the heavy, herby scent began to fill the car Kate recognized the smell of cannabis.

While the evening outside the car was warm, inside was warmer still thanks to the Saxo's rudimentary air-conditioning. Kate, sticky in the mustard linen suit, felt her feet and ankles swelling like dough. The reek of the joint was beginning to make her feel sick.

Such had been the rush to set off, she'd had time only to grab her notebook, shake out her suit, and bundle her hair up in the hope of disguising its lack not only of definite color but of definite style as well. In the heavy evening heat, she could feel it slowly, determinedly, unfurling at the nape of her neck.

At least Celia and Lance seemed to have stopped rowing. They had, in fact, stopped talking altogether. Celia looked pretty and cool in a flowing cream silk dress, a pale pink pashmina, and a pair of vertiginous heels that raised her diminutive stature by a foot. Her blond hair shone in the rich evening light and a vast pair of Jackie O sunglasses added the final sophisticated touch.

"Spliff?" Lance asked Kate suddenly, shoving the smoking paper cylinder in her direction. She took it. It was supposed to have calming qualities, after all. She raised the joint to her lips.

Just then, a gust of sea air buffeted through the open window and blew the burning end of ash straight on to her linen jacket. Before Kate could brush it away it had scorched a gaping, black-edged hole the size of a nickel into the mustard expanse. She wailed in horror. The jacket was ruined. All she had on underneath was a bra, and not the world's most glamorous one at that. Worse, the hole could hardly be more noticeable, being exactly over her nipple. The ruination of her appearance was total. What were the impossibly glamorous guests at this impossibly glamorous party going to think? Not to mention Nat.

Celia twisted round. "Oh *fuck*."

"Never mind," said Lance, grinning, eyes slitty with amusement in the rearview mirror. "No one's going to be looking at you anyway."

*     *     *

Long before they got there they could see the party. The large pink
villa it was held in was perched at the very top of the Cap Ferrat penin-
sula, and lights and movement were visible from all along the main
road. Lance parked the Saxo round a corner a couple of hundred yards
from the entrance. "Don't want to get hemmed in," he explained as
they got out.

"By cars a hundred times more expensive, you mean," Celia observed astringently, pressing herself against the hedge-lined roadside as
a stream of blacked-out limos flowed past. "Well, I wish you'd bloody
well warned me." She looked regretfully at her footwear. "These shoes
*weren't* made for walking."

As Lance strode eagerly on ahead, Kate helped a tottering, cursing
Celia to round the corner after him. Her crushed spirits rose at seeing
the party entrance, a pair of gates topped by two dishes in which dancing yellow flames flickered against the deepening blue of the evening
sky. A chattering crowd of onlookers watched the shining procession
of cars pass, bending close to the dark windows to see who sat behind.
The odd cheer burst out. At the gates, a bevy of wigged and costumed
flunkeys straight out of Mozart leaned into car windows to check tickets.

Beyond the gates Kate could see a red carpet, lined with jostling,
shouting photographers, stretching up a palm-tree-fringed drive.
Those getting out of their limos were greeted by a flurry of flashbulbs
and shouts. "Leonardo! Over 'ere! Hugh! Renée! Give us a smile!"

Stomach muscles rigid with excitement, Kate stared at the flaming
gates reflected in the gleaming limos. She could hardly believe that she
was here. She was agog, swept away, until a small, uncomfortable voice
reminded her that admission to this enchanted world was in serious
doubt.

The voice was Celia's. "Go on," she was hissing to a clearly-reluctant
Lance. "You've got to get Kate in, remember!"

On sufferance and under his wife's burning eye, Lance brandished
his press accreditation at the flint-faced flunkeys and began to explain
the circumstances of her presence. Kate held her breath. Doubt suf-

fused the flunkeys' faces. They examined Lance's invitations, badges, and directions—a folder-full, from what Kate could see—and muttered to each other.

Then came an earsplitting roar. All eyes swivelled to the violently-revving vast black motorbike that had arrived at the gates.

"Hell's Angels!" breathed Celia excitedly, as the hugely thickset and heavily bearded biker tugged off his helmet to reveal long greasy hair, a handlebar moustache, and an uncompromisingly fierce expression.

The backseat passenger, a slender figure in clinging, shining black, removed its helmet and tossed out long blond ropes of hair.

"Hell's actress, more like," muttered Kate, watching as Champagne D'Vyne swung one long PVC-covered leg, tipped with spike heel, over the bike seat and on to the ground. Had she, Kate wondered, watching her unzip her front almost to navel level, been *welded* into that catsuit? Not only did it fit without a wrinkle, but revealed not as much as a gram of spare flesh.

"She's certainly got the first rule of celebrity right," Lance remarked admiringly, as the security men, watching Champagne flashing teeth and cleavage for the cameras, waved them through with no further murmur. "Make an entrance. Turn up on a motorbike if everyone else is arriving by limo."

"Or Saxo," Celia reminded him waspishly as they approached the crimson river of carpet. "She's been no slouch about the second rule of celebrity either. Her tits are up round her throat."

"Cleavage gives leverage," retorted her husband, looking meaningfully at Celia's unabundant frontage. "She's certainly going down well," he added, as popping flashbulbs accompanied Champagne's progress up the red carpet.

"*You'd* know all about that." Celia remarked acidly.

"They're not taking pictures of her anyway." Kate was craning to see. "Sharon Stone's behind her. Champagne looks furious."

Her heart swooped with joy as she stepped on to the red carpet. If only Gran could see her now. Even Dad would be impressed. Her ruined suit was temporarily forgotten. Until Lance pointed to more flaming torches planted between the palm trees, sniggered and told her to watch out.

"Shut up," snapped Celia. "Can't you see Kate's upset about it?"

"Aw, sorry." Lance grinned. "But fortunately I've got just the thing to cover it up." He paused, rummaged in his pocket and passed her something. "There you go. Someone gave it to me at a TV launch party the other day."

Kate gazed at the badge in her hand. *I'm A Pussy On The Piss*, it declared in neon-pink capitals against a glaring yellow background.

"Not the launch of the new-look *Newsnight*, I take it?" Celia said dryly.

"You're too kind," Kate said archly, handing it back.

"Use this." In a brave move, given her heels, Celia bent shakily, plucked a white rose from a nearby bush and gave it to Kate. "A buttonhole."

As Kate and Celia scuttled up the carpet, Lance, hanging back, walked deliberately slowly and beamed about him. The photographers pointed their lenses to the ground, folded their arms, and talked among themselves.


The long, wide drive to the villa sloped upwards, revealing through umbrella-like pine trees glimpses of a pearly blue silk sea. The air was heavy with scent from the bordering jasmine bushes. Kate drew a heady, happy breath.

Lance, who had caught up with them again, ruined the mood by pointing to a large pale-colored building on the coastline and saying it was the hotel where Michael Winner stayed. "He'll probably be at the party," he added.

"Can't wait," Celia groaned.

A crowd milled at the villa entrance. Kate, looking eagerly about for Nat recognized a thin, white-suited man with gold flashing at cuff, buttons, and sunglasses. He was, she thought, much more delicate in the flesh than in photographs. "So old P. Diddy's here." Lance grinned, fishing out his notebook. "But of course he would be—his yacht's in

Monaco at the moment. Wouldn't mind being invited on it, I must say. *Hey! Puffy, you old bastard! It's Lance, remember?*" he yelled with boisterous camaraderie. The white-suited man stared, evidently didn't remember, and turned immediately back to his conversation.

Lance's jaw tensed in annoyance. Then it relaxed again. "Wouldn't you just know it?" he called, striding forward to a group of people arriving at the top of the red carpet. 'Here's the old Riviera gang! David Coulthard, Ivana, Lady Victoria Hervey . . . *Victoria!*" he shouted at a tanned, horse-faced blonde wearing a top little more than a large necklace. She gazed blankly at him before stalking off.

To Kate's disappointment, Sharon Stone, Leonardo DiCaprio, and Renée Zellweger had disappeared into the party. Lots of short and frog-like men with brittle-looking women, however, hadn't.

"Studio executives," Celia murmured. "Much more powerful than the actors. If not quite as attractive to look at."

"*He's* certainly no oil painting," Kate agreed, as a monolith with oily skin, pitch-black sunglasses, and greasy hair caught her eye. Beside him was a skinny blonde in a sequined dress.

"Marty St. Pierre," Celia told her. "And that's his wife Mandi."

Kate couldn't help staring. There was something startlingly unpleasant about the man's hooked nose, spade-shaped beard, and shiny aubergine suit. All the hair no longer resident on his thinly populated head seemed to have slid down the sides and over his collar. "What does he do?" she asked.

Celia rolled his eyes. "International man of mystery."

"Sssh!" said Lance, looking nervously round. "He's got fingers in all sorts of pies. Property, mostly, but he also dabbles in film. Those Bastard Mafia films—you know—*Bloody Bastards, Bad Bastards, Mean Bastards*? He helped produce them. Put up some of the money."

"Oh." Kate vaguely recalled seeing the titles at the local multiplex.

"But everyone says the real reason he got into film," Celia added, "was so he could take a keen and informed interest in the casting process. If you get my drift."

Kate did. "Wow. I didn't realize the casting couch still existed."

Celia stared. Lance guffawed, long and knowingly. Kate shrugged. Perhaps she *was* being naive. On the other hand, it was difficult to imagine a man the size of Marty bouncing around in ecstasy on a chaise longue. The only structure she could imagine supporting him—bouncing or otherwise—was a suspension bridge.

"Well anyway, he's utterly ghastly," Celia added. "Practically a gangster."

"Ssh!" Lance hissed again, frantically flapping his hands.

"And those stories about his poker parties," Celia continued irrepressibly.

"Poker parties?" Kate asked. "You mean cards?"

"Well, she doesn't mean fire irons," Lance whispered, eyes darting everywhere. "*Celia!* Do you want to get my kneecaps shot off?"

Celia folded her arms. "It's certainly a thought."

"What happens at the poker parties?" Kate asked, intrigued.

"What *doesn't*, you mean," Celia said loudly, at which point Lance decided to cut his losses and leave. "Marty gets together a gang of movers and shakers in the film industry. Plus a few of his friends in the organized crime world. Plus a bunch of wannabe actresses to be the waitresses."

"And then they play cards?"

"On and off, yes. When one of them wants a sandwich, he points to his plate. When one of them wants a drink, he points to his glass. And when one of them wants a blow job he points to his—"

"*Don't tell me!*" yelped Kate, looking with horror at where Marty St. Pierre was now deep in conversation with a fawning Champagne D'Vyne. She was all but thrusting her breasts into his face.

"His poor wife," Kate said, noticing Mrs. St. Pierre looking on with a sour expression. "Does she know about these . . . er . . . parties?"

Celia looked at her. "You're asking me if Mandi knows about the poker parties?"

Kate nodded.

"How do you think she met Marty in the first place?"

"Oh. I see."

"Come on," Celia urged. "Are we going inside, or aren't we?"

The villa had been impressive from a distance. Up close, it was extraordinary. Commanding the highest point of the Cap Ferrat promontory, it was a pink fairy palace that looked good enough to eat. Against walls like rose fondants appeared numerous huge windows framed with slender twisted columns in contrasting white. A carved fantasia topped with delicate finials soared lacily around the entrance.

"It looks," Kate remarked, enchanted, "like the door into a cathedral."

"Funny you should say that," said a voice at her side. "Actually, it came from a medieval Spanish monastery."

Kate looked to her right. So busy had she been taking in architectural detail that only now did she see the numerous waiters flanking the entrance, bearing trays of pink champagne. Waiters who, like the flunkeys at the gate, sported white wigs with black-ribboned ponytails, lace at throat and wrist, satin breeches, brocade coats, and buckled shoes, all in shades of white, silver, and rose. The breeches, Kate couldn't help noticing, were extremely tight; clinging silk stockings revealed lean and shapely calves. Each waiter wore high heels, beauty spots, and had his face half hidden by a black mask. From what she could see of the neat chin and nose, not to mention the dark eyes, the waiter talking to them about the doorway was handsome. He proffered his tray of pink champagne.

"Thanks." Celia took a glass and passed one to Kate.

"From a monastery?" Kate asked. "How come?"

"The woman who built this house was very rich," explained the waiter. "She was a great collector. Antiques dealers from all over Europe would bring furniture, paintings, and even great carved doorways by train to the station at Beaulieu. She would come down from the villa and choose things right there on the platform."

"How *amazing*."

"She loved the eighteenth century best. Most of the furniture is from that period. That's why we're wearing these clothes." He shook a lace-edged wrist and grinned. Kate smiled back, not sure whether his perfect English or ability to carry off tight breeches was more impressive. Together, they were a powerful combination.

Beside them, Celia cackled loudly.

Kate turned. "What's up?"

"Lance." Celia pointed. "Just look at him trying to talk to Russell Crowe."

Lance was indeed lurching in the direction of the Australian actor, who shot him a suspicious glance before moving off as swiftly as the crowd allowed. "Russ!" Lance yelped. "Don't you remember me? At the Oscars that time? *Mr. Crowe!*"

"Come on." Celia seized Kate by the elbow.

She stumbled as she tried to mount the marble steps and simultaneously take a gulp of champagne.

"Steady." Kate grabbed her arm. "Your shoes are very high, you know."

"They have to be at parties."

"Why? They look like agony."

"They are, but so's dancing at three in the morning with your face in the sweat-soaked armpit of some bloke who's been leaping about since eight. These get me to shoulder level at least."

As they moved off, Kate swept an assessing glance around and touched the notebook in her pocket. In her eagerness to find Nat she mustn't forget why she was here. She needed to start taking down some details for the *Mercury.* Some faces she recognized, some she didn't, and some of the ones she didn't were sure to be important. Thank goodness she was with Celia who seemed to recognize everyone. "Who are they?" she asked, jerking her glass towards two men talking nearby.

"Well, one is Ridley Scott."

"*Blade Runner* Ridley Scott?" Kate stared with awe.

"And the one with the geeky glasses is Slim Cortez, the latest hot director." Celia yawned. "Made a film called *You, Kant* that made philosophy really trendy. He's a reverse existentialist, or something."

Kate strained her ears to pick up what Cortez was saying. It sounded astonishingly pretentious. "Yeah, but if so-called 'I' so-called 'directed' this so-called 'film,'" he was drawling. Ridley Scott's eyes narrowed.

They narrowed further as a familiar, bounding figure interrupted. *"Ridleeeeee!* Or should that be *Sir* Ridley! Congratulations, mate! *Yo, man!*" So saying, Lance attempted a high five with the celebrated director. Muttering something that sounded terse at best, Scott slipped into the crowd.

"Did you know," Celia remarked, grabbing another glass of champagne, "that wine passes out of the body at the rate of one glass an hour? Shall we go inside, by the way?"

The interior of the villa was even more a dream of luxury than the outside. A lobby whose coffered ceiling was painted with Renaissance heads led into a marble-floored patio crowded with small round tables sparkling with candles, silver, and glassware. No one, as yet, had sat down on any of the small gold chairs circling them.

An arched colonnade ran round all four sides with a balustraded gallery above. Faces laughed and exclaimed in the light of the flaming torches slung from the tops of the pillars. But none, Kate saw, belonged to Nat.

11

Kate took a deep breath, plucked some more champagne off a tray and forced herself not to panic. Nat *had* to be somewhere in the midst of this heaving, glittering crowd. She was *bound* to bump into him eventually. In the meantime, she should relax. Enjoy herself. Observe.

The villa walls bristled with paintings and carvings. Kate moved to examine what the romantic, antique-collecting owner had picked off the station platform.

"What do you mean, you wish you could see the *art*?" Celia pulled her back. "It's social death to look at paintings at parties, darling. Shows you don't know anyone to talk to."

"But what about gallery openings and exhibitions? Is it social death there as well?"

"*Especially* there."

The roar of conversation, bouncing off the marble, echoed from the corners of the flickering ceiling. Snatches—in accents from Brooklyn to Buckingham Palace—floated over.

"*. . . this dress is so tight I haven't breathed since lunchtime.*"

"*Not as tight as Gwyneth's trousers. You can practically read her lips . . .*"

Kate fished the notebook from her jacket pocket and did a little covert scribbling. Fantastic detail—or "color" as Wemyss called it—for her *Mockery* reports, all this. But color wasn't really enough. Given that she had come to the film festival, the first *Mockery* journalist in the paper's 249-year history to do so, Peter Hardstone—and Denys come to that—would be expecting celebrity exclusives at the very least.

It was obvious that such exclusives were not going to drop in her lap. Even a shamelessly thrusting hack like Lance was having serious trouble attracting attention. What she needed was to find a star on their own and swoop. It would surely happen sooner or later, given the way people were flitting from group to group after no more than a clash of teeth.

"Odd thing to do to a prawn." Celia was examining the skewered combination of crustacean and grape she had lifted from a passing tray. "Seafood kebabs, apparently. And have you seen those pink mini-roast potatoes?"

Kate hadn't. She was looking around again for Nat. Still no sign.

"You are admiring the paintings?" Suddenly, the waiter was at her side again. "That one over there is wonderful. *A Venetian Nobleman,* by Carpaccio."

Kate glanced distractedly at the blond sword bearer revealed by Michael Douglas moving his head to kiss Kate Beckinsale on both cheeks. "Oh. Right. Yes, it's great."

The waiter's eyes met hers through the holes in the mask. Strange eyes, Kate saw. Deep-set, dark, and bold. She wondered what the rest of his face was like, then looked sharply aside, her attention caught by someone tall and handsome with dark gold hair. Not Nat, however.

"You are looking for someone?" the waiter enquired.

"Er, yes."

"Your husband, perhaps?"

"Er, no, not exactly. He's more my . . . well . . ."

"Boyfriend?" The waiter's tone was light, neutral.

"Sort of," Kate muttered, suppressing the swoop she felt inside.

He nodded his bewigged head. "Perhaps I can help. I have to keep moving round the party. What does he look like? Is he handsome?"

The champagne swirled warmly through Kate's empty stomach, sweeping away her annoyance and bringing a feeling of woozy reck-lessness. "Ooh yes! *Very* handsome," she giggled.

"Hey, waiter!" yelled some English voices.

Kate turned round. Even if she hadn't known they were Brits she would have guessed. Only Englishmen, after all, thought intensely-black-lensed Ray Bans went well with jowls as pale and plump as dough. Or that sparse mousy hair gelled into a central fin was a good look. And as for those magenta-flowered trousers one of them was wearing . . .

"More champagne, and make it snappy!" commanded Flowered Trousers, whose feet were blue-veined in their sockless loafers.

Kate's toes curled at the rudeness of her fellow countrymen. They uncurled just as quickly when, ignoring them, the waiter flounced off in the other direction.

"Bloody Frogs," roared the Englishmen. "Remember Agincourt!"

"Ick-*eee*!" Kate jumped at a piercing shriek from behind.

A woman who looked like Jabba the Hutt's first wife had slid to the marble floor and was beginning to breast feed an enormous baby.

Celia, beside her again, reached for another pink champagne. "The wonderful thing about a really busy party," she observed, "is that no matter how much you drink, you can't fall over. Everyone else keeps you propped up."

"*Ick-eee!*"

"Who's *that*?" Kate hissed.

Celia groaned. "Jacaranda Thwaites. Married to Ichabod Thwaites, the actor. Makes a point of being a bit bohemian. But everyone puts up with her because Thwaites is so hot at the moment."

Kate watched as, with arms as thick as lampposts, Jacaranda raised her huge child and sniffed its bottom. "Ick-ee!" she yelled again. A goatee-bearded and rather ineffectual-looking young man bent under the weight of an enormous baby bag reluctantly detached himself from a bald-headed, cigar-chewing producer-type who looked, Kate thought, as if he might be important. "Ickee! Quick! Prospero's downloading something."

"Charming," remarked Celia, her black sunglasses glittering in the light of a thousand candles. Or possibly, given the evening's number-one accessory, the reflected light of a thousand other sunglasses. "Look, darling. That's Dora Skinner over there, the actress tipped to be the new Kate Winslet."

"Where?" Kate was momentarily distracted by the old Kate Winslet striding purposefully past, tossing her blond hair.

"In the brown trousers disappearing right up her bum crack with the husband who looks like a frog."

Kate guffawed. "You make them all sound so glamorous."

"Do I, darling? I certainly don't mean to. Look, that's Lord Crisp over there."

"Who's he?"

"Filthy rich English aristo who fancies himself as a film producer. And that's his fiancée, an, *ahem*, Californian glamour model called Tiddles. She's with him for his good looks and charm, obviously."

Kate surveyed a lithe blonde wrapped round something that looked like a sea monster.

"And there's Ziggy Spokes."

"Ah, yes," Kate mused, thinking the name sounded familiar. "Ziggy Spokes."

"Bright young hope of the British literary scene," Celia reminded her. "His first novel, *The Goldfish Funerals*, was a mega-hit. Got *snapped* up by Warner Bros."

Kate stared jealously at Ziggy Spokes. For someone who embodied everything she wanted out of life, he cut a far from glamorous figure. A wild-haired youth in a dirty suede jacket, he had piled his plate with food from somewhere and was busy shoveling it in. Whether or not he looked like the future of English literature, he certainly looked like the future of French catering.

Lance floated past. One hand was clasped firmly on the bottom of an urgent-looking blonde.

"Who *is* that?" Kate asked, outraged. Tall and graceful, the blonde clutched a brilliant red wrap about tanned arms. A chiffony black dress swirled skimpily about slender calves, while a clutch of pink and orange feathers nodded in carefully tousled blond hair.

"Letitia Gardener-Driver-Cooke. Sounds like a small ad in *The Lady*, doesn't it?"

"Who's Letitia Gardener-Driver-Cooke?"

"News reporter. Does all the glam Hollywood stuff for the BBC. Or should I call it the Boo B C," Celia added acidly. Lance was staring straight into the blonde's cleavage.

Kate patted Celia's arm sympathetically. How *hideous* to witness your own husband behaving like that. "Ooh, look," she urged, by way of distraction. "Dinner!"

From the rows of silver-dome–bearing waiters suddenly in evidence, it seemed that food was about to be served. A red-jacketed master of ceremonies was trying in vain to call everyone to the tables. Steering a stumbling Celia towards the nearest one, Kate drew out a gilt chair and deposited her friend firmly on it.

It didn't take long to realize that they were the only ones sitting down. Everyone else, Celia explained, was holding back until the famous had committed themselves. Only then would the hot and happening tables be clear for all to see. The problem was that the famous weren't committing themselves either.

Jodi Kidd tottered up, took one look at Kate and Celia and turned her back. For a while, a woman in a leopard-skin-print dress and increasingly frightened eyes sat three empty seats away. Then her nerve broke and she bolted off. Shortly afterwards, a giggling group approached, listing wildly with champagne, and lurched into the chairs. Some of them greeted Celia cheerfully.

"Who are they?" Kate whispered.

"Newspaper diarists," Celia hissed back. "From the *Telegraph*, the *Daily Mail*, the *Times*, the *Mail on Sunday*, and the *London Evening Standard*. If you're planning to make a fool of yourself, don't do it here. You'll have the piss taken out of you in every paper in Britain."

"They look like fun." Kate watched the shouting, laughing company teasing each other and pouring enormous quantities of champagne. Journalism was never that much fun on the *Mockery*. Until now, of course.

"Not a bad lot," Celia confirmed. "Nowhere near as pompous as Lance. But then, who is?"

The table quietened as a fading star in his sixties approached and appraised it. He looked distinctly unimpressed.

"Come on, darling," urged his companion, a lissome brunette possibly a third of his age. "Do let's sit down."

The fading star petulantly shook his head. "But there's no one I recognize," he complained. "You know I can't sit with a bunch of no-bodies."

As the actor staggered off, Celia squealed with delight. "Bad mistake!" she whispered to Kate.

The hacks hooted. "*Right.*" A plump, short-necked young man in round glasses rubbed his hands together. "Let's take the bastard apart. If I do the hair-dye story, who'll do the built-up shoes?"

Everyone roared. As the laughter subsided, Kate looked again at the passing crowd. Still no solitary celebrity. Still no Nat.

"Go on," Celia said fiercely, seizing another glass of pink fizz from a passing waiter. "Go and look for him. I know you're dying to."

Kate shook her head vehemently.

"Why not?"

"Well, look." Kate nodded her head at Lance and Letitia Gardener-Driver-Cooke. She now had her arms around him and was gazing urgently into his eyes. He, meanwhile, continued to gaze urgently into her cleavage. "Oh Lance," she was saying. "You really think you can get me an exclusive with Russell Crowe?"

"No problem," flirted Lance. "We're like *this*, me and Russ."

Kate ground her teeth. "After all you've done to help me," she told Celia, "I can hardly leave you watching your own husband behaving like that with another woman. Just look at her. It's awful."

Celia nodded sadly. "It is."

Kate's eyes welled with sympathy. "More than that. It's *terrible.*"

"It's worse than that. She's not trying *nearly* hard enough. *Go on, go for it,*" she urged Letitia under her breath. "*Get that creep off my hands for good.*"

"Is your marriage in that much trouble?" Kate asked gently.

By way of reply, Celia ripped off her sunglasses. Revealed was a purple bruise throbbing indignantly through the makeup plastered around her partially closed left eye. "That's what I got this afternoon for insisting you came to the party with me."

A surge of anger flooded Kate. She looked at Lance, mincing off with the TV blonde wrapped round him. "*The bastard.* Why don't you leave him?"

Celia's good eye flashed. "Do you think I haven't thought about that?" Her cut-glass tones were icy.

"So what's stopping you?"

"Easy for you to say, isn't it? But things like this," Celia pointed at the eye, "don't do much for a girl's confidence." She slipped the sunglasses back on and sat heavily down at a small circular table.

"Of course, I know that it's none of my business," Kate said carefully, paving the way for Celia to snap that no, actually, it wasn't. But Celia said nothing. Moodily, she swigged the rest of her glass of champagne.

"But you *could* leave him," Kate urged. "You don't have children, do you?"

"You must be joking. Lance would make the worst possible father. I realized this when we took my nephew Xerxes—he's five—for a country walk. We were in a wood," Celia sighed, "when Lance disappeared and then suddenly leaped out from behind some trees growling terrifyingly and pretending to be a bear. His idea of a joke."

"*What?*"

"Poor Zerky was so scared he was sick. And when his mother, my sister, told Lance her son would probably need therapy, Lance just shrugged and said that coming from a family like ours he would have needed it anyway."

"Nice of him!" Kate exclaimed. "But," he added after a pause, "what did he mean about a family like yours?"

Celia twisted her rings. "Well, I suppose my parents were always rather distant. Literally—they lived miles away at the other side of the house."

"Wow. Must have been a big house."

"It was huge," Celia admitted. "More of a stately home really. Although always less of the home, more of the stately."

Kate was fascinated. Mum being a big stately-home fan, Kate had peered as a child from behind a velvet rope at many a grand and echoing interior and had wondered what it was like to live in such places. She had suspected the inhabitants did not harbor the same curiosity about life at Wits End.

Celia looked at her warily. "Don't be too impressed. The house was freezing, we were never allowed chips and we never saw my parents after tea. I grew up murderously envious of anyone with shag carpet and a duvet. In the end I married Lance less because I longed to be loved than because I longed to be warm." She sniffed and rummaged for a handkerchief. "But a more coldhearted *bastard* . . ."

As Kate rubbed her shoulders comfortingly, Celia dragged the handkerchief viciously underneath shiny, reddened nostrils. "I'm sorry. Could have sworn I packed my stiff upper lip but it obviously got lost in transit. I shouldn't moan. It's all my own fault, and besides it's so lovely to be *here*." Lifting the sunglasses, she scraped at her eyes with the hankie. "I love France. If I could live here, I would."

A waiter placed a plateful of small stuffed vegetables before them. "*Chanterelles farcies*," he announced with a flourish.

"Real food. At last!" Celia exclaimed with forced delight, shoving one into her mouth. "Fantastic." She beamed shakily. "And about the only truly sensual pleasure I have left in life."

"Nah. Can't believe *that*, duchess," someone interrupted.

Kate and Celia stared at the short, stocky figure that had materialized beside them.

"Awright, gels?" he asked in a broad London accent. "Mind if I join ya? I'm bleedin' Hank Marvin."

"You've changed. Lost the glasses and *everything* . . . oh, I see."

Celia colored. "Rhyming slang. You're starving, you mean? Sorry, I'm being thick."

"Nah," said the newcomer, grinning, pulling out a gold chair and sitting down. "Just posh. What's your name?"

"Celia. And I'm not posh . . . well, not very. I used to be, I suppose. I'm lapsed posh, if you like."

"Don't worry. I like a real lady. Gawd knows I've met enough o' the other sort." He looked her up and down appreciatively. "The name's Ken." He drained his glass. "Born an' bred on Shoreditch High Street, I was. All me mates call me High Street Ken, arf arf."

Celia tittered. Kate rolled her eyes. At this particular point of the evening, a cartoon Cockney was all they needed.

"Not bad, this, is it?" Ken's jaw moved vigorously over a *chanterelle farcie*.

"Yummy," Celia said, beaming. "I've never agreed life's too short to stuff a mushroom."

Ken grinned as a passing waiter filled his glass. "Go on, up to the top, mate, if yer don't mind." He thrust out a small foot tightly shod in gray woven crocodile and rotated it with delight.

"Nice shoes," admired Celia. Kate, who thought they looked straight out of the International Pimp of the Year Show, stifled a snigger of disbelief.

"Fanks. These 'ere are my weddin' crocs. As worn to marriages, funerals, bar mitzvahs, and all state occasions in between. "Wannanuvverdrink?" he asked, producing a bottle of champagne from the confines of his jacket. 'Only it's a bit chilly, 'aving it stuffed down there.'"

"Very enterprising." Celia smiled. "A man after my own heart."

Not to mention your own size, thought Kate. No danger of 3 A.M. armpit syndrome with High Street Ken. Celia could stand in a hole and still be at shoulder height.

Ken looked gratified. He exposed a row of sharp square teeth with which he proceeded to tear at the wire on the champagne cage. "Strewth," he exclaimed, as the cork went off like a twelve-bore. "These things need bleedin' silencers on 'em."

"Are you here for the film festival?" Kate probed. It was, after all, *just* possible that he was a character actor in the Ray Winstone mould.

"Nah. Research trip, you could call it. Search trip, more like."

"A search?" Kate was interested. "What are you looking for?"

Ken winked at her and tapped the side of a red and bulbous nose. "Can't say no more about it. If I told you I'd 'ave to kill you, arf arf."

Kate looked at him doubtfully. Was this man for real?

A waiter passed, pushing a cheese trolley. The strong smell hung in the air. Some of what was on board, Kate saw, was making a bid for escape.

"Ooh," said Celia. "I *adore* stinky cheese. Could you leave it here for a moment?" she asked the waiter. "Thank you *so* much."

"Bleedin' 'ell," said Ken, holding his nose. "What an 'onk."

"I suppose," Celia admitted, "that it *is* something of an acquired smell."

"You're not wrong there, love. And I'd like to know exactly 'ow it's acquired." Ken stabbed a beringed and hairy finger at the congealed mass on the plate. "Bleedin' dodgy stuff, that, believe me. Little bit woo, little bit wah. Don't think that's party to them environmental regulations, no bleedin' way."

"What do you *mean*?" Kate asked, irritated. "This place is *crawling* with A-list celebrities. The caterers are bound to be top-notch."

Ken gave her a pitying look. "That's what they'll bleedin' *tell you*. But you've *not gotta believe 'em*." He tapped the side of his shiny nose again. "People'll tell you anyfink. The secret is not to be taken in. Trust *no one*."

"Not much of a life philosophy, is it?" Kate remarked. "Not everyone's bent, you know."

Ken grinned, revealing a flash of gold in the shadowy depths of his mouth. "If I may quote the immortal words of Mr. Bridger, from my all-time favorite film, *The Italian Job*." He took a deep breath before declaiming in a crisp, Noël Coward accent, "My dear, everybody in the world is bent."

Kate rolled her eyes again. Thanks to endless childhood Christmas viewings, sandwiched between Gran and Dad on the sofa, she practically knew the classic crime romp off by heart.

"You're not joking," Celia said, watching Lance, apparently finished with Letitia, shoot past in pursuit of an arrestingly dressed woman. "Hey! *Chloë*," he was shouting. "Miss Sevigny? A word, if you have a minute." It was obvious to all that Miss Sevigny did not have a minute.

"That your boyfriend?" Ken asked.

"Actually, it's my husband. He's an arse."

As Celia began to give Ken chapter and verse on her troubled marriage, Kate wondered about slipping away. Tracking down Nat in what was literally a cast of thousands was obviously going to involve more effort than just standing there. It didn't look as if any celebrities would obligingly walk up and ask to be interviewed, either.

"Can't believe someone would treat you like that, duchess," Ken was saying in amazement. "I wouldn't, I can tell yer."

Celia beamed at him. "Come woo me, woo me, for I am in a holiday humor and like enough to consent," she quoted.

"Yer what?"

"It's Shakespeare."

"I'm just going to the loo," Kate announced, realizing that she really needed to. Ken and Celia acting like teenagers were making her feel queasy, and champagne and excitement was having its expected effect.

"Good luck," said Celia, breaking off her narrative.

"Why, are they very crowded or something?"

"I didn't mean the ladies, darling. I meant good luck finding *Nat*."

Kate looked about hard on the way to the loos. There was, she saw, no shortage of swooningly handsome men with dark-blond hair. Yet none was the one she sought. As she followed the *Toilettes* signs, she felt the sudden, downward pull of exhaustion.

The loo mirrors confirmed that she looked as tired as she felt. The rose Celia had given her had fallen out, exposing the burn mark above her nipple. She yanked the material down hard and in so doing caught the eyes of a cluster of Identikit blondes who stood nearby sipping their drinks and sliding surreptitious glances at their reflections.

"Is my makeup okay?" one emaciated Californian asked another who, for some reason, was washing her feet in the sink.

"Marvellous. The scars don't show *at all*."

Kate returned to the covered patio, where the crowd seemed to have thinned. She could now see past Kate Winsler and Sam Mendes into a room where candlelight glowed on columns encircled by carved wooden rose garlands. She made her way over and stood in the entrance, notebook at the ready to record the Mendes-Winslet conversation while she looked for Nat. Other voices, however, were more audible.

"*. . . you're only supposed to hold that cocktail napkin, not wipe your forehead with it . . .*"

"*. . . you've done so well, though. Congratulations. No, really, you're* *such a success story. Just goes to show you don't have to have looks to make it in the movies."*

*". . . theatrical fake blood, darling. If you blend it into the apple of the cheek it's so much better than any blusher."*

*"Yes, but comedy's the hardest thing in the world to write. Well, it is if you've got no sense of humor, like him."*

*"You like my dress? You really are sweet to say so. I'm going for the Talitha Getty look this year."*

*". . . first she didn't like the color of the towels in the hotel. Then we had to get a thermometer for her assistant to measure the temperature of her bathwater. Then she needed two air purifiers next to her on the plane so we had to book a separate seat for them in first . . ."*

Kate tapped her notebook with annoyance. The champagne was wearing off—or perhaps wearing on—and she was again feeling seriously angry with Nat. Only a near-fatal accident could be accepted as a halfway reasonable excuse for what amounted to nothing less than abandonment.

Her gaze drifted to the pictures and furniture. Celia would disapprove, obviously. But the room really was so beautiful that not to admire it seemed criminal, although most of those present barely gave it a glance. Feminine, delicate, and covered with embroidered padded silk, the oval-backed chairs and elegant sofas looked as if Madame de Pompadour had only just got up from them. The eye fell on something beautiful everywhere it looked. Except over there where Lord Crisp was standing.

"All from the period of Louis the fourteenth," murmured a voice in her ear. Kate turned to see the bright-eyed waiter—*her* waiter—smiling at her over the top of his champagne tray. "You have not found your boyfriend yet?"

Anger and shame flared within her. "Er, no. But I'm sure he's here somewhere. Louis the fourteenth, you say?" she added, forcibly changing the subject.

The face behind the mask smiled and nodded. "Madame

Ephrussi—who built the villa—not only loved the French eighteenth century, she lived it too. She gave fancy dress parties where she'd greet her guests dressed as Marie Antoinette, in genuine period clothes."

"How *glamorous.*" Feeling calmer, Kate looked around at the beautiful women and handsome men, the glossy hair, the perfect teeth, the diamonds, the famous faces. "Like this," she added, excited anew by the glitter of it all.

Behind the mask, the black eyes glared. "*Much* better than this. This is just a job fair. These film people! They think they own the place. Sweeping up and down in their limos, calling Cannes *Karn.*"

"Oh dear." Kate fought the inappropriate urge to giggle. "You don't approve?"

"Certainly I do not," he replied with dignified sincerity. "There is so much more to the Côte d'Azure. Great artists were here long before any actor had heard of . . ." he pulled a face. "*Karn.*"

"Were they?" Besides being the most glamorous party she had ever been to, it was turning out to be the most educational.

"Certainly, Renoir, Matisse, Picasso—they all came here. People like Madame Ephrussi built great collections and made living an art form. Of course there are still *huge* amounts of money about on the Côte d'Azur, but no one does anything good with it. No one builds houses like this any more. For example, near where I live the most horrible luxury estate has just been built. The most tasteless place you ever saw. If you tried to leave it to France, like Madame Ephrussi left this place, France would not want it."

"This villa belongs to the state?"

The white wig nodded an affirmative. "Madame Ephrussi gave it to the nation after she didn't want to live here any more."

"Didn't want to . . . ?" Kate was amazed. "But why not? It's the most beautiful place I've ever seen."

"That, you see, was the problem. Her husband died a few years after she had built the villa. She could never live in it after that."

"Oh, how *sad.*" Kate felt her eyes well.

"I see you are a romantic," twinkled the waiter. "But don't be sad.

Good came out of it in that thousands of people a year are now able to enjoy all this—"

"Waiter!" A growl interrupted them. Both turned to see the fat man with the mullet looking angrily in their direction. Writhing and pouting beside him—still—was Champagne D'Vyne.

"Speak of the devil, as you English say," muttered the waiter.

"What do you mean?"

"That estate I was just talking about. He built it."

"Come over here with that fucking tray," roared Marty St. Pierre. "Can't you see the lady wants a drink?"

The lady, however, suddenly seemed to have other things on her mind. Her predatory eyes had focused on Kate.

"You!" she hissed. The light from the garden lanterns slid over her glistening PVC thighs as she detached herself from her companion. "What the hell are *you* doing *here*?"

"Reporting," Kate said shortly, surprised at the other woman's hostility. Admittedly they had hardly got on like a house on fire at the interview, but the end result had been perfectly polite.

"For the old *Slagheap Bugle*, eh?" Champagne smiled sarcastically. "So you got here after all."

"Er . . . yes," Kate replied, puzzled. Did Champagne know she was coming or something?

"And who," Champagne asked, slinking round the waiter, "might *this* Prince Charming be?" She put out a long-taloned hand to touch his thigh. "Sexy breeches," she murmured.

Kate tensed, sensing this to be the moment when, for all his criticisms of film people, her new friend found something to recommend them. Most men would be won over by a caress from Champagne. A smile, even.

To her surprise and delight, the waiter ducked calmly out of the way and took a few steps back. Champagne, arm outstretched, was left teetering dangerously forward on her heels. The weight of those breasts alone, Kate gleefully calculated, would probably pull her flat on her carefully maquillaged face.

Champagne dragged herself back from disaster. She looked Kate angrily up and down. "*Love* the suit," she sneered. "Gave one just like that to my old school umble sale only last week."

"You're just too generous for your own good," Kate retorted with a sweet smile.

"*Drink!*" roared Marty St. Pierre.

"Excuse me," the waiter muttered to Kate as, deliberately slowly, he walked over with his tray. Kate watched the fat man grasp a glass in each huge hand. While the waiter stood there, he emptied one after the other down his throat before banging the glasses back on the tray and belching loudly.

Kate turned away, repelled, to resume the search for a superstar. And Nat.

12

As Nat didn't seem to be inside the villa, it stood to reason that he was somewhere outside it. Kate pushed through the crowd to where one of the huge arched windows led to a terrace commanding a view of coastline and sea.

Outside a night as soft and dark as an indigo *pashmina* was descending on the Côte d'Azur.

The garden rolled endlessly away before her. Fountains, parterres, pools, and exotic foliage of all heights and descriptions glowed both in the torchlight and the setting sun.

There were people out here too. Stagey laughter mingled with seductive undertones; cigar smoke with assertive perfume. Willowy white-skinned blondes sidled past short tanned brunettes. There were small men with no hair and tall men with a suspicious amount of it, all with the same urgent expressions.

"*So it all depends on Cruise, basically. If his new one does big box office, we get greenlighted and we're in production. . . .*"

"*And then she wanted me to foam up her bath bubbles with a whisk. I tell you, sweetie, I felt like fucking Delia Smith.*"

"*. . . my screenplay about the funny side of the war in Iraq. No, honestly, you're gonna love it. Yeah, the soldiers out there had a great sense of humor. Kind of black comedy, especially the ones whose job it was to go out and pick body parts off the road. You know, finding someone's hand in the wheelbase. . . .*"

"*. . . even her vagina's designer . . .*"

"*He was complaining about the traffic from Cannes to St. Tropez. I said to him, 'Darling, what do you think helicopters are for?'*"

Kate wandered off. An Arabian Nights moon as thin as a fingernail paring was rising in a sky in which the last of the sunset gilded the clouds. Fairy lights had sprung up everywhere in the garden, supplementing the flaming torches.

"Hey! You there."

Kate peered into the growing gloom at the side of the path. Beyond it, the other side of the lawn, was the tall wall bordering the garden. Into this, a delicate Oriental-style belvedere had been set to provide a view of the sea. A wild-haired male figure was now emerging from its shadow and staggering towards Kate.

She watched the figure crash through the flower bed in the center of the lawn, then gasped as, up close, she recognized the face of an extremely famous young actor. A hear-throb, as the *Mockery* might have put it. Kate felt like punching the air with delight. At last, here was her interview opportunity. She felt urgently for her notebook and pen.

"Recognize me, do you?" he drawled.

She nodded wordlessly, registering amid the shock that the good looks he was famous for weren't looking all that good. His clothes were stained and dirty, while from beneath a ragged woolly hat his hair hung in greasy clumps. She wondered what he was doing staggering round in the flower beds. She whipped out her notebook. "Mind if I ask you a few questions?"

"Go ahead. Hey, babe, I'll give you an exclusive. Hey *heh*."

"Great!" This was all too good to be true. She took a deep, excited breath. "First of all, can I just ask you how you're enjoying the party?"

His eyes rolled loosely in their sockets. His feet were planted wide apart in the flower bed for balance, yet he buckled and jerked, as if trying not to fall over. He was clearly extremely drunk.

"Party?" He put his finger to his lips in exaggerated puzzlement. "S'okay, I suppose. Full of assholes and women with plastic tits."

"Any assholes and tits in particular caught your attention?" Well, she might as well try. A celebrity insulting another celebrity always made good copy.

"Sure." He was laughing at her now. "But lady, I ain't gonna say which."

Bugger. "Well, can you tell me about your latest projects?"

"Sure. But why waste time with all that boring shit?" He had stumbled over and his face was close to hers. She realized that, besides hitting the champagne with a vengeance, he had been equally unstinting on the garlicky canapés. His breath could have stripped paint.

Kate stepped backwards. "What would it most surprise people to know about you?" she gasped, thinking that it was probably his halitosis.

Then she squealed as, breathing heavily, the actor lunged and clamped a hand on her breast. "Hey, babe," he said thickly. "You're a great girl. You know that?"

"Er, thanks." Kate tried to wriggle out of his grasp. As he slid a hand round her back, she realized he was trying to pull her into the bushes. "You know," he said, leering, "you remind me of J-Lo."

"Thanks very much. Look, can you just let me go?" Abandoning the interview, Kate devoted her energies to freeing herself.

"Only you're a curvier, sexier, more womanly version. With . . ." she felt hot hands on her buttocks ". . . a fatter ass." The world-famous face was almost in hers now. A trickle of spittle was leaking from the corner of that celebrated mouth. His breath was heavy and rasping; besides the garlic, the scent of undeodorized armpits was now pumping into her nostrils. She looked quickly around her. The nearest people were some distance away on the patio. Given the level of talk and laughter they were unlikely to hear her even if she screamed at the top of her voice. And the actor was big, bigger than her. The ground beneath them was slippery. Any minute now and he'd have her down. Shit. Oh, where the *hell* was Nat?

The heart throb lunged.

"*Get off me!*" Kate yelled into his smelly chest. With all her strength she tried to push him away. As she struggled, her notebook— her precious notebook—fell to the ground and was immediately lost in shadowy foliage. Kate wailed.

"Hey!" His face lolled drunkenly at her. "You're fun, man. I like a girl who likes to fight. Grrr!" He cuffed her so playfully on the temple it almost stunned her.

During the ensuring tussle, Kate managed to find his hand and bite it hard. As, with a yell of fury, her assailant released her, toppled over and lay rolling in the flower bed, Kate grabbed her chance and leaped to safety.

She raced across the lawn, blood thundering in her ears, sobbing with fright. Only now she was free could her terror be given expression. On the edge of the grass, she paused and looked regretfully back. Her notebook was there, somewhere.

The actor lay in the flower bed cackling wildly, face up to the emerging stars. "Hey, Miss Modest," he yelled. "Prefer to do it inside, do ya? Ya wanna come and see me at my hotel? I'm in the penthouse at the Eden Roc. Tell reception you're with me in the big room." His voice trailed away into gales of laughter.

Kate abandoned any idea of retrieving her notes. So much for her star exclusive. She'd heard film stars could be diva-like and difficult but hadn't realized they could be positively dangerous. But she was a professional; here in a professional capacity. She could not leave the party without a story even if, following the loss of the notebook, she would have to scribble it on napkins. The night was young; there would be other opportunities. Once she had picked herself up, dusted herself down and had a few large glasses of wine to recover, that was.

She headed deep into the cool, shadowy garden. At the top, amid the dark of pines and cypresses, she could see a waterfall gleaming in the fading light. Above it was a small circle of pillars, a little temple, crowned with a cupola.

She followed the path ascending in its direction. It was bordered with lavender plants and orange-blossom bushes whose heavy fragrance, undercut with a salty whiff of sea, welled into Kate's nostrils. At a fork in the path, a small, deserted bar stood loaded with glasses and champagne bottles protruding from a large and gleaming ice bucket. A number of small chairs stood invitingly nearby, arranged at conversational angles. The possibilities of a romantic, secluded drink amid these beautiful gardens were there for all to see. If only Nat . . . but never mind. What a waste, anyway.

The little temple was now directly above her, perched atop the rocks forming the pinnacle of the waterfall. As she climbed the faux-rustic craggy steps, the bay of Villefranche, its sea puckered and shimmering, slowly revealed itself in the twilight. Around it and beyond were the hills, their villas and settlements marked by starlike clusters of light. In the distance a dark finger of land poked into the sea—the airport, to judge from the flash on the end and the moving lights descending in its direction. Was it possible she had landed only this afternoon?

Now at the top, Kate entered the pillared enclosure with its circular domed roof. A Renaissance marble statue of Venus or Diana stood in its center. A temple of love, Kate guessed, remembering with a pang how the villa's own particular love story had ended.

She leaned briefly against the goddess whose stone remained blood-warm from the daytime sun. Below the temple, on the other side from the waterfall, she could hear voices. A conversation was floating up in the still, scented air.

"Your film career starts here, baby. The only way, okay, is up."

Kate groaned, recognizing the unmistakable timbre of Champagne D'Vyne.

"So I've always understood," the man replied lasciviously. Kate's spine snapped upright in shock. Nat! It was *Nat*. Except that—she frowned—it couldn't be. If Nat were here, he would have come to find her. Wouldn't he? Filled with dread, she tiptoed to where the ivy rambling on the temple's marble floor tumbled over the edge of the small promontory like a waterfall.

Kate peered. She gasped. She clapped her hands to her mouth to prevent the cry of angry surprise. The tops of the heads of two people, very close together, could be seen about six feet below. One, as expected, as all streaming blond hair over black PVC shoulders. The other—narrow, dark-gold, set on wide, elegant shoulders—looked horribly like . . .

"So you're going to talk to the Bond people about a part for me, yeah?" he drawled.

Kate clutched the goddess's ample sides for support. She felt an unpleasant rushing in her stomach, a queasiness in her throat. So it *was* Nat. Nat, who had clearly been here for some time and just as clearly had not bothered to look for her. Nat, who, for reasons already starting to take horrible form in her head, was sitting in a secluded spot with the ghastliest woman in the universe.

"I'll ask as soon as I get on set tomorrow, okay?" she honked.

"Well, make sure it *is* soon, okay? Don't go running up at half past four again or you'll ruin it for both of us."

"Look, leave it to me, okay? I'm seeing the producer tomorrow anyway. That *bastard* Brosnan . . ."

"He's pissed you off?"

"Yes, he fucking well has," Champagne complained. "I get treated worse that a bloody *dog* because of him. He gets his name biggest on the posters. Gets the biggest trailer. You'd think he was the star of the whole bloody *film* or something."

"But he *is* James Bond."

"*So what?*" Champagne raged. "Either he goes or I go."

"Well, I wouldn't . . . you know . . . go quite that far." There was concern in Nat's voice. "Not just yet, anyway."

There was a pause in which groans, moans, gasps, and sighs momentarily replaced conversation.

Up in her perch, Kate felt the blood race boiling through her veins. She was hating every minute yet was as unable to move as the goddess beside her. So loud was the furious pounding in her ears that she could hardly hear the conversation.

"What do you mean, she's *here*?" Nat's voice floated up sharp with shock. "It's impossible, yeah?"

"Well, she *is* here, okay?" Champagne drawled in reply. "I've seen her."

Kate recoiled in panic back behind Venus. She sensed immediately that they were talking about her. But how could they see her from here?

"Look, Champagne, she bloody well can't be here." Nat sounded jumpy. "She hasn't got an invitation or *anything*. I made bloody sure of that."

"It *is* her, okay? Frankly, you can't miss her—she's the worst-dressed person there by a mile. Bloody great hole in her jacket, for a start," Champagne chortled. "Look, sweetie, it's your oiky little friend from Oop North, all right. From the *Eckmuckleslag Times* or whatever it's called."

Kate itched to punch Champagne right between those large and beautiful green eyes of hers.

"She's *not* my friend," Nat said crossly.

Kate clutched Venus's ample sides for support and breathed deeply.

"Well, she bloody well won't be *now*. I expect even in *her* stupid, state-educated provincial little brain the penny's started to drop."

Kate was frowning so hard now that her forehead hurt. *What penny?*

"Your brilliant scheme to get here without her . . ." Champagne added.

"It was brilliant, wasn't it?" Nat agreed proudly.

"Telling her your pa had given her time off to go to the Film Festival. . . ."

"As if he would," snorted her companion. "Dad's so mean he hates his staff taking time off to go to the bloody *bog*."

"So the editor had no idea she was going either?" Champagne clapped her hands. "Brilliant!"

Up in the temple, Kate was bent double in horror. So neither Denys nor Hardstone had been told she was going anywhere. After all Nat's assurances that he would let them know . . . lying *bastard*. Callous, arrogant bastard too—what did he care whether she lost her job?

There was the sound of a cigarette being lit. "What really pisses me off," Nat meditated, "was that it didn't have to be like this. Behind his back and stuff. I mean, I *tried* with Dad, yeah? Was always coming up with ideas for his shitty little paper. Such as when I suggested he send her off on a stripping course."

Kate's eyes bulged. So that had been *his* idea. Not his father's as he had told her.

". . . sometimes," Nat was whining now, "I think that all I really

want from Dad is a bit of respect. That's what the acting thing was all
about really. Make him, like proud of me." His voice was slurred
slightly; champagne, Kate guessed, had opened the never-fully-closed
floodgates of self-pity. "Make him see there's more to me than just a
shagging machine that eats money."

"And is there?" There was a hint of a sneer in Champagne's voice.

"Course there is," Nat replied indignantly.

"Just checking," Champagne said breezily. "Anyway, it was brilliant of you to get old whatserface to stump up for your ticket out here
as well. Putty in your hands, basically."

"Yes, she fell for me pretty hard," Nat said complacently.

"Well, of *course* she did, darling. She's lived in Ecky-Thump-By-
Slagheap all her life. Probably never *seen* a man with just the *one* head
before."

Kate went hot with hatred. So Nat had got her down as a mug
from the very beginning. Darren had been spot-on about his slipperi-
ness. But could it all really have been nothing more than a confidence
trick? The way he had kissed her . . . The way he had . . .

"Must say, though," Champagne added petulantly, "that *shagging*
her was *slightly* beyond the call of duty."

"Don't worry." There was a smile in Nat's voice; a not particularly
nice one at that. "Means to an end, yeah? I didn't enjoy it or anything."

Choking back a cry of fury, Kate scraped her fingernails down the
goddess's side, imagining it to be Nat's face.

"Get your hands off, will you?" Champagne squealed suddenly.

"But you're *hot*, babe. I want to take you here. *Now*."

"Well, you can't. I've got Harvey Weinstein and Steven Spielberg
to schmooze before I leave, and I can't do *that* with grass stains all over
my arse."

"Later then, yeah?" Nat urged.

"We'll see. Wouldn't do you any harm to come and press some
flesh as well, yah? There are a couple of movers and shakers who are
dying to meet you."

"Like *who*?"

"Marty St. Pierre for one—*such* a duck."

"Marty *St. Pierre? He's* here?" Nat's voice was suddenly all switched-on attention.

"I *know* everyone says he's a gangster. But really, I've always found him a *complete* pussycat. One of the nicest men on the planet. In fact, I was with him when I met," she paused, "your little friend."

"Did you tell him I was here?" Nat croaked.

"Yah. Funny really. He was thrilled to meet me, obviously. But absolutely *dying* to see you. . . ."

Kate staggered away from the statue. She had heard enough. It was all clear as day now, of course. Nat's interest in her had never extended further than the money she had. His allowance slashed, he had been casting around for funds to escape his father and join Champagne who had obviously promised to get him into films. Just how had they met, though? And how close had they been?

Of course. As close as next door, for a start—was not Blavatsky's house next to Hardstone's in Slack Palisades? Which possibly—no *undoubtedly*—explained what Nat was doing all the days he was incommunicado. The identity of the groaner on the entryphone was no longer the conundrum it had been, either. Nor was why he had not been at the airport to meet her. Once he had touched down in France, once he'd got where he wanted, she was out of the picture. While he concentrated his energies in getting into one.

The waiter was right. There was nothing fun about this party. For all its promising start, it had been the worst she had ever been to. Furious and humiliated, Kate exited the temple of love.

She came to consciousness in her room at the Hôtel des Tours—the room Celia had insisted she book. Thank God she had. Expecting Nat to arrange a roof over her head was another thing she had been wrong about.

She clamped both hands to her aching head and groaned as the events of the previous evening crawled in procession through her memory.

Hating the world, herself, and most of all Nat, she had stalked from the temple of love straight to the table of drink and methodically set about reducing its stocks.

Hours later, the friendly waiter had found her huddled in a miserable heap at the end of the terrace. A glass had fallen from his tray and he had spotted her as he stooped to pick it up. When he recognized her he had been all concern, dropping to his hunkers to stroke her shoulder. He had not asked useless, stupid questions such as what the matter was. Presumably it was clear to him, just as it was clear to her, that things hadn't worked out with the handsome boyfriend.

His support had been of a much more practical nature. He had set about organizing her. He had pulled her up, asked her where she was staying. Then had come the sharp scent of leather, the back of a large, luxury car.

"Don't worry," the waiter had winked as he closed the door. "This taxi will take you home."

It was a taxi one or two notices upmaket from the kind she was used to. Such as Oh-Jays of Slackmucklethwaite with their morose drivers, tuned-out radios, migraine-inducing air fresheners and non-existent suspension.

Nonetheless, she'd leaped out of the limo as if the leather seats had burned her. "I can't afford to go all the way to St. Jeanne in a car like this!"

"Just get in." He pushed her gently back.

Kate bounced straight out again. "But whose is it? Hasn't someone else ordered it?"

"Yes." The waiter shoved her back again and tried to close the door. "But the Ritchies can get the next one. They're not ready to leave yet anyway."

Kate shot out again, eyes wide in panic. "The Ritchies?"

"Just get in. It's all taken care of." He slammed the door and tapped the top of the car. It pulled smoothly out and Kate was off. She had twisted her neck to see the lights from the party receding through the rear window.

Kate sank back into the bed, her gratitude towards the waiter mingling with embarrassment at what he must have thought. Still, it wasn't as if she would ever see him again. And now here she was, the morning after the night before, stuck in France's answer to the Bates Motel with the hangover from hell.

She lay there, reflecting on the extent of her failure. The trip to France had been an unmitigated personal disaster. It had hardly been a professional triumph either. Not only had Nat betrayed her, she had failed utterly to interview a single megastar for the *Mockery*. She'd even lost her notebook. Not that any of this mattered now; the greatest professional disaster of all was that she had probably lost her job. A sense of defeat pressed upon her like a weight; Kate felt her very spirits sagging downward into the mattress.

Snatches of the conversation between Nat and Champagne burst in her brain like fireworks. *Ecky-Thump-by-Slagheap . . . state-educated little provincial brain . . .*

Suddenly, she felt so angry she almost felt better. Just what, she asked herself, was *wrong* with being state-educated? Or provincial, come to that? Being brought up and educated in Slackmucklethwaite had, for a start, taught her the importance of working for a living. Rather than lounging aimlessly around at other people's expense like Nat Hardstone. It had taught her to treat people with respect and not the contempt Champagne and Nat lavished so unreservedly on their fellow man. It had taught her—which it had manifestly not taught Nat—that education itself was a privilege, and that the best schools were not necessarily those equipped with medieval chapels and lists of famous alumni. It had taught her, too—Dad especially had taught her this—that snobbery was the most boring way possible in which to view a fascinating and frequently amusing world. Most of all, it had taught her the importance of having a family to love her. Something Nat Hardstone lacked, for all his father's wealth. Not that she had much sympathy any more. All that unloved-son stuff was probably bullshit anyway; he was an actor, wasn't he? Or wanted to be.

Head throbbing against the bolster—what was it with the French and bolsters?—Kate was conscious of a longing for home so intense it felt like cramp. What wouldn't she have given, just now, to be back in her Wits End bedroom, with Dad flushing away in the bathroom next door, the prospect of a day covering typically bonkers *Mockery* stories lying ahead? Stories like—Kate smiled—that one a couple of years ago about the Christmas illumination of the parish church. Installing the lights had required the bishop's permission, and Gladys Arkwright, in her other, non-thespian capacity as churchwarden, had duly applied. A changeover in bishops had, however, delayed its being granted. As Christmas had edged ever more dangerously close, the *Mercury* had swung its big guns behind the illuminations campaign with a headline of which Darren had been particularly proud. COME ON, BISHOP, LIGHT MY SPIRE, that week's front page had urged.

Kate chortled aloud. Then she stopped and sniffed. The pangs of homesickness were now stronger than those of alcohol sickness. She should just cut her losses and leave. The South of France may have been a disappointment, but she could always go back to Slackmucklethwaite. Joy flooded through her at the prospect of home—the hills, the Doge's Palace Town Hall, even Gran's knitting, for Christ's sake. Explaining her absence to Denys might be tricky, all the more if he hadn't been expecting it. But she'd get round him somehow. As for Hardstone, well, she wouldn't think about that just now.

What she must do was ring Mum. If word about the strange circumstances of her departure had reached the house—Denys, after all, could have rung up to ask why she hadn't come to work—Mum would be beside herself. At her Wits End in every sense of the word.

Realizing that the hotel phone would cost a fortune she went out in search of a phone card and phone box.

It rang just twice before her mother snatched it up. Kate pictured the scene—the telly blaring in the lounge, steam swirling round the tiny kitchen from a stove of hysterically boiling pans.

"Mum?"

"*Kathleen!*" The rush of relief Kate had expected on hearing her mother's voice lessened slightly. In common with the rest of the family, Mum only called her that when she was angry. Her fears were realized. Denys *had* called and Mum *was* beside herself.

"I'm sorry."

"Sorry!" riposted her mother.

*Poor* Mum, Kate thought guiltily. But lucky her, to have someone caring about her that much. She suppressed a sniff.

"Sorry! So I should bloomin' well think. What the bloomin' 'eck do you think you're playing at, young lady?"

"I can explain." It was worse than she thought. Mum was seriously angry.

"I'd never 'ave thought it of you, I really wouldn't. I never bloomin' *dreamed* that that's what you were up to."

"But I thought everyone knew," Kate wailed. "I thought they'd all agreed it was okay."

"*Agreed it was okay?* Had they heckerslike. And a bloomin' good thing too."

The slow, hideous feeling that they were talking at cross-purposes crept over Kate. She wondered wildly if her mother was referring to the night Nat had come to Wits End.

"Not the way you were brought up at all," thundered the other end of the phone.

But there had been nothing to find in reality. Nat had been interrupted by the bell of his mobile phone text facility. Which, it now occurred to Kate, was no doubt being facilitated by Champagne.

"Yer grandma practically had a fit," Mum boomed.

But what, Kate thought, had Gran *seen*? She had been watching telly at the time. *And* the bedroom curtains had been pulled.

"All we did was a bit o' spring-cleaning," Mum stormed. "Gave that filthy room o' yours the once-over."

Kate's entire body went stone cold. Sweat beaded her forehead. A suspicion worse than any yet entertained began to bloom in her brain.

"None of us . . . *none* of us," Mum ranted, "will *ever* be able to look Doreen Bracegirdle in the eye again."

Kate closed her own eyes. Small microcosms hurtled, panicked, in the red sea of her lids. She knew how they felt. It couldn't be true—but it was. Under the bed, where she had shoved it out of the reach of Nat, *Northern Gigolo* had fallen into the reach of Mum.

". . . *ever* again. As for them bits about the WI . . ."

Kate gulped. Perhaps that fantasy sequence involving the Victoria sandwich *had* been a tad over the top.

"And them bits about Jolene Shaw! Even if she's no better than she should be!" Mum raged. "I'm ashamed of you, I really am, Leaving that . . . that *filth* under your bed like that. *Anyone* could have found it."

Anyone had, by the sound of it.

There was an altercation at the other end. A clattering of the receiver and another voice beside Mum's. "Let me talk to her, Margaret. Come on now, get back in your kitchen.' The sound of a door slamming.

"Kate?"

"Gran?"

"You all right, love?"

Kate blinked. Gran's tone was low, almost conspiratorial. Hardly the blasting she was expecting.

"So-so," she replied cautiously.

"Your mother's a bit upset, love," Gran whispered.

"I'd gathered that."

"Never mind. She'll get over it. *That book*," Gran added with sudden vehemence.

"Oh, Gran. I'm sorry. But to be honest it wasn't really aimed at you."

"I thought it were very funny," Gran squealed. "Eeh, he's a one and no mistake, that lad you're writing about. An' Doreen Bracegirdle. *Tee hee.*"

Kate felt her mouth drop open. "But Mum said you'd had a fit."

"Laughed fit to bust, you mean."

"Oh Gran," Kate said gratefully. "You are brilliant. I can't wait to see you."

"Not thinking of coming back, are you?"

"Well I was, actually." Kate felt her voice break. She willed back the tears.

"What for? Back to that job on t'*Mockery*? You're best staying where you are," Gran said firmly. "Give your mother a chance to calm down."

"But I want to come home," Kate wailed. "I *want* to go back to that job on the *Mockery*."

"Well, I don't think they'd want you," Gran said baldly. "Yon editor were not 'appy to find you'd gone off and not told him. It were your mum who had to tell 'im in the end."

"Ah. Oh. Right." In her mind's eye, Kate was looking through the dark, prisonlike gates of the knicker factory. It had been bad enough as a holiday job, but as a full-time prospect? Although there might be advantages even in that. At least it would be in dear familiar Slackmucklethwaite. Not here, in this glitzy, hot, untrustworthy land where so far she'd had nothing but bad luck. "I still want to come home," she bleated at Gran.

"Don't be so bloomin' daft," riposted the senior relative.

"But what am I supposed to live on if I stay here?"

"And what'll you do if you come back?" Gran countered. "Won't do you any harm to eat a bit less for a while anyway, love. There's a lovely figure in there somewhere."

"Thanks a lot," Kate said, sulking.

"Get a job," urged her grandmother. "Capable lass like you, you'll find something. Enjoy your freedom. Have some fun—a bit of an adventure. Before it's all too late."

"But—"

"Believe me, love, you're better off staying there." Gran's tone brooked no argument. "It's not a good time to come back. Not yet, anyway."

"But—"

"You can carry on with that book, for one thing," cackled Gran. "Can't wait to read the rest of it, I can't . . . Anyway, give me your bloomin' address and phone number. One of us needs to know where you are. Don't worry, I won't pass it on to your mother."

Kate stammered it out. Then "I'm going," she wailed, watching the phone card's last units disappearing into the ether like a drowning man watches a disappearing lifeboat.

"We're all going, love. Some of us sooner than others."

As the other end went dead, Kate sniveled, weakness and self-pity finally overwhelming her.

*Believe me, love, it's not a good time to come back.* Having been desperate to leave, she was now unable to return; banned from home, in effect, by her own family.

Having had a discreet, hopeless weep in the phone box, Kate gathered her wits about her. Another central tenet of a Slackmucklethwaite upbringing was that crying over spilled milk was not only useless but a waste of good milk. And heaven help the spiller if the floor had just been cleaned.

Kate wandered back down the rue du Midi. Having taken on the prospect of a permanent place of residence, the village looked completely different. The bright row of cheerful shops, so picturesque before, now seemed suggestive only of spending, costs, and her post-Nat bank account. Life on the Côte d'Azur was bound to be expensive, that was the whole point of it. Would she have enough to last a month? A week, even?

*Get a job.* All very well for Gran to say that, but what sort of job? What did people usually do in France? Become au pairs in French families? Work as assistants in French schools? She knew enough French, thank God, but she knew no French families. Nor any French head teachers either. She could, of course, type and write articles. But so could thousands of French journalists. Kate bit her lip and furrowed her brow. *Capable lass like you* . . . capable of what, exactly? Apart from making a mess of things.

The shops, with their assumptions of affluence, were depressing her. She ducked into a side alley running parallel to the main street in the direction of the Place de l'Eglise. Here, in the cool and ancient shade, she took a deep breath and slower steps. Here she could think, because there was a lot of thinking to do. It seemed that she, just as much as the hero of *Northern Gigolo*, must now look to the Riviera for her fortune. Although hopefully not in quite the same way.

The ancient street had a dogleg bend; rounding the corner, staring contemplatively at the ground, Kate saw something lying in a heap in the middle of the cobbles. Had someone dropped something? It looked like a pile of clothes. She glanced up at the loaded airers protruding from almost every top window. Was it someone's fallen-down washing?

It was only as Kate got closer that she realized the pile was a person. Moreover, a person she recognized. It was the malevolent crone last seen scowling at her in the bar of the Hôtel des Tours. She had fallen awkwardly, one arm thrown out. A black patent handbag lay some distance away.

The old lady's eyes were closed and her wrinkled skin had the yellow, brittle appearance of elderly baking parchment. She did not look very alive.

Kate crouched down, horrified curiosity stealing over her. She had never seen a dead body before.

"Are you all right?" she said in French, realizing it was a rather silly question. Of course the old woman wasn't all right. She would hardly be lying in a heap in the road if she were.

Kate glanced up at the houses again; everyone, from the sound of it, was occupied with lunch. The volume of clattering plates and chattering people, amplified by the height of the buildings and the narrowness of the lane meant that, even if she called for help, she would probably not be heard.

She took the tiny wrist. To her relief there seemed a flutter of life there. She rubbed the almost translucent hands. "Madame?" she whispered.

Slowly, the frail old head rolled around. Up close, Kate saw, with a mixture of shock and pity, that what she had assumed in the gloom of the bar to be a bad-tempered scowl was in fact some form of permanent disfigurement. One side of the old lady's face was collapsed like a spent balloon; mouth drooping, one eye sealed permanently shut by the flap of skin dragging it down. The other side, by contrast, looked normal, even handsome, with an arched eyebrow, a prominent cheekbone, and a hazel eye as bright as a hen's. An eye, moreover, fastened with an expression of outrage on Kate's own.

The old lady sat up, clasping her head. Then she spotted her bag and snatched it immediately to her.

"Your head hurts?" Kate asked gently.

"A little," winced the old lady.

Kate helped her to her feet. Despite having legs and arms as thin and brittle as sticks, she did not seem to have broken anything.

"What happened? Did you fall?"

"Well, obviously," the old lady said irritably.

Kate felt a stab of anger. Did she have to be quite so rude? "We haven't met. I'm Kate," she said politely.

"The girl from the hotel!"

"That's right. Look, hold my arm. I'll take you home."

Ignoring the offer, the old lady was surveying her houndstooth skirt with fury. "Just look at it. Chanel. And ruined!"

"I'm sure the dry cleaners . . ." Kate soothed.

The old woman's head snapped up. "Send *this* to the village dry cleaners? *Folie!* You know nothing about clothes, do you?" The bright eye rolled over Kate's creased red sundress and flip-flops.

It was tempting to storm off and leave the ungrateful old hag where she had found her. But allowances must be made. Gran, for one, would expect her to do the right thing. This woman was not only tremendously old but had also had a severe shock. What she needed was a lie-down and whatever the French equivalent was of a nice cup of tea. "Where do you live?" she asked, grimly anticipating somewhere miles away involving several impossible-to-negotiate bus trips and hours of irascible old company.

"The Place de l'Eglise," barked the old lady.

"Oh." Kate was surprised. Yet this explained her presence in the bar. It was the old lady's local. "Come on," she said firmly. "Take my arm."

The sharp eye rolled distrustingly over her. For a second, Kate expected the haughty head to shake in refusal. Then a set of bone-like fingers fumbled at her elbow.

"That's my house over there." As she and Kate emerged into the sunshine of the main square, the old woman gestured at the opposite end.

"What—the big one?"

"Yes. The big one," the old lady said testily, leading the way to the shuttered, mysterious house Kate had seen from her balcony. The ornate, intriguing building spotted yesterday, before the party. Before the world, as she knew it, turned upside down.

The five old women who seemed to spend most of their considerable spare time sitting in the square looked up as Kate and the old lady passed. They nodded at the old lady respectfully and looked a good deal less respectfully at Kate.

"You can go now," the old woman instructed as they reached the impressive sweep of steps leading up to her front door.

*That's okay, don't mention it,* Kate thought hotly, turning away.

A voice came from behind. "If you please, Mademoiselle . . ."

"Yes?" Had the old bat remembered her manners? Was she about to be thanked?

"We never introduced ourselves properly. I," said the old lady haughtily, "am the Comtesse d'Artuby."

"And I'm Kate Clegg."

Without another word the Comtesse turned and went slowly up the stairs. Miserable old crone, Kate thought, heading back to the hotel.

13

Kate spent the afternoon on her balcony dozing and thinking about her novel. Jobs and how to get them could wait until tomorrow. As far as today was concerned, she was exhausted, felt sick, and had a team of demolition men crashing around her brain. Considering her financial position was hardly going to speed her recovery.

She had pulled the chair to the edge of the balcony, the better to view the bustling Place de l'Eglise. One foot propped up on a marble-topped table, the other on the tiled floor, Kate stared at the end of the square and the old lady's imposing, shuttered house. It was easy to imagine that bright hazel eye watching her through the slats.

She picked up the notebook on the marble table—she had had the foresight to pack an extra, spare jotter in her luggage—and tried to think about her novel again. Leafing through the book was distracting, however; it contained work notes that immediately brought to life past *Mockery* features. It all seemed a world away now. Even if she'd wanted to go home, Gran had spoken. The doors of Wits End were closed against her. She could not go back—yet.

Kate noticed the owner of the Café de la Place perambulating the margins of his premises. At least, she assumed he was the owner; a skinny little man with graying hair, pointing and shouting at a hapless, scurrying waiter. And when he wasn't pointing and shouting he was bowing and scraping to affluent-looking customers and delivering a vicious kick to any unfortunate animal in search of food. There were several such animals in the square—cats mostly—all of whom invariably found themselves painfully ejected from the premises.

The telephone interrupted her thoughts.

"Darling? That you?" Celia's voice echoed down a distant, crackling line. "Thought I might have missed you. Thought you might have gone back."

"No, still here. How's London?"

"Gray and depressing as ever, I should think."

"Uh . . . aren't you there?"

"No, darling. I'm here. Floor below you, in fact."

Which accounted, Kate realized, for the curious stereo effect she had noticed at the start of the conversation. If she took the receiver away from her ear, Celia's voice could be heard through the floor. It was, in fact, easier to hear it that way. The Hôtel des Tours phone lines were obviously every bit as rudimentary as its staff.

"Let's meet in the bar," Celia bawled up through the ceiling. "I've got lots to tell you."

"But not nearly as much," Kate shouted down through the floor, "as I've got to tell *you.*"


The bar was just as gloomy as before. From her table against the wall, Kate watched the Trout, large hand clamped to the broad, sallow forehead; most of her face covered by a pair of ludicrously huge sunglasses. She was, again, turning the pages of her accounts book, although, given the obviously parlous state of the business, what comfort this could offer was unclear. With her was a bent old man. Despite the heat of the day he wore, in addition to a wrinkled, suspicious expression, a thick red woolly jumper and a grubby white woolly hat. Both obviously handcrafted some considerable time ago.

"Over here!"

An arm waved in the bar's fug. Sitting, smiling at a table, framed by the open door of the bar, Celia looked a different person from the fraught figure at the Cap Ferrat party.

"It's great to see you." Kate hugged her.

"You too, darling. But I can't tell you *anything* until I've got a drink."

"Leave it to me."

The snippy brunette was nowhere to be seen at the bar. The Troll, mooching about the entrance, was looking more forbidding than usual. Kate eyed him apprehensively.

"He'sh crosh," hissed the only other person at the bar counter, an etiolated figure wearing a stained pink bow tie and a panama hat that looked as if someone had jumped up and down on it. On his grubby white jacket was a yellow badge saying *Tours 'R' Us*. It was the man who had fallen off the stool the day before.

"Crosh?" Kate repeated.

"Crosh becaushe his lady love hashn't turned up for work."

"You mean the barmaid? She's his girlfriend?"

"He wishes! Heh heh. No, she'sh not intereshted in him. Thinksh she can do a lot better. But she likesh the attention, sho she encouragesh him. La Belle Dame Shans Mershi, I call her." He seemed to focus on Kate for the first time. "The name'sh Crichton, by the way. Crichton Porterhoushe."

"Kate Clegg."

"Clegg, eh?" He nodded appreciatively. "Good northern name, rhat."

"That's right." Kate felt a swell of pride.

"I'd help myshelf if I were you," Crichton advised, following her gaze. "I alwaysh do. They don't sheem to mind."

Kate picked up a half-empty bottle of wine from the counter, grabbed a couple of glasses and returned to Celia with her booty.

"Cheers," they said, clanking.

"Yummy," pronounced Celia, pale lips stained purple from her first long swig.

Kate sipped suspiciously. The wine tasted surprisingly good. She savored its blackberry fruitiness on her tongue. She could drink a lot of this. And probably would, now she had Celia, all ears, all to herself. Now the Nat episode could finally get an airing. With a sort of burning, resentful pleasure she anticipated her friend's outrage, fury, and sympathy. "I'm not going back to London," she began.

Celia gave a matter-of-fact nod. "Neither am I."

"*What?*" Her thunder conclusively stolen, Kate lowered her glass of wine.

"I'm leaving Lance, darling," Celia announced.

"But why . . . ?"

"So sudden?" Celia grinned. "Why *now*, when I've obviously put up with him for years?"

"Well—yes. But I suppose Lance *was* behaving pretty badly at the party. Flirting with that woman in the tight trousers and the rest of it."

Celia drained her glass and filled them both up again. "Yes, darling, but as I said at the time, not flirting *enough*. In the end I had to take matters into my own hands."

"What do you mean?" Kate was puzzled. "Last time I saw you, you were with that bizarre bloke . . ."

"High Street Ken." Celia smiled happily. "Really, darling, I've never been *so* looked after in my life. What a gentleman. He treated me like a queen." She laughed throatily. "I tell you, it's bloody nice to have your curves appreciated at three A.M. when you'd eaten as much as I had."

Kate's breath caught in her throat. "But—"

"But what, darling?"

"But . . . don't you think he's a bit strange?"

"Not really. You forget, I've been married to Lance for ten years. I've got a higher strange threshold than most."

"But what was he doing at the party, anyway? Did you ever get to the bottom of it?"

"He told us. He's looking for someone."

"But who?"

Celia shrugged. "His business. Can't say I was all that interested, darling. There were other, more pressing matters to deal with." Over the rim of her wineglass, she gave the staring Kate a satisfied smile. "You don't like him because he's short and bald," she accused.

"Er, well, I wouldn't say that exactly, but—"

"So what's so great about good-looking men? I take it you never managed to hook up with yours? Matter of fact, I know you didn't—he had his tongue down Champagne D'Vyne's throat most of the evening. Lance has practically written an essay about it for his paper."

"Thanks for telling me." Kate bit her lip hard, her insides boiling.

Celia immediately looked repentant. "Oh, darling, I'm so sorry. That was unnecessary. But Nat Hardstone is obviously a bastard. You're *so* much better off without him."

Nothing like the zeal of the newly converted, Kate thought sourly. Celia was a fine one to talk, considering she would have presumably been much better off without Lance for years. "Tell me about Ken, anyway. What happened after I left?"

Celia sighed ecstatically. "We were getting on like a house on fire. I told him all about my marriage. Then, right on cue, Lance came back—*completely* pissed, I might say. He was vile to me and tried to make me leave with him. Ken told him that I was staying and also exactly what he thought of him."

"Good for him."

"Gave him a bit of a shove as well. There would probably have been a fight if Lance had been able to see straight. As it was, he just fell in the pond. Which didn't do much for his dignity in front of the A-list—there was quite a crowd watching by this time. Including all those journalists from our table."

Kate giggled. "Wish I'd been there."

"Then Ken told him that if he ever hit me again he'd be swimming with the fishes. Or was it concrete boots—I forget."

"Are you sure it wasn't both?"

"Could well have been, darling. Anyway, Lance climbed out of the pond and stormed off shouting that I'd be hearing from his lawyers. I said that he'd be hearing from mine first. Then the funniest thing happened," Celia said in wonder.

"What?"

"A round of applause! Incredible. Lots of clapping and cheering— everyone thought it was a rehearsal for something, apparently."

"They didn't!"

"Oh, absolutely, darling. Film people are so self-obsessed they think everything is a movie. I heard someone saying that Ken had a three-picture deal with Warner Brothers."

"No!"

Celia nodded, smiling.

"Well, that's great." Kate tried to sound sincere. After all, who was she to cast aspersions on Celia's choice of man? It wasn't as if she was the world's greatest judge of male character herself.

"Where *is* Ken?" Kate asked. "Is he staying here as well?"

Celia nodded. "Should be back any moment. He left early. Something to do with whoever he's looking for."

Kate was unable to resist returning to the attack. "But doesn't that bother you? This bizarre mission of his?"

Celia stretched her arms contentedly above her head. "Like I said, darling. His business."

She was, Kate noted, the epitome of relaxed radiance. The weary cynic of yesterday had been seen off by a small, bald man in a shiny suit. "I need to get a job, of course," Celia added, tipping back her head. "What'll *you* do while you're here, anyway?"

"I'm writing a novel."

Celia clapped her hands together. "Are you *really*, darling? Well, of course you are! What journalist isn't? Lance was always going on about his masterpiece—a ritzy romp set in the world of celebrity journalism, apparently."

"Was he?" Kate wasn't very thrilled to be compared to that particular yardstick.

"Never saw the light of day. But good for you, anyway. Got an advance, have you?"

"Er, no," Kate confessed. "So I'm going to need another job to make actual money—pay for the room and all that. But I'm trying not to think about it."

"Perhaps we can get something together?"

"Perhaps we can."

Just then the heavy door at the far end of the bar opened.

"Ken!" exclaimed Celia.

His grin was a mile wide and his small feet positively twinkled as he shot over the flagstones towards her. "'Ow've you been then, naughty knickers?" he murmured caressingly into her neck.

"Rather hungry, since you ask." Celia smiled. "I'm Hank Marvin, as you might say."

Kate looked on in amazement. Celia was quite obviously potty about this ludicrous little man. It seemed inexplicable, even given the Lance factor.

"Me too," Ken agreed. "I need me lunch." He cast an assessing glance around. "How about 'ere? At Fawlty Tours, arf arf."

Kate remembered the chef with trepidation. Celia looked equally doubtful. "The food here's good?"

"No idea. But we may as well give it a go. *Oy, mate,*" Ken called to the Troll. "*Can we 'ave a menu?* What did he say?" he added after the Troll had grumbled a reply.

"That they don't have menus," Celia translated. "Honestly, what sort of a restaurant is this? He says he'll come and tell us what they're cooking when he's got a minute."

"When he's got a minute?" Kate echoed. "He's only sitting there looking miserable."

"Yes, darling, but looking *that* miserable must take it out of you."

Eventually, the Troll got a minute. His chosen waiting method was to approach, glowering, slam two hairy hands on the table and announce in a fierce growl the available dishes. His manner throughout suggested that Ken and Celia could take it or leave it; his unspoken recommendation being the latter.

"Pâte to start with, then the lamb," Ken announced after several increasingly irritable repetitions of the menu. The Troll wrote nothing down; merely gave Ken a contemptuous stare before turning to Celia.

"I'll have the same, please," Celia squeaked.

"Nothing for me," Kate said hurriedly. "I've got to be off in a minute."

The Troll returned and threw a handful of cutlery down on the table.

"Silver service," grinned Ken. "Can't beat it, can yer? Blimey. Christ only knows what the grub's going to be like."

In front of Ken was plonked a tureen of soup the size of a wash-basin. "But I ordered pâté," Ken bleated, to the Troll's broad, retreating, supremely indifferent back.

Celia looked up from her plate of courgettes covered in creamy sauce. "Actually, this is fantastic."

It was. For a few minutes, only the sound of cutlery on plates and murmurs of approval disturbed the silence.

14

As she emerged from the bar of the Hôtel des Tours, the heat hit Kate like a blow in the face. The blue parasols of the Café de la Place across the square, their miserable owner notwithstanding, not only looked shady but sang a siren song of coffee. A siren song too of sitting watching the world go by over a leisurely lunch.

Not a single table was free at the café, however. Brits in yellow baseball caps took up at least half the available bottom space.

The other seats were occupied by well-heeled tourist couples with conspicuously little to say to each other. Kate loitered on the edge, forced to step out of the way as the harassed waiter dived backward and forward under a laden tray as huge as a cartwheel.

"Excuse me." A dark-haired man in a red shirt stood up suddenly at one of the tables at the front. "If you want to sit down here, I'm going in a minute." He spoke, to her surprise, in English. Was her foreignness really that obvious? Probably. Pale skin. Reddening nose. Mousy hair. And, no doubt, that eternal English air of being slightly ill at ease.

He was in his mid-twenties, brown-eyed, and with rumpled dark hair. He had a lean, tired, and stubbly face.

"Thanks." Kate sat down carefully opposite him. She picked up the café menu.

"Hungry?" he asked.

"Starving."

"Then you have come to the wrong place. The coffee's the only thing that bearable, and only then because it's quicker than over there." He nodded toward the Hôtel des Tours.

"But this is a café, isn't it?"

His broad, spare shoulders shrugged inside his crumpled shirt. "It says it is. But the food here is awful. Soggy croques. Limp salads. You should get something to eat from the *boulangerie* on the corner."

Kate recalled the glimpse she had had of the baker's window. Tomato-loaded pizza, thick squares of egg tart marbled with spinach, golden-baked *quiches lorraine* a universe away from the ones she remembered from childhood—pale, soggy, and smelling vaguely of sick.

"But if the food here's so bad, why's the café so popular?"

He gestured with his head toward the hotel. "There is no competition."

She could see what he meant. Although it was well into lunchtime, no tablecloths had appeared on any of the Hôtel des Tours's wooden tables scattered anyhow under the shadowy arches. Unlike at the Café de la Place, no menu board stood temptingly outside.

"And the service here, it is terrible," the red-shirted man was saying.

It wasn't much better at the Hôtel des Tours, Kate thought, comparing the two establishments with interest. Yet there was no doubt the miserable owner of the Café de la Place was ahead of the game when it came to presentation. His café had branding—the blue parasols. It looked more attractive—flowers, tablecloths, napkins. It had menus. It had a waiter who, though downtrodden, at least accepted he was there to serve.

Her companion, she realized, was making no immediate effort to leave. He seemed, on the contrary, to be eking out the dregs of his coffee for as long as he possibly could.

"I'm Fabien," he said, his face breaking into a smile.

"Kate. Your English is very good," she remarked.

"I know. But it should be. I spent five years at an English school. My father worked in London for a while."

"Really?"

"He was in the diplomatic service."

"Very smart."

"Well," he gestured down the length of his body, "as you can see, I am not very smart myself."

"Er, do you live in Ste. Jeanne?"

"I live just outside. I work here, though. I'm an artist. I paint."

She was struck by the ungrand way in which he said it. As matter-of-factly as if he mended tractors.

"Must be great to be an artist."

"To live and work here, especially. This area has a great artistic heritage."

"I know," Kate said, grabbing the opportunity to show off the knowledge she'd acquired since she arrived. "Renoir, Matisse, and Picasso all came here."

"They did." He was nodding approvingly.

"And then there are the great collections, such as Madame Ephrussi's on Cap Ferrat."

Fabien raised long fingers to his curving lips. "Very good. I am impressed. You know a lot about art, obviously."

"A bit," Kate said confidently.

He smiled broadly. "But what about you?" he asked her. "What do you do?"

"I'm a writer."

"Ah. An artist too, then?"

"Sort of." She wasn't sure whether *Northern Gigolo* came under the heading, exactly.

"This area is famous for writers, you know. F. Scott Fitzgerald, Graham Greene, Katherine Mansfield . . . ?" His voice trailed away. He smiled.

"Does painting pay well?" she asked after a pause.

He gave her a wry smile. "Painters are always penniless."

"Like novelists," Kate groaned.

"But then artists die and their work becomes valuable. But as all that will come too late for me, I do odd jobs as well. Some gardening, building, being a waiter, things like that."

Silence again, apart from the car engines and chatter of the square. Kate glanced about for the café waiter, but he was nowhere to be seen. Fabien hadn't been exaggerating about the poor service.

"You're writing in the Hôtel des Tours?" Fabien asked.

Kate nodded, thinking with a surge of pride how romantic that sounded. The lady novelist in her Riviera hotel. Very Agatha Christie. "The only thing is, I'm not sure how much longer I'll be able to stay there."

"Why not?"

"Money," Kate sighed. "I need to get an odd job myself. To pay for the room."

Fabien nodded slowly. Half a second later, he was on his feet staring in horror at his watch. "I have to go now. It was nice to meet you again—Kate."

As his warm, dry hand rasped across her palm in farewell, she felt a vague shudder of pleasure. Then alarm bells rioted through her system. Nice to meet her—*again*? She stared, puzzled, after the retreating red shirt.

"Oh. One more thing." Fabien turned. "The wine is as bad as the food. You won't get any pink champagne here."

With that he was off, his sinewy feet in battered deck shoes loping through the square.

*Pink champagne!* Kate clamped both hands to her mouth. It was *him*. The waiter from the night before. The art-loving, actor-loathing man in the mask who had looked after her so courteously, so generously. She stared after the bobbing figure, embarrassment and gratitude fighting for dominance within her, as the waiter finally took her order.

Just then, staggering across the cobbles from the direction of the Hôtel des Tours, came the shambling figure of Crichton Porterhouse. His advent was greeted with a chorus from behind her.

"Croyton! Look, it's Croyton. He's back."

Kate twisted round to see the yellow baseball caps shifting with excitement. Only now did she notice that each hat bore, as Crichton's badge had done, the legend *Tours 'R' Us* on the panel above the peak of the cap. Incredible as it seemed, they had been waiting for Crichton. Even more incredibly, he appeared somehow to have sobered up.

"Sorry I'm a bit late, folks," he muttered. "Long queue in the post office, I'm afraid. And you wouldn't *believe* the one I was in at the bank."

No, thought Kate, grinning to herself. She wouldn't.

"We getting any grub or not?" demanded a portly brunette in an Aston Villa shirt. "Them sandwiches we ordered still 'aven't come. Go and sort 'em out, will you, Croyton."

Crichton now noticed Kate. He gave a guilty smile.

"Hello again." She grinned. "So this is what you do? You're a tour guide?" She tried to keep the note of incredulity out of her voice.

Crichton sidled up to her and passed a hand wearily over his eyes. "This is one of my hats, yes," he muttered. "Carting herds from Birmingham up and down the Croisette and traipsing them round the hill villages." He rolled his eyes. "I try my best to interest them in medieval French architecture. But all they really want is a cake and a crap."

Kate jumped at the thump and rattle of something being put on the table. "*Votre demi*," announced a voice different from the waiter's panicked, breathless tones.

"The lager looked flat, as if it had spent a considerable time waiting on a bar counter. Kate looked at Crichton.

This really is a vile place," he said. "But it's not as if there's anywhere else I can take the unwashed masses to." He flicked his eyes regretfully across the square.

Kate said good-bye and headed into the rue du Midi. At the end of the village's main street was the office of something called the *Riviera Gazette*. The local newspaper, Kate realized with a surge of interest.

From various stickers on the window she deducted the *Gazette* was a weekly aimed at the local English-speaking community. Exactly like the *Mockery*. Although admittedly it was a moot point whether some of the dialects spoken in the latter's remoter catchment areas qualified as English, exactly.

She peered avidly into the *Gazette*'s large plate-glass window. Grubby white blinds obscured most of what there was to see, but the cracks between revealed no one around.

The fleeting thought there might be a job for her here had obviously immediately crossed Kate's mind. But no doubt there would be difficulties. Quite besides the obstructive complexities of French employment law, her experience as a journalist would probably be useless. Any parallels between a paper whose beat was the playground of the rich and another whose beat included the playground of Slackmucklethwaite Junior seemed unlikely. As for references, forget it.

Her forehead throbbed. Even without a hangover the outlook would be bleak. With one it was desperate. The longed-for escape to France really had got off to a dream start. One double-crossing, two-timing, manipulative millionheir. One lost job. One alienated family. A stranger in a strange land who had, within a mere twenty-four hours of arriving, provoked a string of embarrassing encounters with the locals.

And what was she anyway? A so-called writer with a hardly started novel. Still, at least she could do something about that now. With no other distractions, she could stop talking about it, buckle down and get on with it.

On the balcony next morning Kate's pen sped across her notebook.

Mark sat at the back of the Slackmucklethwaite and District WI meeting, watching Dorian Bracegirdle as she got up to thank the speaker. "A fascinating talk on energy saving," she pronounced.

Suddenly, the lovely blue and gold day erupted into earsplitting noise. Several cars were backfiring at once.

It took some time to collect herself again.

Energy saving, Mark thought wearily. There certainly hadn't been much of that the night before. Dorian had been even more insatiable than usual—five times including once with chocolate sauce—and still no sign of the soft-top MX5 she'd promised him. It was time he started seeing some rewards for his efforts.

*Whee-eee-eee.* Someone, somewhere had started a tile cutting machine. Kate rubbed her eyes in despair. She was trying to work, for Christ's sake. Harder than she had ever tried before. But concentrating with all this racket was impossible.

"And while I'm up 'ere," Dorian added from the podium, "I'd like to announce the winner of our top energy saving tip competition. It's Mandy Bolsover, who says that if you boil too much water in your kettle, why not decant the surplus into a vacuum flask?"

Three thousand dogs had all started barking in unison. They stopped and were immediately replaced by the loud yowl of a cat. The Café de la Place owner was doing his St. Francis of Assisi bit again, Kate saw, looking down from her balcony just as the unfortunate feline flew through the air. Breakfast was in full swing, but even from here she could see what a miserable affair it was. The coffee was served in small, mean cups; the croissants looked pale and were no doubt stale.

Mark rolled a lazy glance over in Mandy Bolsover's direction. Trim little bird, new to Slackmucklethwaite, rumored, if he remembered rightly, to have a husband who'd made a fortune with SpeciForEyes, a thriving chain of opticians. His gaze lingered on Mrs. Bolsover's plump little breasts. Well, she certainly had the right frame; it would, he thought, be extremely shortsighted to let such an opportunity pass without closer examination. . . .

The loudest conversation in the world had now started up directly underneath her. Resistance was useless. Kate dropped her notebook and pen on to the table and went gloomily downstairs in search of breakfast.

As she heaved open the door to the bar, she reeled back from the almost physical force of the noise. A full-blown row was taking place. At the eye of the storm was the barmaid, screaming hysterically at the old man who was, once again, wearing his red jumper and woolly hat.

In his wrinkled, yellowish hands two plastic bags of toilet rolls shook with the force of his anger.

"How dare you, Pappy! I've worked here for seven years!" she was yelling, her cleavage rearing like a wild horse. The sight of it was clearly mezmerising the Troll, who stood nearby, dodging forward nervously from time to time as if to try and calm things.

"*Worked!*" Pappy exploded. "Nicole, you wouldn't know what work is."

The barmaid's large black eyes blazed in indignation. Seizing a saucer that sat on the bar top, she hurled it with full force at her accuser. It was a bad shot; the missile flew wide and smashed against the wall above a crumpled old man who sat nursing a large cognac.

"*And another thing,*" Pappy bellowed, going swiftly to sketch out not just one, but several areas in which Nicole was, in his view, giving less than satisfaction.

Nicole's reply was to hurl a pretty green pastis jug. Kate dodged and heard it shatter against the wall above her.

"I've had enough of working for you, you miserable old toad," Nicole raged. "I'm going, do you hear me? I'm leaving. I quit!" Lips pulled back in a snarl of anger, she marched out from behind the bar. She paused only to slap Pappy across the face with a force that made the Troll wince even as he stepped forward to lay a massive and restraining hand on her arm. Shaking it off with contempt, Nicole yanked the heavy door back and stormed out.

The ensuing silence was absolute. No one moved for several minutes. The Troll was the first. His sloping shoulders sloped further. He looked, Kate saw with a pang, utterly despondent. Then he jerked his chin up, threw back his massive shoulders and strode over to Pappy. "Look what you've done!" he boomed in anguish. "She'll *never* come back now!"

"And a good thing too!" yelled the old man, the marks of Nicole's fingers red against his papery cheeks. He shook himself, dusted himself down and, in the process, caught Kate's eye. "You!" Pappy exclaimed, extending a shaking digit. "*You!*"

Kate gulped. Was he about to start hurling loo rolls at her as well? "What?" she said nervously.

Eyes burning intensely in his yellow face, Pappy approached her purposefully over the bar floor. Then, suddenly, he dipped, picked something from under the counter and shoved it in her direction. "This." he muttered, "came for you this morning."

It was a small envelope emblazoned with the logo of an overnight courier delivery service. Kate looked at the address on the back—Wits End, Slackmucklethwaite—and froze.

To send it by overnight delivery seemed particularly dramatic. The message within must be something Mum wanted her to see immediately, possibly before more rational and measured thought had interceded. Was she, Kate wondered sickly, being *disowned* now?

Pappy's papery old visage wore an expectant expression, but Kate had no intention of opening the letter in front of him. Holding the envelope as if it were a bomb, she took it up to her room.

Out on the balcony, Kate tore the courier envelope's cardboard cover off. Heart banging, she opened the paper packet and removed its contents. There was nothing from her mother. The envelope contained a letter in Gran's handwriting. Plus a bundle of Euro notes and a considerable quantity of dirt.

*I'm sending you some northern grit,* Gran had written in her loopy ballpoint. *Now stop moaning, spit on your hands, take a fresh hold and get on with it.*

The words wavered before Kate's rapidly filling eyes. *I don't want your gratitude but I do want your letters*, Gran had added, by way of a postscript. *So make sure you send me some.*

Kate smoothed out the notes with a mixture of relief and guilt. Gran's means, she knew, were extremely straitened; such a gift would have financial ramifications for months. She pictured her grandmother asking—as surely she must have done—for her pension in "them Euro things" at Slackmucklethwaite post office.

She leaned over the balcony and looked down into the square. Even Fawlty Tours had its good points if you looked for them. The wonderful balcony most obviously.

Yes. There were worse places to be than this. Even her job prospects seemed less dismal now she had Gran's contribution to tide her over.

Tomorrow she'd start the search; perhaps the Hôtel des Tours might have a spot of chambermaiding? Thanks to her mother, she'd had years of master classes in the art of hospital corners. She'd even be a *plongeur* if necessary. Washing up for a living had literary legs anyway; what about Orwell's *Down and Out In Paris and London*? There was also, now Nicole had stormed out in so spectacular a fashion, the possibility that *her* job was up for grabs.

And perhaps there was another option too.

She had written off the *Riviera Gazette* without even trying. But surely it was worth going to see the editor? Nothing ventured, nothing gained, as Dad used to say whenever she posted off yet another letter to a London broadsheet. Admittedly, nothing ever was gained.

A silvery jangle from the Place de l'Eglise bells revived her spirits further. Kate spat on her hands, rummaged in the envelope of grit, and took a firm hold of the balcony railings. She was bloodied but, for the moment at least, unbowed.

15

Kate woke next day to another perfect morning. Walking, light-hearted, on to the balcony, she admired the sun streaming across the cobbles and loading the vine leaves on the walls with massy light. The church tower, fully in its rays, was a blaze of peach. The only blot on the blue horizon was, as usual, the owner of the café opposite, already busily smarming up to a smart-looking family with glossy hair and all-white clothes.

No time to loiter, Kate told herself. She had a whole new lifestyle to organize and a job to find—starting with a visit to the *Riviera Gazette*. She wondered vaguely about telling Celia of her plans, but she was probably still wrapped up in Ken—no doubt literally—and might resent the interruption. After a shower that doubled as a clothes-washing session, Kate draped T-shirts and some underwear over the balcony rails to dry and went down to the rue du Midi.

The crowd inside the bread shop bore testament to the national addiction. And it certainly did them no harm, Kate thought enviously, as willowy woman after willowy woman left clutching bundles of twiglike baguettes. Thin bread obviously made thin people.

"Kate!" Someone tall and dark was looming at her left. The artist/waiter . . . Fabien. Smiling at her, hair all over the place, brilliant eyes screwed up against the light.

Her face flooded as their encounter at the café came rushing back. "Hello," he said.

"Hello." She looked up at him, embarrassed and defiant. "Look, about the party the other night . . ."

He flashed a line of level teeth. "Ah. The party."

He really was good-looking. In a loose-limbed, long-necked sort of way. Not that, after the Nat experience, looks had any bearing on anything. But for the record, and if you liked your men slightly raggy at the edges, Fabien was certainly no swamp monster.

"I think I owe you some money for the taxi," she told him.

"I wouldn't hear of it. Besides, it was paid for. Luckily the driver didn't know who by."

"But I pinched Madonna's taxi."

He shrugged his thin, wide shoulders. *"Eh bien?* She can afford it. Go and tell her, if you feel so bad about it."

Kate grinned. "Well thanks, anyway. And sorry about me, you know, banging on about myself."

He tilted his head and pulled a so-what face. They looked at each other in silence. Her heart picked up speed.

"Fabien!" A breathy voice interrupted the stillness. A mane of shining hair arced suddenly through the sunshine; a pair of graceful arms wound suddenly round his neck. Standing there between them, all plunging cleavage and tiny waist, was Nicole the barmaid. Or ex-barmaid.

If she looked beautiful when she was angry, Kate saw, she looked even more so when she wasn't. Her plump brown Bardot lips pumped up and down on a piece of chewing gum; the action revealing white flashes of teeth. The look in her large brown eyes was poised somewhere between proprietorial and mocking.

"This is Nicole," Fabien said.

Kate nodded, stiff from the hackles that had automatically risen, and managed a passably warm shake of the proffered hand. "We've met."

Nicole made no sign of ever having seen her before. Let alone of ever having turned a radio up to drown out her voice. She simply ignored her, whilst giggling and dimpling at Fabien like a giddy schoolgirl.

"We met in the Hôtel des Tours," Kate prompted determinedly.

Nicole's eyes flashed sparks. *"That* shithole. Worst bar in the world. That family! Idiots! Beasts!"

"They're not that bad," Fabien said mildly. "And you're very ungrateful," he rebuked Nicole. "I hear one of them is very fond of you."

Nicole's lip curled. "*That* great ugly imbecile."

"It's not the looks that count," Fabien told her.

"Which is fortunate—for some people," Nicole retorted.

Kate felt a pang for the Troll. Not even his own mother could claim he was handsome, but only a heart of stone could fail to be touched by his devotion. Unfortunately for him, it seemed Nicole had just that heart.

"And he'll inherit the business one day," Fabien twinkled.

"Business! You call that a business? I'd rather inherit a crêpe stand."

"Funny you should say that," Fabien mused. "I once saw a crepe-maker in Nice packing up for the evening. He drove off in a Mercedes."

Nicole stared. Beautiful she might be, Kate thought, but she seemed to lack a sense of humor.

"I must go," Nicole murmured breathily, sliding Fabien the kind of glance that removed hair at fifty paces. A stare of mocking dislike was all Kate received as farewell.

As Nicole flounced off Fabien scratched his wild head and gave Kate an easy grin. "What were we saying? Oh yes. Did you enjoy your drink at the Café de la Place?"

"To be honest, I've had better." She explained the lager saga.

Fabien looked horror-struck. "I'm so sorry."

"Really, it doesn't matter."

"Oh, but it does. I have given you completely the wrong impression of the Côte d'Azur. You probably think that all the bars and cafés round here are as bizarre as the Hôtel des Tours or as unpalatable as the Café de la Place. Don't you?"

Kate made polite demurring noises.

"Exactly. So I would like to take you somewhere better to make up for it. Do you like cocktails?"

"Doesn't everybody?" Kate asked, though in point of fact her exposure to the silver martini shaker had been minimal.

Fabien beamed in approval. "Great. There's a bar I know in Antibes that's the mutt's nuts."

"The mutt's nuts! Where did you learn that?"

"Like I said, I was at school in England. When are you free? Tonight?"

Five minutes later, she stood outside the offices of the *Riviera Gazette*. Gratifyingly, the previously empty wire box outside was filled with copies of the new issue. Much to Kate's surprise, the spelling on the *Gazette* was every bit down to *Mockery* standards. Here, for instance, was an interview with someone who the headline described as A VERY BRITSII IT GRL—no, it couldn't be! But it was, large as life and twice as loathsome. Champagne D'Vyne, wearing the same skimpy T-shirt as in the *Mockery*. Same photography too, by the looks of it. A wave of hatred swirled through Kate. Had her ludicrous and undeserved celebrity spread even here? Was there no escaping the woman?

Something at the top of the piece caught her eye. *By Our Star Interviewer Kate Clog*, ran the byline. Kate gripped the paper with both hands. *Her* interview?

It seemed so. A glance at the first few paragraphs confirmed that the article was indeed, word for word, the same one she had written. But how had it ended up in the *Gazette*? Kate's frown deepened. The mystery wasn't so much *what* had been done—the *Gazette*, understandably imagining *Mockery* readers as few and far between on the Riviera, had obviously just lifted it in its entirety. The mystery was *how. How* had a copy of the *Mockery* got to the South of France?

Still, here it was; what was more, its appearance could be fortuitous. En route to the office Kate had lamented the absence of the cuttings book in which she routinely pasted copies of her articles. But now there was no need for it. By a bizarre twist of fate, the *Gazette*'s editor not only knew her work but had printed it already.

Kate tidied her hair as best she could in the window. Then, straightening her back and lifting her chin, she pushed open the glass door and went inside.

The *Gazette* office was small, smaller even than the *Mockery*'s, although possibly even more untidy. Nothing indicated that its beat was the glittering Côte d'Azur apart from a lopsided calendar featuring a picture of a beach and a peeling poster for a long-past Cannes Film

Festival. Bulging box files, straining against their elastic band belts, jostled for position along the shelves, while the two elderly desks that just fitted in the room were piled high with papers. Behind one of the desks was a large and chaotic notice board covered in photographs and scraps of paper.

Facing this, its back to the door, was a large swivel chair. Just visible over the top of this swivel chair was part of a head of grayish hair moving up and down in rhythm to a wet, snoring noise. The editor, it seemed, was asleep.

Kate coughed loudly. No reaction from the chair. She cleared her throat. Still nothing. Finally she banged on the desk and bawled, "Anyone at home?"

A sound like the whinny of a horse rent the air. There were a number of loud grunts and the chair shook convulsively before shuddering round to reveal its occupant.

"Crichton!" Kate exclaimed delightedly.

As his lolling eyes focused, Crichton leaped violently from the chair. The action precipitated a landslide on his desk that shot off to reveal an enormous bottle of pastis. It rolled slowly out to nudge the empty glass beside the battered desk lamp. Hardly past breakfast, and Crichton was hitting the bottle already.

He looked accusingly at her. "You made me jump."

"Sorry. Didn't mean to. I was just looking for the editor."

Crichton dropped back down into his swivel chair—with difficulty as the seat had swiveled away. He flailed behind him for the arms. "Well, you've found him. I'm the editor."

"*You?*"

"Surprised, eh?"

"It's not that exactly," Kate said politely, although it was. On the other hand, given his tippling tendencies, it certainly explained the paper's spelling. "It's just that I thought you were a tour guide."

"And so I am, part-time. You don't think editing *this* finances a luxurious expat lifestyle on the Riviera, do you? Whole thing's run on a shoestring, and a pretty frayed one at that." He screwed up his face in distaste. "Plus, my real background is in journalism." Crichton opened a soft pack of Winstons, tapped one on the packet filter down, put it in his mouth and lit it from a naked lady lighter.

"What sort of journalism?" Kate asked disbelievingly. School magazines, she guessed.

For a second, Crichton disappeared behind a bloom of smoke. "I was trained on the *Times*. *The Times* of London."

"*Really?*" She was unable to suppress a tone of disbelief.

"*Certainly.*" Crichton's bloodshot eyes were suddenly faraway and dreamy. "Those were the days. Editors had their own oak-paneled offices with coal fires in them and every afternoon a nice lady with a tea trolley came round and—oh well." He exhaled regretfully and sniffed.

As this, for Kate, had a familiar Wemyssian ring, she decided to put Crichton to the test. After all, he and Denys were of an age. "How funny, my old boss used to work at the *Times*." She eyed him carefully.

Crichton brightened. "I say, that's marvellous. Name of?"

"Denys Wemyss."

Crichton's eyes narrowed to a squint. His lips moved as he mouthed the name to himself. Kate regarded him cynically. He'd obviously never heard of the *Mercury* editor. So much for his *Times* claims. Then Crichton slammed the table with a mighty fist blow that once more dislodged the Ricard bottle. "Wemyss, *of course!*" he spluttered, diving, to catch it before it hit the floor. "Slightly older than me but of *course* I remember him. Bit of a one for the ladies, old Wemyss. Or young Wemyss as he was then, of course."

"*Ladies?*" It was Kate's turn to be astonished. Wemyss had never displayed much interest in the womenfolk of Slackmucklethwaite.

"Oh yes. Girls loved him. He was so dapper, so well turned out. While I . . ." Crichton looked down into his stained lap ". . . was more of what you might call the maverick sort. Being the crime correspondent and all. Denys Wemyss. Well, well." He inhaled with an expression of wonder. "I'd love to know what he's up to these days."

"Running a local paper in the North of England."

"That *all?*" Crichton's sniff had a gratified tone. "Must say, one always rather fears one's former colleagues have gone on to great things. What's the paper called?"

"The *Slackmucklethwaite Mercury.*" She could not, Kate thought, have hoped for a neater way in which to introduce the subject of the Champagne interview.

"I say, what a coincidence. Funnily enough, I was only looking at a paper called something like that the other day."

"Yes, I know you were, which is why I've come here. . . ."

But Crichton had disappeared again in a fug of smoke and memory. "Oh, the times we had on the *Times.* The stories I used to cover. Big stories. Important stories. *Crime* stories." He clamped both hands in his Beethoven hair and gave an impassioned groan.

"Must be a bit quiet after all that," she agreed. "Don't suppose you get much crime round here. I mean, it's all beaches and film stars, isn't it? Anyway, you're probably wondering what I'm doing here. . . ."

"Beaches and film stars?" Crichton was staring at her in astonishment. "There's a lot more to the Côte d'Azur than that, let me tell you."

"Well, of course, there's the amazing art."

"Bugger the art." Crichton drew emphatically on his Winston. "Of *course* there's crime on the Côte d'Azur. Some of the biggest and nastiest crooks in the world have their headquarters here."

"Do they?"

"Oh God, yes." Crichton was warming happily to his theme. "There's dodgy goings-on everywhere you look. For example, there's an unmarked white plane lands every Wednesday afternoon at Nice Airport. And *I* want to know what's in it." He stubbed his cigarette out determinedly. "What's more, I'm going to find out."

"What do you think *might* be in it?"

"You tell me. But I'm on the trail, believe me. You can take the crime journalist out of the *Times,* but not the *Times* out of the crime journalist," he added triumphantly. "And there's more."

"More planes?"

"More *crime.*"

"Such as people infringing the copyright laws by helping themselves to other people's newspaper stories?"

Crichton's bloodshot eyeballs flexed in surprise. "What did you say?"

Kate grabbed a *Gazette* and turned to the Champagne interview. "I just wondered where you got this from, that's all. You see—I wrote it."

There was a silence. Crichton sniffed. "Ah. *Right*."

"I used to work on the *Mockery*—er, *Mercury*—you see. Under Denys Wemyss."

Crichton's expression was positioned exactly between amazement and shamefacedness. "Good Lord! What a coincidence. So *that's* Denys's paper?"

"Yes."

"And *you're* Kate Clog, are you . . . ?"

"Clegg, actually. Yes, *isn't* it a coincidence? And hardly the most ethical way of getting a story, as I'm sure you would agree." Kate summoned her best stern face.

Crichton rummaged in panic for a cigarette. "Oh dear, I do apologize, but frankly, given the budget and me being so, erm . . ." eyes to pastis bottle again ". . . well, *busy* all the time." He dropped his gaze. "I thought your interview was terribly good, by the way. Really awfully good. I was stuck for a main story and when I found the copy of the *Heckmuckleslag Bugle*. . . ."

"Where *did* you find it?"

"Shoved in a bin just outside the office." Crichton puffed out a fat cloud of Winston. "I'm not normally in the business of rummaging in rubbish, you understand."

"Of course not," Kate said quickly. Perish the thought. There was nothing *remotely* tramplike about Crichton. Not in the *least*.

". . . but it just happened to catch my eye. Seemed like fate, frankly."

"But how had it got there?"

Crichton shrugged. "Mine not to reason why. It had and I was grateful."

There was a silence. Kate sensed her moment had come. "Well," she said, smiling brightly at Crichton, "what this episode shows, I would say, is that your workload is far too much for one person."

"Absolutely." Crichton sniffed emphatically. "It's overwhelming sometimes. Finding the stories, writing them up," he gave her a nervous glance, "er, bodging the whole shebang together on the computer, getting the disk to the printer. Fortunately the ads are done somewhere else, or I'd really be stuffed."

"And you have no help whatsoever?"

Crichton shook his head.

"And you've got all your tour guide stuff to fit in as well?" Her voice had dropped to a sympathetic coo.

"Don't remind me." Crichton's face buried itself in his hands. "I've got to take them to Nice market tomorrow. Not a loo in sight unless you buy a coffee at one of the cafés for about a million pounds. Then it's lunch at Sospel—the road up there's got at least a hundred hairpin bends and I'm down to drive the bus. The last driver had a head-on collision, flew through the window and broke his pelvis. Mind you, he had a serious drink problem."

"Well, I'm willing to do anything I can to help."

"Got an HGV license?" Crichton asked hopefully.

"I mean journalism," Kate said exasperatedly. "Interviews, advertorial, rewrites. You name it, I can do it. I've been doing it for years. I'm the answer to your prayers. And I think you owe me one, don't you? Pinching my interview and helping yourself to my copyright like that." No need to tell him the copyright was Peter Hardstone's.

Crichton puffed thoughtfully on his Winston. "Well, since you put it like *that.*"

"I do."

"I *might* be able to use you. On a strictly freelance basis, of course—I can't afford permanent staff."

"Fine. Whatever. I'm very flexible."

"And of course, the film festival's on at the moment and—"

"*Fantastic!*" Kate interrupted. "Celebrity interviews—I'm your woman." Pierce Brosan, Julia Roberts, here she came. Gran would be *thrilled.*

Crichton looked perturbed. "Well, actually, what I was about to sat was that as the film festival's on, *I'll* be spending a lot of time down there. Networking and all that. You know." He paused and sniffed. "So it'd be useful to have someone else to do all the boring sh . . . the er . . . bread and butter stuff. *Baguette et beurre,* if you like."

Kate stared levelly back at him. So she was to be the backroom girl again. But then, boring shit was better than no shit at all.

"I've got a few pieces coming up I can probably hand over," Crichton added by way of amelioration. "Swing by tomorrow and I'll go through them with you. And now," he said, grinning, reaching for his desk drawer and removing a fresh bottle of pastis, "how about a snifter to welcome you on board?"

16

It was in a mood of boozy optimism that Kate stepped out of the *Gazette* office into the sunshine of the rue du Midi. Things were picking up at last. Besides a date with a dishy artist later that evening, she had the half-promise of some bits of work which, if they came off, would help support her writing. Hardly the lucrative job of her dreams, but a start. In the long term, like Crichton, it seemed that she too would have to do some multitasking.

"*Mademoiselle!*" Kate jumped at the voice from behind.

The Comtesse, last seen splayed on the ground, was today intimidatingly smart in a close-fitting black suit with black buttons rimmed with gold. A jaunty red silk scarf matched her vermilion slash of mouth and the shining red tips of her fingers. Her heels were high and her thick white hair was twisted up into her trademark chagnon. Only her lopsided face was less than perfect.

"A word, if you please," the old lady commanded, hooking a forefinger through the air. Kate hesitated. She had better things to do than dance attendance on haughty aristocrats. Besides, how close did this word have to be? After all the drink Crichton had just plied her with, she must reek of pastis.

"I would like you to come and have coffee with me." Skewered with the old woman's one good eye, Kate considered resisting, then gave up. What the hell. Coffee, besides sobering her up, would be an excellent opportunity to nose round that fascinating shuttered house. Furthermore, countesses didn't solicit her company every five minutes. Something else to write to Gran about.

Kate followed as the Comtesse, inclining her head grandly in the direction of the five old ladies, click-clacked across the square in her high heels. Her calves and ankles were perfect, despite her age. Far better than Kate's own would ever be. She wondered what lay behind the summons. Most probably something had been missing out of the old boot's handbag when she picked it up from the cobbles.

The Comtesse clacked up the steps, produced the huge house key, fitted it into the lock, and waved Kate inside.

The inside was completely different from what the ornate outside suggested. Kate had expected age-worn flagstones stretched beneath a low, beamed ceiling bearing fading traces of medieval paint. She had imagined ancient fireplaces surmounted by carved stone coats of arms and flanked by armchairs upholstered in rotting damask. Instead, white walls stood around a stripped floor. A faint purple glow lent an ecclesiastical air.

In the center of the hall was a staircase, although not the expected one. Instead of carved and age-blackened seventeenth-century wood, a green glass spiral twisted upward like a vast drill bit. Stretching above all at the very top of the house was a glass roof of a deep, medicine-bottle blue upon which red stained-glass birds wheeled and flapped. The origin, Kate realized, of the purple glow.

"Marc Chagall." The Comtesse stabbed her finger upward. "You have heard of him?"

Kate nodded.

"Painter, and worker in stained glass. He used to be a friend. You have noticed the rest of my collection?"

It was then that Kate really looked at the pictures. What had been a blur in the corner of her eye now resolved itself into ten or so canvases, spot-lit from the ceiling and glowing like jewels against the white walls of the hall. She went over to examine them.

They were modern; all apparently by different artists and all portraits of women in different sizes and frames. One, of a girl with red lips, curling yellow hair and a bright green dress, was in a style Kate immediately recognized.

"Like an Andy Warhol screenprint," she remarked.

"It *is* an Andy Warhol screenprint."

Another, all dots, speech bubbles, and primary colors was reminiscent of the Pop Art style of the 1950s. "Roy Lichtenstein, of course," supplied the Comtesse. "And the one next to it's by Marie Laurencin."

Kate examined the Laurencin. It was a striking image. The woman who stared back had a flat, expressionless face, blond hair, and very black eyes. "She's very pretty. It's a beautiful painting. Who was the artist, did you say?"

She sniffed smoke and saw, as she turned, that the old woman was dragging on a cigarette as if her life depended on it. Everyone in Ste. Jeanne seemed to smoke like chimneys. "Marie Laurencin. She was a friend of Picasso. He lived near Ste. Jeanne, you know—down on the coast, at Juan-les-Pins. This is a famous area for painters. Renoir, Léger, Matisse—they all worked round here."

Kate nodded. The list was growing familiar.

"We'll have coffee in the sitting room," the Comtesse announced. Kate scrambled after her up the glass stairs, the rubber of her flip-flop soles slipping on the surface.

The sitting room she entered seemed the size of a sports hall and had a sports hall's pale wooden floor. Facing each other across it was a pair of fireplaces so minimal they were mere black rectangles in the walls, surrounded by thin chrome frames. The only furniture was a couple of black leather sofas that stood in the center with their backs to each other, art-gallery like.

"I keep the shutters closed," the Comtesse waved an emaciated arm towards the tightly covered windows, "to preserve the paintings."

The art-gallery effect didn't stop at the sofas. The walls were completely covered in paintings. Framed, unframed, portrait, landscape, animal, vegetable, abstract, figurative, wildly colorful, utterly monochrome, they jostled for the attention of the viewer, all brilliantly illuminated by spotlights sunk into the flat white ceiling above. It was a blaze of light and color that made Kate's head ache. She longed for the promised coffee.

Coffee, however, had obviously been forgotten. The old lady began to march rapidly round, pointing and firing out a bewildering roll call of names. "This is a Gertler . . . this a Nash . . . here's a Ben Nicholson . . . and this," she flung out a wrinkled hand and stabbed in the direction of one of the fireplaces," is the latest to join my family. You like it?"

Kate's eyes widened as she took in the huge, unframed canvas. A full-length nude. And, of all possible nudes in all possible worlds, the most uncompromisingly unflattering. And of all possible subjects for a possible nude, was it . . . could it really be . . . the Comtesse?

The painting was, frankly, hideous. The artist—Kate squinted but failed to decipher the name from the signature—had emphasized her age by rendering his subject horribly spare, gray, and skeletal. Her lopsided face was caught perfectly in every imperfect detail, while his pitiless eye had reproduced every wrinkle in her body, every expanse of withered limb. The harshest of scrutinies, meanwhile, had been reserved for her bony knees, shriveled breasts, sunken belly, and—Kate swallowed—*pubic hair.*

She lowered her gaze. Among the many social eventualities her upbringing had not prepared her for was coffee under a picture of one's octogenarian aristocratic hostess in the buff.

"Magnificent, *non?*" the old lady demanded. She had lit up another cigarette and was sucking on it with gusto.

Kate made an acquiescent murmur.

"You like my house?" the old lady demanded suddenly.

"Very much."

"It's not to everyone's taste."

"I love it," Kate said truthfully. It was so spacious, so calm, so spare. She had never been anywhere quite like it.

"I like *space*," the old woman said emphatically. "When my parents lived in this house, many years ago, it was crammed with antiques. Stuffed with hideous old tables and gloomy old portraits. Antique clutter everywhere—coats of arms, vases, pictures, candle sconces, fussy little mirrors, ormolu clocks. Horrid painted cabinets, chairs too rotten to sit on, four-poster beds you couldn't sleep in for fear of the assassin's dagger."

Kate smiled. Now what interior designer did *that* remind her of? "What happened to it all?"

"I got rid of it, of course. It was all rotting, gathering dust. I did not want to live with it. So I sold everything. The family was not happy, but I told them the house had been left to me, not to them, and I could do what I wanted. And what I wanted was a place to hang my paintings, which I'd been collecting for years. . . ." She paused and fumbled for another cigarette. "I didn't want furniture. With paintings like this, who needs furniture? Or anything else, come to that."

Speak for yourself, Kate thought. She would now have cheerfully killed for a coffee.

"I am very fond of England," the Comtesse remarked, apparently apropos of nothing.

"You've visited it?"

"Many times."

The old woman proceeded to ask a barrage of questions about her background and life in Britain. Kate answered carefully, unwilling to give the Comtesse cause to look down her aristocratic nose at the eccentricities of life on the *Mockery*. She ducked and dived queries as best she could to create—she hoped—a gracious impression of genteel parish journalism in the kind of fete-holding village that featured on fudge boxes.

The Comtesse paused in her interrogation to grind out yet another cigarette. "And now you are here in Ste. Jeanne, what do you plan to do?"

Kate avoided her eye. It was a good question.

"I hear you are a writer," the Comtesse probed.

"Yes." *How* had she heard this?

"What sort of writer?"

"Novels. Well, *a* novel."

"And you are able to make a living from *that*?"

Kate bridled. "I'm doing a few odd jobs as well," she said grumpily.

"Where?"

"Freelancing for the *Riviera Gazette*."

"The *Riviera Gazette*!" It was obvious from her tone that Crichton's mighty organ did not command the Comtesse's respect.

There was a silence. The old lady crossed the room to examine the nude of herself again.

"I asked you into my house for a reason." She turned from the picture so swiftly it made Kate jump. "I would like to give you a job. A part-time one. To support your writing."

Kate blinked. Coming from left field, the offer was entirely unexpected. "Wow. Well, that's . . . *great*!"

"You haven't heard what it is yet. It isn't very glamorous. I need a cleaner. Can you clean?"

Kate grinned. Could she clean? Did not vinegar and a toothbrush remove limescale from taps? Did not a cut potato help with burn marks on carpets? Had she not attended the Wits End Academy of Cleaning, the foremost institution of its kind in the world? Whose sparkle-endowing, grease-removing graduates even the gruffest and most gimlet-eyed of aristos would find possible to fault. "Yes, I can clean."

"Good. There are many rooms in this house, which become very dusty and I can't get around like I used to. I miss quite a bit of the dirt."

Kate looked assessingly round. No furniture to speak of; you could whizz round with a duster in minutes. "No problem. I'd love to. Thanks."

"I heard you needed a job," the old woman said gruffly. "You helped me when I had fallen. One good turn deserves another, as the English say."

But *how* had she heard? Was the Trout the source of all this information? She had no doubt heard the discussions in the bar. Or one of the others had.

After times and pay—generous—had been agreed, the Comtesse led the way down the stairs. Kate turned outside the door. "Er—thanks." But the door had already been shut.

She crossed the Place de l'Eglise in a rare mood of self-congratulation. Really, she had done rather well. Having woken this morning with no job at all she now had what might prove to be two. With Gran's largesse thrown in, she should be able to support herself quite comfortably whilst cracking on with *Northern Gigolo.* So cheering a thought was this that she even risked a smile at the five old ladies sitting on the long wall that formed the arcade step. They looked back archly and inclined their heads. "*Mademoiselle.*"

The church clock chimed half past five. Kate looked excitedly at its black-and-white face. She had a job and her date with Fabien was in half an hour. This was turning out to be a lucky day.

Kate stood before the mirror, fighting with her hair and trying not to look at the full, depressing extent of her reflection when a knock shook the door of her hotel room.

"Coming," she muttered through a mouthful of hair grips, glancing, panicked, at her watch. Ten to six, her outfit unfinalized and only half her makeup on.

Celia's head poked round the door. "Oooh! Going somewhere, darling?"

"Well, yes."

The sight of her friend made Kate feel more unkempt than ever. Celia's eyes sparkled, her hair shone, and she radiated the bouncy, boundless optimism of a particularly upbeat shampoo ad. She strode into the room with a Mallory Towers rambunctiousness and flung herself on to the bed. "Lucky you! I *am* envious!"

"But you've got High Street Ken," Kate pointed out. She felt stiff with stress: while top-to-toe glamour in less than thirty minutes had always been unlikely, ten minutes with her makeup bag had not seemed an impossible dream. Until now.

"Now and then I have, darling. But he's throwing himself into his search. Out being mysterious practically all the time at the moment. You know what he's like. A little bit woo, a little bit wah." Celia smiled indulgently.

"Celia, I'm sorry, but . . ." Five to six, with one eye to make up, lipstick to apply, and no firm decision made about which creased and slightly damp garment would best pass muster. Kate looked pleadingly at her friend.

"Who are you going out with?" Celia's fair face darkended with suspicion. "Not that bastard of an ex of yours?"

"No." Kate peered, suddenly horrified, into the mirror. Was that huge black spot on the glass or on her forehead? "It's just someone I met in the village."

"*Really?*"

"Yes. And the thing is," Kate looked at the clothes Celia was now rather unhelpfully lying on, "I'm trying to get ready and—"

"Yes, yes, but I've got some *news,* darling," Celia broke in. "You'll never guess what I've been doing. Well you won't, so I'll tell you. *Only* getting us jobs."

"*Jobs?*" The mascara wand shook in Kate's hand.

"I've found the perfect ones for us both." Celia beamed triumphantly.

Kate chewed her bottom lip in alarm.

"Don't you want to know what as?"

What she really wanted to know, Kate thought, was how to break the news that, having two jobs already, she didn't need another. "Er . . ."

"Okay, I'll tell you. As barmaids and waitresses."

"Celia, the thing is . . ."

"Working *here!*" Celia drummed her hands on the bedspread in excitement.

"*Here?*" Kate yelped. "At Fawlty Tours? You *are* joking."

Celia sat up. "I'm not, darling. I've spoken to the old boy—Pappy. You know, the one Nicole was throwing her jugs at."

Kate nodded. The thought of Nicole led immediately to that of Fabien. Last seen, she had been thrusting her jugs at him as well.

"We're replacing Nicole," Celia said proudly.

"What—both of us?"

"I told Pappy he could have two for the price of one, seeing as we both needed work. I wouldn't say he exactly jumped at the chance, but then he *is* rather ancient, poor darling."

"Er . . ." Kate opened and closed her mouth.

"Knew you'd say that, darling. But just hear me out, will you? This place is a gold mine. Once we get our hands on it, old Fawlty Tours will be Fawlty no longer."

Kate continued to look doubtful.

"It just needs a bit of help, that's all," Celia urged. "The ingredients for success, as it were, are all here. The food's amazing, for a start."

"Well, yes." Kate had to admit this was true.

"And the location's just fabulous, right in the middle of the village. With that *incredible* old interior in the bar."

"If you mean they haven't had the decorators in since 1600. . . ."

Celia waved a dismissive hand. "Never heard of shabby chic?"

Never heard of it? Kate looked balefully at her wardrobe-door reflection. I *am* it.

"People in Knightsbridge pay interior designers a fortune to have their houses look *exactly* like the bar downstairs."

More fool them, Kate thought, the image of Marc de Provence flitting across her subconscious.

"And of course there's the arcades bit outside as well. Arches, passageways, romantic shadows. Bags of atmosphere."

"Ye-es." The Trout was certainly a bag of atmosphere.

"Potentially it's *fantastic*," Celia enthused. "If it looked a bit more welcoming, people would come in droves."

"That's a big if." The minute hand on Kate's watch was creeping toward six.

"So when we take over as the new front of house we make it look better. Put checked cloths on the tables. Candles and flowers and things. We could even," Celia added wickedly, "*smile* every now and then. We'd be brilliant. The perfect team. The Thelma and Louise of the restaurant trade."

Kate's toes started to curl uncomfortably. "You're serious, aren't you?"

"Course I bloody am. I need a job if I'm going to be able to stay here. God knows there's nothing for me in London—apart from being financially bled to death by my solicitor, of course. And you need a job too. Don't you?"

"Look, Celia, I'm not sure . . ."

"*And* we'd get all the trade from across the square," Celia was wheedling. "People only go to the Café de la Place because there's nowhere else. Wouldn't you just *love* to see that place lose all of its customers?"

"Of course I would. But . . ."

"But what?"

*But I don't need three jobs.* Three jobs, besides sounding uncomfortably like hard work, would mean zero time to write.

"So you agree that we could transform the place?"

Kate stared at her watch in horror and at her friend in exasperation. "I agree that *someone* could. . . . Oh hell, Celia. You win. Count me in. I'd love to."

Celia clapped her hands. "Fabulous, darling! But are you really, *really* sure?" She peered solicitously at Kate. "After all, I'd *hate* to push you into anything you didn't want to do."

"You're not, honestly," Kate said. "Couldn't think of anything better. And now, I'm sorry, but I *really* have to go."

17

Kate emerged into the square to make the irritating discovery that she needn't have worried, rushed or skimped on makeup. Fabien was nowhere to be seen. Children scampered, dogs barked, people leaned out of windows, strollers walked in the evening sun. Her date, however, was not among them.

Was that car honking at *her*? Kate shaded her eyes with her hand and scowled in the direction of the driver. A tanned arm rose in salutation from behind the white-leather–covered steering wheel. "Kate!"

"Fabien?"

It was a surprise that an impecunious artist had a car at all. Let alone a beautiful ice-blue Mercedes vintage convertible with whitewall tires, its bodywork gleaming in the evening sun.

"Hop in." He leaned over and pushed open the car's long, shining door.

Kate caught sight of herself in the wing mirror. In the end she'd stuffed her hair into a ponytail and hoped it looked like simple chic. She had crammed on her sunglasses in the hope that they would do the work her sketchy makeup couldn't. They were scratched and held together at one side by a tortuously-bent paper clip. Hardly *La Dolce Vita*. Nonetheless, she climbed excitedly into the stitched cream leather interior.

"What a gorgeous car! I had no idea that—" She stopped, sensing she was about to be tactless.

"That a penniless painter would have one like this?" Beneath his sunglasses, Fabien's face split into a grin. "Actually, it isn't mine. It was lent to me by a friend."

Kate immediately wondered who. Fabien had some stylish pals, obviously. "It's very glamorous."

He looked pretty glamorous himself. He had clearly made a considerable sartorial effort. His wet hair was flattened determinedly down and his rose-pink shirt even revealed a nodding acquaintance with an iron. The color showed off his tanned and wiry forearms, just as his sunglasses accentuated the fineness of his features. He obviously never ate, yet his whippet leanness suited him. Artists needed to be skinny anyway. It went with the territory; the burning eyes, the midnight oil, the general creative intensity.

"Ready?" Fabien swung the Mercedes out of the square. Past the staring, muttering old ladies and past someone else just rounding the bend into the *Place*. As Fabien shouted a greeting, Kate looked up from the low seat to meet the gaze of Nicole. She may have been imagining it, but for one brief moment she had the feeling Nicole wanted to leap in the car and scratch her eyes out.

"Nicole looks pretty cross," she remarked casually.

Fabien was weaving through pedestrians on the rue du Midi. None seemed remotely aware there was a car behind them until its bonnet was practically nudging their buttocks. Then they jumped, parted like the Red sea and stared at the Mercedes and its occupants with a mixture of indignation and admiration.

"*Comment?*" Fabien was now negotiating the steep cobbled road leading down out of the village.

"Nicole looks cross. Furious, in fact."

"Nicole's always cross. You heard how she left the Hôtel des Tours? Smashed the bar into pieces. Hit old Pappy the patron!"

"I remember. I was there." What's more, Kate groaned to herself, I'm replacing her.

"Don't worry about Nicole," Fabien advised. "She's *complètement folle* . . . completely mad. She just likes drama."

They had reached the front of the village. Kate's attention was immediately caught by a row of hoardings by the side of the road advertising an enclave of executive homes.

"What's that?" she asked Fabien.

"That?" He looked at the hoardings and grinned. "Les Jardins des Lavabos."

"Les Jardins de . . ?" She frowned. "*Lavabo*—washroom, isn't it? The Gardens of *Toilet?*"

Fabien, eyes back on the road, sniggered. "Their real name is the Jardins de la Lavande—Lavender Gardens. But there's been some trouble with the plumbing, specifically the sewage system." He slowed down slightly. "Have a sniff."

Kate inhaled. A ripe, sulphurous pong hung over the road. "Yuk."

"It tends to be at its worst at this time of day—the warm evenings. Just when anyone who lives here would be sitting outside in their gardens."

As they passed on the road beneath them, Kate squinted at the hoardings. All were covered in blown-up photographs of the properties in the Jardins des Lavabos, along with fulsome descriptions of the joys of living there. Despite the phrase *exclusive individual styling* featuring repeatedly, each house looked exactly alike. Each featured a sweep of cakey yellow-brick drive and was large, boxlike, bulging with vast bay windows, and extraordinarily hideous in all respects. But more extraordinary was the general resemblance to Slack Palisades. This estate could, Kate thought, have been its twin. "Who lives there?" she asked.

"No one."

"*No one?*"

Fabien shook his head. In the force of the breeze over the windscreen, clumps of hair were peeling up from where he had flattened them down. "Apart from the developer and his wife, that is. They've had enormous trouble selling the houses."

"Because of the smell?" Kate asked.

He nodded. "And it's not the only thing about the place that stinks. It's built on land that was supposed to be protected. The developer bribed the Planning Department of the Council, or so everyone says."

Kate's mouth dropped open. More and more like Slack Palisades.

Was there also the Gallic equivalent of Freya Ogden marching up and down waving a placard? A French version of Mrs. Hardstone?

Something stirred in her memory. Something Fabien had said at the party at Cap Ferrat. She pictured the aggressive, greasy-haired tycoon standing with Champagne D'Vyne. The giver of poker parties. "Is Toilet Gardens the estate whatsisname . . . Marty St. Pierre . . . built?"

"Yes."

The shining blue car drove on. This, Kate thought, was the life. The kind of South of France glamour she had anticipated, but which had so far been in short supply. The afternoon sun was fierce on her face, but the slight breeze behind the windscreen took the heat out. She settled back against the pale leather, stretched one arm out along the top of the door and smiled into the wing mirror.

They had now reached the road that ran alongside the sea. As they flew past the glittering expanse, Kate gazed at beaches bristling with sunshades, refreshment vans, men in thongs, and women in bikinis.

They turned off at Antibes. As Fabien drove through the harbor, Kate was entranced by the expanse of liquid silver reflecting a forest of boat masts.

"I've never *seen* sea that color before," she breathed. Actually, she hadn't seen the sea very much at all, certainly not more than once a year. Slackmucklethwaite's cartographical coordinates meant it occupied one of the spots furthest removed from water of any in the British Isles.

"Antibes is famous for its light," Fabien explained, drawing her back to the colorful, hot present. "That's why so many painters choose to work here."

They drove slowly on through the port area. Couples of all shapes and sizes were seeing and being seen. Dressy twosomes looking for supper; the men casually smart in sockless loafers, the women gilded at ear, heel, and handbag. Swarthy deckhand types with curly hair and Australian accents. Big pink-skinned Germans and white-fleshed Brits. Tall and tanned and young and lovely local teenagers. Many of the women, she noticed, were staring at Fabien with interest.

Leaving the port behind, they swung under the archway into the pretty, pale old town. "Where Picasso worked." Fabien pointed upward to the creamy ramparts of a castle, where a line of emaciated iron figures looked endlessly out to sea. "He used the Château d'Antibes as his studio."

"Lucky him," said Kate. As places of employment went, the thick-walled fortress looked as romantic as it got.

The car sped along on new black tarmac that rolled velvet-soft beneath the tires. Behind the high walls and spike-topped security gates they were now passing, odd glimpses could be seen of bulging, balconied, ice-cream–colored Belle Epoque villas, rioting with moulding and shutters.

"Wow," sniffed Kate. "You can almost smell the money."

"People live like gods round here," Fabien said. "These houses are some of the most valuable in the world."

They drove on. The villas became bigger and even more elaborate, the roads shadier and softer, the palm trees thicker. Kate strained to see through gates and up drives, but Fabien was moving too quickly.

Twisting to peer through a gap in a particularly scintillating wall, Kate noticed a shining black limousine gaining on them rapidly.

"*Merde*," Fabien said softly, peering into the rearview mirror. "A bottom-sniffer."

"A what?"

"It's what we call people who drive right up your bottom to try and frighten you into going faster. People do it a lot in France, people round here especially. There are a lot of arrogant bullies on the Côte d'Azur."

"How awful." Kate was not impressed. "What if you're a learner, or an old person or something?"

"Quite." As the limo loomed closer, Fabien looked at her with twinkling eyes. "But there's a way of dealing with them, don't worry. Hold on tight."

She expected him to zoom off; instead he merely reached over and let down the lever holding the back of her seat up. She gasped as she landed flat on her spine, chin level with the dashboard. Then Fabien let his own seat down; thus prone, his long arms still firmly on the steering wheel, he piloted the vehicle along.

The limo behind honked frantically. "This always makes them furious," Fabien chortled. "From behind it looks as if no one is driving."

"But no one is," Kate pointed out, panicked. "You can't see where you're going."

"Don't worry, I only do it for a few seconds." By Kate's watch, however, it was almost a full minute before Fabien decided he had, as he put it, trimmed sufficient years off the limo driver's life expectancy. He turned into a side street. Parping furiously, the large black car shot past. Kate had a vague impression of someone with a beard staring apoplectically out.

They carried on at their former speed. Seat back up, Kate looked out at the soft blue sea and up into the soft blue sky where stars were gathering. Hanging high, waiting for its cue, was a fragile membrane of moon.

Eventually Fabien slowed down and drove the Mercedes through a pair of tall iron gates. At the end of a wide tarmac drive spread a small château painted in the palest of grays and surrounded by dark-green trees. In front, a flight of wide, shallow steps led up to a glassy entrance glowing with light.

"Here we are," Fabien said casually. "The Hôtel du Roc."

Kate stared at him with round eyes. "This is a hotel? It looks like a palace."

"Well it is, sort of. They wash and press all your clothes when you check in and give them back to you wrapped in tissue paper. Every room comes with a servant who wakes you up in the morning, picks your clothes up off the floor, and draws you a scented bath. You don't even have to dry yourself afterwards—they drape an armchair next to the tub with a huge fluffy towel so all you have to do is climb out and sit there."

"Heaven!" sighed Kate. And how unlike the home life of her own dear Fawlty Towers.

"*Bonsoir, Hubert!*" To Kate's astonishment, Fabien greeted the gray-uniformed flunky looming to open the door on her side. "They park the cars for you in an underground car park," he told her. "The manager thinks it spoils the aesthetics to have them in the drive at the front."

"What, even if they're as glamorous as this one?"

"Believe me, this will be the cheapest one in the garage. Although admittedly probably the nicest." He cast an eye in the mirror at an egg-yolk-yellow Ferrari being driven through the entrance by a small and balding man. "But it'll be even nicer when we get it back. You see, they wash the cars as well."

Hubert disappeared with the Mercedes. As Fabien piloted her up the steps into the golden-lit, marble-floored lobby, excitement and fear swept her equally. The people milling around all exuded monied confidence. They looked, Kate thought, as if every last hair on their head had been washed and dried individually.

"Do you come here a lot or something?" she asked Fabien, faintly incredulous.

"My mother stays here when she comes to see me. This is the real reason why I'm a penniless artist."

"What—you pay for her?"

"No, but she adores cocktails in luxury hotel bars. And now, thanks to her, so do I."

Of all the things Kate had heard people blame their mothers for, this had to be the most stylish. "Your mother must be very glamorous."

He did not deny it. "But I am a great disappointment to her. She wanted me to work at the Bourse—you know, the Parisian Stock Exchange—so I would become rich. She was horrified when I decided to become an artist."

As he steered her across the lobby, Kate had a fleeting left-to-right impression of white sofas, high, carved ceilings, large lamps with pleated shades, and a glittering bar where men in white jackets were busy shaking and pouring. She passed a number of large, illuminated cabinets that seemed filled with shoes and diamonds. Then it was outside again, into the warm evening air.

"Look at the view, Kate."

It was, she supposed, a back garden, but unlike any she had seen before. They stood at the top of a wide flight of shallow stairs, the twin of the one at the front. At its foot, a path as wide as a runway led down through emerald lawns to a glittering sea. Out of the sea rose a dramatic, jagged blue promontory.

"The Esterel," Fabien told her. "A small mountain range just to the right of Cannes."

"It's paradise," she muttered, under her breath.

"But the people are not angels," Fabien whispered, ushering her to a table-filled terrace under a white awning. "Which is another reason why I like it. I get lots of ideas for paintings from here. Drink?"

"Yes, please."

As they took their seats, everyone in the bar turned to stare. "They all think the next person to walk in's going to be George Clooney," Fabien murmured. "Or Elizabeth Hurley. Because it's the film festival and they stay here."

"Really? Are they here now?"

Fabien shrugged dismissively. "I'm not interested in *them*. What I really like," he hissed, putting his mischievous face close to Kate's, "are the not-famous people who come to a place like this. The strange couples. You can't imagine what brings them together. Well, actually, you can, as it's always the same two things."

Kate looked around the terrace. A corpulent, sharp-eyed man in his sixties was watching a girl who looked like a teenage Bosnian pop star gulp down something bright pink and fizzy. At another table, a bored-looking Lauren Hutton look-alike pored over a wooden chess set with an obviously wealthy old man. "What two things?" she asked.

"Sex and money, of course." Fabien flicked his eyes toward the couple immediately in front.

A fashionable young man with elaborately messy blond hair was sipping champagne with a woman resembling an aging Bette Davis. Kate was fascinated by the drawn-on eyebrows, red lipstick, emphatic rouge, and impossibly skinny ankles in impossibly high heels. "It could be his grandmother," she whispered doubtfully.

Fabien shook his head.

"You think he's a *gigolo*?" It was all Kate could do not to squeal. An in-the-flesh version of her fictional hero. She stared hungrily, taking in every detail. The inaudible, sketchy conversation. The young man's smooth face and smooth, absent smile, of the kind that never reached the eyes.

A white-jacketed waiter blocked her view. "Monsieur? Your usual?" he enquired gravely of Fabien.

"Yes, please, Antoine."

"And Madame?"

"I'll have what he's having."

The waiter returned with a tray and began to unload enough olives, nuts, and salted crackers to feed a small cocktail party.

Fabien's usual turned out to be a large, frosted champagne cocktail in a long-stemmed glass boiling with bubbles. On top, exactly fitting the glass's circumference, was a thin circle of lemon rind. Kate sipped and felt the potent, freezing alcohol burst in her empty stomach like a bomb.

"Wow. It's got a kick like David Beckham."

She held up her glass, looking through chill-beaded crystal at the gold-blooming evening sky. She steeled back against her white-cushioned chair and breathed in the mixed scents of grass, sea, strong perfume, and the ever-present, indefinable scent of glamour and wealth.

"You see?" Fabien lit a cigarette contentedly against the white cushions of his chair. "There *is* more to the Riviera than the Café de la Place . . . what's the matter?"

Kate's mouth had dropped open with shock. The Bosnian pop star and her elderly friend having, amid much giggling, got up and gone, a new couple was being shown to their table. A very short, very fat, and very annoyed-looking man dressed entirely in black with greasy gray hair, accompanied by a fragile blonde. She realized immediately who had been following them in the black limo. Newly arrived on the terrace was Marty St. Pierre, movie mogul, poker-party host, and builder of unsuccessful luxury estates. Looking, it had to be said, furious.

Clearly it wasn't only a bad development he had in common with Peter Hardstone. A bad temper figured as well.

And the resemblance didn't end there. St. Pierre's wife, up close, was strongly reminiscent of Mrs. Hardstone. She too was a fully-paid-up graduate of the mutton-dressed-as-lamb school. Her face was thick with foundation and her hair blazed with blond highlights. obviously the work of an expensive colorist. Twenty years ago she had probably been pretty in a big-eyed, delicate sort of way, but time and gravity had loosened her jawline and further receded an unremarkable chin. Her manicured hands glittered with diamonds and her jeans, worn with a T-shirt on which *Popbitch* was spelled out in rhinestones, were low-slung and designer-distressed. A tiny denim jacket completed the ensemble.

A waiter came shimmering over. "You're having dinner here tonight, Monsieur St. Pierre?" His professionalism was faultless. Yet Kate had the ghost of a suspicion he would have given much for the reply to be in the negative.

"Yeah," roared the fat man, chomping on a cigar the size of a small tree.

"Could I ask you to look at the menu?"

"No, you fucking can't. You can fucking well wait. We're expecting another guest anyway."

"We *are?*" said his wife in surprise.

The waiter shimmered away. Mr. and Mrs. St. Pierre began to argue in low, urgent voices. Finally, Marty removed his cigar. Smoke streamed from his mouth like ectoplasm. "Fucking shut up!" he roared at his wife.

Fabien raised his eyebrows.

"Champagne," Marty shouted to the waiter.

And so she came. Right on cue, striding confidently on to the terrace, tossing her platinum hair and honking loudly into a small silver mobile. The person in the world Kate least wanted to see. After Nat, that was. Rigid with apprehension, Kate gazed over Champagne's exposed and shapely shoulder. But no handsome, treacherous head emerged from the entrance on to the terrace. Champagne had arrived alone.

Kate slipped on her sunglasses, determined not to be recognized. As the sun had now dropped behind the mountains, Fabien gave her a puzzled glance, but was too busy demolishing his cocktail to ask questions.

She felt relieved, but slightly thwarted. While part of her never wanted to see Nat again, the other itched for a furious showdown, a chance to humiliate him as he had humiliated her. So where was he? The party had, after all, been only a couple of days ago; he was bound to be still in the area exploring routes to superstardom. Possibly, Kate thought sourly, he was doing a screen test that very second.

"It's her!" Fabien hissed suddenly. "That woman who was wearing the black plastic bag at the party."

He was now staring unwaveringly at the blond goddess. She was, if it were possible, wearing fewer clothes even than usual. The negligible inches of flesh not on show were concealed in tiny denim shorts, a halter top in clinging magenta, and a pair of pink stiletto mules.

"I suppose you think she's beautiful," Kate said sulkily.

"A little obvious, perhaps."

"Over here, Champagne!" The fat man waved a plump hand.

The St. Pierres broke off their argument. "Marty! Darling!" Champagne trilled, clacking over. "See you later, big boy," she honked into the mobile. Kate scowled, having no doubt who the big boy was.

Mrs. St. Pierre shot her a glare like a blowtorch. "What's *she* doin' 'ere?" she demanded of her husband in a broad Essex twang.

"I'm here to talk about movie possibilities," Champagne honked grandly as she dropped confidently into a chair. "Work."

"*Work!*" exclaimed the mogul's wife. "The only work people like you ever do is get on the casting couch and open your legs."

Champagne tossed her flaxen hair. "I'm actually here to discuss a *part*." She threw Marty a glance so smoldering it could have caused a wet bonfire to spontaneously combust.

"I'll resist making the obvious joke," snarled Mrs. St. Pierre.

". . . in a possible new Marty movie," Champagne continued icily. "*Ruthless Bastards*."

"Sounds like typecasting to me," the other woman returned. "So what happened to the Bond film we all 'eard so much about?"

Champagne tossed her head disdainfully. "Oh, *that*. Actually, it didn't work out in the end."

"Because Bouncy Castle was all hot air. That's why."

Marty St. Pierre, who had taken a huge swig of red wine, now choked on it. It sprayed everywhere, leaving the table and its occupants looking like the aftermath of the St. Valentine's Day Massacre. He glared murderously at his wife.

Champagne, cleavage beaded with spitty red droplets, screeched in horror. "It was *not* hot air," she snapped, scrubbing furiously at herself with a napkin. "There were . . . *differences*. That's all."

"*Differences!*" The mogul's wife flicked red wine spittle from the corner of her eye. "You bet there were differences. I read about them in the *Hollywood Reporter*. Time differences—four hours between the director turning up on set and you finally appearing. Acting differences—what he thought was bad was what you thought was Vivien Leigh. And now, of course, a different Bouncy Castle, although the name's changed to Peachy Derrière. Britney Spears, isn't it?"

As even Fabien smirked at this and Champagne looked as if she could cheerfully batter the other woman to death with one of the empty bottles, Kate raised her cocktail to her lips, silently toasting Mrs. St. Pierre. The best evening of her life, she thought, had just got better.

18

Kate knocked at the Comtesse's front door as the church bells rippled a silvery nine o'clock.

Should she, she thought, suddenly panicking, have brought her own cleaning materials? Or would the old woman supply them? She felt heavy with exhaustion. Or perhaps with all the cocktail nibbles she had stuffed down the night before. She had lost count of how many times the white china dishes of crackers, peanuts, and olives had been refilled. She and Fabien had outsat all the other guests on the terrace at the Hôtel du Roc. To Kate's delight, following the Bouncy Castle debate, the St. Pierre party had descended into shrieking, acrimonious chaos and left soon after.

As the moon had risen in the sky, and the lights of the boats in the bay had rippled across the moving water, she and Fabien had talked. Or, to be more accurate, she had talked and he had listened. The third—or possibly the fourth—champagne cocktail had opened the anecdotal floodgates and resulted in a rundown of hometown life so full, colorful, and unexpurgated it had rendered Fabien practially speechless.

"This Eckmucklethwaites," he had mused at the end of the "Come on, Bishop, Light My Spire" story. "I would like to come and paint it."

"You should. It could do with it," Kate giggled, remembering some of the town's less pristine areas. "Joke," she added, as Fabien looked blank.

After he drove her back to the Hôtel des Tours, Kate ran up to her room, her heart in her throat and a chorus line in her stomach. It had been a perfect evening.

But merry nights, as Mum occasionally observed, made sad morn-
ings. And this morning felt very sad indeed. After a fitful sleep in
which she dreamed of cocktail shakers full of paint, Kate dragged herself painfully out of bed: dry-tongued, achy-headed and with her face
on fire from driving around in an open-top with no sun protection
whatsoever. The knowledge that the hours ahead would be spent
doing three jobs was not cheering. Kate had felt barely capable of
doing one.

The Comtesse's door, starting to open, yanked her back to the
present. The old lady, dressed in flowing gray, looked balefully out at
her, twitching the cigarette she held aloft.

The Comtesse did not bother with welcomes. She merely held the
door open for Kate to enter the purple-lit hush of the hall.

"This way." The Comtesse stalked up the green glass stairs. There
was, Kate saw, a third and even a fourth floor; a final set of shining
treads leading almost up into Chagall's purple roof.

The old woman paused on the third landing. "You will start with
the bedrooms. This is the main guest bedroom. Excuse me a moment," she added, as somewhere in the depths of the house a telephone rang.

Kate hovered on the threshold of the bedroom. Like the rest of the
house, the room was light, spacious, and serenely peaceful. Furniture
was minimal; a desk, a chair, a large white bed, and a door flush to the
wall that was probably a wardrobe. The wall opposite the bed contained a set of French doors whose drawn cotton curtains contributed
to the sense of hush. From outside, the strong sun pressed against
the panes.

The Comtesse could be heard talking animatedly downstairs.
Kate stepped across the floor, opened the doors on to a balcony and
emerged into the brilliant light. Immediately below, a spacious garden
blazed in the afternoon heat.

It was the tidiest garden Kate had ever seen. Thin, dark trunks of
pines rose elegantly out of grass as smooth and brilliantly green as a
billiard table. At the far end stood a group of what Kate guessed to be

modern sculptures, an unpainted concrete arch stuck here and there with colored tiles and bristling with what looked like marble rhino horns. An oversized fork of spindly black iron stood upright to the arch's left; to its right was a large pottery urn. Down the middle of the lawn ran a thin oblong pond whose bottom was tiled with elongated blue and black fish. Like the Comtesse's house, her garden was a temple to modern art.

Suddenly, the hairs lifted on the back of her neck. Fear trickled coldly down her spine. She felt certain someone was behind her, watching her. The Comtesse? She whirled around, breath held, expected to see the old lady framed in the doorway.

But no one was there. Only the purple light from the atrium bouncing off the shining wooden floor of the landing. She shot across to the door. Nothing. The someone—if someone there had been—had disappeared.

The Comtesse was mounting the stairs again, her breath rasping as she arrived on the landing. Kate found herself waved into another large room with a powdery smell of perfume. "My bedroom." Here, as everywhere else, the Comtesse's devotion to modernity was unflagging. The main piece of furniture was a huge bed covered with a white duvet. From floor to ceiling the walls held white bookshelves loaded with white-spined hardbacks. All, Kate was unsurprised to see, seemed to be about art.

"You will dust the books. And the TV. It gets very dirty with the mistral. The wind," the Comtesse added, as Kate looked blank.

"The TV?" She couldn't see a telly anywhere.

The Comtesse crossed to the bookcase, felt for something and pulled. Kate watched as the middle section of her art library slid back to expose a huge widescreen television on which the words *DVD* glowed in brilliant blue.

"You will also clean the bathroom." With another swift pull, the wall to the right of the bed moved back. Revealed was a large and shimmering chamber complete with basin, bidet, taps, loo, and a shower head the size of a dustbin lid. The expanse of white and silver, illuminated by sunken halogen ceiling bulbs, exactly resembled Kate's idea of a near-death experience.

"My wardrobe too. The clothes need shaking out to prevent moths."

The Comtesse clicked over to the one bedroom wall that had so far not revealed any secret. With a practiced tug, the shelves rolled away. In their place was a long rail of transparent suit bags on coat hangers. Each bag bore a neatly printed label sticking up above the collar on which was written a designer and a date. *Courrèges 1972*, Kate read, eyes roaming at random over the names. *Grès 1961. Chanel 1987. Cardin 1968. Schiaparelli 1955.* When it came to fashion, the Comtesse was obviously a hoarder.

"They all still fit me," the old lady said proudly.

But Kate was only half listening. She had spotted something. Mounted on the wall at the end of the room was a silver-framed photograph of a smiling girl. She wore a bikini and her blond hair blazed white fire in the brilliant sun. Her eyes shone wickedly, there was a jaunty angle to her chin: her bubbling laughter almost rang out of the frame.

"Who's that?" she asked the Comtesse. "Your daughter?"

The old lady's good eye bulged in fury. "*Me.* Me at the age of twenty-one. At the height of my beauty."

Kate shifted uncomfortably. What was she supposed to say? Any resemblance between the misshapen face before her and the perfect one on the photograph was impossible. Ridiculous, even.

"Oh yes," the Comtesse said softly, gazing at the image. "I was lovely then. Artists buzzed around me like flies." The anger had drained from her voice; she spoke almost dreamily. "I was the one they all wanted to paint."

Kate's stomach concertinaed with pity. The old lady was clearly a fantasist; a tragic victim of the delusions of age. Which possibly explained the elegant clothes. They must be part of the playact, props to support the illusion.

"I have made you a list to help you remember." The Comtesse produced some sheets of paper from her skirt pocket. "You will clean every item on it. It should be possible in the time."

She handed over what looked to be at least three closely written pages. "You'll find everything you need in the basement," she added.

At lunchtime, back aching, knees glowing, and fingers every bit as red and sore as her sunburned face, Kate finally left the Comtesse's house.

For all its pristine appearance—an optical illusion engendered by the expanses of sunlit wood and little furniture—the place had been thick with dust. A good quarter inch had lain atop almost every picture frame; it had been like spring cleaning the National Gallery. In the three allotted hours Kate had got no further than the second-floor sitting room. The upper floors, including the purple-lit fourth floor and the Comtesse's bedroom, would have to wait until next time.

Wearily she walked up the rue du Midi to face job number two.

She reached the *Gazette* offices to find Crichton already tipsy. "Hair of the dog," he sniffed, waving a glass in which a yellowish trace of pastis remained. "Bit of a heavy do last night with my Brummies."

"What happened?"

"You may well ask." Crichton produced his soft pack of Winstons, tipped one out, tapped down on the packet in his usual fashion, and lit up with the naked lady. "I had dinner with them at their hotel in Nice." Behind the fat puff of smoke, his eyelids drooped. "Turned out to be a bit of a drama in the end."

"Why?"

"Management told me that I couldn't eat there unless I put a tie on." *Sniff.*

"Couldn't you borrow one?"

"I did. Then I went into the dining room with it on." *Puff.*

"So what was wrong with that?"

"You tell me!" A slight but nonetheless sheepish note could be detected in Crichton's voice.

Kate looked at him suspiciously. "Go on."

"Well . . . *honestly.*" Crichton exhaled in sudden disgust. "Some people have *no* sense of humor."

"What else were you wearing?"

"Er, well, I was slightly squiffy at this point, I have to say." *Puff.*

"Yes. And you were also wearing?"

"Er, nothing." *Sniff.*

"Nothing!"

"Apart from the tie, of course." *Puff.*

There was awed silence as Kate tried to picture this.

"Pandemonium." *Puff. Sniff.*

"I can imagine."

"Clients loved it—very up-for-it bunch, I have to say. But the hotel management had a *slight* sense of humor failure. Bloody Frogs. Oh well." Crichton drained the last of the pastis. "Another day, another dollar. Or should that be collar?" He disappeared, snorting, behind another cloud of Winston.

With a mighty effort, Kate gathered her underslept wits about her. "Look Crichton, about our last meeting. You said you had a few pieces you might be able to hand over to me."

"Did I?" Crichton's hands were rubbing his grayish face and raking through his mad-composer hair. "Well, I think there *are* a couple of interviews lurking. One tomorrow, or is it today? Today, if I remember rightly."

"*Today?*" Kate looked at her watch. It left her next to no time to prepare.

The editor tipped out another Winston and tapped it against his packet. "Not a problem, is it? You're a professional journalist, aren't you? We pros can do interviews from standing starts if we have to. When I was on the *Times* . . ."

"Who's it with?" Kate interrupted, anxious to avoid another session of Down Memory Fleet Street.

"Hang on a minute while I dig out the bumf." Laying aside his unlit cigarette, Crichton plunged his hands into the pile of papers in front of him. Half of them immediately slid to the floor. "Got it!" he declared triumphantly. He squinted at the crumpled piece of paper. "Oh, actually, it's tomorrow."

"What is?"

"Your mission, should you choose to accept it," Crichton sniffed. "A homes piece."

Kate nodded. "Great!" At one time her heart would have sunk at the prospect of a cushions-and-all description of someone's lovely home. But just now, after her failure to get a single celebrity quote at the Cap Ferrat party, not to mention being fired by Denys Wemyss, her professional confidence was low. A little gentle reporting of this nature was about all she felt capable of. She had two other jobs besides this, after all.

"Whose home?"

"Mandi St. Pierre." *Puff.*

Who she had seen in the Hôtel du Roc last night. Giving Champagne D'Vyne a run for her money. "Okay," Kate said, interested.

"You know of Marty St. Pierre?" Crichton asked, applying the naked lady to the end of his cigarette.

She nodded. "The property developer. Owns that estate just outside the village . . . what does everyone call it? Toilet Gardens."

Crichton choked on his Winston. "*You're* jolly well-informed. How do you know it's called that?"

Kate grinned. "Ear to the ground. My job, isn't it? I'm a journalist, remember?"

She was half joking, but the glance Crichton now turned on her was entirely serious. He bent forward conspiratorially. "Can I trust you?"

Kate looked at him, apprehensively. "Well, you've given me some work, haven't you? That calls for loyalty in my book."

Crichton sniffed in satisfaction. "It's just that walls have ears round here."

She looked around. With all the crap Crichton had crammed on his shelves and hung from the walls on various nails and pinboards, there was no room for ears as far as she could see.

"Les Jardins des Lavabos . . . sorry, *de la Lavande,*" Crichton said, "is the most expensive private estate this side of Cap d'Antibes. St. Pierre's sunk a fortune into it. Lots of fortunes, in fact. None of which were necessarily his own."

Kate nodded. "And?"

"He wants the big English-speaking money to live there," Crichton added. "Wealthy Americans. Rich Brits looking for a place to retire, that sort of thing. Unfortunately, no one's biting."

"Because of the smell."

The editor nodded. "And that," he hissed excitedly, "is not the only thing that's whiffy."

"So I hear." By now Kate too was bent over the table, whispering like a plotter. "There's a whole lot of dodginess surrounding the planning, isn't there? Suspicions of backhanders in high places, building regulations bent out of shape, that sort of thing."

Crichton's eyeballs were straining at their moorings. "How the hell do you know that?" He banged the desk in a frenzy. "Don't tell me," he spluttered excitedly. "*You're* investigating him as well, aren't you?"

"*Investigating* him?"

"Oh, don't play the innocent with me! That's why you're here, isn't it? You're an undercover reporter, aren't you? Putting together a dossier on St. Pierre's activities. Are you working for Interpol? MIFive?" Crichton paused before adding, in tremulous tones, "The *Times*?"

"Of course I'm not."

"Oh, I know you can't tell me," he gabbled excitedly. "I know how these things work. It's enough to know that we're rowing in the same boat. Singing from the same hymn sheet."

"Eh?"

"We can work together!" He rummaged furiously in his desk and pulled out a battered file with a nuclear radiation warning sticker on the cover. He beamed at her proudly. "This is what I've been doing over the past few months." He patted the sticker. "Explosive stuff, this. St. Pierre's turning out to be the biggest crook this side of—well—the next biggest crook along this coast. And together we can expose him!" The grayness in his face, she noticed, had entirely disappeared. It now blazed with a brightness that could have been illuminated by the naked lady herself.

"Um . . ." Kate tried to get a word in edgeways.

"Fascinating," Crichton enthused.

"Er . . ." Kate blinked. Hang on a minute. This had been sold to her as a cushions report, not an international crime exposé. She was staying in Ste. Jeanne to write a novel, not get embroiled in some drunken conspiracy theory. Her serious reporting days, if not over, were certainly on hold. Not that she thought for a moment that Crichton was on to anything serious. But all the same . . .

"Look, Cricthon," she began, intending to explain all this. But the editor had built up a near-explosive head of steam: "It's all extremely dodgy. The land that the Jardins des Lavabos are built on was formerly an area of outstanding natural beauty. So how St. Pierre got planning permission to build on it is anyone's guess. Unless you work in the Nice Planning Department, that is."

Kate groaned. It was history repeating itself. Peter Hardstone and Slackmucklethwaite Council all over again. Darren would no doubt have had a fit. Whereas she merely intended to have nothing to do with it.

"And I've turned up quite a few interesting things, as it happens," Crichton added, patting the folder again. "What St. Pierre gets up to in terms of smuggling is outrageous. There's that unmarked white plane that lands at Nice Airport every Wednesday afternoon. I've been monitoring its comings and goings." His fingers danced once again over the cardboard. "And—"

"You want to know what's in it," Kate interrupted. She, on the other hand, didn't want to know anything about it. Still less, do anything. Being drawn into a story that planned to expose the full extent of St. Pierre's undoubted nastiness was something absolutely to be avoided.

"What *great* fun." Crichton was beaming at her. "You know, I've been *desperate* for someone to help me with this. Someone who, like me, knows their way round a proper crime story. Knows what they're doing."

"Crichton!" She spoke with force. Time to bring this conversation to an end. Time to tell him she wanted no part in his lunatic investigation.

"After all," he wittered on, "busting international crime rings is a tough job. Especially when you have to keep breaking off to take groups from Godalming to the Antibes craft market. But with you to help me it'll be like old times. On The *Times.*"

"*Hang on a minute . . .*"

"Such an *amazing* piece of luck," he gloated, "that the first job I had for you was an interview with Marty St. Pierre's *wife*! You'll be able to have a proper look round the Jardins. Really get you on the scent of things, that will—if you get my drift, ha ha."

"*Ha ha. Now just look, Crichton . . .*"

"But no doubt I'm underestimating you. You've probably done lots of groundwork already."

"*No I bloody well haven't!*"

"Never mind. No need to get upset about it—the best of us slip up from time to time. Here's the address, anyway." Breathlessly, Crichton passed a piece of paper so covered with grease marks and coffee rings that it was a challenge to make out what was written on it. "And you'd better take my folders of evidence too. Read through to where I've got so far."

"Look, I really don't think that will be necessary."

Crichton slapped his head hard with the palm of his hand. "Silly me, of course it won't. You'll have got as far as me and even further, I imagine."

Kate ground her teeth in frustration. What was the point?

"Well, if you ever need it," Crichton whispered conspiratorially over his desk. "If you ever want to know anything I've found out, the folder will be in here." He patted the drawer to the left of his chair. "All the folders are kept under the autobiography of Esther Rantzen—the best deterrent I could think of to stop people rummaging. Miles better than a lock."

Kate leaned forward. "There *is* one thing I want to know, Crichton."

"Anything." The editor's ravaged face was radiant with excitement. "Ask me anything!"

"*Why* are *you* investigating St. Pierre? What's in it for you? Apart from potentially a lot of trouble." It had occurred to her that a near-dipsomaniac eccentric hardly fitted the crusading reporter stereotype.

The editor's burning gaze dropped to the desk. "Well . . ."

"Go on."

"Okay." Crichton jerked his head up again. "You want to know?

I'll tell you." His faced ticked with tension. "Because if we, I, you, whoever, expose, St. Pierre properly it'll make international headlines. Editors adore stories about corruption and the Côte d'Azur. It'll be a sensation. All the London papers will be fighting to have me as a crime reporter. So it'll get me off this rag and back on to a proper paper where I belong."

Kate felt a twinge of sympathy. A mere few days ago, after all, she had been in exactly the same position.

"You will help me, won't you?" He stared at her beseechingly.

Kate groaned. At the bottom of her too-soft-for-her-own-good heart, she *did* want to help the poor old sod. And while instinct was warning her against getting involved, rationality pointed out that she needed the money. She may have three jobs but none of them—not even the Comtesse's—exactly paid beyond the dreams of avarice. She slid a glance at her watch. Her first evening shift at the Hôtel des Tours started in forty-five minutes.

"Okay," she agreed. "I'll do the interview. But that's *all*."

"That's the stuff." Beaming, Crichton reached into his drawer and produced a bottle. "Now how about a snifter to celebrate?"

19

"Do you have any tablecloths Madame Tr . . . Madame?" Kate asked the Trout. The first shift at the Hôtel des Tours was not going entirely to plan.

The plan had been Celia's—a five-minute team talk in her bedroom before the two of them had descended looking as clean, capable, and waitress-like as possible. Their mission, she instructed Kate, was to enhance the popularity of the restaurant by improving its appearance, which would in turn draw attention to its excellent cuisine. Due reward—both financial and through the heartwarming sight of reduced business at the Café de la Place—would then be sure to follow.

Kate had been on duty half an hour and hadn't even managed to set the tables yet. "*Des nappes?*" she repeated.

The Trout looked up from her eternal accounts book, sighed deeply and, with the air of one making her last gesture upon this earth, pointed to where, at the back of the bar, steps led down.

Kate descended gingerly into a cavern-like basement and found, in a neglected corner among some stacked chairs, a wicker chest. This, to her surprise and gratification, turned out to contain piles of clean, neatly ironed and thickly woven cotton tablecloths and napkins in bright primary checks. Clearly, at some time or other, *someone* had taken a pride in the restaurant tables.

She carried the pile of linen out into the arcades to shake out and air. Under the squat, cool arches the rich evening sun was slanting. Here, earlier, and without lifting a finger to help, Pappy watched her rearrange tables and rescue chairs from far-flung corners of the square. She had been vaguely encouraged by the fact that he had not stopped her, until it had struck her that he was going to send the Troll to do so. As yet, however, the Troll had not appeared.

But just as Kate shook out the first cloth over the first table, the familiar barrel shape loomed in the bar doorway. "Oh dear," murmured Celia. "Trouble at t'mill. Or should I say grill?"

To look at the Troll was to know he meant business. He wore, along with his customary fierce expression, a pair of shorts revealing diamond-shaped calves and knees the size and shape of cauliflowers. His folded arms as thick as Parma hams, he watched stonily as Kate and Celia continued to cover the tables. The standoff continued for some time before sulkily, eventually, he asked what they thought they were doing.

"Trying to make the place look better." Celia smoothed an expanse of red check with her hand. "And considerably better it's looking. Don't you agree?" She flashed the Troll a brilliant smile. The single thick line of disapproval forming his brow, however, did not lift.

Celia briskly shook out another tablecloth. "Actually, darling," she added to the Troll, "if you're not doing anything, I'd be *so* grateful if you could go into the kitchen and ask the chef for some knives and forks. I want to put them on the tables with the napkins."

Stand back, Kate thought, seeing angry amazement flare in the Troll's small eyes.

Celia left it a beat or two, then turned round. "Oh, and while you're at it, darling, bring some glasses. Glasses and candles."

The Troll looked astounded.

"Move it," Celia muttered under her breath. "We haven't got much time. Everyone'll be starting their evening totter around the village soon, deciding where they're going for dinner. We've got to look like a viable alternative to the wretched Café de la Place."

The church bell had just donged seven-thirty. A few passersby had already paused and looked interested. The Troll, however, did not move.

"*Mais c'est incroyable,*" murmured an amazed but familiar voice behind Kate. "Who has done this?"

Kate whirled round to look into the misshapen face of the Comtesse. Her stomach lurched with alarm.

"You have done this?" the Comtesse demanded, waving her beringed and painted claw at the tables under the arches.

Glancing over her shoulder, Kate saw that the Troll had switched his expression from hostile to expectant. The Comtesse, after all, was a customer as well as a long-established local. Her views on new developments would carry weight. She may, Kate thought, be a mad self-delusionist, but her disapproval could still spell disaster. She swallowed. "Yes. It was us. We did it."

Silence—or as silent as things ever got in the Place de l'Eglise. In the bar doorway, the Troll rocked expectantly from vast foot to vast foot.

There was a sharp noise. The Comtesse, clapping her liver-spotted hands. "*Mais c'est superbe,*" she croaked. "Look at it—tablecloths, napkins . . . *everything.* The restaurant hasn't look as good as this for years. Has it, Bernard?" She suddenly snapped at the Troll.

Bernard's eyes bulged. Under the old lady's topaz gaze, however, the yellow light of battle faded. "*C'est . . . différent,*" he conceded.

"All it needs is cutlery, glasses, and candles," Kate called to the Troll, forcing a dazzling smile across her face. "You wouldn't know where they were kept, would you?"

The Troll hesitated.

"Oh, I'm sure he does," the Comtesse chimed in. "He'll get them for you. Won't you, Bernard?" Bernard looked at first as if he had no intention of doing anything of the sort. Then, muttering darkly, he stomped off to the bar.

The old lady flashed Kate a conspiratorial grin. "So. This is where you work when you are not working for me?"

An exclamation from Celia interrupted Kate's reply. "You *angel*!" she cried as the Troll emerged with a furious expression and a bread basket crammed with cutlery.

"You are a very hardworking girl," the Comtesse told Kate. "I am very pleased with the way you cleaned my house today. Really, you did a fantastic job."

"Thank you."

A rattling from behind. The Troll was now carrying a tray of glasses and candlesticks that he banged down so hard it made Kate's teeth shake. "Bless you!" breathed Celia as he retreated and, arms folded, stared balefully from the bar entrance at anyone who ventured near.

"Poor Bernard." The Comtesse dropped her voice. "He is not very happy, I'm afraid. You see, he is unlucky in love."

Kate nodded.

"I would like to ask you a favor." The old lady fixed Kate with her one bright eye. "I have to go away for a few days. My sister in Paris is not well."

"I'm sorry to hear that," Kate said politely.

"Mm." The Comtesse acknowledged this with a nod of the head. "As you are obviously both reliable and trustworthy, I wonder whether I could ask you to move into my house while I am not here."

"Oh." Kate weighed this up. The old lady's house was certainly more comfortable than her room in the Hôtel des Tours. Those fascinating paintings. That wonderful, light spaciousness.

"I would be very grateful," the old lady pressed.

"Um . . ." Quieter too, a better place to work, particularly on the guest room balcony overlooking the peaceful garden.

"And I'd pay you extra, of course."

"Ohhh." And by moving out of the hotel room, she'd save a few nights' board into the bargain. All in all, probably too good an offer to pass up. "I'd love to."

"Good. I will be going early tomorrow. Move in whenever you like—you have the key." She smiled and clacked daintily off across the cobbles.

Celia sidled up. "Who's your friend, darling?"

"The old lady I told you about earlier. The one I clean for. She's asked me to move in with her."

"Wow. Doesn't hang about, does she? Ken's still at the bunches-of-flowers-giving stage. Bit old for you though, isn't she, darling?"

"Piss off. She wants me to move in to look after the *house*."

"You're sure, darling? Only all those nude paintings you told me about rather made me wonder."

Kate turned back to the tables which, now Celia had made the additions, looked very inviting. Equally inviting were the delicious smells drifting out from the kitchens. "Such a shame we haven't a *proper* menu," Celia complained, darting a glance at the Troll in the bar doorway. "Apart from him, of course. The human menu. If human's the word."

"And he's hardly a proper menu in any case," Kate pointed out. "There's a bit of difference between what people order and what they actually get here."

They looked at each other glumly.

"Oh well," Celia said brightly. "We'll get through somehow. The place looks better, anyway."

Kate had noticed something. "That couple over there!" she hissed, face aflame with excitement. "They look—*interested.*"

From the cobbled no-man's-land in the center of the square, two Scandinavian types were peering at the tables over rimless techno-spectacles. Kate and Celia smiled at them encouragingly. The couple glanced at each other, nodded, and came forward. Celia leaped exultantly to show them to as conspicuous a table as possible.

"Menu? Ah, yes," Kate heard Celia say in artificially bright tones. "I'll get Bernard to run you through tonight's delights." She looked nervously behind her.

The Troll barreled over, his face grim with purpose. Halfway through his growled rendition of what might or might not be coming out of the kitchens, the composed-looking couple's nerve finally broke. They got up and fled across the square to the Café de la Place. The Troll rolled impassively back to his sentry position in the doorway.

It was inevitable, Kate thought afterwards, that Nicole would make her entrance just then. At the lowest point of the evening, when the disappointment just suffered must have been writ large all over her and Celia's faces.

Tonight it was the sexy widow look. Glossy black hair bouncing on her shoulders, braless breasts clearly outlined by a shrunken black cardigan, Nicole slunk through the square like a lynx, her long brown legs barely covered by a tiny black skirt.

"*Bonsoir,* Bernard," She oozed in a low voice to the Troll. He had shot out of the bar entrance and was devouring her with his eyes.

"*Bonsoir,* Nicole," he said hoarsely.

"The business is doing well with the two English girls, I see." Her eyes rolled sarcastically over Kate and Celia.

The Troll shrugged. Beside Kate, Celia bridled. "Bitch!" she hissed.

Like any self-respecting femme fatale, Nicole was accompanied by a couple of shorter, plumper, plainer girls who acted as foils for her beauty. It was to these two that she now stopped and whispered something behind long, brown hands. All three giggled. Then, shooting the Troll a glance of teasing passion and Kate and Celia one of dislike, Nicole, undulating like a seahorse, flounced off.

"What's her problem?" Celia muttered crossly.

"God knows." Nothing compared to theirs anyway, Kate thought.

It was clear that, for all their determination and energy, the Restaurant des Tours was not going to be transformed overnight. More than a few check tablecloths would be needed to turn this particular tanker round. It was bums on seats that mattered and there was no getting away from the fact that the restaurant seats were resolutely bum-free. And looked set to remain so.

At the end of the evening, under the impassive stare of the Trout and Troll, she and Celia miserably removed the unmarked cloths and unused napkins. The night had not been a success. After the Scandinavians, a couple of apprehensive Germans had sat down, taken one look at the approaching Troll and immediately got up again and left. The only other diners to show interest were the mosquitos Kate had regularly to slap from her legs. Her white northern flesh was clearly the biting-insect equivalent of best foie gras. Or perhaps of the chef's poetic *pistou* soup, now sadly going to waste in the kitchen.

"It takes time for word to get around," Celia said with forced cheeriness as she threw the pristine cutlery back into the bread basket. Kate, however, suspected word *had* got round. The wrong sort of word.

"Good evening."

Both girls looked up from their work in excitement—a customer? Even a late one that they had to turn away would be something. But it was only the owner of the Café de la Place sauntering over and asking in pitying tones whether the image overhaul had improved business.

"Talk about putting the patron in patronizing," Celia muttered.

"We've had a lot of interest," Kate snapped loudly, determined to keep up the shop front.

"Ah, yes. *Interest.*" The weaselly café owner picked his teeth. "Not quite the same thing as customers, *non?* Between you and me, the kind of interest I find most useful is the sort that accumulates on my profits in the bank. Good night, ladies."


The gates of Les Jardines de la Lavande juddered open. Stretching before her was an avenue of blocky green hedge like the crumbly substance in which Slackmucklethwaite WI's flower-arranging class stuck carnations and chrysanthemums. Oasis, it was called. Gran had been puzzled but approving that a successful rock band had taken it as a name. "Perhaps they enjoy doing floral baskets," she had remarked at the time. "What nice and polite young men they must be."

These hedges may have replaced Hardstone's *leylandii.* And the weather was completely different—hot and blue instead of cold and gray. But in all other respects the Jardins des Lavabos, as the outside hoardings had hinted, were identical to Slack Palisades. Here, as there, were unlovely angles, cheap materials. Everywhere were brick drives, ostentatiously huge windows, garages big enough for a catamaran, chimneyless gray roofs made of ugly roof tiles, and a thick sprinkling of heritage lamps and weather vanes. And, hanging like a canopy over it all, a sulphurous stench so powerful it made her eyes water.

Kate had initially thought the site differed from its British counterpart only in the lack of gaping chasms in the lawns. But as she walked down the central artery, from which all the brick drives turned off at sharp and military right angles, she noticed a number of large, deep holes. Pipes were dimly discernible in the gloom at the bottom. Someone had evidently attempted at some stage to address the drainage question; just as evidently, there had been no answer. As at Slack Palisades, Kate was struck by the way in which the abused land had managed to wreak its own revenge.

As she walked, Kate looked apprehensively about for Marty St. Pierre. But there was no sign of a fat and frightening financier in an equally fat car; no sign of anyone, in fact. The place was every bit as deserted as Crichton had said it would be.

Using the logic of Slack Palisades, Kate knew that the biggest, ugliest house with the vastest garage would be the one she was looking for.

The front door was opened by a fierce-looking Filipina in an apron. "*You girl!*" the small woman stated accusingly.

"That's right," Kate confirmed.

"*Madame St. Pierre, she expecting man.*"

"Man?" Crichton had made the arrangements with Mandi. Had he had a brainstorm and said he would come himself?

"*House decorating man! Designer man!*"

"I've come to do an interview. I've nothing to do with design." Some confusion, obviously.

"*Madame St. Pierre, she in garden in ruin!*" the woman shouted, stabbing to the left of the house before slamming the door.

Ruin? Had she, Kate wondered, heard right? *Room,* possibly. Perhaps there was a summer house where Mandi had massages or did whatever developers' wives did all day.

She followed the direction of the Filipina's finger. It led across a concrete-floored patio crowded with white plastic furniture. She passed an electric-blue–bottomed swimming pool and a large outdoor clay oven whose bulbous base and tall flue were reminiscent of an enormous penis. The only thing moving was a large yellow oxygenator progressing up and down the pool in octopuslike fashion. Plus an automatic lawn waterer whose demonic thrashing twists made her feel anxious.

At the end of the patio, a border of closely planted cypresses stood up like Sitting Bull's headdress—intended, Kate supposed, to protect the pool from the prying eyes of next door. Except that, of course, no one lived next door.

A path ran between the trunks.

Kate followed it to find herself in a completely different landscape. A mass of light danced through silvery leaves. Sloping downwards away from her was a wide glade. Thick and twisted trunks of ancient olive trees rose at roughly regular intervals from untamed grass streaked yellow and red with broom and poppy. It had been an olive grove once.

Kate breathed in the sweet, herby scent of the place. It was magical and deserted. There was no one about at all. No Mrs. St. Pierre, no ruin, not as far as she could see. Kate was about to return to the house when she noticed, at the far end of the field where the olive trees clustered particularly thickly, what looked like a pile of stone.

Closer inspection revealed it as a rambling farm building, a small, partly tumbledown barn. A lizard shot across hand-hewn blocks the exact color of a golden Labrador and Kate thought how much prettier, even in their crumbled and broken state, these stones were compared to the mass-produced bricks of the Jardins des Lavabos.

The entrance was through a wide archway framed by an age-buckled pair of doors that must, Kate thought, have closed behind many a rickety farm cart. An older, slower, simpler Côte d'Azur seemed suddenly very close. Fabien, she knew, would approve.

She stepped into the cool interior. All was shadow apart from where shafts of sun formed pools of light through gaps in the tiles. In the center of the uneven earth floor was a huge, lumpy, Heath Robinson device—a wide pillar of wood and circular stones. Kate wondered what it was.

As she stepped forward for a better view, a stone dislodged itself from the darkness and fell on her flip-flopped foot. "Ow!" she yelped.

There was a gasp and a rustle from a part of the barn screened from Kate's view by a broken wall. "That you, Perseus?" demanded a high-pitched woman's voice.

"Is that *you*, Mrs. St. Pierre?"

"Yeah. Who's asking?"

"The *Riviera Gazette*. I've come to talk to you about your . . . er . . . lovely home."

A figure appeared. It just about *was* Mrs. St. Pierre, Kate saw, although a Mrs. St. Pierre markedly different from the incarnation on the terrace of the Hôtel du Roc. Whereas that Mrs. St. Pierre was all glitter, heels, highlights, and more makeup than an Essex vanity case, this one wore a baggy shirt, her hair scraped back in a ponytail, and not even a hint of lipstick. Under her arm she carried what looked like plans. There was a tape measure in her hands.

"My lovely 'ome?" Mandi St. Pierre demanded. "Where's that then?"

"Well—here, of course. The Jardins des Lav . . . I mean de la Lavande."

Mandi pulled a face. "Oh yeah. Forgot you was coming. From the paper, arntchya?" It seemed to Kate she looked at her with a suspicious expression.

"That's it. My brief is to write a very positive piece," Kate said, her smile suggesting she had heard nothing that cast Les Jardins de la Lavande and its creator in anything but the most pearly of lights.

Mandi put one hand on her hip and sniffed. "Well, it won't do any good," she said baldly. "No one wants to come and live in this shit'ole, and who can blame them?"

Kate hid her surprise by whipping out her notebook. That the St. Pierre marriage was not idyllic had been clear at the Hôtel du Roc. But that Marty's wife shared the general unflattering view of his luxury Côte d'Azur development was a surprise. Kate's sympathy with this woman deepened.

"Don't write that down." Fear flashed in Mandi's eyes as she saw the notebook. "Marty'll croak on the spot if 'e sees I've called it a shit'ole."

"Don't worry." Marty croaking on the spot was the last thing Kate wanted. Rarely had she seen a man on whom the words *painful lingering death* were written more clearly.

"Although from the way it niffs you can hardly call it anything else. No wonder the locals call it Toilet Gardens. Potty Park too."

Kate nodded. "The smell *is* a bit strong."

"Strong? Takes the inside of your bleedin' nostrils off. Down 'ere's the only place you can't smell it."

Kate sniffed. She had imagined the smell had faded because she had grown used to it. Unlikely though that seemed with an aroma of such force.

"All my fault thought, apparently," Mandi said crossly.

"What is?"

"The smell, everything. Marty blames *me* for the estate being a flop." She tucked a stray hair behind a small ear. "Says it were my idea all along to build 'ere."

"And was it?"

"In a manner of speakin'. We was drivin' through Provence a few years ago and I spotted a romantic tumbledown farm'ouse. It looked so pretty—all sunny stone and overgrown ivy an' all that—and I told Marty that I'd love to live there. So he bought the romantic tumbledown farm'ouse."

"Nice of him," Kate said, surprised to hear St. Pierre had a soft side.

"Not really. By bedtime the farm'ouse had been razed to the ground and plans were well under way to build bleedin' Potty Park. It were the land he was interested in."

"Oh."

"And *this* place," Mandi patted the broken stone wall at her side, "is all that's left of that romantic tumbledown farm'ouse. Which is why I'm 'aving it restored, even though Marty don't want me to. Thinks rebuildin' an old olive mill's a waste of time and money."

An olive mill. Which, Kate saw, explained the trees outside. And the Heath Robinson contraption in the center of the room must be one of those things that squashed the oil out of the fruit. She could see why Mandi wanted to rebuild it. It was a ruin, but a romantic one. And the setting—the silver leaves, the sunshine, the lush downward slope of the meadow—was idyllic.

"We're renovating the whole place an' puttin' new rooms in."
Mandi's face brightened.

"We? I thought Marty wasn't keen."

"He's not. But he's a bit . . . um . . . *distracted* at the moment." As
Mandi twisted her lips bitterly, Kate's thoughts flew to Champagne
D'Vyne. "So we're taking the opportunity to get on with it. '*We*' being
me and my designer, not that 'e likes to be called a designer. Says 'e's
an interiors visionary!" Mandi chuckled good-naturedly.

"What's his name?" Kate asked as a hundred loud bells all clanged
at once.

"Perseus Cholmondeley-Chatsworth."

"Oh." *Not* the stroppy friend to the stars she was expecting.

"Amazin' guy," Mandi continued. "Friends with all the local
celebs, 'e is. Whenever I see 'im 'e's just got back from lunch with
George Michael. Or tea with Joan Collins. Or cocktails with Elton. I
was lucky to get him. Stephanie of Monaco was *desperate* for him."

Kate did not comment. From what she could remember, the way-
ward Monegasque princess had been desperate for some fairly unlikely
people in her time. Perseus Cholmondeley-Chatsworth's celebrity address book, in any case, sounded suspiciously similar to Marc de
Provence's alleged links to Posh and Becks. Claimed intimacy with the
A-list was obviously a crucial part of international designer territory.

"Amazing name," Kate observed.

"Very grand. Ooh, 'e's very grand. Went to Eton and Cambridge
and grew up in a huge pile in Derbyshire with three hundred rooms.
Apparently it's got millions o' ghosts."

"Really?"

Mandi's strained expression spread into a smile. "There's a
haunted bog that flushes of its own accord. And when there's going to
be a death in the family, it flushes nonstop."

"I see." Kate was growing increasingly curious about this colorful
character. She hoped Perseus Cholmondeley-Chatsworth would turn
up soon.

"Being brought up in a stately home is what inspires 'is work, apparently," Mandi added. "Big sofas an' gold mirrors and silk curtains, all that sort of thing. Bit over the top for 'ere, I dare say, but I like it. Haute couture for the 'ome, he calls it."

That bell was ringing again. Kate looked at Mandi suspiciously. "What does Perseus look like? Does he," she asked tentatively, "wear *purple?*"

20

"Purple?" Mandi shook her head. "Nah, he looks very sort of . . . dunno. Like Sherlock 'olmes. I suppose. Very stuffy British sort o' look—apparently they love it round 'ere. Anyway, you can see it for yerself. Here he is now."

"Ahoy there, Mrs. St. Pierre!" boomed a voice straight out of P. G. Wodehouse.

As Mandi went out to greet him, Kate peered out of the olive mill's broken doorway. A singular figure was strutting through the sunny field. It wore a large red bow tie, a deafeningly loud mustard checked jacket, and matching plus fours. Incredibly, given the heat and the location, the ensemble was topped by a loudly checked deer-stalker with the flaps down.

"Sorry I'm late," the apparition remarked. "Bit knackered, I'm afraid. Didn't get back from Elton's party until gone two in the morning."

The nearer he got, the more overpowering was the effect of his jacket. Kate stared in open-jawed amazement. Was he for real? Admittedly, in this particular part of the world, reality was relative.

The figure stuck out a signet-ringed hand. "Perseus Cholmondeley-Chatsworth. How do you do." She sensed a chill in his voice. No doubt he had been expecting to find his client alone and resented having an audience. She peered at his face, but could make out little, except that within the shadow beneath the peak flashed a monocle.

"Aren't you hot in that hat?" Kate asked him.

"Not particularly," he returned stiffly. "It's quite cool, actually." This was belied by the fact that what could be seen of his face was obviously pouring with sweat.

"Take your hat off, Perry," Mandi urged. "Must be bleedin' boilin' under there."

The designer put a protective hand on his crown. "I'm afraid that's impossible. I've . . . er . . . got a rather bad attack of head lice."

"Head lice!" Mandi looked disgusted.

"That's right," Cholmondeley-Chatsworth said rapidly. "I got it off one of Hugh Grant's godchildren when we were all having lunch the other day. He insisted on trying the hat on. Kids, eh? Little buggers."

Kate looked at him disbelievingly. The truth must be that he was bald and didn't want to reveal it. Mandi sighed and looked down. "I wouldn't know," she said sadly. "Marty never wanted kids."

Kate felt a pang of pity. Looking at Cholmondeley-Chatsworth, she saw he was suppressing a yawn. Truly the cream on the top of the milk of human kindness.

"Anyway," Mandi said to him brightly. "I've been telling Kate what a design genius you are."

Cholmondeley-Chatsworth nodded abruptly.

"She's a journalist," Mandi added. "She'll be able to give yer a nice mention. You should give 'er one of yer cards. You're always saying you want publicity. Here's your chance."

Perseus Cholmondeley-Chatsworth hesitated for a second. "I don't have cards."

"Don't 'ave any?" Mandi teased. "Been givin' 'em away to all them celebrity friends of yours, 'ave you?"

"Something like that."

Kate looked at the designer in dislike. There was definitely something shifty about that gleam in his monocle.

"Think I've got one somewhere." Mandi frowned and rummaged in her jeans pocket. Producing a small and grubby piece of board, she shoved it into Kate's hand.

The card was cream and edged with a deep leaf-green. *Perseus Cholmondeley-Chatsworth, Englishman's Castle Style for Chic Châteaux,* it announced in flowing script. She suppressed a slight start.

Cholmondeley-Chatsworth regarded her from beneath the peak of his deerstalker. Why was he being so hostile? Or was she imagining it? Well, he wasn't going to get rid of her. Among other things she had an interview to do.

"Mrs. St. Pierre's been telling me about all the plans you have for her olive mill." she remarked.

"Really." His monocle flashed menacingly.

"Well!" Mandi, possible sensing the tension, beamed widely at Perseus and Kate. "I don't know about you two but I need a drink. Let's go back to Potty Park. I suppose," she added resignedly to Kate, "that I should show you round for this great article you're writing. About me lovely 'ome."

Whether Mandi's home was lovely or not depended, Kate supposed, on how one viewed the schizophrenic mix of styles inside it. The kitchen looked like Dr. No's bunker while the master bedroom was dominated by a color photograph the width of the wall in an enormously thick black-ash frame. Kate, assuming first the undulating orange curves were sand dunes, eventually worked out that she was looking at a colossally enlarged image of a woman's naked bottom. Was it, she wondered, Mandi's?

Shortly after the show-round it emerged that Mandi had to leave for the hairdresser's. The interview was at an end. Finding that Kate had arrived by bus and foot, Mandi suggested that Cholmondeley-Chatsworth give her a lift back to Ste. Jeanne.

"But I've got no business in Ste. Jeanne," the designer said rudely. *Very* rudely, Kate thought, for one allegedly brought up in a stately home. "*And* I've got to get over to Cap Ferrat. Andrew and Madeleine— Lloyd Webber, of course—are expecting me."

"Oh—don't worry," Kate was beginning to say. She really wasn't imagining it. For some reason the designer had taken an instant and savage dislike to her.

"It's only a few minutes out of your way," Mandi pointed out. "I'd take you myself," she added to Kate, "only the sylist is in Cannes, in completely the opposite direction. So I'll say me good-byes here. It's been lovely to meet you."

"And you," Kate smiled, meaning it.

"I'm parked round the back," Cholmondeley-Chatsworth huffed. They walked round in stony silence.

"Why does Mandi need a limo to go to the hairdresser's?" Kate asked chattily, watching a large, sleek black car with darkened windows crunching up the gravel drive. "Sounds a bit excessive to me."

Cholmondeley-Chatsworth looked pointedly at Kate's untidy mane of mouse. "Yes," he said shortly. "I can see that it would."

Parked round the back of Mandi's house was a small and scruffy van. Chatsworth bundled her almost physically in the vehicle. "Come on," he growled, in a voice suddenly more arc-welder than aristocrat. "I haven't got all bloody day, you know."

They lurched violently along the roads. Kate, in the absence of a seat belt, clung to the door handle and felt sick. Then, as they rounded a bend and the heaped roofs of Ste. Jeanne slid into view across the windscreen, Cholmondeley-Chatsworth cursed loudly and twisted the steering wheel violently away from an oncoming vehicle. His head collided with the rearview mirror. Kate yelped as they plunged into the verge, reversed violently and sped off in the opposite direction.

"What's the matter?" she demanded as the village receded behind them. "Where are we going—*Oh*!"

Cholmondeley-Chatsworth was busy steering with one hand and, with the other, cursing and grappling with his headgear that had fallen off in the argument with the mirror. He did, she saw, have hair after all. And not just any old hair either. It was short, brassy, and sticking up like a cockerel's. And there was no doubt, now the face was finally exposed, as to whom those small, shiny and rather spiteful features belonged.

"It's *you*, isn't it?"

He was driving even faster now, darting agitated glances into the skewed rearview mirror. "I don't know what you're talking about," he snapped.

"You're not Perseus Cholmondeley-Chatsworth at all," Kate accused. "You're Marc de Provence. *Aren't* you?"

He looked across at her. His face was contorted with indignation in exactly the same way as when she had last seen him in Slack Palisades. His teeth were bared, his eyes blazed, his jaw was angled at the same aggressive tilt. His cod French may have been replaced by cut glass; the purple Pimpernel transformed into Mr. Toad. But it was Marc de Provence all right.

She squealed with laughter. "It *is* you. Come on, I know it is."

"You can bloody well get out of my van. *Now.*" He skidded violently to a halt, reached over her and jerked the handle of the door. Within seconds, Kate found herself sitting with a thump at the side of the road. She picked herself up and dusted herself down, unhurt but very shocked. Could Marc de Provence have *really* pushed her out of what was practically a moving car? Because she had guessed who he was?

But this, of course, only begged another question. Why had he stopped being the hottest thing in French interiors since radiators and at the drop of a deerstalker become Perseus Cholmondeley-Chatsworth? With such an impeccable English accent, more to the point? Kate puzzled over this for a few dazed minutes, but came to no conclusion.

What she knew for definite, on the other hand, was that her instincts had been exactly right. Getting involved with the St. Pierres—even the apparently harmless Mandi—was a bad idea. She'd write the interview, file the piece, and then call it a day with the *Gazette*. Whatever Crichton said.

Her ponderings were interrupted by a vehicle screeching to a halt beside her. She looked up fearfully and found herself staring at a familiar, balding head.

"What you doin' 'ere, sweetheart?" Ken gave her a flashing gold grin. His sunglasses were circles of profound black in the middle of his large red face. "Sunbathin'?"

Kate looked at him warily.

"Wanna lift? I'm on my way back to Fawlty Tours."

Kate's instinct was to refuse. But the heat was beating down and the interior of Ken's car looked cool. Or as cool as a bottom-of-the-range rental with faux-denim seats and the legend *Blue-Jean's* on the back could look.

"What've you been up to, wandering about down 'ere in this 'eat?"

"Just out for a walk." Kate had no intention of telling Ken anything.

"Down there?" Ken gestured at the bushes at the side of the road.

Jesus, the man was nosy. "Yes. I was, um, looking for inspiration for my novel."

They drove along for a while without talking.

"Look," Ken said, turning to her, his hand gripping the gearstick. "About Celia and me . . ."

"It's none of my business," Kate said primly. Her insides were twisting with embarrassment.

"I know you don't approve, but . . ."

"Look Ken, I've only known her five minutes. And you even less. I'm hardly in a position to judge." Judged she had, however, as well she knew. He was not worthy of Celia.

The set of his mouth as he looked at her suggested he knew what she was thinking. His voice, when he spoke, was regretful, almost appealing. "Yeah I know," Ken said. "But she sets great store by what you think. So I was 'oping, you know, that we could be . . . well . . . friends . . ."

Kate closed her eyes. Her nerves, twanging already with in-transit ejection, were unable to sustain a nail-bitingly embarrassing conversation with a short and ludicrous Cockney. "Like I said, it's none of my business. You and Celia are both grown-ups." Although actually, she doubted the latter at times. Especially when they were together.

"'Ave it yer own way then." They entered Ste. Jeanne in frosty silence.

"'Ere you are," Ken said in a cold voice as he dropped her in the square.

"Thanks."

"Just one more thing."

"What?" Kate said suspiciously.

"That walk you was 'aving behind the bushes." His tone was sarcastic.

"What about it? It's a very inspiring spot."

"Yeah? Funny book it must be," Ken snarled. "Neighborhood garbage dump down there, that is." He drove off. She stared after him with dislike.

Kate decided to spend the afternoon making her move to the Comtesse's house. Once installed, after a quick whisk around with the duster, she could spend a few hours writing on the quiet garden balcony. The *Northern Gigolo,* she was guiltily conscious, hadn't seen action for days. On the other hand, she had managed to send off Gran's promised letter.

Kate packed and dragged her worldly goods some twenty or so yards across the cobbles to her new home, entered the house and closed the door quietly behind her. The hall was all violet hush; the noise, chatter, and light from the square sealed completely away. There was something about the smooth, modern space that seemed to eat noise; even the suitcase slid silently over the wooden floor.

Kate look doubtfully at the glass staircase. The chances of getting the case up them without damaging both herself and the treads looked remote; still, she could leave it in the hall. With the Comtesse away and the house to herself, there would be no artistic sensibilities to offend.

She jerked her head up suddenly. What was that? Something moving in the upper recesses of the house? She strained to listen, the silence singing in her ears. Nothing.

Jumpily, Kate glanced at the pictures. They glowed from the white hall walls, so many different eyes—some narrow, some exaggeratedly wide, some a single Cyclops stare—their expressions ranging from the curious to the challenging, the critical to the downright creepy. She grappled with her rioting nerves. They were only pictures. She was being silly. What she had heard was a squirrel running over the tiles. Or a cat. Or something.

In the bedroom, she turned her back to open the French doors and immediately felt the hairs rise on the nape of her neck. Twisting round to the doorway, she saw it was empty.

Unpacking her ancient sponge bag in the bathroom, Kate discovered huge, fat, new-looking towels and a bar of soap on the tubside that smelled deliciously of orange blossom. She examined her reflection in the mirror. Despite strenuous efforts with Mum's Vaseline, her face was peeling. She sighed. It looked unlikely that, as she'd hoped, it would settle down into a mahogany tan.

Then came a noise. A *definite* noise. A creak, a footstep, directly above her head. Kate caught her breath and gazed at her shocked reflection. Not a mistake this time. Someone—or something—was up there on the fourth floor. The purple-lit top floor where she and her duster had yet to penetrate.

Was it a burglar? Some casual thief who had seen the Comtesse leaving and decided to grab the opportunity? Her ears bongoed with the panicked pounding of her heart. Every nerve in her body urged her to run away. But the old lady had trusted her. With her house, with the paintings she loved. There was no choice. She had to go and investigate.

The door on the top landing looked blank and innocent. Kate put her ear to it and listened.

At first, she heard nothing but the thundering of her own heart. Then—yes—a sound. A scratching noise. Something sharpening its claws? Or a knife?

Kate placed her shaking hand on the doorknob. Her only weapon was surprise. She could look in quickly—before whatever it was could react—then shoot off down the stairs to raise the alarm. Suddenly, determinedly, she twisted the knob.

Her first impression was of a blaze of light, flooding in through windows that made up the whole of one wall. Her second was of a man standing in its center, pale-blue shirt glowing against his tan, smiling at her as if nothing could be more natural than his presence or her sudden appearance.

"Fabien!"

21

"You didn't know I was here?" He stepped back from his easel and looked at her in amazement. "Odile has not told you I paint here sometimes?"

"Odile?"

"Madame la Comtesse d'Artuby," he said smiling, putting down a pink-tipped paintbrush and rubbing his hands with a filthy-looking rag.

*Odile.* Kate's eyes widened slightly at this familiarity. "She didn't mention it, no." She felt the blood heat her flaking cheeks. "Well—perhaps she meant to but she kept rushing off to answer the phone. But she *did* say she'd heard I needed a job from a friend. Would that be you, by any chance?"

"I mentioned it to her, yes. She told me she needed someone to help her and I thought you would be just what she was looking for."

"I didn't realize you knew her."

"Yes. She loves art, as you have probably gathered. She encourages my painting." He clapped his hands, spread them wide, and bowed. "So, now you are here, come and have a look at my studio."

It faced the same direction as her balcony, over the garden and the roofs of the village. Yet in other respects, the wide, light attic room could not have presented a greater contrast to the rest of the orderly house.

It was cluttered beyond belief. Junk had fallen, junk on junk and had bred, so it seemed, yet more junk. Pushed up against a once-pristine, now heavily paint-smeared wall was a trestle table covered with piles. Piles of magazines, newspapers, hats, pens, a plastic—or so she hoped—skull and several large and dusty geological crystals. There were no chairs. Fabien didn't seem to go in for sitting down.

"It's an incredible mess," she remarked.

Fabien shrugged. "Artists are messy." He gestured around him. "A shame, perhaps. But it is like that." He picked up the plastic skull, tossing it from hand to hand. "Alas, poor Horace."

"Yorick," Kate corrected. Well, you couldn't really expect a Frenchman—not even one as cultured as Fabien—to be up on his Shakespeare.

He looked at her in surprise. "Yes. I know that, of course. But I call this one Horace."

Shoved untidily beneath the tables was a bundle of rags on which Kate guessed he wiped his brushes. Until she spotted, among the heap, the red shirt he had been wearing when they first met. "That's not your wardrobe, is it?"

He grinned. "I keep some of my clothes there. Messy, you see." Against another wall was a low daybed covered with a rumpled, grubby white sheet.

"Yes," Fabien said, following her eyes. "That sheet needs to be washed. It all does really. My hair most of all." It was streaked with purple paint. Kate thought of Darren and wondered how his bid for world domination was going. Swimmingly, no doubt.

Fabien didn't seem to go in for palettes either. His paints seemed to be mixed on whatever came to hand—plates, plastic bags, bits of old newspaper. On the floor and sideboard, a number of dusty candle stubs suggested that, on occasion, he painted through the night. A forest of brushes stood in jars on a filthy and paint-caked piece of furniture that might once have been a sideboard.

Spotting a row of jumbled canvases leaning unevenly against the wall, Kate took a delighted step forward. One was a half-finished image of a cock crowing lustily. She marveled at the way in which, with bold strokes of color and economy of line, Fabien had captured the very essence of vainglorious fowl. There was no actual image of sunshine, no barnyard, yet the cheerful chaos of a busy farm was somehow conveyed.

"It's wonderful," she breathed softly. "How incredible, being able to paint."

"But writing must be a lot like painting," Fabien insisted. "They're both about balance and form and rhythm. You have to structure a story just as you have to structure a painting. You have the contrast of light and dark just the same. Only you use words and characters, good and evil, funny and sad, instead of colors."

Kate's eyes were round. She had never thought of it that way.

"To do either well you have to put your whole self and experience into your work. You have to really live, really observe things," Fabien said.

Kate wondered if she had every really lived or really observed anything. It felt as if she was only starting to do so now.

"Drink?" He pulled a bottle of wine from an ancient and battered fridge that also lived under the trestle table, and poured it into mismatched tumblers. "Not very elegant," he apologized, handing her one.

"Thanks." The rosé inside it was unexpectedly chill and delicious.

"Better than Billee's, *non?*"

*Billy's?*

"Billee's!" Fabien nodded. "Where you 'ad lunch in England. You told me about it the other night. At the Hôtel du Roc."

"I told you about Billy's?" Kate said disbelievingly.

"The café in Ockmucklethwaites," Fabien grinned.

"Slackmucklethwaite."

"I remember it all." He smacked his lips delightedly. "The newspaper, the pizza restaurant. Doreen Bracegird-*ell* and the WI. Gladees Arkwright in *Roméo et Juliette*."

"I told you about *that?*" She'd been more pissed even than she thought. How *embarrassing*. Thank God she hadn't told the Comtesse about any of this.

"You did. It was fascinating. And Odile, she thought so too when I told her."

"You told *her?* About Gladys Arkwright and Doreen Bracegirdle?" Kate imagined the sagging face twisting in disgust.

"*Mais oui*. Why not? She thought you must be a very interesting person. She is an Anglophile, as I am sure she told you. She speaks excellent English."

"Does she? I've always spoken to her in French."

Fabien nodded. "Oh yes. We often speak in English together. For the practice, you know. And I too love England. As I said to you at the Hôtel du Roc, I would like to go and paint this town. Eckmucklethwaites."

"Slackmucklethwaite." Surely he was joking. What, after all, could he possibly paint? A nude of Gladys Arkwright? A still life of Billy's cheese-and-chip special? A nude Gladys Arkwright tucking into one of those cheese-and-chip specials?

"I could paint your grandmother. Knitting. She likes knitting, no?"

Kate nodded. He really had an elephantine memory.

"Or your mother cooking. Or your father standing in front of the television. Or I could paint Slack Palisades," Fabien chortled. "Champagne D'Vyne. *Nat Hardstone.* Or perhaps," he mumbled, eyes flicking to Kate's suddenly stricken face, "that's not such a good idea."

"No," said Kate, thinking that the only desirable interface between Nat and art was his either being drowned in turpentine or battered to death with an easel. She had drunk a lot of rosé, but the mention of Nat was sobering. More sobering still was the reflection that, if Fabien had retained every detail of what she had told him at the Hôtel du Roc, he must also remember everything she had said at the party.

All the time they had been talking, Fabien's hand was dancing across a tiny sketchpad. Kate realized now that she was being drawn. She tensed, tried to suck her cheeks in and show her good side, all at the same time.

Fabien stood abruptly. "Ah, now you are posing. Your face is not as interesting. Relax," he instructed, "and carry on talking."

"Er . . ." Kate groped for a subject that wasn't Uncle Graham and Auntie Joan. Or Nat Hardstone. "Tell me about the Comtesse," she said.

"Odile." Fabien's pencil whispered over the page. "Very interesting woman. She's had a fascinating life."

"Oh?" Kate braced herself for the artist's model routine. No doubt the old woman had spun Fabien the same line.

"A *very* interesting woman. She used to be a painter herself, as well as a model—a very beautiful one. Everyone wanted to paint her."

"Look—about all that beautiful model stuff. It's not true, is it? I mean, just look at her face. Her features are all twisted and lopsided."

Fabien sketched on in silence.

"She showed me a photograph," Kate felt mean but determined to get to the bottom of the matter, "of a beautiful young girl on a beach. She said it was of her but it *couldn't* have been. It didn't look anything like her."

"It *was* her."

"I don't believe it," Kate said firmly. "The girl in the picture was beautiful. Really stunning. The Comtesse, well—she's . . ."

"Had a stroke."

"Had a what?"

"A stroke. Some years ago. The rest of her made a good recovery, but it completely destroyed her face."

Kate's hands flew up to cheeks stinging with blood. "Oh God. You're joking."

"I am afraid not."

She dared not look at him now. Shame scorched through her like fire. She knew little about strokes, but enough to realize they came scything out of the blue, ruining lives, reducing healthy, active people to helplessness. Transforming sun-kissed beauties into slip-faced, one-eyed crones. "But how?" she whispered. "And why? *Why* did it happen?"

Fabien lifted and dropped his shoulders. "No one really knows for certain. But I'm pretty sure—and so, I know, is she—that her smoking had something to do with it. However, she refuses to give up. Says it's her only pleasure and that lightning doesn't strike twice. I hope she's right."

Kate kept her eyes cast down. It was too awful.

"Well, I say her *only* pleasure," Fabien corrected himself, "but she does have others. She still likes to be painted, and she's still a great model—one of my favorites . . . look."

Striding over to the canvases, he pulled one out with a flourish.

Hair scraped back, devoid of makeup, the Comtesse stared out of her painted, lopsided face in a manner that seemed to challenge the world. From the way Fabien's brush had lingered on her cheekbones, sketched in the elegant line of her jaw, Kate could see that here, indeed, was the ghost of loveliness; a woman who had once been beautiful. A lump swelled in her throat.

"I paint her all the time. There are lots," Fabien said breezily, turning round image after image. The Comtesse in a yellow dress against a background of powdery blue. The Comtesse in a red shirt in front of rose-patterned wallpaper. The Comtesse naked, her skin the color of haddock and breasts like wrinkled satsumas atop a rib cage of protruding bones.

Kate felt things sliding into place in her brain. "That picture downstairs," she said slowly. "It's by *you.*"

"The one in the sitting room is by me." Fabien nodded. "But none of the other paintings of Odile are. The ones in the hall . . ."

Kate gaped. "In the hall? They're of her as well?"

"Of course. Who else did you think they were of?"

He must think her stupid as well as cruel. To hide her flaming face, Kate crossed to the wall of long windows. The one at the end was open; she leaned out, grateful for the cool breeze on her cheeks.

A pair of brown arms snaked round her from behind and held her fast. Kate twisted indignantly. She had not heard him approach.

"*Attention,*" Fabien murmured. "I don't want you to fall." He smelt strongly of turpentine. "I've got something else to show you."

"What?" she grumbled, fighting her way upward. As he pulled her erect, his hands ran up her back, over her shoulders, downward and lightly, possibly accidentally, over her breasts. He met her eyes, then strode to the end of the room where the canvases were.

"This," he said, pulling one out. Kate looked at the portrait of a woman. With pale hair and wide-apart eyes.

Then she realized. The pale hair, the white skin, the small, but full round mouth. All as familiar as her own reflection.

"Yes," said Fabien. "That's you. You see it, don't you?"

Kate nodded, momentarily too overcome to speak. He had painted *her*. What was more, he had done it exquisitely. The image was spare but romantic; the painter had clearly found the combination of features attractive. She looked, indeed, almost beautiful. But . . .

"How?" She had only met him a few days ago. There had been no sittings. Had he really done it all from memory?

"That's the strange thing," Fabien said, approaching her softly. "The thing that struck me when I first saw you at the party. I painted this picture ages ago."

"Ages ago? But you've only just met me."

"I know," he murmured, his mouth drawing close to hers. "It was a sort of vision. I've always been haunted by a certain few faces. Yours is one of them."

Kate was late for her shift at the restaurant. "I'm sorry," she told Celia.

"Doesn't matter. We're hardly overrun, darling."

As usual, there wasn't a single customer in the Restaurant des Tours. As usual, business across the square at the Café de la Place was booming. The misanthropic owner could be seen patrolling the borders of his flourishing empire.

"Where've you been, anyway? Your new des res?"

"Moving, yes. Lost track of time."

"Sure." Celia grinned. "And I can guess what other sort of moving you've been doing."

"Meaning?" Kate challenged.

"Your artist friend helping you—move, was he?" Celia teased back.

Kate reddened. After Fabien had kissed her he had announced he was taking her out to lunch tomorrow. Somewhere very special, he had said. Telling Celia any of this felt like tempting fate, however. If the whole thing ended in disaster, she'd prefer it, this time, to be private disaster.

"I'm glad it's going well, anyway." Celia grinned, her eyes trained closely on Kate's face. She sighed. "Wish I could say the same for Ken *et moi*."

"What's the matter?" Guiltily, Kate remembered the scene in the hire car. But was it her fault she couldn't quite see what Celia saw in him?

"He's getting a bit depressed, poor darling."

"Oh dear," Kate said dutifully. Hopefully he'd get so depressed he'd leave. "Why?"

Celia pressed her hands against the small of her back. "This search of his. He's not saying much about it. . . ."

"You don't say," Kate could not resist cutting in. Celia flashed her a cross look.

". . . but it's not going well. He spends his whole time following up leads, but I don't think he's getting anywhere."

"And he *still* hasn't told you what he's looking for?" Kate said impatiently. "If *anything*."

Celia looked at her. "Well actually, he *has,* darling. There really is something. Or someone, rather. But I promised not to say anything. He's terrified that walls have ears."

"And you believe him?"

"I think so, yes."

"Oh." Kate looked disbelievingly at her friend. "And whoever it is is definitely down here somewhere? Who is it?"

"I can't say."

"*Celia!* Come *on!* Tell me."

"I can't. I promised."

"But . . ."

Celia put down a fork and straightened up. "Look, Kate, I'd prefer it if you didn't ask me any more. I know you don't believe a word of it anyway."

There was a silence. She may not be wild about Ken, Kate thought, but she was genuinely fond of Celia. "Tables look great," she remarked placatingly. In addition to the full complement of cutlery and napkins, they now bore small glass bottles prettily filled with sprays of country flowers.

"Try telling *them* that." Celia nodded towards the bar where, if she inclined her head just slightly, Kate could see Pappy, the Trout, and the

Troll huddled in conclave round one of the tables. The Troll was ges-
ticulating furiously and banging the wooden top with his fist while
Pappy, knitted hat pulled low over his brow, muttered violently to
himself. The Trout, as usual, stared tragically into space.

"What's the matter with them?"

Celia grinned. "Just had their biggest shock for a generation."

"What—they're cross about a few flowers?" It seemed unlikely,
even by the Hôtel des Tours's legandarily grumpy standards.

"Slightly more dramatic." Celia beamed. "They're cross because *I*
wrote a menu."

Kate noticed the small white cards on each table. "My God. So
you did."

"Well, we needed one. Now that the tables are looking so fantastic it's the only thing we're lacking. There used to be nothing to show
people the sort of food we serve and how much it costs. I'm sure the
lack of a menu's the only thing standing between us and phenomenal
success."

Kate's eyes flicked doubtfully towards the Troll's massive, forbidding outline inside the bar. The only thing?

"And now we've got one. Basically, the world's our lobster."

Kate picked up one of the cards upon which Celia had written the
evening's available dishes in both French and English. *Soupe au pistou,
raviolis faits à la main, aubergines gratinées, fleur de courgette farcie.*
"Sounds fantastic. But how did you find all this out? The chef never
tells anyone what he's cooking."

"Until now."

Over the course of the next few minutes Kate listened open-
mouthed to the tale of how Celia had bearded the Trout in her den
and suggested—as politely as possible, darling, naturally, that the
Troll's tried and tested method of confronting potential diners with his
growled, incomprehensible, and inaccurate list of dishes might not be
for the best in the best of all possible food-serving worlds.

"You didn't say that!"

"Well, actually I *was* a bit more diplomatic. I said that even the world's best-run hotel owned by the world's most talented hoteliers occasionally needed an outsider's eye to identify possible areas for improvement."

Kate sniggered.

"And that, while the restaurant was obviously perfect in every way, one *could* arguably gild the lily by giving it a menu. That, dull, boring, and conventional though it seemed, a simple list detailing what food is available and how much it costs might be useful to diners, who tend on the whole to be an unimaginative bunch whose dullest and most unimaginative aspect is that they tend to expect such lists. I was hours with the phrase book working that one out, I can tell you."

"What did the Trout say?"

"To be honest, she wasn't terribly responsive." The wrinkled lids of the Trout's fishy eyes, Celia added, had closed, as if brooking no argument. Shudderingly she had inhaled, and shudderingly she had sighed back out.

"Business might increase," had been Celia's next tack, hoping to appeal to the Trout's fondness for her accounts book.

The eyelids had snapped back open to reveal a hard black stare. "But how?" demanded the Trout. "We cannot draw up a list of food. We never know ourselves. The chef," she pulled down the corners of her wide, flabby mouth, "he never tells us what he is doing. Or he tells us the wrong thing. We have to wait and see, like everyone else."

"How ridiculous," interjected Kate, thinking that even the Italian Job kitchens managed some form of communication with the waiting staff. Even if most of that was verbal abuse.

At this stage, Celia confided, she had—reluctantly—accepted the necessity of confronting the huge and terrifying chef in his kitchen.

"Rather you than me," Kate breathed, awed. "What was it like? Blackened cauldrons stirred by urchins?"

"Not a bit of it." It had been, Celia reported, surprisingly clean and orderly, with acres of white tiling, steel hob tops, and chopping surfaces. The chef himself had not been immediately in evidence. Celia had eventually discovered him behind a heap of boxes of vegetables, snoring, feet up, on a vast drum of olive oil. He had not welcomed her interruption. Still less her mission.

"A menu?" he thundered, pink face deepening to puce. "What do you mean, a menu? What do we need a menu for? We've never needed one before."

Celia coughed politely and agreed it was a shame, but that was the nature of the business these days. Tourists needed—and expected—a great deal of help.

"Tourists!" the chef spat. "What do they know about food? Nothing! They eat in their hundreds at that shithole across the square. I would not let my dog eat there."

"I didn't say," Celia told Kate, "that given the lovely café owner's take on animals, his dog would be lucky to escape with its life anyway."

"So what did you say?"

"That a man with his talents was duty bound to show the light to poor blunderers in the gastronomic darkness."

The chef had looked, she said, almost gratified at this until, once again, the subject of a list had come up. His blue eyes bulged in fury. "I don't work with lists," he had thundered. "I am an artist in food."

"Sure," Celia sighed patiently. "But for all the reasons I mentioned, I need to know what particular dishes you're turning your artistry to this evening. That way, more people would enjoy your wonderful food."

The chef had shrugged massive, white-clad shoulders. "I don't care whether people enjoy my food. I don't even care whether they eat it. Eating is," he had made a gesture of disgust, "nothing. *Nothing.*"

As she listened to the saga Kate's eyes were wide with amazement. "He doesn't look as if he thinks eating's nothing. He's *huge.*"

"He says eating spoils everything. What matters is the cooking."

Kate whistled. "With attitudes like that, it's hardly surprising that the business is going down the loo."

Celia admitted she had despaired at this point. It had been obvious she was getting nowhere. Then, just as she was about to give up and go, the boxes of vegetables gave her an idea. "Are you making *pis-*

*tou* soup?" she had guessed, spotting green lengths of courgette with large orange blossoms hanging off the end.

"Stuffed courgette flowers," corrected the chef huffily.

"Lamb?" Did that white polystyrene box contain meat?

"*Bourride*," snapped the chef.

"That comes with green beans, right?"

"*Bourride? Bourride* is a soup made with white fish, wine, herbs . . ."

By this method, Celia had managed to extract details of everything the chef planned to bend his artistry to that evening.

"Brilliant!" applauded Kate.

"But then, of course, I had to drag the prices out of the Trout."

She described the scene. The Trout's lips had parted in astonishment. She had snatched the notebook from Celia's hands and scanned it. "*This* is what he is cooking? I have *never* seen such a list before." Then she wrote down the prices without a murmur. "So—*taran-tara-* menus!" Yet Celia's triumphant expression faded as she looked across to the bustling Café de la Place. "But there's *still* nobody here."

It was, Kate agreed, frustrating. The restaurant, after all, could hardly look more inviting. Above the ancient arches, the ivy hung lushly against the sun-warmed stone. In the picturesque shadows of the passages the bright checked tablecloths glowed.

The square too looked idyllic, every age-worn brick radiating charm. The evening air was balmy, pleasantly weighty, and reverberating with the silvery peal of just-rung bells. On the ancient tops of the higgledy buildings shone the rich orange of the setting sun. It glinted off the higher windows and turned the curlicued iron bell tower to molten copper.

Everywhere but the Restaurant des Tours was a bustling, contented scene. Villager, pausing to chat to villager, was wound instantly in a cat's cradle of dog leads. Horns honked, children shouted, men laughed, women exclaimed. From the windows above the square, from second- and third-story windows where pans clanked and TVs thundered. From every direction, strongly delicious cooking smells competed for dominance. The strongest and most delicious of all came from their own restaurant.

"Come *on!*" Celia growled softly to the passing knots of people. "The place looks right and smells right. We've even got a bloody menu. So why aren't you all queuing up? What are we doing wrong?" She smiled encouragingly at a group of Japanese tourists who had paused to admire the ancient arcades. As they came closer, Kate curled her fists in excited suspense. Then suddenly they scattered, like a school of fish surprised by a shadow.

Or by a Troll. Right on cue, even as the group leader was stretching out a hand to examine the menu, the Troll barreled out of the bar into the passageway and glared. The Japanese fled.

"That's what we're doing wrong," Celia groaned. "*Him.* We'd attract more diners with . . . oh, I don't know."

"Someone walking up and down with a bell shouting 'Bring out your dead'?" suggested Kate.

"I brooked death and danger with that bloody chef for my menus," Celia wailed. "Not to mention taking on the Trout."

"And you did fantastically," Kate assured her.

"Yes, but it's all been for nothing."

Tears of disappointment were welling in Celia's eyes. "As long as *that* great lump's around." She shot a vicious look in the direction the Troll had disappeared in. "The whole thing's a complete waste of time."

"Not necessarily," Kate soothed. "If we had lots of customers, no one would notice him. It's the fact that the place is empty that's doing the damage."

But of course Celia had a point. Not even the most upbeat assessment of the Troll's customer liaison skills could describe them as barely adequate. His status as the son of the owner, moreover, made him immovable object and irresistible force combined. Keeping him away from the restaurant was not an option. Kate gave her friend a comforting squeeze.

But Celia was not to be comforted.

"Pappy'll sack us pretty soon and then I'll have to go back to *bloody* London. . . ." she whined.

Just at that moment, slinking across the square, clinging shirt dress showing every curve and line, came Nicole. She flicked an amused stare at Kate and the wailing Celia. She had obviously come to gloat at the further-declined fortunes of her former place of employment.

"*Her* again," Celia hissed. "Has she nothing better to do?"

"Well, it's a small place and there's probably nothing on the telly."

The Troll had shot out of the bar on seeing her. Nicole called, a sneer on her darkly beautiful face, "Busy evening, Bernard?"

His reply was to gaze at her with dumb longing. Laughing to herself, Nicole sashayed off.

Celia, meanwhile, seemed to have rediscovered her stiff upper lip. "Oh, pull yourself together," she was muttering to herself.

Kate wondered darkly what there was to pull together. While her northern spirit deplored the idea of giving up, northern practicality deemed that effort on dead-horse-flogging was effort wasted. She steeled herself to suggest that perhaps they had overestimated what they could achieve with the place. From the rattle behind her she guessed the Troll was gathering glasses from the tables. He, for one, had given up on the evening's trade.

"Something wrong, ladies?" Head on one side in an attitude of mock solicitude, thinning eyebrows raised in patronizing enquiry, the weaselly owner of the Café de la Place was grinning at them. It was not a nice grin.

"Oh piss off," Celia snarled, stomping back inside the bar.

"Everything's fine," Kate said determinedly. "*Thank* you," she added.

"If you say so." Smirking, he crossed back to his own bustling establishment. Kate watched him, eyes burning. There, in a nutshell, was the problem with giving up. The satisfaction it would undoubtedly give *him*.

22

Eyes fixed resentfully on the retreating back of the café owner, Kate did not notice the dishevelled figure approach.

"I say," an unsteady voice piped up. "Is that you, Kate?"

Kate blinked and refocused. Standing before her was the editor of the *Riviera Gazette*. Crichton was in travel-guide mode, accompanied by at least twenty of his yellow-baseball-capped flock. He was swaying slightly.

"Crichton!"

He was clearly one over the eight already. His trousers were crumpled and his white linen jacket liberally spotted with red wine. He gave her an uncertain grin, came right up and whispered loudly in her ear, "Get on all right at the St. Pierres', did you?"

Kate remembered her resolution to underplay the afternoon as much as possible. "Fine, thanks."

Crichton looked disappointed. "Nothing fishy at all?"

"Nothing," Kate lied. Only a disguised designer who showed her out of a van, and that was just for starters. She pressed her lips tight with the effort of saying nothing.

"Not even . . ."

"No. Honestly, it all seemed fine to me."

"Oh." Clearly disappointed, Crichton stepped backwards into the square again. He cleared his throat and looked about him with mild surprise. "All looks very smart here, I must say. Under new management or something, is it?" he asked. "Oh, I see not," he added as the Troll rolled massively out of the bar.

"It's been upgraded," Kate gabbled, sensing a great opportunity.

The chance that Crichton might bring his group here was staring her in the face. She did a swift head count; twenty at least. All the outside tables filled at one go. It would be the liftoff the restaurant was waiting for. "We've got a menu and everything—look." She grabbed one of Celia's cards from a nearby table and shoved it into Crichton's hand. The tour group pressed round.

"Homemade ravioli, it says," one woman informed another in a broad Midlands twang. "Like a bit of ravioli, I do." Her friend nodded. Both directed meaningful glances at Crichton.

"And it's *very* good," Kate urged. She felt, behind her, the Troll pause to listen. Doubtless with his usual friendly, accommodating expression.

"I'm sure it is," Crichton remarked, sounding anything but. He clapped his hands. "Well, folks. We'd better be off."

There was a discontented murmuring, led by the ravioli fan.

"Where to?" Kate gasped. Was the restaurant's big break about to slip through her fingers?

"Oh, you know. Pre-trough stroll sort of thing. Before we head for dinner."

"Where are you having dinner?"

"Er . . ." Crichton shifted from battered shoe to battered shoe. "Well, since you ask, at the Café de la Place, actually."

At the mention of the enemy her stomach muscles, tight with tension, now slumped in defeat. Then, slowly, they started to tighten again. This was an opportunity and she wouldn't let it pass without a fight. Determination gathered in her heart.

"*Why* the Café de la Place?" she demanded. No point beating about the bush, after all. This was a matter of restaurant life or death. "It's awful."

There was a brief silence. "Of *course* it's awful," Crichton agreed. "Always has been. Service is desperate, prices outrageous, and you wouldn't give the food to pigs."

There was a stir of consternation among the tour group. "*It's awful, it's awful . . . dispirate . . . pigs.*"

"So why go there?" she repeated, encouraged.

"Yes," murmured the ravioli-loving woman. "Why go there?"

Crichton looked at her. There's always one, Kate could see him thinking. And thank God for that, she thought herself.

"Because there isn't anywhere else, of course," he said. "Not in Ste. Jeanne, anyway."

Kate spread out her hands to take in the tables under the arches, the candles twinkling cheerfully, the scent of rich, savory food wafting from the kitchen windows. "There's *here*."

"There's *here*," echoed Ravioli Woman. Crichton darted her an irritated glance.

"Yes, well of course there is *now*," he sighed. "But my point is that there wasn't *before*. And anyway, I had to book us all in as a group at the Café de la Place."

"Come here for dinner instead," Kate suggested. Her tone was casual but she was crossing her fingers so hard her eyes watered. "The food's wonderful."

A stomach-juice-rioting waft from the kitchens chose just that moment to release itself into the air. Ravioli Woman looked sharply at Crichton.

"But they're expecting us." Crichton glanced anxiously over at the café. "Really, we should . . ."

Ravioli Woman and her friend, meanwhile, were reading out the menu to the others amid murmurs of approval.

"Our prices are very reasonable," Kate pressed. "We will, of course, offer a special discounted rate for a group booking." She ignored behind her the sound of the Troll's glass tray rattling ominously. "We can," she added, "certainly better any discount you've been offered by the Café de la Place."

Crichton's confused look confirmed Kate's suspicion that the word *discount* did not feature in the rival establishment's vocabulary. She moved closer to the editor. "What was the Café de la Place charging you per head?"

Crichton named a sum that made Kate whistle. "But that's extortionate!"

"Certainly doesn't leave much over for me, I can tell you."

"Well, how about this?" Kate named a sum which, while much lower, was well within the bounds of what the Hôtel des Tours might expect to charge for a meal. Particularly if multiplied by twenty. What the Trout would make of it was anyone's guess, but Kate decided not to think about the consequences.

Crichton, in any case, had taken the bait. His bloodshot blue eyes kindled. Kate was clenching her fists in victory when she saw the light die away. "Only thing is . . ." Doubt swept his face and he tweezled his moustache in a troubled fashion. He looked unhappily over at the café.

"What?" Kate strained to keep the urgency out of her voice. No point panicking him.

He looked at her pleadingly. "I'd love to, honestly I would. Really, Kate, it looks great here. But I really don't think I can."

"*What?*" Was defeat about to be snatched from the jaws of victory? Then, in a flash, Kate realized what the problem was. "I'll ring the Place for you and cancel the booking."

Relief swept Cricthon's features. "Are you sure? It's just that that owner . . . he can get rather nasty."

"Quite sure. In fact," Kate said, beaming, "it will be a pleasure. Bernard," she added briskly, turning to the Troll. "We have dinner for twenty. Kindly inform the kitchen."

There was a crash as the tray full of glasses hit the floor of the arcades.

The evening was a triumph. Kate's early fears that the grumpy Trout and the terrifying Troll would have a dampening effect proved unfounded. So buoyant, indeed, were the spirits of Crichton's group, particularly after a few bottles of the local rosé, that, as dampeners went, the Trout and Troll at their grumpiest had all the impact of a thimbleful of water on a bonfire. After the rosé came *digestifs* in abundance; Kate hid a smile as, thick brows drawn in disapproval, the Troll barged past for yet another café cognac. Which, it must be added, Pappy dispensed with what almost approached willingness, although without anything that approached a smile.

The presence of the raucous group soon attracted other customers. Couples who previously would have walked hurriedly past, intimidated, now lingered, emboldened, and then asked for tables.

When, much to Celia's delight and Kate's disappointment, the short, solid form of Ken appeared some time after ten, it was to discover that not only the tables outside and in the bar, but also those hurriedly set out in the basement were full. He whistled in amazement. "Christ on a bleedin' bike. What the bleedin' 'ell you done to this place? Didn't realize it 'ad turned into the bleedin' Ivy."

"Good, isn't it?" Celia dimpled, drawn into his arms for a passionate kiss.

Kate pulled a face and turned away. Then guiltily she realized Ken had seen her.

She glanced across the square to where the owner of the Café de la Place was standing, arms akimbo, in front of his unusually sparsely populated establishment. He was staring at the newly-bustling Restaurant des Tours with an expression of unmistakable fury. It was hard to subdue a thrill of triumph.

The battles within her own camp were still far from won, however. The chef, incensed at a menu having been tricked out of him and that someone actually intended to *eat* his masterpieces, sent out the wrong dishes at every opportunity.

This had led to a few sticky moments. Persuading people that the *pistou* soup set before them was the courgette flowers they had ordered, but done in Chef's own very special way, was particularly sticky. But not the stickiest.

"I ordered lamb," complained half of a couple from Penzance, looking crossly at the salmon plonked before him.

"And you've got it," Celia lied with aplomb. "In old Provençal, salmon is known a the 'lamb of the sea.'"

Luckily, everything was of equal deliciousness. In addition, by the time the food appeared, most people were unable—through drink or other distractions—to remember what they had ordered in the first place.

Naturally, there was no intimation from the hotel's owning family that the success of the evening was in any way remarkable. Or in any way due to either Kate's or Celia's efforts. Their silence verged on the Trappist. Yet Kate, becoming as she was something of an expert on the proprietors' moodiness, sensed something different about this one. Rather than disapproving, it was shocked.

And there were signs, to one who knew where to look, that almost approached appreciation. The Trout's face, as she had collected the credit cards proffered by Crichton's twenty happy tourists after three courses and at least one bottle of wine each, had radiated the extreme world weariness that was her version of ecstasy. This expression endured now as, by the light of a single candle, she sat poring lovingly over her accounts book.

But it was from Pappy that the biggest concession came. As she and Celia carried the last trays of dirty glasses into the bar, he slid two small glasses of armagnac silently across the counter in their direction.

Kate chinked her glass triumphantly with Celia and sipped it gratefully, feeling the fire roar down her throat and explode in her stomach.

Meanwhile, at his table outside, a Crichton in an advanced state of inebriation was submitting with bashful enthusiasm to the attentions of the two ravioli-loving ladies. They seemed to be seeing their tour leader—if not the entire world—through rosée-tinted wineglasses.

"'Smarvellous," Crichton called unsteadily to Kate as she emerged from the bar. "Food's fantastic. We'll have to do a special on the place in the *Gazette*."

"That would be great."

"You must write it the next time you're in," Crichton declared, waving his glass expansively. "Come in and see me about it tomorrow afternoon."

Kate hesitated. Tomorrow afternoon was the planned trip with Fabien. Still, if she did her cleaning quickly, there should be time to drop in at the *Gazette*.

"'Smarvellous," repeated Crichton. With that, he fell facedown in the *tarte au citron*.

Much later, Kate awoke with a start from a delicious dream. She was splashing in the warm blue sea with someone tall and tanned with untidy hair and intense dark eyes. A glow of anticipation radiated through her. Of course—the mystery outing with Fabien. That was later today.

Today, however, seemed a long way off. It was not yet light. The night was still and warm; the air close despite her having opened the windows on to the guest-room balcony. Perhaps it was the heat that had woken her up. She lay in the darkness listening to herself breathe.

Or perhaps it was the light that had disturbed her; through the open window, a shaft of brilliant moonlight sliced in like a brilliantly polished blade. Soft breezes eddied in from the garden. All was scented, pearly peace. Yet her spine felt stiff with tension, her ears straining as if expecting to hear . . . something. And, actually, she *could* hear something.

Anxiety pounded within her. Her palms had broken out into a sweat before she realized the steady, rhythmic scraping was caused by her own eyelashes brushing against the cotton surface of the duvet. What a fool she was.

She closed her eyes and settled back to sleep. Seconds later, she was on the alert again. A faint creak beneath the singing silence. Another creak . . . of foot on floorboards? Slowly, she raised herself on an elbow, suddenly scalp-tinglingly certain that Something was in the room.

"Who's there?" she demanded shakily, peering into the felty blackness by her bed. The light from the moon did not fall this far. The air continued still, the silence its high-pitched singing. Yet the hairs on the back of her arms and neck trembled with the continuing message that she was Not Alone.

Then—suddenly—she saw It.

It began as an impression of a movement at the side of her bed. A ripple in the dark. But as it passed through the shaft of light, Kate's entire body jolted in shock. She couldn't be seeing this. This Gothic novel fantasy. This cloaked figure, hooded like a monk.

Her first reaction was a nervous laugh. It had to be someone dressing up, surely. Some sort of joke.

"Ha, ha," she said uncertainly. "Very funny. *Très amusant*," she added for good measure, in case the perpetrator was French.

There was no reaction from the figure. It stood tall, dark, and utterly still in the shaft of light.

Kate gathered her sleep- and fear-scattered wits determinedly about her. It had to be some trick. Although who? And why? Fists clenched at her side, wide-eyed and alert now, she ran, panicked, through the possibilities. Could it be Nicole? She was certainly cross about something—but *this* cross? Or the owner of the Café de la Place? Her wrist still ached, after all, from where he had seized it. But did one night of good trading at the Arcades—no doubt the first in decades—merit this sort of extreme action? Then Ken's red face loomed in her mind's eye; Ken, snarling in his sunglasses as he drove away; Ken, features contorted with annoyance as he spotted her pulling a face in the restaurant tonight. Might it not be him, trying to scare her? Trying to rid Celia of her disapproving influence so he could have her to himself?

"Ken!" Kate snapped at the phantom now moving across the window. "Come on. I *know* it's you. Don't you think this is all a bit childish?" Even as she spoke it occurred to her that the shape was rather taller than the diminutive balding Cockney. Slimmer too.

In the moon's spotlight, the figure paused, then turned and looked at her. Kate gazed in horror into the gaping blackness beneath its hood. There, in the inky dark, glowed the whiteness of a skull.

She swallowed hard. "*Ken?*"

The icy, sick feeling that this might, after all, be something other than human suddenly seized Kate. Transfixed with terror, she gazed for a second before diving under the duvet with a shriek. When she emerged a few minutes later, face hot, head pounding, hands shaking, the figure had gone. The flimsy curtains of the French windows rippled in the night air.

Kate leaped out of bed. The clammy soles of her feet stuck to the floorboards, as she rushed across the room and out on to the balcony. There was no sign of anyone or anything. The figure had apparently melted into thin air. Trembling, Kate went back inside and shut the windows, twisting the handle closed as tight as she could. She paused for a minute, pushing her face against the panes and willing her heart to slow down. Her auricles and ventricles, however, seemed to have other plans.

There had to be a logical explanation for what she'd seen. She'd had only one glass of wine with supper and Pappy's not-terribly-large armagnac. She was not usually given to hallucinations. Nor did she, as a rule, believe in ghosts. Was that what she had seen? Some unquiet spirit, pacing the Comtesse's spare room? In search of . . . what?

Sleep, of course, was impossible now. Kate decided to apply her racing mind to something active; bustle and light, after all, might discourage whatever it was from returning. She switched on the bedside lamp. By the time a pearly pink dawn stained the sky Kate had not only written up—as blandly as possible—the interview with Mandi St. Pierre but completed the best part of a scene in which the Northern Gigolo, disguised as a handsome artists, seduced a lottery winner on the terrace of the Hôtel du Roc. She put her pen down tired and satisfied.

Out on the balcony, watching the rising sun turn the TV aerials of Ste. Jeanne into light sabers, Kate's nervous state finally dissolved into peaceful exhaustion. A few early birds wheeled in the heavens. An opalescent sea glimmered in its cleavage of hills. The day of the outing with Fabien was to be blessed with fine weather.

"Racy stuff, this." It was a few hours later and Crichton was looking up from the handwritten pages with a gleam in his bloodshot eyes. "Not sure how it'll play with the readers though. The majors in Menton might not like it. But I bet their wives jolly well will."

Kate looked down at her bag in panic. Poking out of it was the handful of pages with *MANDI ST. PIERRE* handwritten in large capitals at the top. In her bleary state of underslept exhaustion she had, on arriving in the *Gazette* office, presented a bushy-eyed but otherwise perky Crichton not with the Jardins des Lavabo interview but the latest chapter of *Northern Gigolo*.

"Aw, shame," he protested as she hurriedly snatched it back. "I was enjoying that. Exciting stuff. Particularly that bit where he smears the oil paint all over—"

"Thank you," Kate snapped as she stuffed *Gigolo* back in her bag and passed him the Mandi interview. "This is what I meant to show you."

Crichton's eyes rolled across the lines. Under the table, Kate's toes were curling slightly. Was there anything worse than someone reading your copy in front of your face?

"It'll do," the editor pronounced eventually, tossing the sheets on his desk.

"What's wrong with it?" Kate felt a stab of indignation. She'd done her best with the bad job that was Mandi's house. A job admittedly set to get worse once Marc de Provence got his hands on it. "What's the matter?"

Crichton puffed on his Winston. "Well, I suppose I *was* a bit disappointed in the restaurant last night."

Kate blinked. What did the Hôtel des Tours have to do with anything? "But I thought you enjoyed your *gigot d'agneau*."

"I meant," Crichton removed the cigarette from his mouth, "what you said about Mandi St. Pierre. That you didn't notice a single strange thing about the entire setup."

"Well, no, I didn't," Kate said uncomfortably. "Not really."

He sighed. "I just thought it was a bit odd, that's all. What with all the evidence I'd collected in my dossier. Which you haven't even *looked* at, by the way. And you being a professional reporter and all that. But I suppose if you don't want to help, or don't think it's worth it . . ." His voice tailed regretfully off. He sniffed.

Kate felt guilty. Much as, in the interests of a quiet life, she wanted to keep yesterday afternoon's bizarre events to herself, there was no ignoring the fact Crichton had done her an enormous favor by bringing his entire tour group to the restaurant. He had single-handedly set the place on the map.

"Well, actually . . ." she began. The sun was high in the sky now. There wasn't much risk in telling Crichton about the apparition in her bedroom. She was now almost convinced she had imagined it all anyway. The heated fantasies of an overloaded brain, no doubt.

Kate was therefore unprepared for Crichton's reaction as she described the cloaked and skull-visaged visitor to her room.

"Marvellous!" he exclaimed.

"Why's it marvellous?"

"Because it's something else to solve, of course."

"But you've got Marty St. Pierre," Kate faltered.

"Yes, but there's always room for more," Crichton said excitedly. "I can start a new dossier and everything."

She looked at him disbelievingly. "So you actually think there's something in it?"

"Certainly," Crichton said matter-of-factly. He placed his fingers under his chin in the shape of a steeple. "One thing is abundantly clear already."

"Is it?"

"Someone," Crichton told her gleefully, "is trying to scare you."

Kate gazed at him in horror. All her fears, which she had lulled and calmed as a mother calms a fretful baby, were now awake and screaming in their cot. They were standing up in it, shaking the bars. Examining them, Kate saw they bore a passing resemblance to a short, red-faced Londoner. Had it been Ken, then? After all? "*Scare* me? *Me?*" she croaked.

"My dear Kate," Crichton said, grinning. "As we investigate types know, everything is possible." He started to scribble notes.

"Bit far-fetched, isn't it?" Kate said nervously.

Crichton continued to scribble.

"Who would want to scare *me?*" Kate demanded. "Anyway, it might," she tried to sound casual, "be a *real* ghost."

Crichton put his chewed pen down. "Now that really *is* far-fetched."

"Why?" Kate howled.

"Everyone knows that spirits don't really walk the earth."

Unless they're inside *you,* Kate thought hotly. Crichton must be 50 percent proof most of the time. "Or it might," she said desperately, "be just a *joke.* Nothing more sinister."

"Something more sinister, definitely," Crichton said with satisfaction, making more notes on his pad.

"But what?" Kate yelped. "And what for?"

"Never forget that the criminal mind is one particularly rich in invention." His ears were fairly pink with pleasure.

*But nowhere near as rich as yours.* She looked at Crichton in frightened fury.

Crichton put down his chewed ballpoint. "There! This *really* gives us something to go on. I'll start making enquiries straight away."

"Enquiries to whom?"

Crichton shrugged. "Well, to costume shops to begin with, obviously. See who's hired a monk outfit recently. The skull might be more difficult." He twirled his pen thoughtfully. "Medical supplies shop, perhaps? Millions of those on the Riviera. Every other persons's a galloping hypochondriac." He drummed his fingers on his chin in excitement.

"Well, I'm glad *you're* pleased," Kate said sarcastically.

"Pleased? Of *course* I'm pleased. Something to get our teeth into, this is. We can start this afternoon!" He beamed.

"Er, the thing is, Crichton, I've already got something I have to do this afternoon."

"Have you?" The editor looked amazed. "What could possibly be more important?"

"A lunch, actually."

"A *lunch!*"

"Noncancellable, I'm afraid."

"You young people," Crichton grumbled, good-naturedly. "It was never like this in my day. On the *Times.* Oh well. Suppose I'd better soldier on alone for now." The prospect clearly gave him enormous pleasure. He flashed her a grin. "Great story, though. In fact, I'd say this calls for a snifter to celebrate. Wouldn't you?"

Kate returned slowly to the Comtesse's house. Her feet dragged over the cobbles as she approached. Keen as she was to get ready for lunch, she felt less keen to be back inside. She glanced at the Hôtel des Tours.

The bar was much busier than usual. People were even drinking outside. Crisp-cotton-clad tourists with shining lunchtime hair were sipping wine in the sunshine alongside the handful of hard-bitten, small-spending regulars who had previously comprised the hotel's entire customer base. And who possibly hadn't been outside for years.

Kate was overwhelmed with a sudden urge for caffeine. She went into the bar. The Trout, locked in her diurnal struggle with the coffee machine, gave her an unsmiling nod that Kate, as she ordered a cappuccino, rightly interpreted as a fulsome greeting.

"Over 'ere!" An arm waved at her from the smoky fug. Kate started with shock. Ken! The very man. The prime suspect. She glared at him. He waved back.

The cheek of the man. Hailing her as if it was the most natural thing in the world and that he absolutely hadn't been wandering around her bedroom last night dressed as a monk.

Certainly, she thought sourly, he had not deviated much from last night's color scheme. He wore black shirt and black trousers and of course black sunglasses. She marched over, carrying her cappuccino.

He looked her up and down. "You look knackered."

"I am," Kate said meaningfully. "I didn't sleep all that well." She tried to look into his eyes behind the sunglasses. But so profoundly black were the lenses that this was not possible.

"Dintcha?" Ken's jaws worked busily over his croissant. "Me neither, to be honest."

"Is that so." Kate's mouth tightened with angry triumph. The man was practically admitting it, for Christ's sake!

"You ask Celia. Tossing an' turnin' all night. I was." He was, she realized, establishing his alibi. Celia, admittedly, was a good one. He must have crept in and out of bed very skilfully to fool her.

"You were there *all night*, were you? In *bed*?"

"'Course I was. Where else would I be?"

Kate gave him a "you tell me" look.

"Trying to decide whether to stay 'ere, I was. In France. Whether there was any point."

Kate's eyes flexed in surprise. Surely last night's exercise was all about encouraging *her* to leave. Was this some sort of double bluff? Her eyes narrowed suspiciously. "Really?"

"*Really.* An' this is why." Ken gestured at a letter beside his plate. It was covered in shaky old-lady handwriting; the looping, faintly pressed blue biro suggesting the frailty of the writer. "From me old mum," Ken explained.

"Oh." A red herring now, on top of the double bluff? What did his old mum have to do with anything? Kate was starting to feel confused.

Ken sighed heavily.

"What's the matter with your old mum?" Kate asked irritably.

"She's not well. Not been all right for a long time, she ain't. Things are going from bad to worse in 'er flat. Her boiler's knackered. Run out of steam. I've rung the bleedin' landlord five times." As he removed his sunglasses, she noticed he looked gray with exhaustion. His head hung so low over the table his chin was almost in the butter. "Truth to tell, princess, I'm beginning to run out of steam meself a bit. You get to the stage where you begin to wonder what you're doin'."

Why was he telling her all this? It wasn't as if they had much mutual trust or rapport. Then Kate remembered her earliest theory, that Ken was an actor. And a very good one too if this was anything to go by.

Ken looked at her, his forehead crumpled with creases. He rubbed at the shiny purple swags beneath his bright, round eyes into which a look of desolation had crept. "Celia not told you about this then?" He sounded surprised. "About what I'm doin' 'ere?"

She shook her head, no longer sure now what was acting and what wasn't. Certainly, Ken was exhibiting every sign of being at an extremely low ebb. Not quite what you'd expect, Kate thought, of someone hell-bent on getting rid of me. And there was always the possibility—certainly it had seemed so at the time—that the figure in her bedroom was not Ken. Not human at all, in fact. She swallowed, uncertain which was worse.

Ken nodded slowly. "I suppose I didn't really expect her not to, though. Almost restores yer faith in 'uman nature, it does."

"Celia's no flake," Kate said loyally.

"She's a wonderful woman." Ken's head raised above the butter slightly. "Only reason I'm still 'ere in many ways."

Kate said nothing.

Ken looked at her assessingly before shaking his head. "S'pose I may as well tell yer. At least that way you won't think I'm some sort of fantasist nutter any more." As she looked abashed, his shiny red face split in a grin. "Come on. That's exactly what yer thought, innit? I could see it in yer eyes. Got a very expressive face, you 'ave."

Kate looked hard at her knees, determined not to capitulate to his friendlienss. Whatever Celia thought of him, whatever the truth about the phantom, he *still* wasn't to be trusted.

"The reason I'm 'ere," Ken lifted his coffee cup to his lips and drained it, "is because some dodgy bloke ripped off me old ma. She won arf a million quid on the National Lottery and 'e swindled it all out of 'er. *All of it.*" He banged down the cup for emphasis.

"All of it?" Kate frowned. "Half a million pounds? How the hell did he do that?"

"Bleedin' confidence trickster, wasn't 'e? Wangled 'is way into her affections, didn't 'e? Not that it was too 'ard; me old mum 'ad gone a bit funny with all that money. Started puttin' on airs an' graces. Takin' bleedin' taxis everywhere and buyin' 'er food at 'Arrods. That's where Mr. Slimy met 'er. By the vegetable section. Notorious gigolo pickup spot, according to the Old Bill."

Kate felt her suspicions melting. Her *Mockery* experience had proved that the more bizarre a tale, the more true it usually was. Moreover, this had given her an idea. Apart from finding time to work on it at all, the main sticking point with her novel at the moment was getting her fictional hero out of the North and into Knightsbridge. Here, in front of her, was the answer.

"Oh yeah. You can 'ardly move in 'Arrods for dodgy blokes prey-ing on rich old ladies 'oo are losing their marbles. Mr. Slimy were all over 'er like a rash in seconds. Fell for 'im 'ook, line, and sinker, she did." He shook his head. "Nothing I could do about it, though. Me ma, bless 'er, she might be eighty, but she won't be told. By the time I'd found out, Mr. Slimy 'ad moved into this posh new flat she'd rented—she's a widder, you understand—and that was bleedin' well *that*."

"Eighty!" Kate's eyes were out on stalks. "You mean they were hav-ing *sex*?"

"Blimey, you don't mess about, do you? Well, since you ask, per-sonally I was never sure whether the bloke was Arthur or Martha, but he knew 'ow to lay on the charm wiv a bleedin' trowel. I offered to send the boys round to get rid of 'im but she was 'avin' none of it. Told me I was jealous she was finally 'avin' a good time after all these years wivout me dad and 'avin' to scrimp an' save." He crumbled the re-mains of his croissant.

"So what happened?"

"Next thing I know, 'e's scarpered, 'asn't 'e? And 'e's taken 'er bleedin' money wiv 'im an' all. Being the old-fashioned sort, Mum kept it under 'er bed, see."

"Hundreds of thousands of pounds, *under her bed*?"

Ken nodded. "I know. I told 'er. But would she listen? Anyway, it was the last we ever 'eard of bleedin' Slimy."

"But that's appalling. That's theft."

"Too bleedin' right it is. An' from what I can gather, my old mum's not the only one this bloke's ripped off." Ken ground his teeth. "Any-way, last we 'eard 'e was 'eaded to France, but Gawd knows where 'e is now." Ken sighed heavily and stared at a blob of jam on his plate. "I've 'ad a couple o' near misses but nothin' definite."

There was a silence as Kate took this in. Guilt was welling in her. Poor Ken. All the time she had been imagining him a self-aggrandizing inadequate with a psychopathic, haunting streak, when he had in fact been a concerned and dutiful son. "So what happened to your mother? Where is she now?"

"Sheltered accommodation in Limehouse," Ken said shortly.

"'Ad to leave her fancy flat pretty sharpish. Not a penny to 'er name now. Only good thing," he sighed, "is that she's too doolally to remember all that much about it. I tell yer though." he bared his teeth threateningly. "If I ever meet that bloke again, I'll 'ave 'is bleedin' legs orf."

"I'll drink to that." Kate smiled, raising her cappuccino.

23

Fabien drove her along the motorway, never out of the fast lane, the speedometer a good 10 over the 170km/h warning signs at the roadside. France, Kate concluded, clinging on to her sunglasses, didn't go in so much for speed limits as speed targets.

Her present unease, however, had more to do with Crichton and his conspiracy theories than Fabien and his accelerator. Was someone really trying to frighten her? She had tried hard, now Ken was no longer a suspect, to return to believing she had imagined the whole thing. Yet the more she thought about it, the more Ste. Jeanne seemed peopled with potential disturbers of her nocturnal peace. Perhaps it *was* the vicious owner of the Café de la Place. Or Nicole. Or the other prime suspect, of course—the decorator who had already demonstrated his willingness to go to dangerous lengths to protect his identity. But if it had been any of these, how had they reached the balcony? Or roof, or however else entrance had been gained? Kate examined the scene carefully; both were some considerable distance from the ground. And there were no handy trees and drainpipes nearby.

Catching sight of her worry-wrinkled forehead in the side mirror, Kate determinedly put the brakes on her paranoia. Apart from anything else, anxiety was not a good look. Carpe diem, she told herself. And it was a day well worth seizing. Blue and gold and beautiful. Nothing was going to stop her enjoying herself. She had left it all behind her now—for this afternoon, at least.

"Merde." Beside her, Fabien was battling to overtake a series of large white campervans bristling with bicycles. It was not long before the blue Mercedes—which she now knew belonged to Odile—slid triumphantly past.

Eventually, they turned off the motorway. The coast road now taken wound through small, cream-painted towns full of apartment buildings and neon signs—pink for bakeries, green crosses for chemists'—and out again. The rocky outcrops bordering the sea had changed color, Kate noticed, from the butterscotch of Antibes and Cannes to a deep, rusty red.

Abruptly, Fabien swung off the road and came to a halt. Kate got out, wriggled her shoulders, flexed her leg muscles beneath her sundress, and sniffed the sea. They had stopped by a long crumbling wall that looked like the border to some estate. In it was set a doorway almost hidden by a beard of shining vine leaves. The door's sun-blistered, salt-split surface was cracked to reveal an entire history of colors. Fabien pushed aside the tendrils, unlocked the door, and pushed it open.

He turned and smiled at her. "I want you to walk through this door and not turn round for at least five minutes. I've got a surprise for you."

Kate passed through the doorway and found herself in an enchanted land. Bushes whose leaves shone brilliantly in the sun cascaded down to sand delicately tinged with pink. Deep rose-colored rocks tumbled into swirling crystal waves coming in from a large, blue, horseshoe-shaped bay.

"Don't turn round yet," called Fabien.

Kate slid her feet out of her flip-flops and felt the warm beach press beneath her soles. She breathed the salt and seaweed and looked across to the small town on the other side of the bay. She wondered what the picturesque cluster of ice-cream–colored buildings was called.

"Ready! You can turn round now."

Kate gasped in amazement. "I don't believe it."

"You like it?" Fabien grinned.

Kate could not speak for the lump in her throat. No one had ever gone to such lengths on her account before.

He sat, one long leg swung over the other, on a director's chair in the shade of a large parasol pine. Before him was a small folding table that had presumably been concealed in the boot of the Mercedes. Another director's chair was turned invitingly towards her.

Kate opened and closed her mouth but still no words came out.

"Lunch is served." Fabien smiled.

"It looks amazing." She shook her head in wonderment. "A Provençal feast."

"Well, it's certainly Provençal—but I can't claim to have cooked it. I bought it all from Nice market this morning."

Nice market was obviously quite a place. Never in a million years could one imagine procuring such a haul from the Market Arcade, Slackmucklethwaite.

The table was filled with an artist's flair for color. From a platter of marine blue stripes, a pink mountain of prawns rose above a small pot of mayonnaise. A plate of warm red held two small, brown-skinned roast chickens. Radishes and tomatoes clashed beautifully in a lilac bowl; small white goats' cheeses held their own against an apple-green dish. Completing the scene were two hard, shining baguettes whose crusty ends Kate longed to break off.

"It's wonderful." She looked around her. "It's all wonderful."

"Glad Madame is satisfied. It's not easy to find a deserted beach on the Côte d'Azur in high season."

"But how did you?"

"Belongs to some friends of mine."

He twisted in his chair to point over the wall and up into the hills. "They have a lovely old *bastide* up there. This used to be the vineyard. Stretched all the way down to the sea once, before they built the road. So now it's just a beach really."

But not like any beach she'd ever seen before. Not with the tumbling remains of the vineyard, once-orderly rows lost in a romantic rumpus of waving tendrils. She wondered what the wine had been like.

Fabien produced two cocktail glasses. "*Apéro?*"

"Yes, please." She sipped the champagne and pomegranate juice cocktail and squinted over the glittering bay. "What's that village over there?"

"St. Tropez."

"*The* St. Tropez? But it's so *tiny.*"

"That's its problem. It gets very crowded, particularly at this time of year."

Kate turned to him eagerly. "Could we pop in on our way back?"

"What I would prefer," he said, "is to show you *my* Côte d'Azur. The artist's Riviera."

"I'd love that." Kate glowed at the prospect.

Fabien nodded with satisfaction. "We could start with the Fondation Maeght, the wonderful modern art collection at St.-Paul-de-Vence. We could go for lunch afterwards at the Colombe d'Or . . ."

"Ooh, yes please." Kate felt as excited as a five-year-old.

A pink landslide of prawns cascaded on to her pale-blue striped plate. "Here." He snapped off the head of one, peeled off the shell, removed the thread, and dunked the body in mayonnaise. "Open your mouth."

She savored the salty burst on her tongue as he reached over and pushed the prawn against her lips.

"Have another." He was leaning closer now.

She parted her lips and felt fire between her thighs as he pushed piece after piece of firm pink flesh into her mouth. As, with the final one, he traced her lower lip slowly with his finger.

She opened her eyes to see him looking at her meaningfully. He silently passed her the plate of chicken and poured her a glass of chilled rosé. They ate and drank in a silence broken only by the dry rasping of the leaves and the swishing sea. She felt the atmosphere between them thicken and tighten. Beneath the chirping crickets, the air buzzed with tension.

After the chicken and salad, Fabien dipped into his basket again and produced a beribboned box. She watched him lift out a lemon tart, position it on a plate of deep blue and place strands of lavender across the top. "From Odile's garden."

"It looks beautiful—like one of your paintings. Wish I had a camera."

"This is your camera." He tapped his glossy head.

The knife flashed Excalibur-like in the sun. The tart was sharp yet sweet, with a velvety filling and a thin, crisp base. Her tastebuds in delicious riot, Kate stared meditatively out toward St. Tropez, wondering whether anyone there, however rich, was eating a lunch as delicious as this. Or as romantic. She doubted it.

She looked over to see him watching her. "I want you to help me," he said. His tone was brisk and matter-of-fact.

"How?"

"I want to see you naked."

"*Oh.*" Kate blinked. No one had ever *asked*, as such, before.

He slipped a cigarette into his mouth. "I want to see," he said calmly, "if your body corresponds to the mental image I have of it."

Kate forced her alcohol-fuddled brain through the apparently contradictory facts. He was asking her to take her clothes off. All the signs were that he was about to seduce her. And yet his attitude was of almost medical detachment.

"I also want to see how your body relates to your head," he added.

Oh. Not a seduction then. Kate felt vaguely disappointed but mostly relieved. The fact he intended to look at her from the point of view of an artist meant at least that he would take her shape on its merits. He would be looking at the effects of light and shade, one color against another. Not her underwear.

A giddy recklessness swept her. Why not, after all. Especially if it was for Art's sake. Her hand reached up to unbutton the front of her dress. Three buttons down she paused and looked at Fabien. His face was blank. She reached for the fourth button.

Eventually she stood before him, the sun warm on her bare skin, feeling oddly unembarrassed. She pictured herself, skin pale against the russet rocks behind, hair flying like a dull-gold flag against the brilliant blue of the sea.

He said nothing for a few minutes. "It's amazing," he murmured eventually. "You look exactly as I thought you would."

"Meaning?"

"Beautiful."

He reached out, took her hand, pulled her swiftly into his arms and kissed her.

She felt real, yet unreal; there and yet not there as he pulled her down on to the sand. The wine whirled in her head; she arched her back luxuriously as his hand worked slowly, gently, over her skin. It rounded her breasts, rubbed her nipples, reached up between her thighs, exploring every curve, every secret place; licking and flicking into light a thousand tiny flames of longing. Kate turned her head from side to side, hearing her hair scrape the sand, feeling herself swell with desire, all senses blending with the warmth of the sun, the sigh of the waves, the salt tang of the sea.

Then she jerked her head up. "Er . . . Fabien . . ." Her face flamed as the gut-twisting embarrassment of getting Nat to use condoms returned.

His teeth flashed as, between finger and thumb, he held up a small silver packet. "It's okay. No problem."

Moments later, she was savoring the delicious savagery of his thrusts. From a distance beyond the rushing in her ears, Kate listened for some moments to the yells of delight before realizing they were hers.

Afterwards, Fabien raised himself on his elbow to look into her eyes and smile.

"Come for a swim." He pulled her to her feet and strode ahead on long brown legs to where a russet, tongue-shaped strand lapped the water between two miniature headlands of red rock. She watched as, without hesitation, he plunged into the white-blue curve of the waves. She stood gingerly on the edge, testing the temperature, bending to rub her arms with water colder than expected.

"Hurry up," he urged from the sea, hair black and shiny as a seal's amid the crashing waves. "Skinny-dipping is the best. You feel part of the elements."

Kate waded in up to her calves, trying to remember the last time she had swum naked. A strong, cold, wet hand suddenly grabbed her ankle and she fell forward. Water like freezing silk rushed about her body, over her breasts, between her still-throbbing thighs. A pair of strong arms drew her further into the water; she laughed, gasped, screamed, splashed. Spray flew between them like feathers. They flung themselves down on to the sand.

"Happy?" he asked her.

"Oh yes. And you?"

"Of course. I have everything to be happy about. I have met you. We have had a wonderful afternoon together. And last night I had a fantastic piece of news from Odile."

"Odile?" Kate's thoughts swirled immediately back to the house. Last night had been not nearly so enjoyable for her. A bass note of apprehension boomed through her stomach.

"She's found an art dealer for me in Paris. A very prestigious gallery. It could make all the difference to my career. I could make some money at last!" He grinned.

"That's brilliant," Kate said, genuinely glad. "Er . . ." she tried to sound casual. "Any idea when Odile's coming back?"

"Not for a while. She asked me to let you know. Her sister's not improving much, apparently."

"Oh." Kate could not disguise her disappointment.

Fabien's brows rose questioningly. "There is a problem, Kate?"

Kate shook her head violently. She was determined not to mention her midnight visitor to Fabien. It was, after all, unlikely he had seen the apparition; he would hardly paint through the night if he had. What was, on the other hand, very likely was that he would think she was either mad or paranoid. Or both.

"Sure?" Fabien pressed.

"Sure." Kate smiled. "Really—it's nothing."

24

W ord that diners had, within living memory, been spotted enjoying themselves at the Restaurant des Tours had swept the town like wildfire. Everyone in Ste. Jeanne seemed to want a piece of the action, not to mention the chef's *tarte tatin*.

Every available table was already full as—fifteen minutes after the official start of Kate's shift—she and Fabien bowled up in the Mercedes, attracting admiring glances from those already queuing. Kate scrambled out of the car and tried to slink into the restaurant without Celia seeing her.

She failed. "Get your order pad, dirty stop-out," Celia hissed, whizzing past with armfuls of *pistou* soup. "You're in charge of all the tables to the left of the bar."

The evening flew by. After the first sitting there was a second and, incredibly, a third. Kate, rushing back and forth between arcades and kitchen was too busy to think. Except to register, with an intermittent thrill of fear, the sour presence of the Café de la Place owner outside his denuded establishment across the square.

"Wow," Celia muttered, dashing past with plates of *tarte tatin* just after the clock had struck half past ten. "We really must be the talk of the town. Look at who the cat's dragged in. On your side, thank God."

Completely ignoring the queue and sitting at one of Kate's just-vacated tables was a familiar fat man dressed entirely in black. He was accompanied by a nervous blonde of a certain age. A younger, more beautiful blonde was honking loudly into a small silver mobile. "*Yah,*" she bawled. "*It's like, a typically French place. Tray sheek, darling. Hottest place to eat on the Riviera at the moment. So of course we had to come. It's*

*amazing, okay? Makes the Caprice look like a truck stop. It's simply
packed with the A-list—in fact if I bend forward I can see Julia Roberts."*

What Champagne actually could see was a couple from Hampshire who had requested their steak very well done. The Andover list, presumably. Not that Kate noticed any of this. Her eyes were riveted on one thing only. The fourth member of the St. Pierre party. *Nat.*

He wore white jeans that exactly matched his teeth, and what looked like a pair of flat silver mules. His chest was bare and tanned a deep brown. His hair was lavishly streaked—by the sun presumably, although Kate would not have put money on it—and his eyes blazed with satisfaction at the stir created among the diners.

Battered by a storm of conflicting emotions, Kate clung to the lee of one of the arcade pillars, well out of the group's sight.

"What's going on?" demanded Celia, whizzing past. "What are you skulking there for?"

"It's him. Nat." Kate was now shaking violently.

"Oh God. *'Course* it is. With Champagne D'Vyne!" Celia's mouth was a tight line of disapproval.

"Striking couple, aren't they?" Kate gulped.

"Only in the sense that I'd like to strike them. With one of Chef's cleavers, preferably."

"Oh God, Celia." Kate was dry-mouthed with panic. "I know this must sound really pathetic, but I just don't want to see him."

"But darling, *why,* when you can pour the evening menu all over his nasty deceitful *lap?*" Celia stood on her tiptoes and squinted in Nat's direction. "Those lovely white jeans are just *crying out* for a generous dollop of tomato. And think how lovely scalding hot *pistou* will look on that manly chest. Or red wine. Or whatever."

Kate hesitated. From time to time she had visualized such a moment. Wreaking revenge on Nat by whatever method came to hand. But now the moment was here, she shrank from it. What struck her forcefully was how unpleasant it was to see him again. That deceitful mouth, those knowing, self-satisfied eyes, that miserable, bitter heart. He looked handsomer than ever, but even more thoroughly pleased with himself. How could she ever have found him attractive?

"Always remember, darling," Celia was saying, "revenge may be a dish best eaten cold, but a hot one thrown everywhere comes a close second."

Kate smiled faintly. There was another consideration too. After her blissful afternoon with Fabien and the promise of a wonderful new friendship starting, pouring soup over someone seemed banal. Cartoon vengeful. In a way, after all, she felt grateful to Nat. If he hadn't been quite so selfish and manipulative, she and Fabien would never have met.

"Look, Celia, I just want to forget it all ever happened. But I can't serve that table. I just *can't.*"

Celia glanced assessingly over. Several members of the queue were muttering restively. Marty St. Pierre, meanwhile, had spread his enormous legs either side of his chair and was banging the table. "What do you have to do to get fucking served round here?" he was roaring.

"Don't worry." Celia squeezed Kate's arm. "We'll swap sides. You do mine, I'll do yours." A second later, she was gliding authoritatively up to St. Pierre.

"I'm afraid there's a wait," she informed him with freezing politeness.

"We don't *do* waits," said the fat man challengingly, removing his cigar from his mouth and fixing her with cold, hostile little eyes.

"You don't?"

"No."

"I see."

"So what you gonna do about it?" St. Pierre growled menacingly.

"Marty, darlin'," murmured Mandi, flashing Celia a nervous, apologetic smile.

Champagne giggled and pouted at the developer/financier. "Oh Marty. You say the funniest things." From the safety of distance Kate saw Nat too snigger sycophantically.

"Look, lady," Marty snarled at Celia. "Do you know who I am?"

"I do." A hush had fallen over the restaurant as everyone followed the drama. Celia's voice rang clear and unintimidated over the tops of the diners' heads. "But I'm afraid we operate a strictly first-come, first-served basis here. It's the only fair way."

Marty St. Pierre rose slowly and threateningly to his feet. Towering massively over tiny Celia, he placed his florid jowls in her face. "Look, lady. I'm the one guy round here you really don't want to mess with." His mouth was savage with spittle. Kate felt a twinge of pure terror for Celia. "Now you listen to me. This is supposed to be the hot new place, right? So you'd better tread carefully with me. Or," his voice rose to a bellow, *"I'll close you down even quicker than you fucking started up."*

There was a gasp from the restaurant. Kate, sidling along the wall, tried to catch her friend's eye. Celia should retreat while the going was good. No one would blame her. The knowledge that she had precipitated Celia into this situation was agonizing.

But Celia was unmoving. She stared back at St. Pierre with wide, innocent eyes. "Hot new place?" she repeated with loud pantomime incredulity. *"Hot new place?* Mr. St. Pierre, I'm glad to say all this is very easily solved. It's simply a case of mistaken identity. The thing is, you've got the wrong restaurant."

"*Wrong restaurant?*" roared St. Pierre.

Celia stabbed a finger towards the Café de la Place. "*That's* the one that everyone's talking about," she said gaily "You'll be much better off over there. Better food, better wine, better everything. People only come here because they can't get in there."

There was a suppressed titter among the Restaurant des Tours diners, especially those who were refugees from the Café de la Place.

St. Pierre slammed purple, spade-like hands on the table and heaved himself up. "Well, let's get over there then," he roared.

The St. Pierre party lumbered across the cobble square to where the Café de la Place owner was waiting delightedly to greet them. Celia showed the front of the queue to the vacated table and staggered into the bar passageway.

"Christ," she hissed, gratefully sipping the brandy Kate had brought her. "What a disgusting *bully* that man is."

"Celia, I'm so grateful." Kate's tongue was loose with relief.

"Don't mention it." Celia closed her eyes briefly. "A damned close-run thing, as I believe one of my ancestors once said. Now let's get on with it, shall we?"

Despite trying hard, Kate could not concentrate for the rest of the night. Glasses slipped, bread dropped, cutlery went clattering to the ground. It was impossible not to keep glancing over to the Restaurant de la Place, and the distinctive figure in white. Long legs stretched out, arms folded, that familiar sneering laugh twisting in her gut as, from time to time, it rang smarmily out. The occasion was obviously related to Champagne's efforts to get Nat into the film business. No doubt he was pestering St. Pierre for a part.

The mogul's loud, brutal voice could be heard vibrating through the evening air like a plane engine. "*How many times have I told you. You can forget all about that fucking olive mill. It's a waste of fucking time and money.*"

The noise in the Restaurant des Tours dipped as the diners listened. Oh God, Kate thought sympathetically. *Poor Mandi.*

Poor Mandi, however, seemed finally to have had enough. Both restaurants hushed entirely as she rose slowly to her feet. Even the gypsy musicians stopped playing. Then Mandi went off like a bomb. "*You fuck off yourself,*" she shrieked. "*I'll do what I fucking well like.*" Seizing her glass of wine, she hurled it straight into her husband's face.

Then she pushed back her chair and fled across the square. As she entered the Restaurant des Tours, and disappeared inside, spontaneous applause broke out among the diners.

Across the square, there was a crash, as of chairs being hurled backwards from a table. Marty, Nat, and Champagne were leaving. "Food's bloody crap anyway," St. Pierre was snarling. "A shithole, like the rest of this bloody village."

Seeing Nat loping out of the square, Kate felt her entire body sag in relief. So that was it. An unpleasant coda to an unpleasant experience. Now, hopefully, she would never, ever see him again.

"Great news, by the way," Celia muttered, passing with a stack of empty soup bowls. "The Troll's disappeared. He hasn't scared anyone off for ages."

"Disappeared?" Kate flicked a glance to the bar doorway. The Troll was indeed absent from his usual station. "Disappeared where?"

"God knows," Celia called over her shoulder. "According to Pappy, he was last seen helping poor Mrs. St. Pierre find the loos. Just what she needed to push her over the edge completely, I imagine. Talk of the devil, here they come now."

Kate stared over at the bar entrance. An emerging Mandi St. Pierre was beaming into the face of the Troll. Who, it had to be said, looked a good several degrees less forbidding than usual. "Thank you," she was saying to him in halting French. "You've been very understanding. It's been lovely to talk to you."

Kate rubbed her eyes hard. She really was seeing things now. Hearing them too. The Troll? Understanding?

It was dark when Kate awoke. She fumbled immediately for her watch. 4:30 A.M. The dark hour before the dawn. And the feeling, once again, that she was not alone.

The silence in the room was absolute. The companionable croaking of the toads in the valley had ceased hours ago. All Kate could hear now was a high, taut note of tension. Her rasping breath echoed hotly in the dark space beneath the duvet.

Fear hammered at her temples and banged in her ears. Remembering, as a breath-squeezing weight gathered in her heart, that fear itself was more terrifying than whatever she might be afraid of, Kate raised her head slowly from the dark, protective fug.

She was wrong. Fear itself was a breeze compared with what now met her eyes.

There, as before, silhouetted against the faint but growing light in the French windows, stood the cloaked figure. She stared with horrified fascination at its impossible tallness and blackness, the way it transmitted malevolence like a radio mast. As before, it made no sound. The white circles of the empty eye sockets and the rictus smile stared from beneath its shadowed hood.

Kate knew she ought to be rational. Ought to measure the figure against the remaining list of suspects. Was it taller than Marc de Provence? Less bent than the café owner, less curvy than Nicole? Her brain, however, was refusing to work. Logic and sanity shredded and dissolved before the hideous actuality of the sight.

"Who is it?" she croaked from a throat dry with fear.

The figure neither replied nor moved.

Kate slid a shaking leg clumsily to the floor. "Who are you?" Her voice was trembling. "What do you want?"

As she moved, the figure stopped. It seemed to get bigger. Kate realized with a mighty jolt of the heart that it was *approaching*. Gliding slowly, soundlessly towards her as she cowered against the mattress.

Kate snatched up her leg and pressed back against the wall. She tried to wrench her terrified gaze away, but her eyes remained bolted to what she least wanted to see. The bone-glow and the moving shadow.

She tried to scream. Nothing emerged but a broken-chorded squeak. The dark figure was almost on her now; she could see the gaps in the grinning white skull. Kate squealed. All attempts at bravery abandoned, she dived beneath the duvet, expecting any minute to feel the freezing hardness of dead bone on her own, living skin.

When she emerged some time later, her arms were stiff and numb with the force of pressing her hands protectively to her head. She had clearly been in this position for some time. Had she fainted? Sticking her head cautiously above the duvet, she saw the sun spilling across the pale wooden floor. The air outside was full of blueness and birdsong. The apparition had disappeared.

After some minutes' deep, restorative breathing, Kate decided to get up and doing. The house by daylight was not a frightening place. Keeping busy would take her mind off things and there was certainly plenty to do. Several days had passed since she had given the Comtesse's house the thorough clean it was due.

Walking around, she saw it needed one. The dry weather seemed to produce an extraordinary amount of dust. As before, it lay thinly on the floor of the sitting room and spread gray and gritty along the tops of the picture frames. Dust danced like champagne bubbles in the golden wedges of sunshine slanting through the windows. Even the gleam of the glass staircase treads was dulled.

Kate decided this time to work in approved Mum and Gran fashion, from the top of the house and working down. Her starting point would be Fabien's studio. Which was fine, obviously; was he not always saying he wished he were tidier? Well, that much at least she could do for him. Armed with her second-to-none cleaning skills, she could tackle the mess currently rolling like the Mississippi across his work area. And in doing so, thank him for the unforgettable lunch he had so generously given her.

Mop, bucket, duster, and arsenal of household products in hand, she ascended the staircase. She felt exultant. What better or more practical way to thank Fabien for the most wonderful afternoon of her life?

After an exhausting two hours hard at it, Kate sat back on her aching heels. Gran and Mum, she thought, would be proud of her. She had scrubbed the wood of the trestle tables until they gleamed and, dusting and wiping everything carefully first, packed the jumble on top into the many battered empty boxes and crates lying around. She had sharpened blunt pencils, arranged paints according to the spectrum, and thrown away the mountains of thickly color-smeared newspaper lying about the dusty floor.

Next she started on the canvases. Compared to the rest of the studio they were arranged reasonably tidily. But Kate had the organizing fire in her blood. They could be stacked straighter and take up less space. She began to pull out the pictures at the front, pausing to admire the one of herself that was not herself. "*I've always been haunted by a certain few faces,*" he had said. "*And yours is one of them.*"

Kate delved further into the paintings. More of Odile; smiling, stern, naked, clothed. A study of a village square that was recognizably the Place de l'Eglise, with three familiar figures at the side. She smiled. In a few witty lines, Fabien had expertly sketched in that nerve-racking triumvirate of the Trout, Pappy, and the Troll.

Her delight was short-lived. Halfway down the row of canvases, she turned back a painting and gasped aloud in horror. The image was conveyed with Fabien's signature lack of fuss. Yet the black-eyed, full-lipped face was unmistakable, as was the lithe, long-legged body which, naked, revealed full and springy breasts. It was Nicole.

As the first shock subsided, Kate stared miserably at the picture.

Nicole looked beautiful and desirable. And, by the looks of it, desired. The way she had been painted seemed supercharged with sex. Stretched invitingly across a background of rumpled sheets, her back was arched slightly and she was looking at the artist with eyes full of seductive intent. The expression on her face didn't strike Kate as the kind of look the average model trained on the average artist. The queen had never looked that way at Lucien Freud; at least, not as far as anyone knew.

What had gone on between these two? At the very, very least, the beautiful Nicole had been here, naked, alone with Fabien. Here, in this very studio. She glanced suspiciously at the chaise longue, whose previously rumpled sheet now lay in the corner en route to the washing machine.

"Kate!"

She had not heard him come in. The canvas clattered noisily back against its bedfellows as she whipped round so fast the muscles of her neck crunched. Fabien stood in the doorway, a surprised look on his handsome face.

"You have found my picture of Nicole."

"She's very beautiful," Kate muttered.

"Exquisite," Fabien corrected.

His tone was reverent. To her jealous ears, regretful too. She had no difficulty jumping to the most obvious and unpleasant conclusions. Had the breakup been recent? Who had split with whom? Was he on the rebound? Yet did men on the rebound routinely lay on afternoons like yesterday? The memory fluttered in her mind like bright ribbon. It had seemed radiant with possibility. But possibility was obviously all it was.

"I didn't realize you were such a fan of hers," she said stiffly, remembering how offhand he had been about Nicole when they had all met in the street. Rude, even. He had said she was mad. All bluff, obviously.

Fabien shrugged. "We had a relationship, if that's what you mean," he said easily. "But it is over now."

Kate felt sour with jealousy. Over, was it? Did he seriously expect her to believe him? Were relationships with people who looked like Nicole ever entirely over? She doubted it. Unless, that was, you were the Troll, in which case the relationships never began in the first place.

Her swift train of bitter thought was derailed by a long, sharp intake of breath from Fabien. He was staring round the studio in amazement.

"It cannot be true," he murmured, apparently to himself.

Kate arranged her sulky features into an expression of grudging anticipation. It was, after all, her moment of triumph. One she had worked hard for. She watched him walk about the room, pulling out boxes and riffling agitatedly through them.

"It *cannot* be true." His voice was louder now, fractious almost.

Kate blinked. Something about this scenario was at odds with the way she had imagined it. Instead of being delighted with the results of her efforts, Fabien looked perturbed. Actually, he looked angry.

His eyes glowed as he stared at her, but not with desire and affection in the way they had yesterday. "What," he asked, in a low, level voice, "have you been doing in here?"

Panic bubbled within her. "I thought, er, that you'd work better if . . . I just, well, tidied it up a bit, that's all."

"Tidied it up. *A bit?*" He spat the words out as if they were bile. His face, drained of color, was pale and hard.

"But you were always saying how messy you were."

His hands flew to his hair and tugged it in fury. "*Yes, but I didn't mean* . . ." His hands dropped. "It is destroyed," he said flatly.

"Destroyed?" Kate echoed in horror. She felt sick, weak at the knees, despite the fact she was still kneeling on them. "But I was only helping. Putting your colors in order. Sharpening your pencils."

"Sharpening my pencils!" Fabien exploded. "Do you not realize I keep some of them blunt on purpose? As for the colors, I store them like that because I know where they are. And you've thrown away my newspapers, which I keep to remind me of how much of which color went into the mix to make other colors!" His eyes were sparking, his mouth a hard and furious line.

As he stood, moaning and clutching his hair, Kate hastily reassessed the situation. It had been a mistake. She accepted that now.

But she had meant well and Fabien was definitely overreacting. "I did it with the best of intentions," she defended herself. "I thought you'd like it."

"*Like it?*" yelled Fabien. "Do you not realize what you have done? *Ruined* my studio, that is what. Made it absolutely *impossible* for me to work here."

It was at this point that Kate decided he had overplayed the temperamental artist card. She'd spent all morning on her knees, for God's sake. Didn't that count for anything?

"Oh, don't be such a bloody drama queen," she spat back, goaded by the mocking, triumphant gaze of Nicole at the other end of the studio.

He was at the trestle table now, staring at its clinical neatness with horror. "And where is my skull?" he roared. "What have you done with it?"

"*Nothing!*" Kate bellowed in reply. "I haven't seen your bloody skull. Apart from that thick one sitting on your own bloody shoulders."

He gazed at her with icy fury. "Get out," he snarled. "Get out of here *now*. You have done enough damage. *Get out!*"

"It'll be a pleasure," snapped Kate. Turning on her heel, she stormed out of the studio, leaving the arsenal of cleaning products on the newly gleaming wooden floor. As she stomped furiously down the stairs she heard the clank and crash of Fabien kicking them savagely about.

25

"*Bonjour, Mademoiselle!*" The shock of the Trout's unprecedentedly friendly greeting, plus teeth-revealing beam, almost had Kate falling down the stairs as, red-faced with fury, she left the Comtesse's house. She gaped at the broad receding back as the Trout swept on through the Place de l'Eglise, carrying, Kate noticed, a heavy-looking bag that jangled slightly. She was obviously bank bound.

"*Mademoiselle,*" someone else grunted as Kate hurried along, staring fiercely at the cobbles to discourage angry tears. Glancing up, she saw, to her surprise the Troll, heading busily out of the square with a box of tools in one huge hand and wearing an unusually cheerful bright yellow shirt. He was twitching his mouth about in a peculiar way that Kate incredulously realized was a smile. Even more amazingly, was not that peculiar smell, which trailed in his burly wake, the unmistakable whiff of aftershave?

She headed grimly for the shadows. The world was out of joint. Any minute now, Pappy would come out of the bar dancing the cancan.

The leaden feeling that lay on her heart felt quite different from the hot rage that had followed the discovery of Nat's betrayal. Which was odd, as the situation was so similar. Only a self-deluding idiot like her could have supposed Fabien to be any different. In the great scheme of things, after all, she barely knew him. Not long enough to see that, emotionally, reliably, trustworthily speaking, he was all gong and no dinner, to use a favorite expression of Gran's.

She leaned against a nearby wall and lifted her head to roll back the pricking tears. She must move on. There was nothing special about Fabien—the blissful afternoon on the beach was obviously one of many spent with similarly willing girls. No wonder his routine—

chairs, table, picnic, cocktails, and of course *condom*—had seemed so polished. Typical of a Frenchman. And, no doubt, most typical of all of a Frenchman whose job was getting women to take all their clothes off.

Sniffling in the shadows, Kate, shoved both hands into her jeans pockets. The sensitive tips of her fingers touched something lumpy and hard in the bottom; small stones. The northern grit that Gran had sent, she remembered. While Kate had no doubt that it originated in the local garden center, was imported and probably no more northern than Fabien was, that was hardly the point. Smiling, she looked up at the ribbon of blue sky visible between the tops of the tall houses. She wasn't finished yet.

She mooched along to the *Gazette*. Hopefully Crichton would have got over his excitement about the ghost by now. Or perhaps he would still be so obsessed with it that he might actually delegate something interesting. She had so far not managed to get so much as a sniff of the film festival. Beyond the first-night party, of course.

Kate was surprised to see a small crowd gathered in front of the *Gazette*'s plate-glass window. What could be interesting them so much she had no idea; the *Gazette*'s window, after all, lacked even the curling photographs of the *Mockery*'s. But then she recognized the yellow baseball caps. It was Crichton's gang of tourists from Birmingham. They looked hot and had clearly been there for some time.

"Are you waiting for Crichton?" she asked.

The Ravioli woman nodded. "We don't know where he is. He's supposed to be toiking us to the perfume museums at Grasse this morning. Roilly looking forward to it, we were!"

"Well, I'm sure he'll turn up if we all hang on and wait," Kate said encouragingly.

"Woit!" exclaimed a formidable assisted blonde. "We've been woiting for over half an hour as it is. He told us to come here at eleven. It's twenty-five to twelve now."

There was a murmur of discontented agreement. Crichton, Kate realized, had a putative mutiny on his hands.

"Bloody shoime," added the auburn-haired woman. "I was looking forward to that perfume factory. Was going to do all my Christmas shopping while I was there."

"But it's *May!*" Kate exclaimed.

"Don't remoind me. I'm late doing it this year. Normally I've got the whole lot wrapped and labeled by now."

The blond woman looked at her watch and sighed.

"He'll be along in a minute," Kate assured them. "Bound to be. Unless something's come up." No amount of peering down the bright, bustling rue du Midi resulted in Crichton's appearance, however. The shambolic, linen-jacketed form stubbornly refused to materialize. Kate decided to look inside for clues.

To her surprise, the office door was open. Inside, everything seemed even more of a mess than usual. All the signs were of a hasty departure; the phone was off the hook and a half-eaten *pain au raisin* sat next to where an overturned takeaway coffee cup was leaking brown liquid over a heap of unopened post. Touching it with a forefinger, Kate found it was still warm. Crichton had obviously been here recently and had gone out for some reason, clearly in a tearing hurry. Odd. Especially when he was expecting his tour group.

Replacing the receiver, she noticed that the drawer to the left of Crichton's desk had been pulled out. It lay overturned on the floor surrounded by a muddle of papers, books, and general jetsam. Kate riffled through and noticed that the editor's precious St. Pierre dossier with its distinctive nuclear sticker did not seem to be among them. Wherever Crichton had gone, he had obviously taken it with him.

Suddenly, Kate spotted her name. It was on a Post-It stuck on a brochure for something called the Musée Palais Cascari, which appeared to be in Nice. *Kate?* Crichton had written on the Post-It. *Piece for "Out and About" column?* It was clear that the next job he had in mind for her had not been reporting on the film festival. It had been describing for the benefit of readers in need of ideas for visits this gloomy-sounding edifice which, according to the literature, contained a reconstructed seventeenth-century apothecary's shop on the ground floor. Fascinating.

On the other hand, it would be somewhere to go. Fabien was no doubt still kicking Monsieur Muscle in blind fury round the penthouse, so Odile's was obviously out of bounds at the moment. And would probably stay that way—rowing with Fabien was hardly likely to endear her to his adoring Comtesse. She'd be out of that job on the old lady's return; possibly before.

She decided not to dwell on this. Her immediate duty, Kate realized, was to help her boss and benefactor out of an even stickier patch than that currently accumulating on his post.

She went to the door. "Come in," she invited the crowd. "Come in out of the sun."

They shuffled inside, entirely filling the office. Kate, rummaging in the grubby kitchen, discovered a stash of lumpy dried milk in a somewhat rusty tin, ancient tea bags, and stacks of plastic cups. With a cup of tea in each of their hands, Crichton's group began to look more mollified, especially when Kate unearthed a packet of elderly Jammie Dodgers whose price sticker bore the address of *Ethel's English Food Emporium, 3 rue de Londres, Antibes.*

They waited. And waited. Eventually, at the point when all hope of Crichton's arrival had finally faded, Kate suggested to the group that they visit the Picasso Museum at Antibes. After racking her brains for the details of the drive with Fabien, she was even able to give them directions. Contentedly, they began to drift away.

Beset with memories of that first velvety evening with Fabien driving to the Hôtel du Roc under the Picasso Museum's ramparts, Kate leaned pensively in the *Gazette* doorway for some time after they had gone.

Eventually she sat down opposite Crichton's messy desk. He had left his naked lady lighter behind, which seemed odd. Next to her generous chrome form lay a bunch of car keys. Curiouser and curiouser: wherever the editor had gone with his dossier, he'd gone on foot.

The keys belonged, Kate knew, to the battered, dusty blue Renault Crichton kept parked round the corner. It was a vehicle of so disreputable an appearance that various Ste. Jeanne wits had written *Nettoyez-Moi* with their fingers in the thick dust on the bonnet.

She regarded the keys thoughtfully. If Crichton was otherwise engaged, then surely he wouldn't mind her borrowing his car for the trip to the Musée Cascari? Particularly as she had just saved the day with his tour group. And it wasn't as if he would be driving the car himself today; it was approaching lunchtime, after which he would be unable to drive. Unable to walk, quite possibly.

The Palais Cascari Museum, the brochure informed her, was in Nice Old Town. After a few wrong turnings and misunderstood directions, she finally arrived in the orange and ocher maze of ancient, narrow streets. The streets wound between shady buildings as high and sheer as cliffs. Washing dangled from the shuttered upper stories. Kate sensed a whiff of piracy in the dark doorways, an atmosphere of skulduggery and rundown romance.

The lane where the museum lay was a lane even danker than the rest. Kate hurried down its chilly length, starting at the occasional figure looming out of the shadows. Far above, in the narrow space between walls almost close enough to shake hands, a hot blue sky could be seen. It was, Kate thought, like looking up from the bottom of a well.

In the gloomy succession of buildings along the lane, the Palais Cascari stood out as a dwelling of importance. Carvings distinguished the windows and there was a large stone crest above the doorway. No amount of exterior splendor, however, could conceal the building's air of profound and threatening gloom.

Kate entered apprehensively into a vaulted courtyard. To the right was the apothecary's shop. Kate shuddered as she spotted arsenic and belladonna among the names painted on the china urns. The suggested threat of agonizing death rather set the tone for the place. As did the cadaverous—not to say ghoulish—information assistant.

The leaflet he handed over with bony yellow fingers had more information than the one she had. Kate learned now that the Palais Cascari had been built by one Jean de Cascar, a rich seventeenth-century merchant. Rising from the cobbled entrance yard, flights of wide white marble stairs, edged by fat balustrades, led to upper floors. The staircase ceilings were painted with a stylized, chalky design of red and white leaves, interspersed with a shield bearing a bloodthirsty black eagle. De Cascar's personal symbol, Kate read.

De Cascar might have been cash rich, but Kate considered him taste poor. Everything in the reception rooms was heavy, over-ornate, and thick with gold. He had obviously employed the seventeenth-century version of Marc de Provence to do his interior decoration, and subtlety had not been among the specifications.

The chapel, a small, windowless room painted sticking-plaster pink and full of shabby gilt reliquaries and rotting hangings, had an impressive air. Standing before the tarnished gilt altar, Kate swallowed as she felt, once again, someone's eyes on her back. But it was impossible, surely; the Thing could not have followed her here. What was possible was that she was becoming obsessed. Becoming paranoid. Gathering her courage, she twisted round to meet a moody, malevolent stare.

According to the typewritten label beside the painting, the gaze belonged to Jean de Cascar. He looked, Kate thought, every bit as depressing as his decorating; with a thin, pale, and bonelike face. Rather like the Thing, in fact. Kate shuddered and left the chapel.

She found herself in a passage painted an unattractive combination of mustard and gilt. It led through a sequence of doors propped open on oddly long hinges. Kate, already jittery, yelped in surprised terror as, entirely without warning, a figure appeared from nowhere, swiftly joined her and walked in step alongside. Then, with relief, she realized a mirror formed one entire wall of the passage. The other figure was the reflection of herself.

Time, Kate told herself, getting out her notebook, to calm down and pull herself together. And concentrate on the job in hand; writing down the place's finer points for prospective visitors. Presumably it had some, somewhere. She clicked her pen and looked round for something to recommend.

At the end of the mustard passage was a magnificent if somber bedroom. At its far end was an alcove announced with carved and gilded caryatids. Here, a four-poster bed with hangings the color of dried blood stood behind a floor-to-ceiling partition in which antique glass panes the texture of cloudy ice sat in a frame of age-darkened gilt.

She felt her heart break into yet another panicked gallop. This time, she knew, no mere painted pair of eyes were staring at her between the shoulder blades. Someone—or something—was in the room behind her.

She turned slowly. Nothing.

She paced to the bedroom entrance and glanced down the corridor. Again, nothing. Kate walked quickly back along the route she had taken. No one else arrived to break the swathed, antique silence. Even the sounds from the street below failed to penetrate the tightly closed windows. Apart from the ghoul at the desk on the ground floor, Kate seemed entirely alone in the building. The Palais Cascari was deserted.

She had come to a halt by one of the propped-open doors. Pausing, breathing in the stuffy, airless smell of dust and age, she sensed a swift, swishing movement behind her. As something painfully tight and bony grasped her arm above the elbow, her ears reverberated to a high-pitched scream. Her own.

Kate saw lava-lamp patterns of panicked pink and orange whirl wildly before her eyes. Then the survival instinct kicked in. She tore away and ran, heart thudding in unison with her heels. Jean de Cascar's ornate gold, tapestry, and painted ceilings blurred overhead as she sped back across his sequence of state reception rooms. Could she hear or was she imagining the heavy swish of cloth behind her?

She ran in the direction she hoped led to the stairs, only to find herself back in the chapel with the blood-caked Messiah. She doubled back again into the mustard corridor, racing alongside herself. Her eyes, she saw, were wide with fear.

And something other than herself, now, was moving in the mirror. Something immensely tall, clad in a long black cloak and clutching the neck of its cowl about its grinning skull face. The Thing.

Kate crashed in terror down the corridor, skidded round the corner and found herself back in the forbidding bedroom. Too late she realized the room led to nowhere but itself.

She looked wildly up into the corners of the room; could no one see what was going on? Were there no CCTVs, for Christ's sake? Sensing rather than seeing the cloaked figure glide into the bedroom entrance and pause, Kate seized the carved gilt handles of the boudoir's double door. After some energetic shaking, she succeeded in wrenching them open.

The air was filled with the dusty smell of ancient material. The only way out was through a window to the right of the bed which, Kate feared, and as a glimpse through its cloudy panes confirmed, led only to the steep downward plunge of the central atrium. The room she was in was at least three stories up. The drop was a good seventy feet.

But she had one chance. To her left, at right angles to the window, a side of the atrium wall opened on to one of the staircase landings. All she had to do was leap from the sill of the bedroom window and over the landing balustrade. The angle, admittedly, was awkward. She looked down again at the gulf below. If she wobbled on the ledge, or failed to jump high or far enough . . .

She had never been very good at heights. Or jumping. Sports of any kind, for that matter.

Behind her, the Thing was approaching rapidly. Kate scrambled on to the window ledge—and leaped.

26

She landed right on the eye of the landing floor's mosaic eagle. One ankle molten with pain—her foot had twisted awkwardly on landing— Kate shot as fast as she could down the wide marble staircase, dashed across the courtyard and out into the shadowy lane. After her came the protestations of the ghoul-assistant, who had been led to believe he would be interviewed later and who now saw his fifteen minutes of *Riviera Gazette* fame disappearing before his sunken yellow eyes.

Kate ran, hobbled and ran until she could do so no longer. She flung herself into a patch of sunshine as if it were sanctuary, bending over to ease her heaving lungs, her dangerously thudding heart. Gingerly she flexed her ankle; a bad sprain, but not broken.

The place where she stood was a junction, the confluence of two busy shopping streets. Incredible to think this had all been going on as usual while, mere meters away, she had been fleeing for her life. She lifted her face in the sunny air and stared at the passing crowds, thankful for the bustle and color after the palatial gloom and doom.

Then she saw him. Tall, deerstalkered and clad from head to foot in his signature ear-shatteringly-loud check. Marc de Provence.

Her stomach jolted in her throat. So had it, after all, been *him* beneath the Thing's flowing cloak? Was he so desperate to protect his identity—or identities—that he was prepared to kill her? It seemed too unlikely for words that this ludicrous figure, already disguised as Cholmondeley-Chatsworth, could have put another disguise on top as the hooded monk. But why else would he be chasing her, as he now obviously was? Except with the intention of finishing what he had started? She stared in dry-mouthed horror as he pushed through the shoppers and sightseers towards her. While he was no longer in a position to push her off a ledge to her death, she had no doubt he had other means about his person. A ricin-spiked syringe. A gun.

With a yelp, Kate fled, limping, into the crowds.

She barged her way through, ignoring exclamations of French fury, Anglo-Saxon outrage, and the occasional American-accented, "Hey, lady, watch where you're going!" She plunged down the busy lane before her and emerged into a lively market square.

It was, Kate guessed, with another twist of the heart, the market where Fabien had bought the picnic. As she sped through into the stalls, she gained a blurred impression of heaps of Provençal cornucopia. The air was full of food smells, sunshine, and lingering shoppers.

Kate moved swiftly through their ranks. Her knees felt about to give out at any moment and her ankle was pounding agony. Flip-flops, she was discovering, were far from being the most suitable of sprint-wear. Despite de Provence having both knickerbockers and a monocle to cope with, he was making up the distance.

Kate barged between the stalls, flinging desperate apologies over her shoulder. Twisting round from time to time, she saw with faint gratification that her pursuer was bearing the brunt of the outrage of those she had bumped into. One old woman smacked him with a large bunch of celery. A fishmonger shook his scaly fist. Others merely gawped at the eccentric figure of Marc de Provence. "*C'est un film anglais?*" Kate heard several of them murmur. "*De Sherlock 'Olmes, peut-être?*"

Then, for a split second, amid the sea of bobbing heads, she saw someone she recognized. A potential savior. Short, thickset, and balding, eyes hidden behind round black sunglasses. Pushing his way through the crowds in a hurry, looking around as if trying to spot someone. "*Ken!*"

They may have had their differences in the past, but surely he would help her now. Eyes straining pleadingly in his direction, Kate regretted every uncharitable remark she had ever made about him to Celia. She had, she hoped, repaired some of the damage to their relationship as they had clinked cappuccinos after the Old Mum revelations. But she hadn't seen much of him since and there was, she knew, plenty of ground to make up.

"Ken! Oh, please turn round. *Please!*"

For Celia's sake, if not for her own, he could hardly stand and watch as she was hunted to her death. "Ken!" she shrieked, waving an arm frantically in the air. But the noise of the crowd drowned her voice. The air, in any case, was full of waving arms, many trying to thwack Marc de Provence. Then, miraculously, Ken turned.

"Ken!" Kate yelped desperately. As he looked in her direction, however, she watched his expression change to a grimace and his mouth draw back in a snarl. Then a couple of taller shoppers obscured him entirely from view. Clearly, he still bore her a grudge. She'd been looking in the wrong place for help there.

*Thanks, Ken. Thanks for fucking nothing. Remind me to do you a favor sometime. If I live, that is.* But, if she were honest, did she have anyone to blame but herself?

Kate turned sharply into an offshoot of the main drag, a space noisy with live chickens in wooden cages and crammed with stalls whose tops were crowded with jars of all conceivable types of preserve. The vendors here lacked the polish of the others; both they and their goods had a more rustic air. On one stall, a woman who looked as if she could bend tree trunks presided over a stall of pickles and brawns whose centerpiece was an entire cooked pig's head.

Kate noticed now that she was not heading, as she had hoped, into the concealing maze of the Old Town. She was running into a cul-de-sac. As with the Palais Cascari bedroom, there was no way out. *Bugger.*

Doubling back and dashing by the honey stall, past the proprietor and his extravagant handlebar moustache, Kate felt her gut jerk with dismay. Flashing triumphantly at her from the other side, over the candles and soaps, was the Marc de Provence monocle.

He launched himself straight at her. Kate's vision briefly filled with noisy check before, a second later, something powerful hit her squarely in the chest.

"Got you," growled the designer.

They fell heavily through the air together, dragging the honey stall with them toward one of farmhouse produce. As they crashed amid jams, preserves, eggs, and goats' cheese, the sound of smashing reminded Kate of the first encounter with Crichton at the bar of the Hôtel des Tours. The stall gave way beneath them and crashed to the ground.

Aware that, just to round things off nicely, she was lying in an olive-studded pool of honey, Kate stared up from beneath a struggling Marc de Provence to find the tree-trunk-bending stallholder glaring down with blazing eyes and a moustache that almost rivaled the honey-seller's. With baleful deliberation she began to roll up her sleeves.

"*Run!*" urged Marc de Provence, scrambling to his feet and yanking Kate upwards.

*Run?* Run where? With *him?*

"Come on," urged the designer. "Quick. Before that bloody saleswoman tears our heads off and makes brawn out of them."

The tweeded arm pulled her to her feet and shoved her forward. "I can't," Kate gasped, swaying on her jelly legs and burning ankle. Then she heard the bloodcurdling roar of the stallholder. There was murder in it. "Okay," she muttered. "Maybe I can."

"You have a car, right?" de Provence shouted as they shot through the market. "Well, let's get to it, for Christ's sake."

Hang on a minute. Her assassin—the cloaked pursuer of the Palais Cascari—was pleading with her for *a lift?* The person she was trying to get away from wanted a getaway car himself? "You've got to be bloody joking," Kate panted.

"Not joking actually." He had dragged her into a small alleyway whose entrance was part-concealed by a large and busy vegetable stall.

"But," she gasped, "aren't you trying to kill me?"

"Kill you?" His monocle swung out in surprise. "Course I'm not bloody trying to kill you."

"Then why were you chasing me round the museum dressed as a monk?"

Marc de Provence's small mouth dropped open. "What are you talking about? I've not been near any museum."

"But . . ."

"Look, I don't give a toss who's after *you*. There's someone after *me*, all right?"

"What—that woman in the brawn stall . . . ?"

"Not just her." His voice was low and urgent. "Bit more serious than that. Let's go, shall we?" He gripped her arm.

"But why should I care?" Kate demanded, shaking off his grasp. "You pushed me out of your car. Why should I give you a lift in mine?"

A second later, something hard and round-ended was pressing her in the ribs.

"Because of this?" he asked, with a slow, evil smile. "Don't give me ideas about killing you. *The car*, if you don't mind."

Her breath coming in short, terrified bursts, Kate was frog-marched all the way back to the Promenade des Anglais.

Crichton's venerable vehicle tore willingly off with a shriek of tires. It had, it seemed, its owner's ability to rise to the occasion despite apparent decrepitude.

Marc de Provence flopped back against the passenger seat and groaned loudly. "Christ. That was a near bloody miss."

Then his eyes, flickering to the driving mirror, suddenly dilated with alarm. "Bugger," he shouted. "He's after us. Put your foot down, can't you?"

*Who's after us?* "But I don't know where I'm going!" Kate yelped back. The low row of shops and villas that faced the sea had given way to a vast and rocky cliff that formed the bend round into a large port.

"Outside lane! Outside lane!" screamed de Provence. "He's gaining on us!" Reaching over, he grabbed Kate's knee and pressed her leg forcibly down on the accelerator.

The Renault shot round the port, Kate weaving wildly through gaps in the traffic to accommodate the velocity. "Middle lane, middle lane," shrieked Marc de Provence, crushing her leg down even harder. The weight on her tender ankle brought tears to her eyes. Kate shot through a red light, flew up a hill, and found herself on a sunny narrow road hugging the hillside above the sea.

"Go, go, go!" ordered her companion, peering in the mirror again.

"Up there," he added, gesturing wildly towards a sign bearing the legend *Haute Corniche.*

Kate knew the name. The highest of the three Corniche roads leading over the rocky hills from Nice to Monte Carlo was one of the Riviera must-sees. She had not imagined seeing it in quite these circumstances.

Kate had never driven at speed on a bendy, narrow road before. Having no choice, however, she pressed down the accelerator, muttered a prayer and ate up the bends like a NASCAR driver. As the road climbed, the blue expanse of the Mediterranean, practically alongside to start with, suddenly seemed an awfully long way beneath. The only object between the car and the ever-more-precipitous drop from the side of the cliff was the barrierless edge of the road. An additional concern was the number of sharp, blind bends. It was impossible to tear one's eyes off the road even to look in the rearview mirror.

"Is he still after us?" she gasped.

"Of course he fucking is," de Provence shouted. "You want me to get the gun out again? Move it, will you?"

Kate glanced at the mirror and saw to her surprise that the car following them was small, blue, and clearly finding the ascent of the Corniche a struggle. The sun on its windscreen made it impossible to see who was driving it.

Another lorry was bearing down on her. Swerving violently, she veered the Renault back into the center of the road. Trees, villas, sides of bare rock, and glimpses of sapphire sea shot past. Kate zoomed on, ever faster. Yet still the small blue car remained in her rearview mirror.

"Get rid of him," de Provence was shrieking. "Get him off our tail. Or . . ." He made a move towards his pocket.

"Okay, okay!" yelped Kate, pressing her foot down.

As the road up got steeper and steeper, Kate decided it was now or never. The Renault's engine sounded as if it were about to explode. She awaited the moment, then, with a mighty wrench of the wheel and a skidding of tires, twisted suddenly into a passing place. The blue car shot helplessly past. By the time their pursuer had turned round and returned, Kate and Marc de Provence had speedily reversed up the overhung driveway of a nearby villa and were hidden entirely from view. They watched as the blue car belted past the drive bottom on its way back down to Nice.

"Right," Kate said, tipping her head back against the seat. "I've kept my part of the bargain. Can I go now?"

The designer smiled at her. It was not a particularly reassuring smile. "I'm afraid not," he said lightly. "In the interests of destroying the evidence, I'm going to have to get rid of you after all."

Kate swallowed. Her eyes fixed on the torn ceiling out of which ragged ends of yellow foam were seeping. She was starting to shake.

"But don't worry. I won't shoot you until you've driven me to where I want to go. Drive on," de Provence commanded.

Kate released the hand brake and slowly piloted the car back out on to the road. So, as long as she was driving, she was safe. The thought gave her a little encouragement. While the urge to scream and beg was tremendous, a still small voice within warned that playing for time was vital. As was conversation. It was not unknown for hostages to talk their way out of these situations. She took a deep, shuddering breath and tried to control her chattering teeth.

"Well, if you're going to kill me, you may as well tell me," she suggested in as controlled a voice as she could manage.

"Tell you what?"

"What's going on. What all this is about."

"Oh. That." Kate noticed now that his voice had a camp esturial twang. His normal tones, presumably. Meaning that he was neither Marc de Provence nor Perseus Cholmondeley-Chatsworth at all really, not that she had seriously thought he was the latter.

"So who *are* you? You're not Marc de Provence and you're certainly not Perseus Cholmondeley-Chatsworth."

"No," he agreed. "I'm Arthur Turtle from Beckenham."

She forced down an explosion of mirth. At this delicate stage in negotiations she could literally die laughing. "And who are you running away from?"

"A short, fat, bald Cockney called Ken Scoggins."

"*Ken?*"

De Provence—she could not bring herself to think of him as Tur-tle, not at this late stage—looked amazed. "You know him?"

"Of course I do."

He just deserted her in her hour of need in the marketplace, in fact. Which was why she was in this bloody mess. "He's a friend of my friend Celia. A very good one."

"Is he now?" De Provence looked at her speculatively.

But Kate, for her part, was looking suspiciously back at him. The ends of her fingers were buzzing. "It's you, isn't it," she croaked. "The one he's been looking for? *You're* the swindling crook."

De Provence looked indignant. "Well, I wouldn't put it quite like that."

"You're the one who stole Ken's mother's lottery winnings."

"Stole? *Borrowed,* perhaps . . ."

"You're not an interior designer at all, are you?" Kate stared at him accusingly. "It was all part of the con, wasn't it? Of course it was. Only an idiot would think that that—what do you call it, *Baroque and Roll?*—was the work of a *professional.*"

As the de Provence nostrils flared, Kate felt a stab of fear. She mustn't forget that she was talking for her life here. One wrong move and . . . she swallowed. "Well, what I mean is . . ."

"I'll have you know that I *am* a professional," de Provence interrupted. "A professional interior designer, more to the point."

"Of course you are. Of *course.*"

"I attended a paint effects course at the Eaton Square School of Design. Under Lady Violet Wincham. Entirely thanks," de Provence added, "to the generosity of Mrs. Scoggins."

"Whom you met in the salad section of Harrods food hall."

"No, I didn't."

"Yes, you did."

"No, I didn't." In the end, de Provence explained, it had been by the *vegetable* counter that he had run into Eliza Scoggins, a purple-haired octogenarian in whose largely visible veins the blood still flowed strongly. He had deduced this much from the avid way she watched him handle, a suggestive smile on his face, a particularly thick organic carrot.

Days later he had moved into Mrs. Scoggins's flat and the rest was history. Eliza Scoggins, certainly, was history after he had persuaded her to finance his Eaton Square course and "lend" him her remaining available funds to start up an interior design business.

But Mrs. Scoggins's entire capital had turned out to be sufficient only for one shop. After, that was, her young protégé's considerable catalogue of debts had been paid off sufficiently for a bank to take him on.

The other problem, de Provence told Kate, was finding the right name to trade under. Something people would recognize and remember.

The name Marc de Provence had leaped out. Pretending to be French in England would be infinitely easier; hardly any British person could speak a word of any language other than their own. That the name's immediate context was a type of clear French brandy couldn't have been less important.

It was a simple matter to launch a website full of thrilled star endorsements in which the nonexistent celebrities were conveniently never named "out of respect for their privacy." This had, as intended, attracted the interest of the *Celebrity Channel*, and thus the business was launched.

Alas, de Provence soon ran into trouble. The kind of wives who wanted his look tended to have husbands who didn't want to pay for it; Slack Palisades being the supreme example. Peter Hardstone, in fact, had not yet coughed up the full amount for the job he had done there.

But this had been nothing—*nothing*—beside the day he received the news that Eliza Scoggins's son Ken was on his tail. Ken had, he was told, been making enquiries at the design school, had discovered the website and knew all about Marc de Provence. He had also vowed bloody vengeance after discovering that, after Marc de Provence had "borrowed" from it, his mother's bank account held exactly thirty-five pounds.

"So," de Provence said in glum conclusion, "I was well and truly buggered after that. Had to put Slack Top behind me pretty bloody sharpish." Choosing where to go next had not taken long; where else, after all, did a young—well, young*ish*, he amended, catching Kate's eye—man on the make go in search of rich, bored, gullible women? The South of France, obviously. Choosing a new disguise had not taken long either. Masquerading as an upper-class Englishman would, de Provence had decided, be much easier in France, where they expected all Brits to look like deranged Sherlock Holmeses.

So to the Riviera had come Perseus Cholmondeley-Chatsworth. He had immediately started combing antiques fairs for suitable victims. As luck would have it, within days he had run into Mandi St. Pierre, who was trying to decide between two elderly commodes. And who, it emerged over a drink or six, just happened to be looking for a designer for a property on a newbuild luxury estate that sounded like everything Slack Palisades was cracked up to be, but wasn't. Arthur Turtle had been unable to believe his luck. Until, that was, he discovered that Toilet Gardens was just as much an abject failure as its British counterpart; that Mandi's husband was some sort of gangster and that the property she wanted working on wasn't her house anyway but some collapso heap in the garden that required skills he couldn't even put a name to, let alone perform. All that had been bad enough.

And then the real blow had fallen. The day before he had run into the one person in the world he least wanted to see. The person who had vowed to leave no stone unturned before he found the man who had, with one flutter of his blue eyes, fleeced his mother of everything Dale Winton had, with one push of his mahogany-tanned hand, given her. In other words, Ken Scoggins. De Provence had known he was in the area—there had been a car chase at one stage, which Kate might remember.

"Of course," Kate said crossly. "The day you pushed me out of the van."

"Well, desperate times, desperate measures, you know," de Provence said breezily. "Anyway, I ran into the bastard on the rue du

Whatsit. He recognized me straight away—not surprising with this blasted deerstalker, I suppose. Been on the run ever since."

"And you're on it again now," Kate said grimly. The blue car—now recognizably Ken's, of course—had reappeared in the driving mirror and was gaining on them. Fast.

De Provence shot a glance over his tweeded shoulder and yelped. "Let's go!"

Kate shot him a speculative look. Her plan had worked to the extent that he seemed to have warmed towards her in the past few confessional minutes. It was a gamble, admittedly, but might now be the time to escape with her life? "Look," she pleaded, spotting a passing place. "If I pull in, you can bail out. Run away. He'll never catch you."

The designer stared at her. "Me? Bail out? On my own?" His arm moved. A second later, the hard, round coldness was pressing against her ribs again. Kate felt sick. She had gambled—and lost.

"Stop the car," he hissed. "And get out. With your hands up." He jabbed the gun painfully against her ribs.

"Why drag me into it?" Kate wailed despairingly as she climbed out of the car on wobbly knees. She looked wildly around for passing traffic; there was none. Where were the lorries and camper vans when you needed them?

De Provence prodded her along as if she were a prize heifer into a clearing concealed from the road by a group of tired and dusty bushes. "Because Scoggins is a friend of your friend Celia. He's hardly going to bump me off while I can do the same to you. *Is he?* So get out and put your hands up."

27

Occasionally and horribly frustratingly, a car swept past just the other side of the bushes. Mere feet away from where, the de Provence weapon in her ribs, Kate stood gazing down at this scrappy patch of sandy ground. She wondered whether the cigarette stubs, chewing gum and, more worryingly, scrunched-up clumps of toilet paper were the last things she would see on this earth.

The blue car, with Ken in it, was parked some distance from where she stood in the scorching afternoon sun, arms up against a rock with Marc de Provence behind her. From time to time he prodded her in the ribs with the weapon. Things had reached stalemate. There had been an initial, shouted conversation, in which de Provence threatened to shoot both his hostage and himself if Ken didn't immediately surrender his Saxo and allow them a getaway. Ken had refused and since then the situation had not advanced. Neither Ken nor Marc de Provence seemed to have any ideas about how to progress matters.

Sweat trickled down Kate's brow. From somewhere at the bottom of the hill, she heard a vehicle engine grinding as it struggled up. In a moment it would draw parallel with the bushes, then go past. Another chance of rescue lost. Yet what could she do? It wasn't as if she had any emergency flares on her, still less a whistle.

"I'm baking in these fucking tweeds," de Provence complained. She looked at him. Did he expect her to sympathize or something? She, after all, was baking, too.

It seemed to Kate she had stood for hours beneath a sun beating relentlessly down on her from a sky of sizzling blue. The approaching engine thrummed in her brain. As it crawled painfully up the ascent, her entire being throbbed painfully in response. Her eyes drooped, her tongue felt dry and leaden and nausea was beginning to rise. She groaned, and felt Marc de Provence poke her warningly.

The car, van or whatever it was had almost reached the little clearing. The noise was pounding so violently in her ears now that Kate longed for it to go past, get it over with, give her some peace. Instead of which, the noise ceased. The vehicle had stopped. Just the other side of the bushes.

She lifted her head and felt Marc de Provence stiffen behind her. The weapon was thrust harder than ever into her side. Then followed the blare of a radio, quickly switched off, the slamming of car doors, the sound of jaunty voices, of scuffing and twigs snapping beneath feet. The sound of people, Kate incredulously realized. People coming in their direction.

Then, amazingly, a man called her name. "Kate?"

It was a familiar voice, which her swirling brain, fumbling unsuccessfully for its Rolodex, couldn't quite place. It called again, sounding closer this time. "Kate? What the hell's going on here?" From the shocked yelp of the final question, she knew that he was in the clearing now. He could see what was going on.

"Help me," she muttered deliriously, expecting but no longer caring about the final explosion that, in a shower of vermilion gore, would shatter ribs and vital organs at any moment. In the event, she heard no explosion and saw no gore. Everything simply went black.

Kate opened her eyes slowly. She was lying amid soft whiteness in a room full of dim, diffused light. Had she died and was this heaven? Or hell?

Something—or someone—was putting its face up to hers. The eyes were black, delineated to hideous effect. The ebony hair was arranged in alarming spikes. The lips were metallic blue. It reminded her of painted skulls at the Mexican Day of the Dead. Or else . . .

"She's awake!" it exclaimed in a voice she recognized.

"*Darren?*" She raised a hand to her throbbing head. "Why are you here? Why am I in bed?"

Celia's voice. "You've had ghastly sunstroke."

Kate smiled slowly in relief. That explained it. Nothing had happened at all. She had merely been ill, here in her own bed in the Comtesse's house all the time. Suffering from hallucinations. She sat up gingerly. "I've been having the weirdest dreams. I dreamed that Marc de Provence was holding me hostage against a rock and sticking a gun in my ribs."

"That wasn't a hallucination," Darren said.

Kate puckered her pounding forehead. "Sorry?"

"And it wasn't a gun. It was a banana. He was holding you hostage with a banana."

"A *banana?*"

"That's right. An unripe one. Very hard."

"But . . . how could he have shot me with a banana?"

"He couldn't have. He was trying to scare you. He didn't have a gun, that's the point. Only a banana, which was left over from his lunch. He hadn't eaten it because it was so hard, or something. But as you couldn't see it, you thought it was a gun. As you were supposed to. In fact," Darren added, "we all thought it was a gun at first."

"Until Ken found out it wasn't," Celia said proudly.

"What did Ken do?" she murmured.

"Can't you remember?" Celia sounded disappointed. "I suppose you must have fainted by then, darling. Well, when Darren and his friends came round the corner . . ."

"We gave Marc de Provence a shock and so Ken took advantage of the moment," Darren butted in. "Real action hero stuff. You wouldn't have thought someone of Ken's age was up to it."

"*I beg your pardon,*" Celia said indignantly.

"He's obviously extremely fit," Darren said hurriedly.

"He's certainly that, darling."

"Anyway, he snuck out of his car and shot across the clearing while de Provence was still dealing with us. Then just like that," Darren snapped his fingers, "de Provence had bitten the dust and Ken was sitting on top of him. Holding de Provence's weapon."

"What a hero!" Celia sighed. "So brave."

"Which was when we found it was a banana."

"But Ken didn't know that," Celia pointed out loyally.

"'Course he didn't," Darren enthused. "He thought it was a gun too. He was a star. A complete hero. Amazing."

Kate was not sure, even so, that she agreed. She raised herself on her elbow. "Look, I hate to stick a spanner in the works and all that, but why did he leave me in the market? I mean, he saw me being chased and he just ignored me."

"He didn't, darling. He saw Marc de Provence, although I suppose we should call him Arthur Turtle now. He'd been chasing Turtle through the back streets but had lost him. Which was presumably when *you* bumped into him. And then he saw you both in the market, realized Turtle was chasing *you* and chased after *him*. You probably couldn't see him because . . . well . . ."

"He's small but perfectly formed?" Darren was obviously choosing his words carefully.

"Something like that."

Kate looked guiltily at Celia. The time had clearly come to stop assuming things about Ken. She had been wrong on every count so far. "That's fantastic," she said weakly.

"Ken *is* fantastic, darling," Celia said simply.

"So where's Marc de Provence . . . I'm sorry, but I just *can't* call him Arthur Turtle . . . now?"

"Ken's . . . ah . . . taking care of him, darling." Celia grinned. "Along with the police, from what I can gather."

Kate touched her pounding head. It was all too much to take in.

"Hurting, darling? That swindling bastard, making you stand for hours in the blazing sun. You were delirious. Sick as a dog. You should have seen the amount of green bile . . ."

"Er, thanks, Celia. I get the picture."

"Anyway, you've been out of it for ages. Eaten practically nothing too."

Beneath the covers, Kate slid a hand to her stomach. Or where her stomach had been. The precipice of her rib cage descended to a flat plain below.

"Chef's been cooking up lots of lovely, delicate things to tempt your invalid appetite, but you've barely touched them."

"*Chef* has?"

"Darling, he's been really rather worried about you. Turns out he's a complete hypochondriac—nothing excites his sympathies so much as a good illness. Everyone at the restaurant sends love, by the way."

"*Love?*"

"Yes, *love*. Really. We're all dying for you to come back. Er . . . Nicole's been helping out with the serving while you've been ill," Celia added casually.

Kate was appalled. "*Nicole?*"

A cagey expression crept over Celia's face. "To be honest, she's actually been rather good. Has quite a way with the customers."

"Yes." Kate thought sourly of Nicole's spectacular curves and almost as spectacularly short skirts. "I know the way you mean."

"So she's *thrilled* to be back at the Hôtel des Tours, let me tell you. As a matter of fact, I was thinking of asking her to stay on. We need another pair of hands now the restaurant is so busy and Bernard's spending all his time somewhere else."

"*Bernard* is? With Nicole back on the scene?"

"Oh, that's all over, darling. History. There's someone else now."

"Someone else?"

"I'm sure of it."

"Who?" Scuttling into Kate's mind came her last sight of the Troll. Grinning and smelling of aftershave as he carried his toolbox out of the square. To where? Or to whom?

"Search me, sweetie. But wherever it is he goes, he certainly comes back with a smile on his face. Look, darling," Celia stood up. "Now you're a bit perkier and we don't think you're going to die any minute, I'll just slip across to the restaurant and see if Ken's come back. And whether Cheffy has anything for you. I'm sure you'd appreciate a nibble, wouldn't you, darling? I know I would." She grinned wickedly.

As Celia slipped out of the door, Kate looked tiredly up at Darren. He was looking bewildered; the recent exchange of information had plainly meant nothing to him.

"What I don't understand," she murmured, "is how you knew that I was there." Impossible, surely, that he just happened to be driving past, just happened to stop and discover that someone who just happened to be his former colleague was being held hostage with a piece of fruit.

"Well, that's sort of what happened," Darren admitted. "The van's been on its last legs for a while. It conked out just by the bushes."

"But what are you doing here in the first place?"

"We're down here on tour." The dark eyes sparkled. "In case you'd forgotten."

Kate clapped a hand to her clammy forehead as it all came rushing back. "Oh God. The Chip Shop Records thing." The Punch Out, the Denholme Velvets gig, Nat Hardstone, Slackmucklethwaite itself, even, all seemed like a thousand years ago. "How's it going? Are you megastars yet?"

"Not exactly."

"So?" Kate probed. "Tell me."

Darren shrugged. "Well, we've gone down okay as a Velvet Underground cover band." He sighed. "But, to be honest, I'm not sure mainland Europe is up to speed with our particular sense of humor."

"Oh Darren." Kate bit her lip, imagining his disappointment. "I am sorry."

"Don't be. It's fine. It all worked out brilliantly in the end, anyway."

"But it was going to be your big break and everything, wasn't it?"

Darren nodded solemnly. Then, most unexpectedly, he grinned. "And actually, it still might be. Only not in the music business."

"*Really?* What other business then?"

Darren raked his long, ringed hands through his spiky hair, in the familiar old gesture. "Journalism. All being well, I'm on the verge of a major story."

Kate sat up and hugged her knees. Her eyes gleamed. "Tell me!"

Darren looked doubtfully over his shoulder at the door Celia had left ajar.

"Come on! Don't tell me, let me guess. Is it the Peter Hardstone story again?"

"Sssh!" Darren looked at the door once more.

"*It is*, isn't it! You're working on it again."

His eyes were wide with eyeliner and panic. "Look . . . walls have ears."

"Honestly," Kate said, grinning, "you sound just like Crichton." A shame that Darren wouldn't have the faintest idea who Crichton was. They would have got on well together.

"I've been trying to get hold of Crichton," Darren replied unexpectedly. "But it seems he's disappeared."

Instantly, Kate remembered the scene inside the *Gazette* office. The unlocked door, the spilled coffee, the sense of a hurried departure. "He's *disappeared*?"

"Yes. Hasn't been seen for a couple of days. Which is a bit frustrating, as my sources tell me he's been doing some investigation work along the same lines as me."

"*What* sources? What investigation? Why do you want Crichton?"

"Can't tell you. All I can say," Darren hissed, leaning closer, "is that I was hoping that me and Crichton could hook up. Work together. I want to join the team. Apparently he's got some shit-hot London journalist working with him already . . ."

"Er, no, he hasn't."

"How do you know?"

"Because that was me."

Darren barked with laughter. "You?"

"Don't ask." Kate put her face so close to Darren's that their noses briefly touched. She imagined a dot of white makeup on the tip of hers. "But Crichton was investigating Marty St. Pierre, not Peter Hardstone," she hissed. "He had a dossier . . ."

"Yes, I know. I was very keen to get my hands on that dossier." Darren drummed long, black-nailed fingers on the bedside table.

"But why?"

"Why? I've been *desperate* for someone to help me with this. Busting international crime rings is a tough job, you know."

"International crime rings? But aren't you after Peter Hardstone?" Kate felt as if she were going round in circles.

"I am."

"So what does Marty St. Pierre have to do with it?"

Darren leaned back and with a rattle of bracelets put both hands behind his head. "Only everything!"

"How do you mean—everything?"

Darren arranged himself more comfortably on his chair. "Hardstone's company's going down the pan," he said abruptly. "He heavily overinvested in Slack Palisades. The Inland Revenue are after him, not to mention Customs and Excise. And now there's an investigation into exactly what went on with Bracegirdle, the Council, and the Planning Department. Hardstone's in deep doo-doo, basically."

"Trying to hide it as well," Kate chimed in, remembering what Nat had told her. "Misstating the profits on the company accounts, every trick in the corporate book. But the banks are going to foreclose on him soon, unless he can come up with some kind of rescue package."

Darren's eyes were wide. "How the hell do you know all this?"

"Nat Hardstone told me," Kate confessed.

"Well, thanks for telling *me*," Darren snapped. "Anyway, the plot's moved on since then."

"But what does Marty St. Pierre have to do with it all?"

"He's Hardstone's brother."

"Hardstone's *brother*?" Kate yelped. "Why isn't he called Hardstone as well then?"

"Martin Hardstone had to change his name and leave the country after some nasty business with Scotland Yard a few years ago."

"So they're in business together?"

"Yeah. International media, property, and filmmaking. Well, that's the front at least. We're still investigating what really goes on."

"I suppose," Kate said consideringly, "it explains why the two housing estates are so similar. I did think that was rather a coincidence."

"So crap as well."

"Literally, in the case of Potty Park."

"They've never been big on consequences, it seems," Darren said. "Not thinking things through seems to be their business hallmark.

They were okay when they were dealing with papers, films, and a spot of narcotics and armament smuggling."

"What?" exclaimed Kate.

"Oh yes. Anyway, but property's a different ballgame. Between them Slack Palisades and Toilet Gardens have brought the company to its knees. Hardstone and St. Pierre are desperate for money to keep it afloat. They're desperate in general. Especially as they know that certain people are starting to piece the whole story together. The bribes over planning permission being just the start of it."

*Certain people.* Kate swallowed, picturing Crichton's ransacked office. The phone off the hook. The open drawer, pulled out and emptied on to the floor. With no sign among its contents of the folder with the nuclear sticker. She remembered too what had happened to Freya Ogden. "You don't think that Crichton's disappearance has something to do with all this? That Hardstone and St. Pierre have found out about the dossier and—"

Darren raised his eyebrows. "It could have," he said gravely. "It may well be that either Hardstone or St. Pierre got wind of what he was up to."

Kate sank back on her pillows. *Poor* Crichton. Where was he now? Had he been puffing and sniffing away, ploughing happily through his papers, when someone large and nasty appeared through the door? She pictured him, tied up and gagged, in the pitiless grip—probably literally—of St. Pierre and his equally bullying brother.

"After all," Darren added with relish, "they've got a lot to hide. What St. Pierre alone got up to round here in terms of contraband is outrageous. Unbelievable. You name it. Apparently there's an unmarked plane that lands at Nice Airport every Wednesday afternoon. And .."

"Oh God, not that again," Kate murmured. "Don't tell me. Crichton wanted to know what was in it as well. And now he's disappeared."

"Yes." Ignoring the last remark, Darren drummed his knees in excitement. "Things are definitely hotting up now. According to my intelligence, the Hardstone brothers are on the point of trying something really big and really daring to get the money to keep the company afloat."

"What?" Kate asked.

"Dunno. But I'm going to find out."

She looked at him with concern. "Darren, those men are dangerous. Especially Marty St. Pierre. He's a vile, cruel bully. Believe me—I've met him. And just remember what happened to Freya."

"Oh come on, Kate," Darren said scornfully. "It's the best story of my life."

"It could be the last story of your life as well." With an effort, Kate heaved herself up in the bed. "Please, Darren," she said earnestly. "Keep away from him. From both of them. Unless you want whatever's happened to Crichton to happen to you. They're dangerous, and if they're desperate they'll be lethal. Anyone who gets in their way will be swatted like a fly."

"She's right," boomed a deep voice from behind them both.

28

"Odile?" Kate stared into the gloom over Darren's shoulder.

The old lady came closer, high heels tapping softly over the floorboards, wrinkles silvered by the soft light filtering through the curtains.

"You are right," she announced. "Those people are dangerous and it is time to stop them. Before something dreadful happens."

"Who's this?" Darren stared at the collapsed face and back to Kate.

"My, er, landlady," Kate muttered. "Sort of."

"Well, what does she know about Hardstone and St. Pierre?" he hissed.

"I don't know," Kate hissed back. "Ask her."

"I know enough," Odile interrupted in English, "to be able to guess what they might be trying to do. That big and daring thing that you mentioned, in particular." She turned a glittering eye on Darren. With compressed mouth and raised eyebrow she took in his blue lipstick, inches of bracelets, spiked hair, and tight black jeans festooned with a multitude of studs and chains.

His eyes widened. "You do?"

Odile nodded. As she bent over Kate, a discreet, expensive, peppery whiff swirled around the pillow. "My dear, I have something to show you. To show both of you," she added, drawing Darren in with a glance. She smiled down at Kate again. "Are you well enough to come for a short walk?"

Kate swung her wobbly legs out of bed. She was relieved to find that someone—Celia hopefully—had had the forethought to put some pajamas on her. Not the most beautiful ever, admittedly, striped red-and-blue flannel, short in the leg and wide in the back. No prizes for guessing who they belonged to, she thought, seeing Odile eyeing them doubtfully.

"This way, then." The Comtesse clacked out of the bedroom, Kate following and a rattling Darren bringing up the rear.

They followed the smart brown-and-black–check back across the landing to her bedroom. Here, with the same practiced tug as before, Odile pulled away the bookcases concealing the entrance to her wardrobe.

Darren whistled when the rows of transparent clothes bags were revealed. "All vintage," he breathed, rattling forward excitedly and examining the labels.

"Didn't know you knew anything about fashion," Kate muttered.

"Part of my A-level history of art course, wasn't it?"

"I can see you would be interested," Odile interrupted. "It's obvious from your clothes. You have," she added graciously to Darren, "a most unique sense of style."

Darren looked gratified.

"And what period of art did you study in your course?" Odile fished out another cigarette.

"Modern," Darren replied. "Did a lot of the people you've got down there in your hall, as it happens. Laurencin, Lichtenstein—that collection of yours must be worth a bit."

Odile nodded, eyes screwed up against the smoke. "A bit, yes. But essentially they're a decoy. Like this collection of vintage clothes. It's a well-known trick to deter thieves. You use something less valuable to . . ."

"Distract attention from the *really* valuable thing you've got?" Kate guessed, tremulous excitement welling within her.

Odile nodded. "Only in this case," she lamented under her breath, "it doesn't seem to have worked."

Clicking smartly to the end of the room, she reached up and removed the picture of herself. Beneath was a small control panel, flickering with red and green lights. At the press of a switch, the wall slid away to reveal another room.

There were no windows. A wooden floor reflected a plain white ceiling. The room was completely empty apart from the pictures. About ten enormous canvases stretched down either side of each wall. Huge, colorful, bold—and unmistakable.

"Oh. My. God." Kate had recognized the artist immediately.

Darren looked at the Comtesse. "They're Picassos, aren't they?"

Odile nodded. She blew a nonchalant plume of smoke.

"But, I mean . . . how . . . did you . . ." Darren's voice faded helplessly away.

"Get hold of so many? Picasso gave them to me, of course. And some I bought—he did not like to give too many away, not he!" The Comtesse smiled, a faraway look in her good eye. "He was a friend. I modeled for him. That one, that one and that one," she pointed, her rings flashing in the lights fixed above each picture, "are of me."

Kate and Darren stared at the canvases indicated. One was of a dark-haired woman in profile. Two huge eyes with blue and green lashes, a pair of red lips and two black eyebrows were arranged on the exposed half of her face. Another showed a dark-haired, dark-eyed woman as a flower, her face the plant head and her body the stalk. Despite the abstraction, both were recognizable as Odile.

"Looks *much* more like me now than it did then," Odile smirked, pointing at the lopsided face.

"When did he paint you?" Kate asked, her brain teeming with other, more personal questions. Was Picasso nice or nasty? Had they been lovers? He was, after all, famously randy. And Odile *had* been very attractive.

"The fifties—when he came to live in Juan-les-Pins."

Darren's Adam's apple was yo-yoing with awe. "Must be worth . . ." Behind his mascara, his eyes were huge and speculative.

"Millions," Odile said flatly. "Tens of millions."

Darren was pacing up and down the rows of paintings like the surveyor of the queen's pictures. "They come from every stage of his career, don't they? It's a wonderful collection."

"And it has been gaining in value the whole time, sadly."

"Sadly?" Kate exclaimed. "What's sad about having something worth tens of millions?"

The old lady shrugged. "That depends how you look at it. You see, I don't care about the money. All I ever wanted was to hang my beautiful paintings on my walls. And then just look at them. But that isn't possible now. Everything Picasso touched is worth a fortune today. And probably quite a lot of things he didn't. If anyone knew I had these paintings, I would never be able just to look at them. I would have to wire them up to alarms, put Perspex cases over them, mount an armed guard—probably place them in a bank vault." She paused and sighed. "And now, of course, I *do* have to."

"You do?" Kate echoed. "Why?"

"Because someone *does* know I have them."

"Who?"

There was a silence, followed by a muffled explosion from Darren. "*Yes!*" he squealed, near-hyperventilating with excitement. "I get it. This is it, isn't it? *This* is what the Hardstone brothers have been after. *This* is their big plan."

"You mean . . ?" Kate gaped at her former colleague.

"The Picassos, of course," yelped Darren. "The Hardstones were planning an art heist. Stealing these paintings, then selling them in secret to some private collector. Stealing to order, I bet. The paintings would have disappeared without trace, without even touching a saleroom. I'm right, aren't I?" he appealed to Odile.

"I think so." Odile's elegant black shoe pawed at an imaginary mark on the varnished surface of the wood.

"*Yes!*" Darren punched the air. "Mystery solved at last. Christ, I wish Crichton was here to see it."

"Me too," Kate said sadly, realizing that that wasn't the only conundrum explained. Presumably the Thing was connected to all this as well. She looked at Odile. "Someone has been in the house trying to scare me. Crichton was right about that too."

"I owe you an apology, my dear," Odile said. "I rather suspected someone had guessed the paintings were there before I went to Paris. You remember when you first met me?"

"When you'd fallen on the cobbles . . . Oh, I see. You hadn't fallen at all, you mean?"

The white chignon twisted slowly from side to side. "Not until someone hit me over the head from behind, no." She tapped her skull. "Fortunately I have a very hard head. And they were in too much of a hurry to do it properly. They were rummaging in my bag looking for the keys to my house just as you were approaching round the corner."

"I see," Kate exhaled slowly. "But surely it was pretty high risk for them to do that? Anyone could have seen. It was broad daylight, after all."

"My dear, you forget. It was lunchtime." Odile smiled faintly. "Everyone's mind was on *much* more important things. So you see, I asked you to stay in my house. I thought a younger, stronger person would discourage the thieves."

"Thanks a lot," Kate said indignantly. "So you left me to the mercy of the Hardstones."

There was a pleading look in the old lady's good eye. "I did not—and you must believe me—know who the thieves were at that stage. None of it made sense to me until I heard your friend just now. But if he is right—and I am certain that he is—the situation is very serious. Marty St. Pierre is a very unpleasant man."

Tell me something I don't know, Kate thought. "Well, just look what's happened to Crichton."

"*Exactement.* My dear Kate, I do not want anything to happen to you."

Which makes two of us, Kate thought. "But how *did* the Hardstones find out about the paintings?" she mused. "I mean, if they've been hidden for decades and all that. Who else knows about them?" She looked speculatively at the Comtesse. "Fabien?" Of course, he was bound to know. Odile must have told him. And the fact the news had spread was the ultimate proof of his untrustworthiness. Surely even the Comtesse, previously his greatest fan, would see that now?

"Fabien?" Odile looked puzzled. "But of course Fabien did not tell them."

"How can you be sure?" Kate challenged.

"Because he has no idea. I have never shown them to him, although I would have liked to. He is a very talented painter. One day he will be great, I am sure of it."

Kate frowned. "But if you think he's so fantastic, why didn't you tell him?"

"Because so enormous a secret is impossible to keep, of course. It would have come out sooner or later. Fabien is very hot-tempered—"

"Isn't he just." Kate spoke with feeling.

The Comtesse raised her eyebrows. "He told me about the disagreement. I hope you can make up your differences soon."

Kate did not reply.

"Such a shame if you don't," Odile continued. "I thought you were quite well-matched."

*Yes*, Kate wanted to burst out. *I thought so too. Until I found he was also well-matched with Nicole and God knows how many other women.* But she remained silent and hoped Odile would drop the subject.

The Comtesse, unfortunately, seemed to have no such intention. "But you were quite right, my dear. That studio of his was a disgrace. Even Picasso's wasn't that messy, and that's saying something."

Kate was aware of Darren looking puzzled and trying to catch her eye for an explanation.

"The only other person who knows about the paintings is my sister Odette," Odile told them. "She also modeled for Picasso—that's her over there in the middle. The one with the foot coming out of her head and the hand out of her ear. But she has said nothing either. Until now."

"Why?" Kate asked, curious. "What's happened now that's so different?"

"Odette is ill, as you know, and has been for some weeks now. What I didn't know—until I went to Paris—was that she rambles a lot. Talks all the time, especially of the past, and reveals a lot of things she is unaware of. It would not take long, with some of the people she knows," Odile pinched her lips in disapproval, "for such news to get around. Collectors hear, galleries hear. My sister still has a lot of acquaintances in the art world. Not all of them very pleasant ones."

"Oh dear," said Darren.

"Just one thing." Kate's brow puckered. "Why are you telling *us* about the paintings now?"

Odile's shoulders slumped. "Because I can't keep them here any more. So it doesn't matter now *who* knows about them. Before long, everyone will."

"Won't they just!" Darren was licking his shiny blue lips and rubbing his hands together. His bracelets rattled deafeningly. "When the Hardstones are caught red-handed and my version of what happened is all over the broadsheets."

The Comtesse turned her glittering eye on him. "That's not exactly what I meant."

The wind drained from Darren's sails. "It's not? You don't want to catch them?"

"No. I am going to give the Picassos to the nation. Right away— now. I will make the necessary phone calls this very afternoon."

Darren's blue mouth dropped open. "*Give* them away?"

"Yes. Along with all the other pictures in my house. The house itself too. The inside, as I'm sure you have noticed, is a classic example of Modernist design." The Comtesse brought her veined, liver-and-diamond spotted hands abruptly together and clasped them. "I always intended it to be a museum of modern art in the end."

"Like the Musée Ile de France on Cap Ferrat," Kate said slowly. "The owner of that left her house and everything in it to the nation."

"Exactly that, my dear. The Ile de France is not my style, of course. But it's the same idea. I want this house and its garden to be a Mecca of modern art to rival the Fondation Maeght at St.-Paul-de-Vence. Which of course, with my Picassos, it will."

*The Fondation Maeght.* One of the wonderful places, Kate remembered, that Fabien had promised to take her to plus lunch afterwards at the Colombe d'Or. Well, obviously none of that was going to happen now. Under Odile's stare, she buried the sting of regret.

"But the Picassos, they're worth . . ." a stunned Darren was repeating.

"I don't *care* what they're worth," the old lady snapped, exasperated. "Do you think of nothing but money?"

"But what about the Hardstone brothers?" Darren tried a different tack. "Don't you want to see them brought to trial? Put in prison?"

Odile tapped her foot impatiently. "What difference will it make? The Côte d'Azur will be full of crooks just the same. So long as none of them get my pictures, that's all I care about."

"But you can't," Darren repeated stubbornly, "just *give* them away."

"Why not? They're no longer safe in my keeping. Why shouldn't the nation see what I have had for my own pleasure for so long? Besides, I won't be here much longer to enjoy them."

"Why, are you going somewhere? Moving house?"

"*Of course I'm not moving house!*" Odile barked. Darren leaped backwards, rattling with alarm. "What I mean is that I'm an old woman now. I smoke too much. It is likely I'm not long for this world. . . ."

"*Not long for this world?*" grumbled a voice from the doorway. "What sort of silly talk is that?"

Everyone whirled round as one to stare at the newcomer.

"There's nothing wrong with *you*," the voice continued briskly, addressing the Comtesse. "Nothing that a good meal wouldn't sort out. Just look at you. No wonder you're feeling peaky. So skinny you'd disappear if you turned side on. I've seen more meat on a lolly stick."

As Odile's mouth dropped open, Kate stepped forward, rubbing her eyes. "*Gran?*"

The hallucinations were obviously back. Of course, this could not possibly be her octogenarian relative. Though it looked astonishingly like her. Standing, mere feet away, on the upper landing of the Comtesse's house, carrying her familiar large white handbag and dressed in her familiar blue raincoat. Completing the ensemble was a cream-colored hat with a transparent plastic rain bonnet tied over the top. Odile stared at the latter in amazement.

"Of course it's blooming well me." Thrusting one strong tea-colored leg in front of another, Gran marched into the room. "By 'eck, it's warm," she added, removing the rain bonnet. "I always wear this just in case, but it's fair crackin' t'flags out there."

"But how . . . ?" Kate's jaw dropped even lower than the Comtesse's.

". . . did I know where to find you here? Got your address, haven't I? From the one letter—*one* letter mind, that you sent me. Since then, nothing. *Nothing*—for all your fancy promises!"

"Sorry," Kate mumbled, aware of Darren and Odile staring.

"So I got up off my you-know-what and came straight here," Gran continued, broad, capable hands firmly planted on broad, capable hips.

"I didn't even know you had a passport."

"Oh, I've always kept that up to date," Gran twinkled. "You never know when it might come in handy for something. I went up to the library, got on the Internet—"

"Internet?" Kate gasped. She had always imagined her grandmother's library visits to revolve around the Mills and Boon section.

". . . and found one o' them cheap flights. Twenty-five pound—not that cheap, but never mind. You can't take it with you. There's no pockets in a shroud." Her grandmother looked Kate critically up and down. "By gum, you've got thin."

"Do you think so?" Kate smiled, distractedly.

"Wasting away, you are," the old lady confirmed. "Not that it doesn't suit you, mind. Your hair's gone a bit blonder with the sun as well. Look like a completely different person to when I last saw you, you do."

"Believe me, I feel like one." Kate smiled ruefully. "Is that all your luggage, Gran?" She gestured at the huge white handbag.

"It certainly is. Travel light, that's the key. One of the things I learned during . . . anyway, never mind that now. Here I am. Found out you'd moved to here from the hotel. Very nice young man at the hotel showed me where the house was. Very well-built. Bernard, I think his name was."

*The Troll!* The thought of her grandmother and the Troll actually meeting—nay, actually *conversing*—was almost more than Kate's overwrought sensibilities could absorb.

"Nice woman he was with as well. Mandi, I think she said she was called. Looked a flighty piece. Turned out to be very down-to-earth though."

Mandi? With the Troll? Was this what the mysterious disappearances with his tool kit were all about? Was he—in the teeth of all opposition—helping Mandi with her olive mill?

"Spoke very highly of *you,* she did," Gran added.

"*Who's Mandi?*" Darren was mouthing. Kate, meanwhile, was staring open-mouthed at her relative.

"Surprised to see me, eh? *Tee hee.*" The old lady rubbed her shiny red hands. "Well, you never write—well, hardly. You never phone. What else did you expect me to do?"

"Does Mum know you're here?"

"Your mum thinks I'm on the Slackmucklethwaite pensioners' annual trip to Blackpool!"

"How *is* Mum?" Kate's tone was apprehensive.

"Worried sick, of course, yer daft 'ap'orth. Hasn't slept properly since that bloomin' row you had on the phone with her."

"Really?" Kate swallowed. Tears were never far away where the subject of Mum was concerned. And here they came, pressing hard against the corners of her eyes. She blinked furiously.

"Not that she'd say so, mind," Gran was adding. "Stubborn as a mule, she is when she puts her mind to it. You and her, cut from the same cloth you are. But that's why I'm here. Someone's got to break the bloomin' deadlock. As well as find out whether you're still alive or not."

"Is she still cross about *Northern Gig*—the book, I mean?" Kate ventured. The book, moreover, that she hadn't picked up for ages, and seemed unlikely to ever again. Hardly worth alienating her nearest and dearest for.

"Cross?" Gran lifted off her hat. Placing it carefully on the dressing table, she shook her shining white curls. "Course not. She's got over it. She's been too worried to be cross. Matter of fact," she chuckled, "I even found her reading it the other day. Engrossed, she was. Shut it up sharpish when she saw me, though."

The piercing relief of the next few seconds was quickly canceled out by the sudden, disturbing delusion that her grandmother had turned to Odile and was now speaking fluent French.

I am, Kate thought, *definitely* going mad. What else but an insane fantasy explained Gran offering to cook the Comtesse *un vrai pudding de Yorkshire avec boeuf rôti, et comme dessert un Richard avec des boutons—ou* Spotted Dick, *comme on dit en Anglais—servi avec* . . . "what's the French for custard?" the old lady suddenly demanded.

"Crème anglaise." Kate remembered Dad's fagash joke. She was relieved Gran hadn't.

Gran nodded. "Of course. *That custard with fagash in,*" she quoted and turned back to Odile. "*Bon. Je vais le préparer pour vous. Il sera un repas vraiment* . . . rib-sticking!"

"*Rib-sticking?*" Odile repeated faintly.

"I didn't know you could speak French." Kate stared at Gran in admiration.

Gran lifted her chin, revealing inches of wrinkled ivory wattle. "There's a lot you don't know about me, love."

Kate smiled. "So you keep saying. But I'd still like to know where you learned French."

"In France, of course," the old lady returned smartly. "Where else?"

"But I always thought you'd never left Yorkshire."

"Well, you know what Thought did, don't you?"

Kate grinned at the familiar sally. "When?" she pursued. "*When* were you in France?"

"Oh, back when God were a lad. Before you were born. Before your mother was, even."

She must, Kate calculated, be talking fifty, sixty years ago. "You don't mean during the *war,* do you?" Her grandparents had always been uncharacteristically silent on the subject of what exactly they had been doing during their country's finest hour.

"As I say, it were a long time ago. It doesn't matter any more." Gran's lips tightened. Yet something urged Kate to keep probing.

"You were in France during the war," she mused. "Were you a nurse? A Wren?"

Gran shook her head.

Kate rummaged through her general knowledge. Munitions? Digging for Victory? But if Gran was in France, though . . .

"Don't tell me, Mrs. Gawkroger," Darren bounced in. "You were one of those Special Operations Executive women who parachuted into France and helped the Resistance."

His tone was jokey. Yet Odile looked up sharply, her one good eye slamming into focus. Gran said nothing. Her lips merely tightened further.

"*Gran?*" Kate whispered, as the amazing possibility took hold. "*Were* you?" Gran, leaping out of planes for king and country! Gran, scrabbling through the undergrowth with her hair in a forties roll, a knife in her teeth, and secret papers in her bra! Gran, alone in a foreign country, living by her wits and enterprise—rather, come to think of it, as she had urged her granddaughter to.

"I'm saying nowt," was Gran's maddening reply. "But I will say this. Whatever your mother seems to think, I've had a more interesting life than most folk."

Kate's eyes swirled. It was all too much to take in. Everything that had happened recently—the Palais Cascari, the banana stickup, the unveiling of the Picassos—all these were unbelievable enough. But that her no-nonsense, much-loved but presumed parochial aged relative was a war heroine—that was the most extraordinary revelation of all.

"*Gran!* You should write it all down."

"You should, Mrs. Gawkroger," Darren agreed.

"What would I be wanting to write it all down for?"

"People have made millions out of novels about less."

"Well, bully for them," said Gran.

"But Gran! You've never said anything about it before."

"And I'm saying nowt now."

"But you should."

"Should I heckerslike. Far too many folk talk about nowt else. Whenever you switch on the telly, open a paper, there it is. The bloomin' war. You'd think it had never ended. All the bloomin' stuff about Nazis and the like. Everywhere. How are we all supposed to put it behind us and go forwards when there's almost as much about it now as there was at the bloomin' time?"

Odile, Kate saw, was nodding in agreement. She seemed to be blinking a lot.

"But it's part of our history," Kate urged. "World history, come to that."

Gran's lips tightened again. The subject, they implied, was dropped.

"Is this that young man you were raving about in your letter?" she demanded, peering at Darren with a ferocity that made him start. His bracelets rattled in alarm. "François or whatever his name was?"

"Fabien," muttered Kate through gritted teeth, hoping Odile, who seemed lost in thought, would not hear. "No, Gran, of *course* it's not."

"Oh." Her grandmother sounded disappointed. "Haven't fallen out, have you? He sounded a nice lad."

"He was. Is, I mean," Odile interrupted. "I agree with you," she added to Gran. "It's a shame they're not seeing each other any more."

"Fair looking forward to meeting him, I was," Gran complained.

"You'd have liked him," Odile rubbed it in.

Kate said nothing, outraged at being ganged up on by two octogenarians.

Gran screwed up her face and peered at Darren again. "So who's this then? How come 'e knows me name?"

"It's *Darren*, Gran."

"Mrs. Gawkroger." Darren inclined his head respectfully.

"You've met him," Kate prompted. "He's from the *Mercury*. I used to *work* with him. He's been for tea now and then."

"But my hair was probably a different color then," Darren added helpfully.

"So long as he's not your boyfriend," the old lady said. "Couldn't imagine you pining like you obviously are about someone who looks like they've put their finger in a socket."

As Odile looked amused and Darren indignant, Gran started to unbutton her coat. "Better take this off, or I won't feel the benefit when I go outside. Come on, love," she commanded the Comtesse. "Take me to your kitchen and let's get cracking. You'll be feeling better in no time with a good square meal inside you, let me tell you. Not long for this world . . ." the old woman paused for a suitable exclamation of disgust . . . my *foot*!"

"You are very kind," Odile smiled. "I am very interested in this spotted dick."

"It's no wonder you're in a state," Gran chided. "Besides never eating, you've no furniture in this house. Need to get yourself some nice comfy chairs, you do. And some nicer pictures while you're at it." As she led Odile out of the room, Gran swept an unimpressed glance over the Picassos. "Give me nightmares, them will."

"Me too," said Odile with a faint smile.

29

"Darling!" Celia exclaimed. "You haven't noticed yet, have you?"

It was mid-morning at the Restaurant des Tours. Kate was helping Celia to lay place settings for the newly launched lunchtime opening. As usual, and much as she tried to stop herself, she was thinking about Fabien.

Hard as Kate worked at keeping the fires of her resentment stoked, she was finding it difficult to think of the stormy artist without melancholy. Regret even. Should she have stomped off like that during the cleaning row? He had, admittedly, been *extremely* rude about what had been intended as a labor of love. But, if he really had kept the studio messy on purpose, were his objections to her blitz so surprising? Still, the damage was done. It was all quite literally done and dusted.

"Have I noticed what?" Kate looked around. "Oh, right. You mean Old Grumpyknickers has got himself some new sunshades?" Across the square, the irascible owner of the Café de la Place was taking delivery of some new outdoor umbrellas. "White ones too. Like ours."

In acknowledgment of the fact that the number of regulars now far exceeded the space under the arcades and spilled out nightly into the square, the Restaurant des Tours had invested in some large white shades to mark the lunchtime opening. Celia had been very particular about the right size, right shape, and right kind of teak support to shelter outside diners from the broiling sun. That the Café de la Place had done the same was, however, a cause for joy rather than indignation; an indication of the huge and growing success of the hotel restaurant was the large spillover of business for the establishment opposite.

"He's certainly taken your advice to heart," Kate observed, watching Mr. Café de la Place liberating his sunshades from their plastic scabbards. Unable to bear the sight of a business opportunity going to waste, Celia had some days ago marched over and pointed out to the café owner that, instead of standing there sulking, he should be making hay while the sun shone. Or profit while the Restaurant des Tours was open. After some initial arguing and accusation, the café owner had simmered down, seen reason, fired his inadequate chef, and hired a whizzy graduate from a local catering school. He was now churning out "Provençal with a witty twist" to all comers. Kate wasn't entirely sure about such inventions as "naked ravioli," which was the stuffing without the pasta. Nonetheless, the Café de la Place's new, lighter menu was, as Celia who had suggested it had intended it should be, the perfect complement to Chef's more solid offerings at the Restaurant des Tours. Trade at the Place had been brisk ever since. And, while he could hardly be described as a reformed character, there were notable changes in its owner's attitude. He had grimaced a smile at her a couple of times and had, since Celia had pointed out it could upset some customers, entirely stopped kicking domestic animals.

The café owner had, of course, been one of the suspects for the Thing, although a question mark had always hung over his having the necessary fitness. The dash in the Musée Cascari, certainly, had been beyond the scope of a man with varicose veins like his. The phantom had ceased appearing anyway, or so Kate assumed. News of Odile's intention to give the Picassos to the nation would have reached the Hardstones by now.

She herself had moved out of Odile's; now the Comtesse was back, the need for her to stay there was over and Gran in any case had enthusiastically accepted Odile's invitation to take her place. Kate had been glad to leave, and not only because of free-range apparitions. The longer she stayed there, the greater became the odds of her bumping into Fabien. Not something she especially wanted to happen.

Gran, certainly, had not mentioned seeing any ghosts. She was generally too busy singing Fabien's praises for that. "Why can't you two just make it up?" she would demand.

"Because Fabien hates the sight of me."

"Gerrawaywithyer," Gran exclaimed in disgust. "You need yer 'eads banging together, you two."

A shame, Kate thought, twisting her musings determinedly away from the artist, that she would never properly get to the bottom of who the ghost had been. First Ken had dropped out of the running, then Marc de Provence. Even Nicole had been ruled out now, Celia having revealed that she had been working nights in a twenty-four-hour Texas theme bar down on the Antibes road ever since walking out on the Hôtel des Tours. But if, as seemed most likely, it was linked to the Hardstone brothers, why had it been such a different shape from them? One of their henchmen, she supposed.

"I'm not talking about that bloody café owner," Celia was saying. "Haven't you noticed anything *else*?" She waved a hand around above the table she was setting.

Kate sighed and made an effort. "Well, the wineglasses look great." They shone like the sun, it had to be said. Getting the five old ladies who sat on the step to help with the ever-increasing amount of washing-up had been the inspired idea of Gran.

Gran had, within hours of her arrival, become practically the sixth member of the coven. She had discovered that they were by no means averse to the idea of a little gainful employment. Some had drifted elsewhere in the kitchen and were now engaged in vegetable-chopping for Chef, whose repertoire they swelled with various long-held recipes of their own. Everywhere Kate looked, things were perking up for the most unlikely people. Apart from her, that was.

"Well?" Celia demanded.

"Why are you waving your arm about so much . . . *Christ*, Celia!" Kate's astonished gaze finally settled on what she was meant to see. A diamond the size and brightness of a car headlight on full beam. "That *ring*!"

"Not bad, is it?" Celia was puce with satisfaction. "Ken gave it to me."

"Where'd he get it? The Tower of London?"

"Very probably, darling," Celia trilled. "No, seriously, someone in Hatton Garden who owes him a favor, apparently. It arrived by courier yesterday."

"So you're getting married?"

"Yessss!" Celia's voice lingered ecstatically on the *s*. "Once my divorce from Lance comes through. And afterward we'll stay in Ste. Jeanne. Now Ken's—ahem—sorted out the business with his old mum, he rather fancies trying his hand at running the bar here. While I, of course, carry on running the restaurant."

"Great," Kate said, rather leadenly. "Congratulations." In the nick of time, she steered the tanker of her thoughts from running aground on the sandbank of her lamentable luck in love. She grinned shakily at her friend.

"Darling, you *do* approve?" A tremor of suspicion darkened Celia's bright face. "Only, and I may be utterly wrong here, but I always rather got the impression you weren't awfully keen on Ken."

"I wasn't at first. Partly because I thought . . ." Kate hesitated. Much for the same reasons she had never told Fabien, she had left Celia unenlightened about the apparition in the bedroom.

"Thought *what*?" Celia fixed her with a beady blue gaze. "That he was a fantasist, basically."

"No, not that—I know I got him all wrong about that."

"Then what?"

"You won't believe me." Kate grinned sheepishly. The nightmare was over now, after all. Surely Celia could be told?

"Try me."

"Well, a funny thing happened while I was staying at the Comtesse's." As she began to tell the story, Kate derived a certain dark enjoyment from watching her friend's expression change from cynical to surprised to amazed.

"Someone dressed from head to foot in a swishing black *robe*, darling?"

"That's it. Oh Celia, it was *hideous*. You can't imagine."

"With a *skull* face?"

"Yes. *So* scary."

"And you haven't seen it since?"

Kate nodded.

"Well, I've got news for you, darling," Celia directed a narrow squint over Kate's shoulder into the square. "Something answering to that description is walking this way right now. What's more, it's with your grandmother."

"*You're joking.*" Kate whirled round, oblivious to the tray of glasses she held in her hands. Oblivious too to them sliding in an earsplitting stream to the floor. "I don't believe it. I don't *bloody* believe it."

Walking across the cobbles of the Place de l'Eglise, just as Celia had said, was Gran. She wore her blue raincoat, her hat, and a grim expression. One large and capable hand was clamped tightly round the arm of someone dressed from head to foot in a black swishing robe. Someone carrying Fabien's missing skull underneath their arm. Someone looking furious and apprehensive in equal parts. Someone with dark-blond hair, full red lips drawn sulkily downwards, and cheekbones possibly visible from the moon.

"Nat!" she screeched, amazed and outraged in equal measure. "*Nat Hardstone!* Fuck! It was *him!*"

"Language, young lady," Gran chided as she drew level with the restaurant. "I've had enough of that sort of thing from Lord Fauntleroy here."

"But . . . how?" Kate gasped. "How did he do it? How did he get in?"

"Through the balcony doors, 'e says."

Kate looked hard at Nat. He stared coolly back, no hint of apology in his features. His obdurate, arrogant face seemed as untroubled by guilt as the first time she had met him, the afternoon they had spent in Billy's. A lifetime ago, that seemed now. She should have known not to trust him. The signs had all been there.

Gran glared at her prisoner. "And to think I thought you were such a nice boy when you came to our house," she snapped. "I was led astray by your knitwear, I suppose. Still," she sighed, "it wouldn't be the first time."

Kate boggled. What was *that* supposed to mean?

"Your father was right," Gran told Kate. "Didn't take to Lord Muck 'ere at all, he didn't."

"I remember," Nat said, with feeling.

"Shut up, you." Gran stared at him fiercely. "I've had a bellyful of you as it is."

"I should have listened to Dad," Kate wailed. "Or Darren. He couldn't stand him either."

"That so?" Approval twinkled in Gran's eye. "Maybe 'e's not as peculiar as he looks, then."

"No," Kate said loyally, "he isn't. I wish I'd listened to him."

"You were never going to listen to anyone, were you heckerslike," the old lady said firmly. "You were head over heels. Plainer than the nose on yer face it were."

Kate looked at Nat. He glanced sulkily back before his gaze slid to the floor.

Despite being a good two feet shorter than Nat, the old lady quite clearly had a grip of iron. He was obviously incapable of wresting himself free.

Kate asked her grandmother, "What happened? How—"

"Did I get hold of him? You may well ask. There I was, last night, lying in bed minding my own business, with me curlers in an' all. Just finished me bit o' knitting to send me off to sleep. I 'ad, and were settling down when who should hove into sight but summat that looked like a monk. Gave me the fright of me life, it did. So I sat up in bed and shouted at it to go away, but it didn't. Just stood there, starin' at me, like. So I got up, grabbed one of me knitting needles and a few seconds later I had him on his back on the floor."

"You mean you overpowered him?" Kate gasped. "How the *hell* did you manage that?"

"*Language!* You're not too big to go over my knee, you know," warned the old lady, despite all visual evidence to the contrary. "But since you ask, it's not all that difficult. Not with a pipsqueak like him." She threw a contemptuous glance at Nat. "Fought much bigger than him in me time, I have. Soldiers an' all."

"*Have* you?" Celia and Kate chorused.

"All part of me war training, weren't it?" Gran said breezily. "Overcoming the enemy."

"Your . . . ?" Kate yelped. So it really *was* true, after all?

"I'm saying no more about it. Already said too much, I 'ave."

"So is that how you spent the night?" Celia chipped in. "Holding him at knitting-needle point on the floor?"

Gran snorted. "Course not. I dragged him up by his hair and shoved him in my bathroom. And locked the door. Spot-on place to keep a prisoner. No winders an' a slidin' door that you can't pick the lock of. Then I went back to bed to get me eight hours."

Celia went to the edge of the pavement and looked accusingly down at Nat. He stared defiantly back at her. "But what did you think you were doing?" she asked him. "Why were you dressed up like that? Did you think Kate was still there?"

"No point talking to him," Gran butted in. "He's saying he won't talk to anyone but his solicitor now. But I got the whole story out of him earlier, let me tell you. Chapter an' verse. Interrogation techniques!" She shot a teasing glance at Kate. "That were part of me training an' all."

"So what was it all about?" Celia interposed, seeing Kate still grappling for words. "Why was he haunting poor old Kate?"

"Well, it's a bit complicated." Gran jerked a shiny, wrinkled thumb at Nat. "He's here because he wants to be an actor and his uncle's in the film business . . ."

"Marty St. Pierre," breathed Kate.

"That's the chap. But his dad . . ."

"Peter Hardstone."

". . . is none too happy he's over here. So his uncle said that he'd make it all right with his dad for him to stay. But only on condition that he did a very particular little acting job for him."

"Dressing up as a ghost to scare *me*," Kate said slowly.

"That's it!" Gran nodded emphatically.

"So I'd leave the house and clear the way for his uncle to—"

"Run off wi' them bloomin' awful paintings of Odile's," Gran nodded. She rolled her eyes. "I can't understand it, really I can't. Give me *When Did You Last See Your Father?* any day o' t'bloomin' week. That's a proper painting, that is."

"So he obviously didn't realize I'd left Odile's," Kate reasoned.

"No. His uncle had decided it were worth a final go at them paintings before all the hi-tech security for the art museum gets installed. But he'd reckoned without me being there."

"So what happens now?" Celia asked, getting, as was her way, to the point.

"He gets delivered into the hands of the authorities," Gran announced. She lifted her chin. "Bernard, if you please."

There was a movement at the back of the arcades. Kate and Celia turned round to see the Troll loom massively out of the bar doorway. As they watched, he rolled onwards towards Gran and, with a respectful nod, relieved her of her prisoner. Registering his huge bulk and impassive features, the expression of alarm in Nat's blue eyes deepened to terror.

"Odile made the necessary telephone calls," Gran explained. "Bernard volunteered to take our friend here down to the local police station. An' then, if I'm not very much mistaken, it'll be home to Daddy after all."

"If Daddy's still at home," Celia murmured. "He'll be in a police station himself soon by the sound of it."

Kate gazed numbly at Nat. There he stood, glowering in the sunshine. The man for whom she had thrown up everything she had known, because of whom she had lost her job and risked alienating her family. The man who had abandoned her and betrayed her, and who had, in addition, tried literally to frighten her to death, both in the Comtesse's house and, more frighteningly still, in the Musée Cascari. She should, she knew, probably hate him.

And yet, standing there, in the custody of her octogenarian grandmother, dressed ludicrously in a cowl under the scorching Provençal sun, Nat cut a pathetic figure. A comic one, even. The chain of events he had set into motion had brought misery and very nearly tragedy, but it was impossible not to see its humorous side. The thought of him spending the night in Gran's bathroom after being forced to confess at knitting-needle point . . .

Her shoulders started to shake. Then Celia's. Next to capitulate was Gran and finally even the Troll. As Nat stood, burning with heat and humiliation, the four of them, and a number of amused passersby, stood helpless with laughter around him. Which was, Kate knew, the ultimate revenge. For someone who took himself as seriously as Nat did, being laughed at in public was the unkindest cut of all.

It was late afternoon of the same day. As she and Celia set the tables for the evening sitting, Kate spotted a plane rising into the sunny sky. Did it, she wondered, contain Nat? He was due to be deported now she had decided not to press charges; Celia had thought she was mad. Kate felt, however, that being sent back to his father, his film career in ruins, was punishment enough. She had no wish to see him again anyway, in a witness box or anywhere else.

They finished the tables in silence. "Aren't you going to ask me?" Celia asked eventually.

"Ask you what?"

"What you were about to ask me before we got so rudely interrupted."

"Erm . . ."

"Where we're getting married?" Celia prompted.

"Where are you getting married?" Kate asked obediently.

"Here, of course. At the church in the square." Celia ducked out under the arcades to gaze happily across at the slab of peach-colored bell tower shining in the sun. "Bernard has set it all up for us, the poppet."

"That was nice of him to help. Some of that ecclesiastical jargon must be a bit tricky in French."

Celia's smile suddenly lost some of its heat. "My French is *quite* up to it, thank you. I was educated at a convent school, after all. No, it's more the fact that as Bernard is planning to get married there himself, he thought he might as well sort us out at the same time."

"*Bernard's* getting married?"

"Yes, didn't you know? He and Mandi really hit it off."

"He's getting married to *Mandi*? *Mandi St. Pierre*?"

"Sweet, isn't it?" Celia cooed. "It's her he's been helping with that building work, apparently. They're converting some collapso old shack—an outside loo or something—at her house in Toilet Gardens."

Kate was speechless.

"It seems," Celia continued blithely, "that love bloomed among the sand and cement."

Her words fell like weights on Kate's heart. Everywhere she looked, the most unlikely people seemed to be fitting snugly into happy little holes. Except for herself.

Kate stared at Celia's retreating back as, swinging her empty tray, she disappeared back inside the bar. Finishing the last of her napkins, Kate sulked into the square. She was thrilled for everyone, really she was. But had none of these happy lovers any consideration for those among them with *slightly* less good fortune on the love front? On the other hand, no one could argue that Mandi and Celia, both of whom had been wives to utter shits, had not served their time in the gulag of marital misery.

She wasn't jealous. No, really, she wasn't. But surely she could be forgiven for being slightly bitter and twisted over the fact that *everyone* in sight seemed to be finding life partners. Or, failing that, bosom friends. Take Gran with Odile. The old Northerner and the elderly aristocrat had been inseparable since the afternoon they met, and were to be seen constantly about the town, walking arm-in-arm and either giggling away like schoolgirls or conversing in low voices as if they were plotting something. Particularly when they saw Kate, for some reason.

"*Bonsoir*, Kate."

At the husky voice, she looked up. Nicole had arrived for the evening shift. As ever, she looked as beautiful as the day—or the night, rather. Kate regarded her warily. She never looked at Nicole without those images Fabien had painted snapping instantly, infuriatingly, to mind.

Shading her eyes against the blaze of Nicole's smile, Kate nodded abruptly back. She instinctively distrusted the barmaid's new veneer of fulsome charm, which no doubt had little to do with genuine fondness for her new colleagues and everything to do with her unwillingness to be returned to the Texas Truck-In.

"How's it going?" Nicole spoke in a saccharine trill, brushing her Everest-like cheekbones against the flat planes of Kate's face. Kate submitted to the kiss, thinking she rather preferred the malevolent old Nicole to this butter-wouldn't-melt new one. At least you knew where you were with the former.

"Did *you* know Bernard was getting married?" she asked her.

Expecting a scornful toss of the head, Kate was surprised to see an expression of regret sweep the perfect features. "I'd heard something about it," Nicole groaned. "My fault," she added. "He was in love with me for so many years. And I let him slip through my fingers."

Kate glanced at Nicole's thin fingers and tried to imagine the Troll slipping through anything less snug than the Blackwall Tunnel. She wondered what had brought about the change in attitude. Nicole had not been the least bit interested in the Troll before.

"He is a good man. He would have made a good husband," Nicole lamented.

Kate grinned as the real reason for Nicole's disappointment struck her. "And of course," she reminded Nicole silkily, "he *is* heir to all this." She nodded towards the front of the Hôtel des Tours.

As Nicole's eyes narrowed, Kate knew she had struck home.

"And of course the hotel is worth *so* much more now. Now the restaurant is doing so well. It's a gold mine." Kate was unable to resist a revenge-twist of the knife in that beautiful back. "Such a shame, as you say. Fabien, of course, was a *much* less safe bet."

The perfect chin jerked sharply up. "*Fabien?*"

"Fabien."

"Fabien!" Nicole gave a humorless chuckle. "All he is interested in is my body."

"That's rather what I thought," Kate said, tight-lipped.

"Not in that way," Nicole snapped. "Not any more. Only for painting now." She frowned. "But why are you asking? Why *you*, of all people?"

"What do you mean, why *me*?"

Because Nicole knew everything, Kate guessed with a clench of shame. The afternoon on the beach, the cleaning disaster. Impossible to imagine Nicole on her elegant knees with a scrubbing brush. Or those beautiful hands, red with water and soap suds. Kate burned. How Nicole and Fabien must have laughed. She imagined Nicole's husky, mocking voice: "*Frumpy little English housewife . . .*" Or something equally cutting. And, damn it, equally true.

"Well, Fabien, he . . ." Nicole paused, before hurling out the next couple of sentences. "He seemed to like *you*, that's all. I cannot imagine *why*." She tossed her head and stalked into the bar.

Kate watched her go with a tug in her insides. It was, she realized, her heart being dragged upwards by the raising machinery of Hope. But was there any point in hoping? After all that had been said, not to mention done, Fabien was unlikely to want even to speak to her again.

She was almost grateful when the earsplitting sound of a car engine backfiring burst these morbid thoughts asunder as well as prompting every slumbering dog in the square to bark its annoyed disapproval. Shading her eyes with her hand, she peered to see who it was.

"Hey!" cried a familiar voice.

30

The voice was Darren's.

Dazzling in a new pair of reflector shades, he leaped out of Crichton's ancient car and bounded towards her. Not inappropriately, the theme from *Beverly Hills Cop* pounded out of the elderly speakers behind him.

"Hey," he repeated, seeing her expression. "As the barman said to the horse—why the long face?"

"I'm fine," Kate grumbled.

"Looks like it," Darren said. "Well, you will be. I've got something exciting to show you. Two exciting things really. Get in the car. Come on."

"I can't," Kate informed him with a triumphant sort of flatness. "It's the lunch shift."

"Bugger that. Look at *this*." Diving into the car, Darren emerged with a familiar-looking newspaper and flashed it before her eyes.

Kate frowned. "It's a copy of the *Mockery*." *This* was exciting? Why would anyone, least of all *Darren*, imagine that she would want to see a copy of the *Slackmucklethwaite Mercury*? But, as he continued to shake it insistently towards her, she took the proffered journal, unfolded it to look at the front page and read the headline.

"*Fuck!*" she exclaimed.

"Quite."

Kate looked down, head shaking, at the paper again. "PALISADES SCAM EXPOSED," she read out in incredulous tones. "HATED DEVELOPER FACES COURT ACTION." She looked up at Darren. "It's about Peter Hardstone."

"Read on."

Kate obeyed. Seconds later, her head shot up again. "It's all about his dodgy property deals! But why is his *own paper* printing it? I don't get it."

Darren snatched the newspaper back. "Just come with me and all will be revealed."

"Come with you? Where?"

"Wait and see."

Kate glanced swiftly over her shoulder. Neither Celia nor Nicole were anywhere to be seen. The tables were all set and no customers were expected for an hour. Chef, moreover, had a platoon of willing octogenarian helpers in his kitchen. "Okay," she hissed. "But I've got to be back in half an hour."

With the help of another mighty cannon blast from the engine, Darren screeched out of the square.

Kate took the *Mercury* out of the driver's footwell where Darren had stuffed it. The Renault swerved dangerously, first toward a couple of women with powerful calves struggling up the slope with their shopping, then back toward a couple of cats. The cats looked, if anything, even more outraged than the women.

"It's all here," Kate said, reading on incredulously. "Everything you were working on. Slack Palisades, backhanders to the Council, jerry-building, dodgy business dealing, the lot." Her eyes snapped back to the columns of type again. "Even the connection with Marty St. Pierre . . . Toilet Gardens . . . it's all here."

"That's right. It's caused a sensation at home, apparently. All the broadsheets have followed it up." His eyes now firmly on the road, Darren beamed through the windscreen. They were, Kate vaguely noticed, heading for the coast road. The one she had, on those two happy occasions, taken with Fabien.

All the broadsheets . . . Amid the excitement, Kate tasted the sour tang of frustration.

"Typical," she groaned. "You and I slave for years to get a national-headline–grabbing story. And the minute we turn our backs, the

*Mockery*—the bloody *Mockery*—hits the news jackpot. With a story you were working on *yourself*!"

"That's right," Darren agreed mildly.

"But don't you *mind*?" Kate demanded. "Doesn't it piss you off?"

"Look at the editorial page," Darren said, smirking.

"*Editorial?* But Hardstone made Denys drop it." Kate riffled breathlessly through the paper. "It's back," she gasped. "The editorial page is *back*. And what's this?" Her eyes devoured the headline that spread across both pages. A PROUD PLEDGE TO OUR LOYAL READERS.

"Read it," Darren squeaked, bouncing up and down in the driving seat.

Kate read. A few seconds later, she looked up, eyes shining in wonder. "It's about how Denys and the other editors in the group have—and I quote—*thanks to some imaginative, understanding, and committed bank managers . . . been able to buy the local newspapers comprising the Hardstone Holdings . . . proud now to assure their legions of loyal local readers that they aim to return to the proud old days of campaigning local journalism, as exemplified by the proud tradition of the* Slackmucklethwaite Mercury *in particular, which in its great days was proudly known as the—*"

"Thunderer of the North!" they chorused.

"Yes, and look," Kate yelped, stabbing the increasingly battered front page with a finger. "The old strapline is back. FIGHTING LOCAL BATTLES FOR LOCAL PEOPLE. Good old Denys! So, basically, he's led a management buyout!"

"*Yee-hah!*" Darren slapped his skinny black-trousered thigh. "Apparently, the minute he realized Hardstone was about to be arrested and the *Mockery* about to go into receivership, he was in there like a flash."

"And the minute he got back in charge he was straight back to campaigning local-issue stuff. Good-bye *Carpetmania* and *Use Your Noodle*."

"Yes. Sad, isn't it?"

"'*Hated*' *Developer* . . . it's true, of course, but a bit *strong* for

Denys. And why is it in quote marks?" Kate's finger ran down another column of the story. "Ohmigod! *I see!* . . . *Hardstone, whose questionable and oppressive business practices came under close national scrutiny last week when he was voted 'Most Hated Boss in Britain' by listeners to Radio Four's* Today *program.* Wow!" She sank back against the rickety headrest. "Incredible."

"The Hardstones are in deep shit, basically," Darren sang. "They'll be getting their comeuppance, whether Odile likes it or not."

They were, Kate now saw, driving along a seafront fringed by palm trees on the one side and huge wedding-cake hotels on the other. It did not look like Antibes, lacking its small, shabby intimacy. It looked bigger and grander altogether.

"There's just one thing I don't get." Kate looked at Darren. "I didn't realize Denys knew about Slack Palisades—let alone about Marty St. Pierre and all that stuff. How did he find out?"

"You still haven't looked at the front-page byline, have you?"

Kate looked. "*By Our Special South of France Correspondent, Crichton Porterhouse . . . Crichton!*"

"He knows Wemyss," Darren explained, grinning. "They used to work together on the *Times.*"

"But that was a thousand years ago."

"They spoke recently."

"Spoke?" Kate frowned, picturing the abandoned office, the telephone off its hook. Had Crichton, aware that he was being hunted down, phoned Wemyss and told him the whole story before the Hardstones struck?

Slowing down marginally, Darren pulled the car's hand brake up with a protesting shriek. "We're here, by the way. The Hôtel Carlton, Cannes."

The glamorous name made no impression on Kate. She completely failed to recall its position as epicenter of the still-current film festival. Her mind was on other things altogether, and one thing in particular. *Poor* Crichton. Everything he had been working for had finally come to pass. But he had missed his day of triumph altogether.

She stumbled out of the vehicle scarcely noticing where she was. A

vague impression of palm trees and sea on the one hand and a glistening stucco edifice on the other was all she took in as she followed Darren. He leaped, bracelets ringing, up a shallow flight of marble stairs
and across a terrace buzzing with people, one or two of whom seemed
familiar.

At the table nearest her, a knot of speculative-looking men with
rimless glasses were trying to impress some airbrushed, blank-faced
blondes. "My screenplay," one of the men was saying. "It's about the
funny side of the war in Afghanistan."

"Like, wow," replied one of the airbrushed blondes, her jaw
clamping furiously up and down on a piece of invisible gum. "Like,
when *was* that?"

Darren turned in delight to Kate. "God, how stupid some people
are . . . oh *sweetie*. What are you sniveling at?"

"What do you think?" she snapped, fighting back the tears. "Poor
Crichton, *that's* what. Oh, I know he got his wish, sort of. His story in
print, in *all* the broadsheets. It's what he would have wanted. But . . ."
She stopped, bit her lip, and looked down.

"You're absolutely right," a voice by her elbow assured her. "I'm
thrilled skinny about the whole thing." Into Kate's amazed ears slid a
sniff, followed by the click of a lighter.

"Crichton!"

"For my sins." Crichton grinned from the midst of a swirl of Winston fumes. His Beethoven hair rioted in the sunshine; one chino'd
leg, folded over another, swung a battered desert boot happily in her
direction. "Lovely to see you, dear. Sight for sore eyes, you are, let me
tell you."

"Where have you *been*?" she groaned to the editor, pulling out a
white scrolled-iron chair and sinking down. "We've been so worried.
We thought you were . . ." She stopped. "In a real mess, anyway."

Crichton sniffed. "Well, as a matter of fact, a mess was exactly
what I was in."

"What happened?" Kate's eyes and voice were melting with concern. "What did they do to you?"

"I'm not sure it's the sort of thing ladies want to hear about."

Kate smiled, touched by his courtesy and impressed by his modesty. "No, really," she encouraged gently. "You forget I'm a journalist. You can tell me. I won't be shocked."

"You sure?" There was an uncertain expression in Crichton's blue and red eyes.

Kate nodded apprehensively. She quailed slightly at what she might be about to hear. Falling into the brutal clutches of the Hardstones would not have been a pleasant business. She hoped it didn't involve nipple clamps or electric prods.

Crichton tipped out another Winston and tapped it on the side of his packet. "You must understand that I was unconscious to begin with. . . ."

"Of course." A blunt instrument, no doubt.

". . . But when I came round, I realized I was completely in the buff. They'd stripped me naked. Bound and gagged me as well."

Kate nodded, eyes dewy with understanding. She was aware, in the background, of Darren's bracelets rattling as he waved for a waiter.

*Puff. Sniff.* "And I was locked in, of course. Couldn't get out."

"No." Where, Kate wondered, had the torture cell been? She pictured a damp cavern with bloodstained walls. Somewhere up in the hills, probably.

"Two champagne cocktails and a large Jameson's on the rocks," Darren instructed the waiter. Kate's lips tightened. How could he think of anything so trivial at a time like this? In the presence of someone who had suffered as Crichton had?

"How long were you locked in?" she asked gently.

Crichton's eyes flexed in surprise. "Oh, just the usual time."

Kate frowned. Was there some sort of internationally agreed length that ruthless criminals allotted to torture and interrogation sessions?

"Well, it's always the same, isn't it? Give or take half an hour for delays."

The drinks arrived. As Crichton seized his eagerly, Kate pushed hers away.

"So," she probed softly. "How did you escape?"

"Well, it wasn't an escape, exactly. I just lay there and the cleaners came and found me."

"*Cleaners?*"

Crichton sniffed. "Yes. Bit embarrassing really. They had to call the police to take me away, as I didn't have any clothes. Otherwise I'd have been walking stark naked through the commuters at Waterloo."

"*Waterloo!*"

"Well, what's so surprising about that? It's the Eurostar terminal. isn't it? Where the train stops." *Puff.*

"Yes, but why were you on the Eurostar with the Hardstones?"

"The Hardstones?" Crichton looked blank. "What on earth would I be with them for?"

She was beginning to feel silly. From the way his face was determinedly twisted away, it was obvious that Darren was suppressing a torrent of laughter. "So the Hardstones weren't torturing you?" she muttered lamely.

"*Torturing* me? Er, no. Not at all. Heavens, whatever gave you that idea?" Crichton fumbled for his whiskey.

Darren was making squeaking noises now. Kate avoided his eye. "So, let's take it from the top," she instructed Crichton grumpily. "Why *did* you disappear?"

"Ah." Crichton puffed on his Winston and looked rather ashamed. "All a bit of a mistake, you see. I was supposed to be taking the gang––my Brummies––to Ventimigbog, as I call it."

"*Where?*"

"Ventimiglia. A town just over the Italian border. Jolly good market . . ." He cleared his throat. "Anyway, I'd forgotten to sort out the tickets, which I was supposed to buy the day before. So I left the office in a bit of a hurry to shoot down to Nice station. Luckily the mayor was driving past and gave me a lift––he's got a much faster car."

"But the folder had gone," Kate bleated.

"Yes. I decided to take it with me."

"But why? You normally leave it in your drawer."

"True," Crichton admitted. "But it struck me, what with your ghost and all, that things were hotting up. So I took it. Anyone could have popped in and helped themselves, after all."

"Quite," Kate said through gritted teeth. "*So*, there you were at the station . . ."

"Oh. Yes. So there I was at the station, minding my own business. When who should pole up but a gang of Scottish rugby supporters. Including—would you *believe* it—a couple of old muckers I was at college with in Durham." He took another slug of whiskey. "Anyway, we went for a quick snifter and one thing rather led to another . . . you know how it is." He darted a swift look at Kate.

"I know how it *was*," she said crossly. "Your group were waiting outside the office expecting you to take them to Grasse."

"Were they *really*?" Crichton said guiltily. "Suppose they would have been . . . oh dear. Well, they didn't miss much. Awfully touristy, Grasse." He cleared his throat uncomfortably. "Anyway, next thing I knew I was waking up in the London-bound Eurostar, naked, handcuffed, and gagged and, according to the fuzz, with something unrepeatable written on my forehead."

"What?" Darren asked instantly.

Crichton shrugged. "Rozzers wiped it off." He grinned apologetically. "Those rugby players, eh? Crazy bunch of guys. Total nutters."

"Bonkers," Kate said acidly. "Do go on."

"So there I was in a London nick with no clothes, no dosh, and no bloody passport." *Sniff.* "So the boys in blue let me make a phone call to someone to bail me out and the first person I thought of—not having been back to the homeland in ages, you see—was old *Denys Wemyss*. Because you and I had been talking about him, I suppose." He shot a look at Kate.

She nodded. "And?"

"He always was a brick and sure enough, he was a complete star. Sorted me out with the Old Bill, got me up to Heckmucklethwaite-by-Slagheap or whatever it's called, and looked after me for a bit. I'd got a touch of flu, being starkers and all that. That Eurostar air-conditioning is pretty powerful. Anyway, ahem, one night Denys and I were talking about his paper—he's led a management buyout, you know, great stuff—and the whole Hardstone thing came up. Turned out he had half the story already, thanks to Darren here, but was looking for the missing links to make the first front-page splash for his first issue. So once he'd promised me the sole byline, *ahem*," he grinned apologetically at Darren, "of course I was delighted to oblige. Then I came back and here I am." *Puff. Sniff.*

"I see." Kate stared down at the marble terrace.

"Don't you want your cocktail?" Darren asked her. "Only it's getting warm and I'd hate to see it go to waste."

"Help yourself."

Darren knocked it back in one and stood up. "Come on, Crichton. Time we made tracks. We've got this week's edition to lay out."

Kate looked up. "You're working at the *Gazette*?"

Darren nodded, his purple hair swaying merrily in the sunshine. "Just for the next couple of days. Then it's back to the *Mercury* for me."

"You're not serious."

"Am too. And why not? The old place is buzzing now. National headlines, fired-up editor desperate for as many muckraking stories— sorry, campaigning local issues—as I can lay my hands on. What's not to go back for? I've had a couple of calls from the nationals already about freelancing." He paused. "You should think about going back to the *Mercury* too."

"To the *Mercury*?" Kate stared at him. "But Denys wouldn't want me. He was furious when I disappeared without permission. Not that I knew it was without permission," she added hotly.

"Oh, he got over that ages ago. He'd love to have you back. Hot reporter like you, who knows the beat backward."

Kate swallowed hard on the lump forming in her throat. While it was lovely, if odd, to have Gran in Ste. Jeanne, she really couldn't imagine staying here forever. Unlike Celia, she didn't want to run a restaurant; unlike Mandi, she had no real desire to live in a romantic ruin. Nor was the *Riviera Gazette* the end of her particular career rainbow. All she really wanted to do was write. Novels, preferably. Yet, despite the picturesque hotel balcony, despite all the color of the village, despite having time to write even with all her commitments, *Northern Gigolo* had, for one reason or another, failed to take shape under this hot, blue Mediterranean sky.

And now, suddenly, Kate realized why. It wasn't that she had lost both will and ability to write, as she was starting to fear. The chilly, cheerless skies of the frozen North were what was needed to continue, and most importantly of all, the everyday presence of the material she had once taken so utterly for granted. And perhaps she had been barking up the wrong tree all along. Perhaps what she really wanted to write about wasn't gigolos and steamy sex, but something taking full advantage of the humorous, earthy, wise, and wonderful material in which Slackmucklethwaite abounded.

Material in which the *Mockery* especially abounded. And while she had no doubt that the more eccentric stories would continue, who wasn't to say, under the new, improved, fired-up, campaigning Denys, that the proud old paper wouldn't now blaze a trail of its own? Slack Country Chickens, for example, might at last get its comeuppance. Which in itself was worth going back for. Darren was right. From where she was sitting, the once-despised paper looked like a sexier proposition even than that man sitting nearby who looked amazingly like George Clooney.

And the reasons for returning didn't end there, Kate realized. All her friends in Ste. Jeanne were happily in love—Celia with Ken, Mandi with the Troll. Worse, they were about to get married. Whereas all *she* had were the ruins of a relationship with Fabien. There really was nothing to stay for.

"Hang on," Kate said, pushing her seat back. "Look, I think you might have a point about me going back to the *Mercury*. I want to talk about it properly. You can give me a lift back up."

Darren's eyes dilated. "Er, actually . . ." He looked at Crichton with a curiously panicked expression.

"As it happens, we can't," Crichton finished. "You have to stay here."

"Stay *here?*" Kate looked round at the sunshaded terrace, the carved-cherub-rioting, balcony-bulging facade of the hotel, the gentle tinkle of glassware and expensive crockery as the waiters served lunch. At the table nearest her, Kate half-noticed, was a woman with startlingly white skin and red hair who looked very like Nicole Kidman. "Why?" she asked, distractedly.

"Your, er, grandmother's instructions. As well as Madame La Comtesse's," Crichton warned.

"Oh." It didn't look like Gran's sort of place but, egged on by Odile, she was getting some fancy ideas these days. "Coming for lunch, are they?"

"They didn't say," Darren said carefully. "Anyway, give them my love when you see them. Tell Odile as well that our exclusive interview with her about giving the Picassos and the modern art museum to the nation will run this week. That should get the Frog national press going," he added with a grin. "The *Riviera Gazette* breaks the first big story of its career."

"The cheek!" exclaimed Crichton. "A story I once wrote about food-throwing at the mayor of Vence's fondue party was picked up by *Le Figaro*, I'll have you know."

Kate watched them lurch off across the terrace. As the waiter approached, she waved him away. Funny. The man sitting opposite really did look *unbelievably* like George Clooney. She glanced across the palm-tree–lined boulevard to the glittering sea. With a pull of regret she recognized how beautiful it was here. Although that didn't mean she didn't want to leave it.

Yes, she *would* leave. After lunch with Gran and Odile, she'd head back to the Hôtel des Tours and pack. In the meantime, though, she'd enjoy this last taste of Riviera glamour. Sit here and wait for the two old ladies with the sun on her back and the breeze in her face and just—melt. She closed her eyes contentedly, relieved at having made her decision. In the end, it hadn't been so difficult after all.

The sunlight through her eyelids glowed red. The excitement of the past few days had taken its toll. She was tired. So, so tired.

She sensed someone at her side. "No," she murmured sleepily. "I don't want another champagne cocktail. I'm waiting for someone."

She lapsed back into her dream. Fabien's face was looming before her. "Oh God, I'm sorry," she told him. "Your studio—I didn't mean to ruin it. I was only trying to help, that's all."

"I know, I know," murmured the Fabien of her dreams. "I'm sorry too."

"I stormed off like an idiot," Kate groaned. "I shouldn't have. I thought—you know. You and Nicole . . ."

His dark eyes were so tender. "Understandably you thought so, with that painting of her. It was obvious to me afterwards exactly how it must have seemed to you."

Kate liked this dream. All the miserable misunderstandings straightened out. How liberating fantasy was; she'd never dare be this frank in the flesh.

She smiled at him. "So why didn't you tell me?"

He raised a dark eyebrow. "Apart from the fact that I never saw you, because you were obviously keeping out of my way?" He sighed. "I was too angry about the studio, I suppose. Angry too because the way you stormed out seemed to say that the time we spent together meant nothing to you."

"But that's exactly what I thought about you!" Kate exclaimed.

"And I was too proud to come and explain myself," Fabien said ruefully. "I was an idiot."

"And I was an idiot about Nicole. Thinking you were in love with her."

"You *were* an idiot," Fabien agreed. "In love with *that* shrew! We had a relationship, as I told you. Which is when I found out that the only thing she is interested in is money."

Kate smiled. "Yes, and she's beside herself at the moment because she's missed the boat with Bernard. All that lovely cash now the hotel's making a profit."

"Bernard, he has had a lucky escape," Fabien remarked. "But Nicole needn't worry. She's bound to pick up some rich producer—the film festival's still on, after all. Lots of movie types go to the Restaurant des Tours now. All she has to do is lift her skirt a bit."

"If she can get it up any higher . . . *film festival*, you say?" Kate looked around her, blinking. George Clooney *was* opposite, broad, handsome, genial, and sipping a cup of tea—*the real George Clooney!* And Nicole Kidman—*it really was Nicole Kidman!*—was impatiently crumbling her bread roll at the next table. Kate's eyes flicked up to the front of the hotel. Those shining, narrow black domes pointing up into a flawless blue sky. The ornate balconies rippling across the front of the famous facade with *Hotel Carlton* written across it in azure letters.

Snatches of conversation drifted across like cigarette smoke.

"*I know. Her face has had more lifts than the Empire State Building and yet she beat everyone to get the part. They say she's screwing the producer but you know he's really a woman?*"

Here she was at deal-makers' central. The epicenter of the most glamorous festival in the world. And, by definition, right here, right now, the most glamorous place in the world. A hum of excitement raced along her intestines. It was *real*.

Which must mean . . .

Oh dear.

She slotted her eyes to the side. Fabien *was* there. In the flesh—what there was of it. He looked skinnier than ever. But three-dimensional— just. "*Oh*," she said. Embarrassment stung her cheeks.

Fabien, however, was not looking at her. "You know," he mused, eyes fixed on the Carlton's domes, "they're supposed to be modeled on the breasts of the first hotel-owner's mistress."

Kate stared round. *Nicolas Cage! Judi Dench! Champagne D'Vyne* . . . oh *no*. She dropped her eyes in horror.

"Well," she said nervously, "I can't think where my grandmother is. She's supposed to be meeting me for lunch. With the Comtesse." Hurry up, Gran, she urged silently. Apart from bailing her out of an embarrassing situation, Gran would adore the chance to celebrity spot.

"About that lunch." Fabien looked at his hands. "They're not coming."

Panic flared in Kate's eyes. "Why? Has something happened?"

"They're not coming because they never were. It's a setup." Fabien grinned. "Your grandmother and Odile had an idea. None of them thought you'd go to my studio and I could hardly go up to your room. So Darren drove you here and I came along afterwards and . . . *voilà!*"

"A setup." Kate savored the words. Gran and Odile, playing Cupid. "Why?"

"Because I've got some news for you," Fabien said. "Odile's just given me a big portrait commission. My biggest ever, in fact."

At the shy pride in his face, Kate felt her heart contract. "That's *fantastic.* Congratulations! I'm so glad!" But did the world really need another near-ninety-year-old nude?

"I am very pleased to hear you are glad. You see, it's a portrait of you."

"*Me?*" Kate reeled at this bombshell. "You are *joking.* Why would Odile want a picture of *me?*"

"She thinks you are very beautiful. And so, as you know, do I."

Her embarrassment melted, to be replaced by thrumming excitement. He was to paint her portrait. The glory of it! If everything Odile said about him was true—and she seemed to know her stuff—in what great gallery might she not hang in future years? She would be the Giaconda to his Leonardo. The Fornarina to his Raphael. The Mother to his Whistler—well, perhaps not that. She shot a triumphant glance at Champagne D'Vyne, currently thrusting her turbo-charged frontage at a man—no doubt from celluloid high command—whose face looked as if it had been squashed by a truck. In the image-immortality stakes, Kate knew, she had won. *Top that*, she thought, exultant.

"So you agree?"

"Yes!" she squeaked. Clever old Odile. And clever old Gran too probably. So *this* was what they had been whispering and giggling about all the time. Not so much about a painting as how to repair a relationship. What better way than art, they had no doubt reasoned, to enforce two young people into each other's intimate society, alone, for hours on end? With one of them, at least, in a state of undress. If not outright nudity.

"That's fantastic," she breathed. And, then, she remembered. She actually stopped breathing as she stared at him in horror. "Oh. My. God. Actually, Fabien, that's not fantastic at all. I'm sorry, but——"

"But *what*?" His eyes were huge with alarm. "Look, Kate, I swear there was never anything between Nicole and me. Nothing that ever meant anything. Not like . . ." he plucked pleadingly at her hand.

"Oh Fabien, it's so sweet of you to say so." Kate swallowed. "But really, I can't." She felt almost angry with disappointment. Why was he choosing *now*, of all times, to tell her this? *Now*, when she had just decided—happily decided, moreover—that there was no future for her here.

"Why?" Fabien cried in despair.

Kate took his hand, searching for the words. She knew with nerve-stiffening certainty that she had no intention, however heartbreaking the decision, to throw away her career and vocation for any relationship. Let alone one of such recent vintage as this one. Not now she had finally realized how important career and vocation were to her. Not to mention home and family.

"Because," she said gently. "I'm going back home."

"*What?*"

"I'm sorry, Fabien, but there it is. Ste. Jeanne—well, it's lovely. Beautiful. But," she sighed, "it's not home."

"But, but . . ." Fabien was stumbling for the words. Her heart squeezed with pity. "That is *wonderful* news, Kate."

"*Wonderful?*"

"Yes, because you see," he was gabbling now, "this portrait. It is not just of you."

Kate bent forward. "Fabien, you are talking in riddles," she said patiently. "Perhaps I'm not understanding you. It is not just of me? What do you mean?"

Fabien beamed. "You know, Odile was very taken with those stories you told me about your family. About your mother and father and grandmother. And aunts and uncles."

Kate stared at him. "Ye-es?"

"She wants a group. *Les Cleggs*."

"You mean . . . *my family*?" Kate whispered.

He nodded. "It will be by far the biggest and most important picture I have ever painted. And before you say they won't all come to the Riviera, they don't have to."

"They don't?"

"Odile wants it painted in your home surroundings—what's the house called again?"

Kate's mouth snapped open and shut in shock. "Wits End."

"That's it. So, with your family's permission, that's what I would like to do."

"Oh, *Fabien*! Fab—"

He had leaned over and was kissing her very long and very slowly. Coming up for air, he added: "I am so happy. You know I've always wanted to see Eckmucklethwaites."

"Slackmucklethwaite."

"And to meet, as you say, the in-laws. And seeing what I think of them."

"*In*-laws?" Her grin widened. "Well, that depends."

"On what does it depend?"

"On what Slackmucklethwaite thinks of *you*."

"*Parfait*. Let's go and pack *now*."